THE KARMADONT CHESS SET

*Books are the lives
we don't have
time to live,
Vasily Mahanenko*

THE WAY OF THE SHAMAN
BOOK 5

MAGIC DOME BOOKS

THIS BOOK IS ENTIRELY A WORK OF FICTION.
ANY CORRELATION WITH REAL PEOPLE OR EVENTS IS
COINCIDENTAL.

The Karmadont Chess Set
The Way of the Shaman, Book # 5
Copyright © V. Mahanenko 2017
Cover Art © V. Manyukhin 2017
Translator © Boris Smirnov 2017
Published by Magic Dome Books, 2017
All Rights Reserved
ISBN: 978-80-88231-03-5

TABLE OF CONTENTS:

CHAPTER ONE

ALTAMEDA

PLEASE ASSIGN a new location for your castle...

As soon as I took my rightful seat on Altameda's throne, a fairly elaborate castle management interface popped up before me. The first thing that caught my eye was the damage percentage. At the moment Altameda was at 88% of its nominal Durability and needed repairs—but I was in for a real shock when I checked the list of required materials. The castle's repairs called for tens of thousands of stacks of Imperial Granite, Oak and Steel. And that was just for 'preliminary'—i.e. cosmetic—repairs. According to the system, I'd need to bring in an Architect of at least Level 350 to get a more accurate list of resources.

Harsh...

I could roughly gauge the cost of the Imperial materials and knew that I simply hadn't the right to withdraw seventy million gold from the clan coffers to repair this place. Naturally, I'd call some Carpenters to repair the castle gates, which were below 50%. But everything else, including the walls, the buildings and the interiors would have to wait—as in, about another three hundred years or so...

The castle's personnel was managed in a separate tab of the interface. There were positions available for various stewards, guards, butlers and servants. Craftsmen and gatherers were not included here. Considering that a Level 24 castle required servants of all but Imperial level, the majordomo alone would cost my clan two million gold per year. A cheaper steward wouldn't be able to cope with the amount of work the position entailed. It was the same with the castle guard—ordinary guards wouldn't be able to keep the castle secure. I'd need advanced, Level 300 Warriors and Mages, as well as a Level 350 chief of security. I took another glance at the tab and couldn't help but curse under my breath. Even a skeleton crew of NPC guards would cost my clan 27 million gold a year.

The next tab in the castle management screen brought me some relief—there was at least one thing that didn't require immense investment—the castle's passive defense systems. It turned out that the castle had a moat which, when activated, would appear around the castle for several days. The magic that had repelled Geyra and her warriors from the walls was a property of the castle itself and not of its level. It was also maxed out so no one would be able to sneak into my place by stealth. The same thing held true for the overflight protection—no one could fly over or into Altameda's airspace. This included players, NPCs and even mobs like the Rukh birds that Anastaria had told me about. In this sense, Altameda was impregnable.

The next tab detailed what needed to happen before the castle reached Level 25. I took a glance at the requirements and immediately moved onto the next tab. To level up, I'd need to improve the castle's Spartan interiors—install statues, fountains, paintings, glass, chandeliers...I'd have to make a maddening amount of various improvements to the place that would all amount to tens of millions gold in materials alone, not to mention the cost of labor. And anyway, where would I find the craftsmen to do all this?

Wait just a second...

Closing the management interface, I opened my mailbox and jotted down a letter. Beside me, Anastaria and Plinto looked on in surprise. If I remembered correctly, Sakas and Alt were going to be released from Pryke Mine fairly soon. Being released on parole isn't very entertaining, I know from my own experience—so I sent them an offer to join my clan. A Carpenter and Painter of my own would come in handy. The Pryke Mine governor hadn't praised them for nothing.

"Mahan, is it normal for the walls to be shaking?" Plinto asked in an utterly neutral tone of voice. It was as if the shaking didn't bother him or anything, but still, the Rogue had decided that perhaps he wouldn't like to be buried alive in this place after all.

"I'm still getting a handle on how to manage the castle and I haven't gotten to the teleportation function yet, so we're merely in a holding pattern, getting ready to teleport," I reassured the Vampire.

"Teleportation function?" Anastaria instantly perked up upon hearing two words that didn't normally appear together: 'castle' and 'teleportation.'

"Uh-huh. Our castle can teleport to a new location every three months—either automatically or if we tell it to. What, did you not receive the notification? I thought we're all equal owners..."

"We may be equal, but some are more equal than others," Stacey smiled. "I didn't get anything like that at all. If you choose a new location, don't even think of situating us anywhere near a large city. It may be prestigious to have a castle near a large settlement, but it's very dangerous too."

"Dangerous?" It was my turn to get hung up on words.

"Treasure hunters, thieves, robbers, raids by clans who want to level up at our expense...There's a variety of things players could do with a castle that sits there in plain view, making their mouths water. Especially if it belongs to someone who's caused you to respawn twice before—in the Dark Forest and with the Armageddon spell. So all in all, I recommend you place it somewhere close to the Free Lands. We'll buy a static portal, install it in the castle and live the good life quietly and to ourselves."

"There's already a portal here. It's simply not activated," I replied, checking the castle's properties. "But yeah, I agree—we've got no business near Anhurs. Any suggestions for where we should go?"

"What about here?" Stacey opened her map, zoomed in and poked her finger at Lestran Province. "We have Exalted Status with them after Krispa, Kartoss is on the other side of the mountains, the Free Lands are nearby and so is Sintana, the Dwarven capital. And since we'll be near the mountains, we might stumble across some ore to mine."

"But you said yourself that we should stay away from large settlements..."

"We won't be that close," replied Stacey, zooming in one more time and bending over the map. "Sintana is here. We can teleport to this site here, on the other side of this mountain range that branches off from the Elma Mountains. Players don't enjoy climbing mountains very much, so there won't be many people wandering around. And whoever actually wants to find us will do so anyway. Check it out—the castle doesn't have a moat surrounding it, so if we site it here on the shore..."

"There is a moat too, it just hasn't been activated," I interrupted Stacey. "In fact, this castle has basically everything we could need—it's just not activated at the moment."

"Hmm..." Anastaria took a moment to think things over and then confidently pointed at a spot on the map. "In that case—here. It's a perfect location for harvesting timber, mining ore and developing agriculture."

"All right. I'll try to teleport us over there," I agreed with the girl and returned to the castle management interface. I hadn't bothered to glance at the tab for the castle vaults yet. It wasn't likely that someone had hidden something in Altameda...Hold up!

"Magdey, Clutzer—emergency meeting!" I called my raid leaders with the amulet. "I need your people here ASAP! You have two minutes to cast a portal to the following coordinates..."

Your castle (Altameda) is under attack! Hurry to its aid! Attackers: Narlak City Guard and the Azure Dragons clan (Undigit, Donotpunnik, Unber, Untoucan, Donotmanic, Untzold, Un...

I'd have to adjust my notification settings because the list of players who had decided to find out what had happened to the phantoms filled my entire screen. I swatted it aside like some annoying fly and turned to the Rogue:

"Plinto—get over to the gates and try to take them on one at a time."

"Ahem..." the Rogue cleared his throat, evidently so that he could sound as sarcastic as possible: "Did you forget that we don't have any of our class abilities until we speak to our teachers? It's not even clear whether we'll get them back after we do talk to them. And you want me to go fight someone right now? If I show up as a mere Vampire, they'll wipe the floor with me in a second. And, remember, there won't be anyone to heal me—Stacey is in the same boat. In other words, sorry to use your favorite quip against you but, 'Like hell!'"

"I'm going to trademark that," I muttered, "and then you'll have to pay me royalties whenever you want to be funny at my expense."

And yet, Plinto was absolutely right. I really had forgotten that we'd lost our class abilities. I still had to go talk to Prontho...

"What do you need Magdey and Clutzer for? Do you really think they can keep the attackers at bay?" asked Anastaria, apparently unclear about my plan.

"Among other things. Our storage vaults are entirely empty..."

"If they tear down the gates, we won't even have empty ones."

"Okay, I'll give you another hint. Where exactly is Altameda located right now? Rather, on top of what..?"

"That's a dumb question. We..." Stacey first furrowed her brow and suddenly broke into a smirk. "Plinto! What are you standing there for? The enemy is at the gates and Glarnis lies untouched beneath our feet! On your mark, get set and pillage all the things! We're taking anything that isn't nailed down! And anything that is nailed down—we're taking it with the nails! Mahan, you're a genius!"

"WHAT DO YOU THINK YOU ARE YOU DOING?" Leite's voice blared in my amulet when I withdrew fifteen million gold from the clan account—half of the castle guard's annual salary. I only parted with this sum after a lot of heartache and after I'd read up on the guards' capabilities. The phantoms could only fight outside of the castle gates, while my new boys could sit back comfortably on the battlements and rain death from above. They would effectively make us invulnerable to any raid. In addition to all this, I was pleasantly surprised to discover that the XP the castle guard earned from killing players or NPCs went either to repair the castle or, if the castle was already at full Durability, to special crystals that could be used to repair it in the future.

Achievement unlocked: 'Guards! Guards!'
You have hired a sufficient number of warriors to defend your castle. -5% off guards' yearly salary.

"I'm saving you money, you miser!" I shot back at our outraged accountant—and hung up. I wasn't about to leave my castle defenseless and was prepared to spend good money on keeping it safe. Thirty million a year really was a terrifying amount. We'd only earned six million in clean profit since Leite had begun to manage our budget—and he was a financial genius. It follows that unless our clan gets some lucky break, we'll all end up working simply to pay the guards! A fun little present the Emperor has made me with this Level 24 castle! It looked like an Imperial gift from afar, but it was turning out to be more akin to Imperial servitude...

"Orders, boss?" said Vimes, my new head of security. Since Altameda was initially a Kartossian castle, its personnel appeared in the form of enormous, anthropomorphic bulls that resembled minotaurs—or 'Taurens,' as Anastaria informed me in a reverent whisper. I gathered by her surprise that this wasn't a very common race in Barliona.

"The castle needs to be defended. Your orders are to kill anything that threatens it, while doing your utmost to minimize our own losses. Loot is priority number two. I want you to transfer whatever the assailants drop to the castle vaults. On the double!"

"Whoa! You sound like a real commander!" quipped Plinto. "Halt! At ease! Left, left...left, right, left! You're giving me the shivers here, Mahan!"

I was about to send the Rogue packing when two portals flared open simultaneously in the middle of the hall and began to disgorge Magdey's and Clutzer's troops.

"Hello, hello!" the Rogue nodded amicably to the newcomers.

"Magdey, Clutzer—it's my pleasure to introduce you to Plinto. He will show you where to go and what to do. Our main objective is to strip Glarnis of everything it has. We're at Hatred status with Narlak anyway so there's nothing to lose. We don't have much time. The castle is being attacked by some players. They're weak at the moment, but we can expect a larger assault in the near future. We need to make our escape before then."

"We're going to abandon the castle?" Magdey asked surprised.

"Nope. We're bringing the castle with us," I smiled at the puzzlement on my players' faces. "Come on people—time is loot. Off you go to Glarnis!"

Still pretty puzzled, the troops followed Plinto, while I returned to my throne and continued to study my castle's abilities. Ah! Here's the tab for managing the phantoms...Initially I wanted to hang on to them, but the Dark Lord was a bit too adamant about setting them free, so—well, be free, my darlings! All is forgiven.

"Where should we store the loot? Where are the storage vaults?" one of the raiders asked me, tearing me away from my studies.

"The vaults?" I shot the player a puzzled look. "I haven't the slightest idea..."

"No one does. We looked all over Altameda and couldn't find any. What are we going to do? If we dump the loot on the ground, it'll vanish instantly..."

"Leite will kill me," I grumbled, returned to the castle management interface and hired some more personnel—a castle majordomo. That's minus another 1.5 million...an expensive bit of fun. A good majordomo who also happens to be...

"Master," said Viltrius in a slightly squeaky voice and bowed. "What are your orders?"

...a goblin.

Green all over and with prominent ears that stuck out from his head, Viltrius was wearing such whimsical, circular glasses that one glance at him told you that you'd never eke any gold or items from him. It was also clear that in his charge, the castle would be so spotless that it would sparkle like the sun itself on a clear day. No doubt he'd count even the dust and dirt, pack it away in tidy little baggies and store these on their proper shelves until they came in handy.

"We're doing inventory today," I told Viltrius. "My players will bring you items to catalog and store. Basically, I need you to make sure that we don't lose anything."

"Yes, sir!" The goblin shut his eyes for a moment and then said, "There are twelve vaults available in this castle. Two of them are currently active. Shall I activate the rest as well?"

"Do as you see fit. If activating the others costs money, there's obviously no point in wasting funds."

"I understand the task required of me," Viltrius bowed again and after a pause, uttered a phrase I did not expect: "I am extremely pleased, Earl, to have been put in charge of such a high-level castle. I am grateful to you that you have chosen me. Believe me— all your items will be perfectly preserved."

Stunned, I couldn't think of a reply to the bowing goblin. The raider standing beside us didn't seem to think any of this was odd, but to me, the point was crystal clear: The NPCs generated by my castle were endowed with medium-level Imitators—at least! These weren't your ordinary toy soldiers who would follow your orders like zombies. No, these were almost fully-formed individuals with their own personal histories. So this is what a high-level castle could do!

Meanwhile, Altameda's walls continued to tremble. The castle seemed to be waiting impatiently for when I would finally input its teleport destination. But no one was paying any attention to the shaking anymore. Anastaria showed up about thirty minutes after the plundering of Glarnis had begun and basically forced me to ask Ehkiller for help. We needed high-level miners, smiths, lumberjacks— anyone who could help us strip the Imperial Steel from the Glarnis throne room. By that point, we had already summoned all of our gatherers and craftsmen, yet their levels weren't high enough to do the bulk of the job. I was forced to agree and call Stacey's dad...

Over the next eight hours, my castle sunk in two great jolts, crushing several tarrying players but also indicating that we were making progress in our plundering activities. The Altameda guard wasn't sitting by idly either. They fought off three assaults and picked up all the fallen loot. According to Barsina who had stayed back in Anhurs, Undigit was running around like mad trying to assemble yet another raid, gathering players for what he billed 'an exquisite caper—the annihilation of the Legends of Barliona castle.' Judging by the number of players pooling on the ridge across from our walls, he was making good progress. I was beginning to get the impression that we were not much loved in Barliona...

"Dan, we might not survive the assault," Anastaria remarked, climbing up to join me on the battlements. "I checked out the gates. They're at 24% Durability—not enough to handle a full-scale attack. Glarnis has been almost picked to pieces. They're clearing the last of the vaults down there. So...well, we are cutting it close here..."

"Did you see the loot that Vimes and his warriors won?" I asked the girl. Every five minutes, Viltrius was reporting on the incoming inventory, the activation of new vaults, the allocation of funds, and various other tidbits of info. My head was beginning to spin and yet I did manage to notice one interesting notification among this torrent of news: Several Legendary items for players of at least Level 300 had found their way to the shelves of our vaults. "I'm sending you the description," I sent Stacey a link to one of the more curious finds, which would serve a Paladin-Healer extremely well. "What do you think— shall we return them to their rightful owner? For a finder's fee of course..."

"You poking fun?" Anastaria almost yelled. "These are the bracers of Donotmanic, one of the leading Paladins in the Azure Dragons! If you return them or even sell them back to him, I'll never speak to you again! Have you seen the ones I've been wearing? They're boring old Level 280 Epic bracers! Dan— where'd you put them?"

Ding! You have received a message from your private circle. Do you wish to read it?

"Tell Viltrius that I'm green-lighting the third vault," I said in Stacey's wake and reached for my mailbox. Something tells me that even if Viltrius and I had been against it, Anastaria would still have her way. Me she could negotiate with, and the majordomo could always be replaced...Well, whatever, I wonder what that letter says?

Hello Dan!

A massive assault on your castle is scheduled to begin in twenty minutes. They are planning on using the Black Death spell along with several catapults— they were just now procuring them. Keep this in mind as you marshal your defenses.

Mirida the Farshighted.

Damn! I was trying to avoid you! What the hell are you warning me for and—what's more interesting—when the hell did I add you to my personal circle? Now, whether I liked it or not, I'd have to see Marina and have a chat with her. I'd really prefer to avoid the topic of how I ended up in Barliona. At any rate, for the moment—who knew what the future would bring? Perhaps even in the near future...

"We only have ten minutes left!" I warned Magdey and Clutzer and thanked Vimes for the good work he'd been doing. After that, I headed to the throne room—the only place where I could activate the castle's teleportation. It turned out that there wasn't anything complicated about this process. If I wanted, I could even keep the castle in its current location by simply inputting its current coordinates.

"Stacey, heads up—we're about to jump. Listen,

they're sure to find us—that's a given. So what's our plan after we teleport? If they launch a full-scale assault, we can kiss the castle goodbye. They'll raze it back to Level 1 and we'll have to rebuild it from scratch."

"That's exactly why we're teleporting to Lestran— you're an Earl, after all! As soon as anyone attacks you in Lestran, you'll be able to summon not only the local NPCs but also the Governor and the Imperial army to your aid. You really need to study the laws of this place, Dan! At the moment, it's true—we're at Hatred with Narlak and so they're trying to kill us while the Guardian sits idly by. By the way, it occurred to me that the Narlak Council must have been under Geranika's control. He didn't merely pay them off—he owned them. And you know what put me onto this idea? Or rather, who? Geyra! She managed to hide her Shadow alignment somehow—to the point that even Urusai who had access to the phantoms didn't know it. Remember—as soon as the phantoms saw Cain, it was like they lost their minds and paid Geyra absolutely no attention. How did she manage to remain invisible to them? Something tells me that if we manage to answer this question, we'll be able to get our class abilities back."

"Okay, we'll get to the bottom of it..." I reassured the girl and opened the clan chat in order to welcome everyone on board *HMS Altameda*:

"*We are scheduled to depart in a minute. Anyone outside of the castle will remain here at the mercy of the mob. Hurry up!*"

I let a minute elapse and turned to Anastaria, grinning:

"...And we'll get to the bottom of this mystery so thoroughly that they'll make another movie about it. We don't know any other way of figuring things out. Let's go!"

Castle location has been updated. Please submit relevant taxation documents.

Taxation?

The castle's jump from one location to a new one wasn't much different than an ordinary teleportation. There was a flash and a very quick loading bar and we were already at our new site—'strangers in a strange land.' I'd give quite a bit right now to see the looks on Undigit's and Donotpunnik's faces. They'd assembled a huge army, equipped it with catapults, called in warriors from Narlak and mercenaries and—all of a sudden—there's no one to fight! I'd be pissed...

"Earl, allow me to congratulate you on acquiring such an excellent castle." I hadn't even stepped off my throne when a Herald appeared in the throne room. "Your request has been approved. I have been sent by the Emperor to notify you of this and to accept the payment for the property taxes. In view of the castle's location, the nominal rates in Lestran Province and the province's relations with your clan, as well as the current level of the castle, the total amount comes out to 24 million gold annually. Or, one million for each level. There are two methods of payment—a one-time sum, subject to a 5% discount, or a monthly installment. Which of these methods do you prefer?"

"Forgive me, Herald..." I said, stunned by such insolence. A few more tax payments like this and my clan won't have any money at all! "Why should I pay anything at all if Altameda was a gift made personally to me by the Emperor himself? Does the Emperor wish to bankrupt my clan?"

"If you are unable to pay the taxes, or if you do not wish to, your castle shall be put up for auction within the next two months. No one wishes to compel you to do anything, Earl. You could have refused to accept ownership of Altameda. You could have chosen the castle located near Sintana which would have incurred a tax of a mere 1.5 million gold per year. However, you chose Altameda and now you have two options available to you: Either the castle is sold and you receive half of the proceeds from the sale, since under the laws of Malabar, the remainder belongs to the Empire, or you can pay the taxes on your property. As you see, everything is quite simple, transparent and lawful. Please make your decision!"

"Monthly payments it is," I seethed through clenched teeth. "You may withdraw the first installment from the clan's treasury..."

Eight million four hundred and forty thousand. That's exactly how much money our clan had after the Herald vanished. My amulet came alive vibrating once again, but I didn't rush to answer it. I knew very well who was calling—Leite. I knew very well what he wanted to say too, but I didn't have any other choice at the moment. Minus two mill every month—I would simply have to accept this as a fact of life from now on.

"Leite, I'm sorry, I really hope that this is the last major outlay," I said, finally answering the call. It seemed that my accountant refused to be ignored because my amulet kept ringing for an entire minute. "At any rate..."

"Mahan!" Leite's voice didn't have even a hint of anger in it. To the contrary—it sounded like my accountant was even pleased..."Have you seen our storage vaults?"

"Not yet," was my honest answer. "All I've been doing the past ten minutes is paying various taxes for the castle..."

"Listen to me!" Leite interrupted, impatient with my bumbling. "We have three vaults active in the castle at the moment. I looked up the properties and we have another nine available. I've already been contacted by several clans who want us to help them guard their property. What do you think? Should we agree? We managed to hold out for eight hours against a siege by none other than the Azure Dragons—that's a very long time for a castle that specializes in storing valuables. And everyone can still remember that the castle survived the Armageddon spell with hardly a blemish...I have two contracts before me right now and there are another seven clans waiting for your decision. Our storage vaults are enormous. All of Glarnis fit into just two of them, so...How does seventy thousand a month from each clan sound to you? If we scrounge up about thirty clients, we'll be able to cover our tax burden and then some."

"You've already crunched all the numbers?"

"It's the first thing I checked. I figured the taxes would be higher actually, but you chose a good place to relocate to...And that's not all!"

"Why, what else is there?" I asked surprised. As the clan treasurer, Leite had full access to everything located in our vaults. I guess he'd spent the past eight hours familiarizing himself with their contents.

"I already sent Ehkiller his share, but even after that we still have about twelve thousand stacks of Imperial Oak and Steel in there! One unit at auction at the moment brings in 200 gold and a stack has 40 units in it...I suggest that we sell half of the steel and oak—very slowly, mind you, so as not to flood the market—and thereby recoup our costs for the guards. But I need your permission to offload the materials. Give Viltrius the order. And in general—will you change the castle settings so that I don't have to pester you every time I need to take something out of the storage vaults? Am I your treasurer or not?"

"Done," I grinned, having granted Leite full access. "Don't I remember you trying to refuse the post?"

"When was that? I must have woken up on the wrong side of bed that morning. Okay, I'll set up a company to advertise our services. Mahan—our situation isn't as bleak as it seemed at first glance! By the way, you should stop by the first vault. Take

Plinto and Anastaria with you. I think you'll like what you find in there."

Leite hung up and various notifications began to pop up about payments he was making for advertising—it seemed that the Warrior had already prepared everything ahead of time and called me strictly to obtain my formal approval. Well, as long as he wasn't cursing up a storm like usual, I was happy...

"Stacey, what are you doing?"

"I'm exploring the castle, why?"

"Let's go look at the first vault. I've been told there's something we'll like in there. We'll bring Plinto with us..."

Altameda's storage vault was quite the epic sight—I had never seen one before and imagined them like the Dragon's treasure vault—a huge space housing heaps and piles of all kinds of stuff amid which only the vault keeper knew how to find the item you needed. Like hell...I don't know what it's like in other castles, but Altameda's vaults contained orderly rows of shelves upon which various goods were organized according to a clear logical pattern. Judging by the description of the vault, each place on the shelves had its own three-digit address and included the name of the items stored in it as well as their quantity. This was effectively an inventory management system! I see now why Leite hadn't objected in the slightest to my hiring of Viltrius.

"Are these the fruits of your labor?" I asked the goblin to make sure and received only a satisfied smile and a bow in reply. "Leite told me that there's something for Anastaria, Plinto and me here. Any idea what that might be?"

"Yes, Master. As I mentioned earlier, the castle already had three onsite vaults activated..."

"Onsite?" I asked puzzled.

"Located within Altameda. If you look at the map, you will see that currently we are deep within the Elma Mountains. The doors to this vault are merely static portals with an altered appearance. If the castle is captured, one of the owners—that is, you, or the honorable Anastaria and Plinto—may revoke access to the vault. Then the captors won't be able to get any of the items stored here. Even if the castle is destroyed, you may access its vaults from the trade guild. All the necessary legal documents can be found there too."

"Got it...So then about our items..?"

"Please follow me. At the risk of repeating myself, Altameda had three storage vaults active, two of which were entirely empty. However, the third one held three items whose purpose was unclear to me. When I made my report to Treasurer Leite, he designated each of the three items for you, for Anastaria and for Plinto. He then asked me that I bring you to them. And here we are—and there are the items in question."

The goblin indicated a row of shelves among which three spots immediately drew my eye. Three items rested on three red velvet pillows among the clutter of Imperial Steel and Oak, Stone and various other loot that we had pillaged from Glarnis.

"This knife is for you, Master," added Viltrius, gingerly picking up a small knife from the pillow and offering it to me. "In any event, such is the opinion of Master Leite."

Until the item reached my hands, its properties remained hidden as I hadn't felt like digging around the vault's database. But as soon as I took a hold of its hilt...

'Almair.' Description: Knife used during the creation of the Chess Set of Karmadont. Item class: Legendary. Information for owner: Remember the majesty of Emperor Karmadont and do not forget about time!

"This horn is for you, Anastaria." Viltrius picked up the next item and handed it to Stacey.

'Narlashtar.' Description: Horn used by Shatrizal to summon the armies to the final battle with the Dragons. Item class: Legendary. Information for owner: Remember the majesty of the Great Mother of the Sirens, Shatrizal, and do not forget about time!

"And finally, this ring must be yours, Plinto," the Goblin concluded, handing the Rogue a ring that seemed to be leaking fog.

'Kragnistal.' Description: The ring of the

Vampire who sacrificed himself to save life in Barliona. Item class: Legendary. Information for owner: Remember the majesty of the first Vampire Patriarch and do not forget about time!

"It is time to return to Altameda," said Viltrius, after giving us a moment to appreciate our presents. "As I see it, Treasurer Leite was not mistaken."

"All right guys, here's the situation: I need to head over to meet the Patriarch ASAP," Plinto began as soon as we returned to the throne room. "I have this one quest to do and this ring makes it clear that I can't put it off any longer."

"Just as the horn does for me and the dagger does for Mahan," Anastaria echoed the Rogue. "I too need to go to Laertol Island to meet Nashlazar...Mahan, it looks like you're going to be without us for a few months. We have to do these quests on our own."

"But I can still count on you in the event of an emergency, right?"

"If there's an emergency, yes," smirked Plinto and offered me his hand. "It was fun adventuring with you, but it's time to part ways. My amulet is on. I'll be in-game 12–14 hours a day. If you need anything holler and I'll come flying. But okay, I don't like long goodbyes...Bye all!"

The Rogue cast a portal and stepped through it. Anastaria and I were left on our own.

"Dan, I have to go too, but before I do that... Want to go check out our bedchamber? It must be quite sumptuous in a Level 24 castle..."

* * *

Before leaving, Anastaria forced me to sit down with her and make some plans for the future. According to her, it made sense to follow my premonition but it wasn't productive to do so all the time. You can't really argue with a girl who's pressing her body to you, so I opened my notepad and began to write.

And so...

First—the Second Dragon Dungeon, which would require a massive raid party. Since there wouldn't be any bonuses in there for us, I'd have to take Magdey's and Clutzer's raids with me. Then, when we'd reach the last boss, I'd summon Anastaria to my location so that she could get a First Kill too. She was quite the collector it turned out...

Second—the Skrooj Dungeon quest that Ishni had given me. Essentially, this is a place in which I have to acquire all of the materials I need for the Chess Set, so completing it ranks up there with our most urgent objectives. Again—this is a job for Magdey and Clutzer's boys, with Anastaria called in at the last moment.

Third—a visit to the pirates. Here I'd have to team up with Evolett, since we'd agreed to do this quest together. We were supposed to meet the pirates not near Narlak but much further west—they were expecting us in the city of Cadis, which lies on the coast right beyond Kartoss. There weren't any deadlines for this quest and Evolett wasn't pushing us to go, so I could comfortably delay this one until I had less on my plate.

Fourth—the Eye of the Dark Widow. A quest that required at least twenty-five players of Level 100 or higher. At the moment, I had more than that at my disposal, but Stacey suggested we keep the Eye quest as a backup in case it turned out that I couldn't manage the Chess Set quest. That way, she said, we'd have another way of getting into the Creator's Tomb. I agreed with her, put the quest aside and forgot about it for the time being.

Fifth—I had to sift through the loot in my inventory as well as the piles of it that we'd extracted from the Glarnis Dungeon. Since this was a new Dungeon that had never been completed before, there was a very high probability that there would be some valuable item among the general clutter we had picked up. Anastaria took all of the meat I was carrying and sent it to the Alchemist she knew, asking him to create Merlin's Potion. According to the girl, I'd be very pleased with the results.

Sixth—the Wolf quest in Farstead. Anastaria looked at me like at a madman when I told her that I wanted to complete this quest. Even taking into account that Farstead now belonged to Kartoss, I didn't wish to abandon the Gray Death. She had very cute wolf cubs and being a Shaman, I'm quite fond of wolves in general...But, uh, well, under the girl's withering glance, I filed this quest in the low importance folder...and yet, I did not forget it about it.

Seventh—I needed to visit Prontho to find out what was happening with my Shamanic powers. Why were they blocked? When would I get them back? And how come neither Anastaria nor Plinto nor I had received a quest for killing Geranika? Had we really been counted out and excluded from this coming scenario? Like hell! An army of players wouldn't pose much of a problem to Geranika now that he had the Heart of Chaos...the Dark Forest had shown as much. Surely the assistance of a Siren, Vampire and Dragon should be very welcome..?

Eighth—I needed to find Kreel. I was very curious to know how this player had managed to bring Rogzar's Crystal to Altameda and avoid the curse at the same time. And why Altameda specifically and not some other castle? Anastaria supported me in this and told me to call her once I'd found this guy. She too was very curious about this player.

Ninth—the Chess Set of Karmadont. More precisely, the Giants from the Chess Set. I had been struggling to learn the least bit about them for a week already without any progress. At this point, Anastaria called me a moron, explaining that I could have simply asked her about it and she would have dug something up. I was forced to prostrate myself and promise that this kind of thing wouldn't happen again. But in any event, I'd need to start working on the Chess Set—I couldn't procrastinate with this quest any longer.

Tenth—(oh my god, there is so much to do!

When am I going to manage it all?)—I need to develop my Jewelcrafting and earn my third Gem Cutter rank. It was safe to assume that the next two months would bring some intense battles against Geranika. The players would need upgrades to their weapons and armor. This was therefore an opportunity to earn a lot of gold for our clan. Although Stacey was the one who mentioned the idea, I'm sure that Leite was the one who put her up to it. That cunning spider tried to make a buck on anything and everything.

Eleventh—I needed to find a student. Regardless of what Prontho would tell me about my Shamanic powers, I would take on a student and begin to teach him the fundamentals of Shamanism. I had no idea who this would be, but I knew that he would have to have a certain attitude to playing this game. He'd need to be ready to act in contradiction to the game's established logic. Where I'd find someone like that I had no idea, but I'd do my utmost. I certainly didn't want to just take on the first person who came across my path.

Twelfth—I needed to allocate my unused stat points. At the moment, I had 490 of them and saw no sense in growing my collection further. To my surprise, however, Anastaria categorically forbade me from doing this. She explained that the main stats maxed out at 500 points. This limit could only be exceeded by adding the unused stat points, so if I had the opportunity, it was better to leave them unassigned for now. To my question of how I was going to hit the max limit without pumping in my unused points, Stacey simply smiled enigmatically and asked me to wait. She added only that I'd be very happy with the present she was going to make me. As a result, I happily struck this twelfth item from my already lengthy list.

Thirteenth—our training with the Patriarch. Unfortunately this would have to be put off for now, since I couldn't leave Altameda for more than a day and commuting every day would be too expensive, especially in view of our recent expenditures. The important thing here was for the Patriarch to meet us halfway. He could easily tell us to either get on with the training now or forget about the whole thing.

Fourteenth—I had to go see Renox. I don't know when I'd be able to—it was looking like only after I reached Dragon Rank 10—but I desperately needed to talk to my in-game father. Nashlazar's words still rang in my head: Renox had sacrificed Draco to the Tarantulas. It was an impossible thing to believe and yet the Siren had sworn an oath that she was telling the truth...All in all, this was a complicated issue and it was better to deal with it slowly.

"Is that really all?" quipped Anastaria, running through the list one more time. "I'll admit I only figured there'd be three or four points to keep you busy for the next couple months, but now it looks like you have your work cut out for you for the next year. We may as well go ahead and add the Geranika quest, the destruction of the Heart of Chaos and the future development of our clan to the list while we're at it..."

"I think I'll be able to figure out what I need to do

now and what I can put aside on my own. You're right—there really is a lot of things to do, but at least now it's clear what they are."

"Especially the Chess Set one. All right Dan. I'm going to get going. Make sure to check in and tell me how you're doing...Try and have a good time here..." Anastaria cast the portal, gave me a farewell kiss and vanished to an unknown destination.

"Master," said Viltrius, appearing suddenly beside me as if he had been waiting for the right moment. "Dinner is ready. Do you wish to dine in the bedroom or the dining hall?"

"Dining hall," I told the goblin. Being an Earl was pretty fun, I decided. All I had to do was figure out the money problem and then I'd enjoy being an aristocrat so much that I wouldn't even want to leave Barliona after my seven years were up. Life's not bad when people fawn over you...

"Honorable Earl, there is a visitor here to see you," Viltrius announced triumphantly as soon as I finished my meal. Even though the goblin had done his best, it was clear as day that I'd need to hire a chef for the castle, as well as a wait staff and several chambermaids. As hard as it is to admit it, there was no alternative. And yet even here, Altameda surprised me yet again. The salaries of a waitstaff of seven, including three chambermaids, only amounted to two million gold per year. And that was taking into account the high levels of these NPCs to match that of the castle. Making a mental note to compensate myself as soon as the clan earned some more money, I paid the six-month sum out of my own pocket. But who was this visitor, and where had he come from? Altameda had been at its new location only about two hours... "Do you wish to receive him today or shall I inform him that the audience will be held tomorrow?"

"Let's do it today," I confirmed my payment, and watched as the goblin's eyes flared with joy—now he'd have some personnel to manage.

"As you wish, Master," the goblin bowed. "I shall usher the visitor into the throne room..."

As soon as I sat down on my throne, the wide doors opened and Viltrius proclaimed in a grandiose voice:

"The Alderman of Happy Moss Village to see His Highness!"

Why look at that! It turns out there's a village nearby. Recalling the fundamental principles of Barliona, I knew that where there was a village—there was a quest! I'd been a bit naïve, making out my schedule for the next several years and not considering all the opportunities that might be awaiting me at my new location. My fourteen-point plan for world domination would have to wait...Hmm...world domination...I grimaced a little at the thought—Cain had mentioned that there wasn't much time remaining to take over this world, and he wasn't equivocating or being sarcastic either. Geranika's warrior had been honest and sincere all along, and I had paid little attention to him...All I could do now was sigh bitterly and recall the mistakes of the past.

A smallish man meekly entered the hall. He kept glancing about himself as if unsure of whether he should fall to his knees or hazard another step. Fiddling with his hat as if it were the source of all his troubles, he froze halfway between the entrance and the throne. He was dressed in a simple outfit, with a rope instead of a belt around his waist and scuffed boots...The Alderman of Happy Moss Village looked nothing at all like the Beatwick Headman. Even taking into account that the Beatwick Headman had since then become the Emperor of Malabar, the difference was immense.

"Sire! Myrrh they call me." The alderman decided to hazard an address. "Our village that lies yonder bears the calling Happy Moss. A peaceful place of a hundred homesteads. We are properly registered in the provincial registry of settlements. Have you come to rule us, oh Sire? I assure you we pay our taxes regularly and follow all the laws to the letter."

Having finished with his speech, Myrrh sighed with relief and peered at me inquisitively. Hmm...Does this mean that by teleporting to this new location, my castle has taken the surrounding villages under its protection?

"*Stacey, I need some emergency advice. Can players govern villages?*"

"*No...What's going on?*"

"*There's a village alderman here, asking me*

whether I'm the new boss. I can't call you because he's right here staring at me. My Energy's almost out..."

"Got it...Dan, summon a Herald and ask him about the status of the village. You won't be penalized for the summons, since you have a visitor. Only, make sure that you make it clear that the man came to you and that you didn't summon him yourself. All of the player castles I know about are located far from Barliona's villages, so there's simply no precedent for this. When your Energy returns, tell me what happened..."

"I call upon a Herald, I request your assistance!" I said, trusting in Anastaria's experience. I can't make my own decision of whether I'll govern the village or not—I'd definitely be punished if I chose wrong, so better let someone explain my rights to me.

"Earl! You called me and I came," the Herald's bell rang in the throne room and the alderman of Happy Moss fell prostrate to the floor. If he wasn't sure how to act in my presence to begin with, then the appearance of the Herald knocked the legs from under the poor NPC. Given how remote this location was from the Free Citizens' typical haunts and, consequently, the simplified nature of local governance—or rather its utter absence—the simultaneous arrival of a mysterious Earl and even more the Herald—a high Imperial official—amounted to a major blow to the uncomplicated psyche of the alderman's Imitator. He was clearly unprepared for all these changes.

"I'd like you to clarify a legal question for me."

Having listened to the boilerplate about being punished for making an unsubstantiated summons, I explained the situation as it stood while makings sure to emphasize that I hadn't caused it.

"You have done the right thing by calling me, Earl. Please wait a little. I need to consult with the Advisors—this kind of thing has never happened in our Empire before."

The Herald dived back into his portal, which remained floating in the air. The alderman raised his head from the floor but as soon as his eyes met mine, Myrrh immediately planted his forehead flush against the floor again, terrified of displeasing the mighty Earl who had such self-assurance when speaking with Imperial Heralds.

"Viltrius," I called the goblin, noting to my surprise that he was also standing motionless and in awe at the edge of the auditorium, "tell our servants that the esteemed alderman should be bathed, fed and assigned a bedroom. He has no business wandering around the woods at night. Until the question of the village administration is settled, he will stay here as our guest."

"M-master Earl," said the goblin with a slight stutter. "Th-there are two more visitors to see you. The village aldermen of Silent Vine and Lower Creek. Shall I have them bathed and fed as well?"

"And don't forget to issue them beds," I replied with a smile. "Get to it!"

Viltrius approached the prostrated alderman, raised him to his feet as if he didn't weigh anything and nodded at the door, evidently indicating that the audience with the Earl had drawn to a close. I'll have to call the goblin later and ask him why he had responded so oddly to the Herald's appearance. Had he really never encountered such guests before?

"Thank you for waiting, Earl," said the Herald, returning after ten minutes. "This situation is truly out of the ordinary. The laws of Malabar clearly state that a Free Citizen may not govern any settlements or manage their resources. However, considering the various factors at play...Well, in short, the Emperor wishes to personally communicate his decision to you. Please follow me."

The Herald moved aside and it was my turn to step through the portal. As soon as the Herald had reappeared, Viltrius, who had returned by now, turned into a statute again. But when the Herald mentioned that the Emperor wished to see me, something must have gone wrong in the poor goblin's head because he simply collapsed to the floor unconscious.

"Hi, Mahan!" The first thing I heard upon appearing in the Imperial palace was the happy voice of the Princess. After what had happened in the Cliffy Forest, my reputation with Tisha had reached Esteem, while my Attractiveness to her (I paused specifically to check it again) was now at 83. Slate should be resurrected very soon—this time in human form—and no one will be able to stop him from becoming the Princess's legal husband. "Are you going to see dad? Stop by to see me later please. Take this amulet. When you're free, call me."

Quest available: 'Conversation with the Princess.' Description: The Princess is incredibly happy that Slate has become human and wishes to express her gratitude to you. Quest type: Rare. Restriction: Have at least status of Esteem with Princess.

Item acquired: 'Disposable Amulet of Communication with Princess Tisha.'

"Of course, Tisha. As soon as I have time, I'll meet with you. Excuse me right now though, I believe your father is expecting me..."

Since the Herald could have delivered me directly to the Emperor, I could assume that the meeting with the Princess had been arranged for me ahead of time. Well, then...My to-do list was beginning to burst at its seams. With every passing hour more quests piled on and I was beginning to hope I wouldn't have to start a new list to fit them all.

"Free Citizens of Malabar! Earl Mahan, Ehkiller, Ankir and Karrar!" announced the crier, opening the doors to the throne room. Three portals appeared and the three other players emerged from them. We exchanged greetings and paused in anticipation—the Emperor doesn't summon such an odd combination of people without good reason. Ehkiller I was acquainted with, but the others were dark horses as far as I was concerned. Who are they, I wondered, and where'd they come from? Judging by their clan symbols—

Ankir was in Phoenix and Karrar wasn't in any clan at all. Odd...

The last time I was in this room, Geranika's Dagger had still been stuck in the throne, which had been surrounded by the Stones of Light. Now, it was occupied by Naahti, who looked down upon us majestically. All six of the Advisors, the Duchess of Caltanor, the toad-like Governor of Serrest and several dozen unfamiliar NPCs, all imparted a certain formal quality to this meeting. Accordingly, all four of the players took on proud, prim postures as we entered the hall.

"Gentlemen, please have a seat," the Emperor said and—as if a magic wand had been waved—a large round table appeared in the center of the throne room. While the NPCs took their seats around it, we remained standing: There were no seats for the Free Players.

"You have come here at my request with a single purpose," the Emperor addressed the assembly, "to decide whether the time has come to change our laws or leave them as they are."

If I understand correctly, the assembled included all thirty-three Governors who remained in Malabar after the Kartossian expansion, the Duchess as the representative of the aristocracy and the Advisors, the highest authorities in the land after the Emperor. This was in effect the Governing Committee of Malabar! The Emperor, meanwhile, went on: "You are aware of the reason for such exigent measures. Before we begin the voting process, I wish to hear your views on the matter at hand."

"Lestran Province fully supports the Emperor's initiative to amend the law," the Governor of Lestran spoke up. "Free residents have long since proven themselves to be competent leaders. A portion of them should be entrusted with the management of villages and even small towns. I understand that there are risks involved—that the Free Citizens will seek to enrich themselves at the expense of the Empire, if not directly, then indirectly, so the selection of suitable candidates and our oversight of their governance must be very careful. But my opinion is that we can give them the chance to prove themselves. If the villages or towns under their administration begin to grow, we could even look the other way when..."

"The position of Lestran Province is understandable," the Emperor interrupted my Governor—with whom I enjoyed Exalted status. "Are there others among the assembly who wish to express their views before we vote?"

"Brantar Province opposes the amendment!" spoke up a very dignified looking man—a military uniform with a plethora of medals, a military bearing, whiskers...the Brantar Governor reminded me a bit of the Mayor of Narlak. It was almost as if they were related. "The Free Citizens, especially after they appeared in Kartoss, have become the scourge of Malabar! Raids, pogroms, brigandage! It's not only the Kartossians either—the Malabarians too have been destroying whole towns, to say nothing of the villages. Lestran's position is unsurprising—the players recently helped save one of their towns, and the Governor has no problem looking the other way. Yet the esteemed Krondavir does not know, or does not wish to know, that in the last three months, seven of my towns were razed to the ground. Seven! Of these, only five were the fault of the Kartossians—the others were the work of our own Malabarians! Why should we trust them with the administration of our villages and towns in particular? Solely so that they can build better bases to launch stronger raids from? Solely so that they work to enrich themselves without a care for the Empire?"

"The position of Brantar Province is understandable. Are there others who wish to speak?"

Another three Governors—of Alyen, Nirriana and Shatil Provinces—expressed their support for amending the law. Four, including Governor Toad there, were opposed. The rest, including the Advisors, remained silent.

"Duchess," the Emperor addressed the majestic lady, "do you have something to say?"

"Yes, my Emperor," replied the lady, without taking her eyes from me. "As the official representative of the aristocracy of Malabar, I too think that the time has come to change, to grow. Not all of the current leaders have earned their positions lawfully," the Duchess glanced over at Governor Toad, who sank into his chair under her glare, "but also not all of the Free Citizens have the right to govern. How we shall determine who is worthy of this honor and who is not—is a matter for further discussion, one at which quite obviously, the Free Citizens should be absent. But since they are already here now, I will say that I nominated these four candidates because they had earned my trust and thus the trust of the entire nobility. My advice is this: Let's grant permission to these sentients to govern several small settlements over the next six months. After the trial period, we shall evaluate their work and make a further decision. My Emperor is well acquainted with each of these four men, so it makes no sense to detail the advantages and disadvantages of each. One should not rush headlong into uncharted territory; one should enter it with caution. I request that the Emperor make a sensible decision."

"Thank you, Duchess," concluded the Emperor, lost in thought. Apparently, the Imitator had begun his upgrade procedure, since it wasn't likely that such a critical change to the game mechanics would occur spontaneously. "I have reached a decision. Advisors, I request you to bear witness and record it. First of all, four Free Citizens of Malabar shall be allowed to serve as rulers of several settlements, with a total population of up to ten thousand sentients, for a period of six months. Further! I confer upon Free Citizens Ehkiller, Ankir and Karrar the titles of Baron! Third of all, if after the expiration of the test period, the results will be positive, this practice shall be extended to all Free Citizens who meet the required criteria, which we shall determine later. Such is my decision!"

A message flashed before my eyes, repeating

verbatim the Emperor's words and culminating with two response options: 'Accept' and 'Decline.' Keenly aware that one does not decline such an offer, I pushed the 'Accept' button and turned to watch what the others would decide. Ehkiller's eyes remained glassy longer than anyone else's. The Mage seemed to be poring over the text and looking for any pitfalls. When he finally rejoined us, the Emperor continued with his speech:

"I hereby enjoin the Free Barons and the Earl here present to arrange their village administrations within the next ten days and summon a Herald to formalize their appointments. I thank all those present. I declare this meeting concluded!"

CHAPTER TWO
SHAMANISM IS A VOCATION

As I strolled through Anhurs, I reflected on my meeting with Tisha. I had beelined for her chambers as soon as I left the throne room. As the assembly adjourned, I had ducked a conversation with Ehkiller—the Mage had made it clear that he wanted to speak with me, but I...Well, I simply didn't feel like hearing another fairy tale about how the circumstances had been beyond him, how he hadn't been able to tell me about his deal with Geranika and how the whole world was tumbling into a perilous unknown...It's not like he'd tell me anything I didn't already know. Plus he'd find some way to make it sound like it was all my fault. So, instead, I hurried off to meet Tisha. I was looking forward to some rare quest. It wasn't every day that the Princess invited a player to a personal appointment. In fact, the whole business was starting to smell to me like a quest chain or another scenario...

Or...nothing of the kind.

In fact, Tisha didn't have any good news for me at all. She didn't have any bad news either, but there certainly wasn't any unique surprises for me like I had expected. Thanking me for my assistance with Slate, the Princess assured me of her full support and friendship in the future. Then she advised me to stop by for an audience in about a month—when the Prince had returned. At that point, this quest was marked completed. I didn't receive a further one, despite all her kind words. After Tisha finished singing my praises, she thanked me for having found the opportunity to meet her, excused herself and went off on her way. I was left alone with a sense of deep dissatisfaction and disappointment. It was a total mystery to me why this meeting had been arranged at all. I was sure that the devs had set it up on purpose—did they wish to show me that the Princess remembered about me but didn't have time to deal with me? All of this gave rise to nothing but further unanswered questions...

Realizing that the palace was closed to me, I went out into Anhurs and headed for the Shamanic compound. I needed to find out when I would get my powers back.

"How can I help you, Renegade?" a Shamanic Mentor addressed me as soon as I set foot on the training ground. Just like that, all of my thoughts were pulled out by their roots and without anesthesia. What did he just call me?

"Renegade." I suppose that I looked so

bewildered that the Mentor decided to repeat the word for good measure. "A Shaman who has been stripped of his class abilities. When Geranika acquired the Heart of Chaos, the Shaman Council assembled and resolved to...Harbinger," the Shaman suddenly stuttered, greeting his elder. I turned around and encountered the cool stare of Prontho, head of the Shaman Council.

"Follow me," barked the orc, He turned around and briskly headed for the only building at the training ground. Hmm...I'm beginning to like this less and less. The Shaman Council is a very powerful institution. It doesn't convene to deal with an ordinary player without some very substantial reason.

"Sit down," said Prontho once he'd led me into his office. He waited until I took a seat in the only available chair, circled his massive desk which was piled high with some papers, and collapsed into his armchair.

One glance around the office sent shivers running down my spine—I was in the exact replica of the Pryke Mine Governor's office. Even the painting of the orc warriors, depicting the glory of the orcish race, occupied the exact same place of honor where I'd last seen it. All this place needed was a horn, the ringing of pickaxes and the cries of prisoners—and I would have felt right 'at home.'

For several moments Prontho remained sitting quietly, staring in my direction but also somewhere off into the distance, as if deciding how to begin the conversation. At last his gaze regained its clarity and he said softly:

"Kornik..."

Almost immediately, my goblin teacher appeared in the office. He looked around, smiled, disappeared and immediately reappeared again, only this time with a chair and a glass full of some liquid.

"So he showed up after all!" Despite the apparent severity of the situation, the sarcasm in Kornik's voice remained undiminished. "Didn't everyone tell you to keep your nose out of Altameda, you dolt? 'And if you do go in there,' they all said, 'remember that you are a Shaman!' But no, all he could think of was getting his paws on his castle. What are we supposed to do with you now?"

"Understand and forgive," I growled the first thing that came to mind, knowing that the goblin's question had been rhetorical.

"The Council has decided that you are not worthy of its confidence," Prontho finally emerged from his meditative stupor. "We therefore decided to temporarily strip you of your summoning powers."

"Temporarily?" I grasped at the lifeline.

"The Council has deprived you of your power for two months," Kornik explained. "As long as it takes for the other Free Citizens to destroy the Heart."

"What a bunch of malarkey," I looked at the Harbingers with bewilderment. "If it's my fault that Geranika got the Heart, shouldn't I be involved in...Wait a second...Did you say that the Council made the decision? Wasn't most of the Council assembled under Shiam?"

"It hasn't even been six months! I'm beginning to suspect that the only time you use your head is when you're cramming food into it," quipped Kornik, confirming my sudden hunch—Geranika had his followers among the High Shamans of Malabar!

"But Anastaria and Plinto..." I began and fell silent, suddenly realizing the much larger plan that the developers had in mind: The struggle against Geranika was to occur not only in his empire, situated in the far western portion of the continent, but also in Anhurs, a place brimming with the spies and followers of Shadow.

"As well as the Warrior Hellfire, the Death Knight Donotpunnik, the Hunter Exodus and a dozen other Free Citizens who are the most skilled in their respective classes...All of them have been deprived of their class powers for two months, opening the way for other heroes. The situation's so bad that the Emperor has decreed that the clan tournament shall be put off to a later date. It doesn't make much sense to hold it when none of the best can participate."

"But why me? What about Antsinthepantsa? And surely there are a hundred other Shamans that could trounce me in a heartbeat..."

"Unfortunately, or fortunately, no one knows what happened to Antsinthepantsa. Last anyone heard of her she had gone to Astrum and became one of its subjects. As for the hundreds of Shamans...You're right—there are many of us in Malabar, but practically every single one of them is stuck at the Elemental rank. You are the only High

Shaman who has a chance, however small, to become a Harbinger. That is why they decided to limit you. Altameda had nothing to do with it."

"So we have to smoke out the traitors?" I decided to take the bull by the horns. All of this really felt like a quest was forthcoming. But it would take forever for these two NPCs to get to the main point.

"Agreed. They need to be found," agreed Kornik. "Only to do so we'll need either Initiate Shamans or Elemental Shamans that have followed the right path. Do you know where we can find any?"

"Why only Initiate Shamans?" I asked baffled. How come I wasn't eligible for this quest?

"Because we need someone who'll smoke out Geranika's followers. We know roughly who may be a traitor, but we need to confirm it to avoid a witch hunt. The only way to identify the traitors is to give them the opportunity to seduce a Free Citizen to Geranika's side."

"In that case, you have no way of ensuring that the Free Citizen won't agree," I went on pressuring them to give me the quest. This just wasn't fair, after all!

"You're right—there is no guarantee. If the Free Citizen decides to join Geranika's army, that'll be his choice. Before issuing such a quest to a novice, we will ask them what is important to them as far as this world is concerned and what they are trying to accomplish in it. We must keep in mind that a time of changes is upon us."

"But that doesn't explain why you can't simply

use me as the bait!"

"Really, you do only use your head as a convenient conduit for shoveling grub into your belly," muttered Kornik. "You, my dear knucklehead, have been marked by the Lord of Shadow. No traitor is going to approach you about joining Geranika. Besides, Geranika has deemed you his personal nemesis, so...Shall I go on or will you try and think for yourself for a change?"

"What do I have to do then?" I asked in surprise, realizing with a slight shock that I had just been removed from the game for two months.

"There's no point in continuing your education at the moment," Kornik said pensively. "You'll forget everything in two months anyway. So I can only recommend one thing—go back to Altameda and work on being a good ruler. Once your ownership of the castle becomes permanent, we'll start your training."

Quest updated: 'The Way of the Shaman. Step 4. Training.' Your training has been delayed for a period of three months.

"Three months? If we don't take the Heart of Chaos from Geranika, then Malabar won't have three months! What're you thinking, Harbingers?"

"Stop acting like a Mage!" Prontho cast me another grim look. "Your Shamanic powers are blocked for the next two months. That's a hard fact we can't avoid. After that, the clan competitions will begin—the Emperor has pushed them back until everyone regains their abilities. Somehow I doubt that you'll choose training over competing alongside your clan. As for Geranika...Bear in mind that what I'm about to tell you is a strict secret. If the other Free Citizens find out about it, I'll know who spilled the beans—and I'll make the appropriate conclusions. If the Free Citizens fail to destroy the Heart of Chaos in the next two months, then Eluna will intercede. No one has any desire to see Barliona sink into the depths of darkness. The goddess is therefore prepared to sacrifice her divinity and destroy the Heart. If she does this, the higher planes will descend to chaos as the various powers fight for control of the empty throne. Despite all that, Barliona will be saved."

"Is there no way at all for me to get my powers back?" I made one last attempt. Prontho had just regaled me with one of his longest orations and I think I was supposed to be rubbing my chin in deep contemplation—but the thought that I'd be without any access to my Spirits for two months gave me such a sinking feeling that...

"Come here, Draco!"

"Coming."

"Heh," I heard Kornik's satisfied chuckle, after which the goblin turned to the orc and intoned unctuously:

"This is why I didn't bother arguing with you. I know my student too!"

"Brother...Harbingers," Draco greeted everyone present. "Nice little conference you're having here."

"Don't bother with the Spirits. They are definitely

blocked," Kornik went on, noticing that I was trying to summon a Healing Spirit. "In fact, theoretically, your ability to summon your Totem is blocked too. If you'd summoned him the way the other Shamans do, nothing would've happened. But Draco is more than just a Totem for you. He is an extension of you and how can anyone prohibit a sentient from using a part of his essence? Shall I tell you about another nice feature of your abilities being blocked?"

"Shoot..."

"Don't interrupt! Since theoretically you cannot summon your Totem, you didn't actually summon anyone just now. As a result...Well? Do you get it?" Kornik gave me a testing look as if I was supposed to experience some epiphany.

"No—you know—with a student like this, I'll lose all faith in the youth of today," erupted Kornik when my eyes didn't go wide from amazement. "There aren't any limitations to the summons, you ninny! Your Totem may remain in this world for the entire two months. He can study, play, interact...Oh Supremes, why do you punish me like this?"

"No limitations?" came the voice of the Totem, who had grown still all of a sudden. "So I can go to the library this very instant and stay there for a whole week?"

"Goblins above! You two dimwits really do deserve each other..."

"May I go, brother?" the excited Dragon turned to me. "I...I need to!"

"Go right ahead," I smiled at the Totem, yet by

the time the last syllable had left my mouth all I could see was Draco's tail vanishing in the busted out window.

"It wouldn't hurt you to study a bit too," remarked Kornik and summoned some kind of Spirit to repair the window. "You need to learn how to manage a castle properly and what your rights and obligations are as an Earl. As I understand it, you've been granted the governance of a settlement. You should read up on how to manage it properly so that you don't find yourself up a creek, so to speak. You won't even notice the two months fly by! That's it for now. You may go. We've wasted too much time chatting here as it is."

Kornik simply disappeared, taking the chair he'd brought with him, and Prontho arched an eyebrow inquisitively as if wondering why I was still in his office. I had no choice but to mutter "thank you for the information" and leave the building. Sitting down on the steps, I tried to process everything that I had just learned. It turns out that all the major players of our continent, which, as I noted with pleasure, included yours truly, had been deprived of their powers for two months. This had been done in order to allow the remaining mass of players to catch up a little to the leaders—if not in level then at least in their involvement in the various events that the Corporation had arranged. I wasn't about to go against the Harbingers' advice and throw myself headlong with the rest of the players against Geranika's Empire. My daily trips to Altameda to renew my presence there would cost so much money that Leite would end up suffering a stroke. So I really would have to stay in place and do some studying ...

"It's no good!" I heard a girl's plaintive voice. "This goddamn race. I'll delete it to hell and restart with something more human!"

"Anger will get you nowhere," said one of the teachers.

Typically, I wouldn't have noticed this scene—students who were having trouble with something were all over Barliona. And yet these people were speaking Kartossian—on the Shamanic training ground in Anhurs, in the heart of the Malabar Empire!

I could see two people near the pond, beside two trees which according to the lore had been planted by the Supreme Spirits themselves many millennia ago. I recognized the Mentor who had called me 'Renegade,' and a girl who outwardly at least resembled a human. The reason I say resembled is because the arms of this lovely creature were unnaturally white. Any race can have blue hair—but only vampires could have such pale skin. Had these toothy beings appeared in Kartoss, depriving Plinto of his claim to uniqueness? If I were the Rogue, I'd be a little miffed...

Trying to make as little noise as possible, I crept closer and stopped ten paces from the pair. Apparently, the Mentor was teaching the girl how to summon a Spirit. He kept pointing at a training dummy and telling her to concentrate while renouncing the surrounding world. The girl was nodding her head—unfortunately I couldn't make out her face from where I was standing—and waving her hands, freezing in place and even hopping around like a goat—all to no avail: Nothing happened and the training dummy remained untouched.

"To hell with this!" the girl snapped after yet another failed attempt. She flared up and barked to no one in particular: "That's it. I give up! Zombies cannot be Shamans! They're not meant for it! I'm done."

A Zombie? Only now did I decide to check the girl's properties: Fleita the Decembrist, Level 8 Zombie, no class.

"Wait!" I managed to call to the girl who had begun to fade—she was leaving the game apparently with the intention of deleting her character. "Don't start over!"

"Why shouldn't I start over if nothing works? Oh!" the girl faded back in, turned to see who was speaking to her and froze in place with a silly smile which revealed a row of black teeth. Hmm...yeah...Generally speaking, Fleita was an attractive girl—shapely and well proportioned—but her face...yeesh! Her face was chalk white, as were her pupil-less eyes. Her blue hair partly obscured her face just like in that ancient horror flick *The Ring*...Jeez...

"Just don't," I replied to the flustered girl. There was a 'no PVP' marker hovering over her head which meant that this cute zombie was under eighteen and, therefore, this was the way she looked in reality, albeit with less 'undead' features...

"*Stacey, I have a question: Can a player start a character without choosing a class?*"

"*That's a new mechanic for new players. They introduced it with the Kartoss expansion. Until a player hits Level 10, he can try out all the classes to choose the one that fits him best. In other words, the tier one skills are unlocked for everyone. Why—did you meet someone without a class?*"

"*Yeah, a very surprising phenomenon. Thanks for the information.*"

"*You're welcome. I'm probably going to pop out to reality for a couple of days. Then I'll spend a week with Nashlazar. After that, we'll have a day to ourselves. A telepathic kiss until then...*"

"So what isn't working out for you?" I asked Fleita.

"Well...I don't even know how to explain it. The teacher wants me to focus and see the Spirit within, but...The spell itself is in the spellbook. When I activate it, an icon appears, but as soon as I cast it at the target dummy, something goes wrong! I've been at it for a whole week already!"

"I see...Show me, please, how you summon the Spirit..."

"You don't get it," forgetting her embarrassment, the girl adopted a more informal tone and began to explain. "The teacher told me that I can't summon Spirits. I can only use the spellbook at the moment. It contains several spells from each class. For the Shaman it has the Spirits of Healing and Lightning. I can activate the spell and aim it, but it all falls apart after that."

"I understand. Show me!"

"Okay. First, we activate the spell." The icon of a lightning bolt in an orb appeared in the girl's hand. "Then we cast it at the training dummy and," as soon as it left the girl's hand, the lightning bolt fizzed out as if it never existed, "the show's over. Damn it all! How much more of this can I take?"

"All right. I saw it. What does the Mentor say?"

"Mentor?" echoed Fleita.

"The one you call your teacher. What does he tell you to do?"

"That I need to find this lightning bolt within myself and imagine that it appears in the dummy on its own. But for this I need to concentrate on my inner self. I understand perfectly well what he is trying to tell me—over the last two weeks I've read every forum post and guide and asked everyone I could...But it all comes down to one thing—Zombies cannot be Shamans. They're not meant for it—they have limits coded in."

"But you managed to create the icon," I reminded the girl.

"Well yes, but when I was trying out being a Mage, I could cast the icon however I wanted too! I had all the training dummies convulsing on the floor, while here...I get nothing at all. It seems that I'll have to start over with a different race, since I'll never become a Zombie Shaman."

"By the way, why'd you choose a Zombie

anyway?"

"Because that's the only Kartossian race that looks remotely human. I don't have the money to be a Dark One and they're charging now to transfer a character from Malabar to Kartoss...so Zombie's all I had. And, I'd like to point out that only the first few minutes feel odd...after that, you get used to it."

"In that case, here's the next question—what is a Kartossian like you doing in Anhurs? Especially at such a low level?"

"There's no one to teach Zombies in Kartoss. Rather, there's no one to teach Zombies how to become Shamans. You can learn how to be a Warrior, a Dark Priest, a Necromancer...whoever you want, but not a Shaman! Everyone I asked, goblins, kobolds, orcs...No one could help me. Then I watched the movies and decided that Shamans have a much better time of it in Malabar. And really, Prontho, who's the boss around here, understood me right away...By the way! How do you know how to speak Kartossian? I've about lost my mind here trying to communicate with other players—no one understands me! They even wanted to attack me several times," Fleita grinned, "the dumb brats...The guards immediately took care of them. You can't hurt minnows like me."

"Prontho," I reminded the girl, trying to bring the conversation back on topic.

"What about Prontho?" the girl stopped in her tracks and looked around in bewilderment. "Is he coming?"

"You were telling me that Prontho understood

you and...?"

"Oh! Right! He speaks Kartossian, so he assigned me one of the teachers who also spoke it and sent me to train. So I've been here two weeks already with nothing to show for it."

"In that case, here's the most important question of all—why'd you decide to become a Shaman? I doubt you've wasted two weeks just to learn the principles of summoning Spirits. Why do you want to be a Shaman?"

Fleita looked down at the ground without replying.

"Okay, I see. Very well. Best of luck to you in your future endeavors..."

"Because I watched the movies!" the girl blurted out with a defiant look.

"That's good that you watched them. But so what?" I failed to understand her point.

"And nothing! When you were pulling Yalininka out, I felt like I was right there beside you! When you sank the dagger into Geranika's breast, I was yelling at you to leave Kornik alone! When...I watched all seventeen Barliona movies, but only those two made me feel like I was in them. I...I can't explain it, but I feel like I simply have to become a Shaman!"

There was so much resolution in the girl's eyes that I couldn't walk away without trying to help her. The Mentor had frozen like a statue several meters away from us, letting us have our conversation, so I seized the initiative:

"Did you try to form the icon directly inside the

target dummy?"

"I did. It doesn't work. The only place I can get it to appear is in my hand...Okay, I'm sorry I bothered you," Fleita switched back to a polite tone of voice. "It looks like I'll have to be a goblin. But one way or another, I'll become a Shaman! It's a matter of principle for me!"

"Don't worry about bothering me, I have a lot of time on my hands at the moment. You should try to forget about the spellbook though, and summon the Spirit directly inside the dummy."

Even though the girl seemed determined to delete her Zombie and switch to a Goblin, I wasn't about to give up. I was growing curious now: Were Spirits really inaccessible to Zombies or not? In the Dark Forest, I discovered an interesting feature of these undead creatures—the plane of reality they occupy lies parallel to the one the Spirits are in. The Patriarch had been unable to communicate with the Supreme Spirits and vice versa. Since I was now faced with a member of the Barliona undead who was eager to become a Shaman, I could use the opportunity to run some experiments—as long as she didn't have a problem with it, obviously.

"I don't understand," said Fleita sadly. "What do you mean by summon a Spirit? According to the forums, I need to enter Spirit Summoning Mode..."

"Forget about the forums," I interrupted the girl. "Just imagine that the Spirit has possessed the dummy and all you need to do is poke it. The only problem is that you have to do so at a distance."

"I still don't understand," Fleita was on the verge of tears. "What do you want me to do?"

"The dead cannot communicate with the spirits, oh Renegade," the Mentor suddenly said to me in Malabarian so that the Zombie wouldn't understand him. "I angered the head of Council and his punishment for me was to make this girl understand—without showing her my irritation—that Zombies cannot be Shamans. They were passed over in this either by nature itself or that mad Mage that first created the elixir of revival. You should not torment her in vain."

"What did he say?" asked Fleita instantly. "He's saying that I'm incompetent, isn't he? I already knew as much...Okay, thank you, but..."

"Silence! Stay right there!" I never thought that I could yell at other people, especially girls, but now for some reason it seemed like the right thing to do. The girl was taken aback and all but snapped to attention like a well-drilled soldier. "Take a seat here," I pointed to the pond's shore, "and wait for me! I'll be right back! And if you even dare to delete your character, you may as well quit the game all together! Is that clear?"

Staring at me wide-eyed, Fleita nevertheless turned around obediently and walked over to the bank. That was good enough for me. Now I needed to have a chat with someone...

"Kornik, I need your help!" I spoke to the empty air. Even though they had removed my ability to communicate with the Spirits, they couldn't keep me from communicating with my teacher...

"You do know that your summoning abilities are blocked, right?" the goblin quipped sarcastically, appearing beside me. "How many times do I have to tell you—you're not a Shaman right now!"

"So how'd you hear me then?"

"I didn't." A wide grin spread across Kornik's face. "I was just passing by when suddenly I see my listless student standing there screaming his head off at no one. What kind of teacher would I be if I didn't stop to find out if he was feeling all right in the head?"

"We can deal with my head later. At the moment, why don't you tell me whether Fleita can become a Shaman or not?"

"You really aren't feeling well, are you? Why don't you take a nap in the shade there?" said my teacher with mock worry and even tried to hop up to feel my temperature. "You're overheated, I see...How many times have I taught you to consider what you're saying? How can a flute become a Shaman?"

"What? Not a flute like the instrument..." I realized that the goblin misheard me and pointed at the Zombie. "Her—her name is Fleita..."

"Heh," grunted Kornik and began examining the girl with such interest that he even cocked his head. "Who would have thought that a Zombie would decide to become a Shaman...What is the world coming to?!"

"You haven't answered me, Kornik," I restrained my teacher from slipping into one of his lengthy digressions.

"My answer..." the goblin began—but fell silent,

struck by something that Fleita was doing. The girl had grown bored of sitting beside the lake. She pulled out a fishing rod and began to fish. A minute passed and Kornik sat down on the ground in the Lotus pose. He continued to study the little angler, as if he could see some profound meaning in her actions. Having grown accustomed to trust the wisdom of this Imitator, I took a seat beside him. If the time had come to observe—well, why not observe a little...

Over the thirty minutes that I meditated on the girl, she caught only two shiny fish—common carp, according to their properties. There was nothing remarkable at all about them, and yet during the same thirty minutes Kornik hummed twice, both times after Fleita caught a fish.

"Now I understand," the goblin said at long last and vanished without bothering to explain a thing. Well, I tried my best, I guess...

"Fleita," I called the girl, "enough fishing. Come over here. Fleita!" I had to raise my voice since the girl didn't seem to hear me at all—or simply pretended not to hear...

"Eh? What?" she asked, looking around, as if not quite knowing where she was. "Oh, I completely lost track of time. What did you come up with?"

"I'm sorry..." I began and shook my head, noting with displeasure the sudden 'extinguished' look in the Zombie's eyes. When our conversation began, they were white, but as soon as I shook my head, a kind of gray dullness filled them.

"Okay, I get it. In any case, thanks for trying to

help...If I start another character in Malabar, will you let me join your clan? Your projections are pretty. I want one."

"Sure, I'll let you join. Just write me and tell me that you're Fleita."

"What—has our blockhead upset you?" Kornik said suddenly and clearly not to me. "He's a good one to seek advice from!"

"Excuse me?" The girl's face expressed complete bewilderment.

"I said, he's a blockhead," Kornik stepped out from behind my back and walked right up to the girl. "How's the fish?"

"Not great. Barely biting. All I caught was two carps."

"Considering that those would be the first two carps caught in that pond in as many millennia— then, yes, 'barely biting' is a fair assessment," grinned Kornik.

"What do you mean?" asked the girl still failing to understand the goblin's point—as did I in all honesty.

"My student will explain," Kornik turned to me as if he could sense my confusion.

It was pointless to ask the goblin dumb questions, so I tried to consider what he had said about the two carps. If they really are the first fish that have been caught in the pond, then...

"Tell us how you caught the fish," I asked the girl. "And I don't mean in the sense of 'I cast my line, saw the fish biting and pulled it out.' I want to know about your feelings."

"Feelings? I...I cast the line and it was like...I don't even know how to explain it...I had this feeling that I was transported to another world. One part of me knew for sure that there weren't any fish here, but another part didn't want to believe it, and stubbornly searched for the fish, reeling it in from somewhere far away...from some place that's at once warm and pleasant and cold and chilly."

A shiver ran down my spine. The girl was talking about the Astral Plane, the abode of the Supreme Spirits! In spite of everything, she had managed to get through!

"Yup, that's roughly what I think too," said Kornik philosophically, giving my reaction a mocking glance. "Looks like we're dealing with another sentient who's decided to ignore all the rules. So you wish to become a Shaman, my dear?"

"I do," said the girl.

"In that case—be one," shrugged Kornik. "You have the power and the desire. Everything else will come with experience. And don't ever listen to anyone when they tell you that you can't be a Shaman. You proved the opposite just now..."

Kornik vanished, as did the Mentor, and Fleita and I remained on our own.

"Mahan, will you tell me what just happened? I don't understand a damn thing..."

"There's no fish in that lake..."

"I already got that, but what does that have to do with me being a Shaman?"

"There's no fish in the lake," I said, this time for my own benefit, "but you couldn't care less about that fact. You used the fishing rod as a focus point and ended up catching two fish through the Astral Plane. Do I need to explain to you what the Astral Plane is?"

"I did that?!" It was looking like Fleita's primary goal for the rest of the day would be not dying from astonishment. "I know what the Astral Plane is. But only High Shamans can enter it!"

"Yes. Kornik mentioned that," I replied, a bit jealously. Ever since I had managed to wrangle my way into the Astral Plane while still an Elemental Shaman, I thought of myself as quite the rarity. But here came Fleita and managed to enter it without even having reached Beginner rank. What would she be capable of when she became a High Shaman? "If you decide to become a Shaman, you will be able to summon Spirits. In effect, you already managed to do just that—you caught two fish."

"So what should I do now?"

"As I understand it, you need to reach Level 10 and choose the Shaman class if that's what you still want. Then you'll have to find a teacher and harass him until he explains the principles of passing the Shamanic trial to you...Or actually, until he teaches you how to be a Shaman. I think you'll manage to pass your trial on your own...Kornik!" I called out again.

"Well, what are you yelling about now? I told you—your ability to summon your teacher has been blocked!"

"Kornik—Fleita has decided to become a Shaman. You should be her teacher! No one but you can teach her properly."

"Heh, have you decided to get rid of me?" the goblin asked wryly. "Tired of your old teacher, huh?"

"Why get rid of? To the contrary, this is a worthy challenge to the great and terrible Kornik, the doom of all mortals! Who else, if not you, will be able to teach the one who cannot be taught?"

"I don't want to study with him," said Fleita, with one fell swoop knocking down all my fantasies. I had almost persuaded the goblin to take her as a new student, when, well, here you go! "If I must have a teacher, I want you to be it. It was you who made me go to the lake!"

"He cannot become your teacher, oh class-less one," Kornik began with his typical snark, and yet, I knew this NPC well enough by now to be certain that this wasn't a laughing matter for him. It's true that I have a quest to become a teacher, which I have to do once Kornik gets done teaching me, but considering my social position back in reality, only an NPC could become my student. And that's not to mention that I've never even heard of players becoming the students of other players. If I'm not mistaken, that would be against the game rules. Either an NPC teaches a player or a player teaches an NPC. There's no other option.

"Why not?" To my surprise, Fleita refused to cave. "He is a High Shaman and he's always involved in events that expose the true values of Shamanism.

Only practice can make a true Shaman—not reading some dusty volume you've stored somewhere in your cellar."

"He can't be your teacher because he's got nothing to offer—no powers, no abilities, no skills. He's not much of a Shaman at the moment, you see..."

"That's only for the next two months," I couldn't help but butt in. There's no need to embarrass me in front of a colleague...

"There, you see?" Fleita said happily. "Mahan isn't against it! I'll spend the two months reading up on the theory and after that we'll start training! Is that all right with you?"

"Heh," was all that Kornik could manage at this juncture. "One more headache for this poor goblin...Prontho—come over here, will you?"

"What's happened now?" As cool as Akela from the *Jungle Book*, the orc appeared beside us and looked us over thoughtfully. It's odd—according to Kornik, the two are constantly arguing over every possible thing, but I'm having trouble imagining this confident, charismatic and renowned Shaman arguing over which end of a hardboiled egg one should crack. I guess such fantasies are beyond me...

"She wants to become a student," Kornik nodded in Fleita's direction and then at me, "of his. She says she wants to have a Dragon, since this is what she's always dreamed of."

"An undead creature cannot become a Shaman," Prontho declared flatly. "You've torn me away from my work over this?"

"No one's arguing about that. Moreover, I'm in agreement with you!" It was looking like Kornik was having his moment of glory. I hadn't heard this much snark in his voice in a long time—and yet the topic was pretty serious! "But you see, Fleita didn't choose Mahan for no reason. Did you see that?" Kornik pointed at the two carps still lying on the pond shore.

"From the pond?" asked Prontho gravely.

"From the pond," the goblin sighed sadly. "The Supreme Spirits say that the time has come to forget prior limits...The Shadows seek to erase everything..."

"He cannot become your teacher, oh class-less one," the orc immediately rejoined as if echoing the goblin.

"I already heard that part," Fleita still refused to back down. "He's got no powers, no abilities, no skills. He's not much of a Shaman at the moment, blah blah blah...I believe he can! And you can all go to hell! Here you all are holding a big meeting and not one of you wants to make a decision."

Having said this, the girl turned to me and said with a smirk:

"Mahan, take me on as a student. I promise to be studious, to argue only about matters of principle, to agree with almost all you tell me and to do most of the quests you send me on! I promise I'll spend five to six hours of the day in-game, except on weekends and during finals. What else...Oh! Please!"

"You know, it looks like she's not getting it," Kornik whispered to the orc, although everyone could still hear him. "Mahan really cannot become a teacher right now."

I hadn't received a notification of a new quest with the girl's offer, which made perfect sense—she wasn't an NPC and couldn't generate quests. At the same time, there had also been no warning that I wasn't allowed to accept her offer. To hell with all this!

"Unclassified Free Citizen Fleita the Decembrist! Since you have chosen to become a Shaman, I am prepared to become your teacher and teach you everything I know and have learned myself. However, you must know something about me which may have a serious effect on your decision—I am a convict who is serving his sentence in Barliona. I escaped Pryke Mine where this orc was the governor," I nodded at Prontho who remained still like a marble statue, "so if you become my student, you will be studying with a criminal."

"If you were a bad person," it took Fleita literally several moments to make her decision, "you wouldn't be standing here. My offer stands—I'll reach Level 10 in a few days and become a Shaman! Then I'll consider myself your student. You promised!"

"I confirm my words," my heart skipped a beat when Fleita told me that my social standing didn't matter to her. "Go ahead and become a Shaman and..."

"She doesn't have to wait until Level 10," Kornik said wistfully. "If your decision is final and you don't intend on seeing reason, Fleita is allowed to become a Shaman this very instant..."

"Oh! What do I need to do?" the girl inquired.

"Prontho?" Kornik cast his melancholy glance at the orc. "I'm through arguing. One Mahan is enough for me. If I have to deal with Mahan and Fleita together, I'll be in the goblin madhouse within a month. I give up. If she wants him as her teacher, let her think he's her teacher..."

"Let it be so!" Prontho proclaimed loftily and vanished into thin air. Boy, I really can't wait to be a Harbinger!

"I'm going to take your student with me for the next eight hours," Kornik told me, taking Fleita by the hand. "I'll turn her into an Initiate Shaman. After that, you can deal with her on your own. Remember— she must undergo her trial to become Elemental Shaman six months from now. Don't let me down..."

Kornik and Fleita vanished, leaving a single anxious Shaman beside the lake—me, that is. Life is strange. I had come here to figure out why I had been stripped of my powers...and ended up becoming a teacher. It'd be nice to avoid Stacey and Plinto for a little while. They'd really let me have it if they found out.

"Magdey, Clutzer—I'll need the services of your raid parties in the coming days. We'll have to complete a new Dungeon which is supposed to contain some tasty bosses. Please, clear your schedules for it—First Kills don't grow on trees!"

After I finished issuing orders, I headed off to get some rest with a clean conscience. With one swoop, I had just struck two of my thirteen tasks from the list—I'd figured out how I had lost my powers and acquired a student. The next step, as I saw it, would be the Skrooj Dungeon, which according to Ishni supposedly contained stones for the Karmadont Chess Set. Since I didn't want to choose between Magdey and Clutzer, I decided to simply take both raid parties with me. If there was some party size limit, we'd cast lots to see who stayed and who went home, but we'd do that only once we'd all be there.

There wasn't any point in staying in Anhurs longer, so I cast a portal and returned to Altameda. Elizabeth and the Jewelcrafting trainer, whom I should probably visit too, could wait a few days until Fleita returned. The eight game hours that Kornik had mentioned could easily add up to several calendar days for the girl. For my part, I resolved to take the girl with me wherever I went—there's no other way to teach a Shaman.

"Viltrius, assemble all the aldermen tomorrow," I ordered the goblin, upon reaching my castle. "We'll preside over their oaths of fealty around ten in the morning. The Emperor has granted permission to administer the villages."

"I shall make the requisite preparations immediately," my majordomo assured me in a neutral voice. "Will there be anything else?"

"Yes, one more thing...Tell me, my green friend, is there a workshop in Altameda?"

Even though it was almost evening, I decided to do some work for the good of the clan. Rings, chains, cut stones—a clan has many urgent Jewelcrafting needs. As a 'permanent' resident of Barliona, I had no excuse to avoid work. Besides, this would push me closer to reaching my third Gem Cutter rank—for which I had to first somehow gain another +31 in Jewelcrafting. I think I recall someone once telling me that nothing happens on its own, so no doubt I had some long, hard work in front of me. Like Mister Geppetto...

A ring? A chain? A stone?

The question of where to begin in my crafting confronted me as soon as I entered design mode. On the one hand, it's high time I made myself some rings. I'm still wandering around with +12 Copper Rings that I'd crafted in a former life. The same applies to my chain: +12 to Intellect is not becoming for a leveled-up character like mine—to say nothing of how it looks on an Earl. I could craft a Gold Ring of Intellect, which I had a recipe for in my book, and thereby increase this stat by +32 with one ring. Yet I wouldn't be able to set a stone into such a ring...Should I maybe forget about my recipes and come up with something more interesting? It wasn't a big deal if I went missing from the game for several days—I was in Altameda after all. And I didn't have any pressing business. Kornik would keep Fleita occupied with something or other...Okay! It's decided. Let's forget about the recipe book and start something from scratch. The highest-level metal that I can Jewelcraft with is gold; the highest-level stone is Amethyst and Tourmaline. I'll use these as my basic materials then!

Having ordered the stones from the auctioneers, I commenced with my work.

To begin with, I decided to craft myself a new ring. The immediate question was whether I should fashion it from wire or cast it? As I understood it, a ring of wire would grant lower stat bonuses, but it would be easier to set a stone in it. A cast ring was the exact opposite and, besides, harder to craft. I was comfortable working with wire, whereas cutting a mold for casting would pose a challenge.

A blinking notification that I had received my order interrupted my thoughts, so I left design mode and opened the mail. After paying for the delivery service, I poured the stones into two large heaps of fifty stones each and began to consider which of the stones I liked better—the greenish Tourmaline or the bluish Amethyst. I would eventually have to craft the Karmadont Chess Knights from Tourmaline, so I knew I should practice working with it.

Darkness again—and again design mode.

Looking at the wire, I suddenly realized that I would no longer work with this material. It's not that I don't like the process of braiding wire into a ring...it's the result that's the problem. I don't even know how to describe it. It's like the ring comes out flimsy or something like that. And that's not to mention that, cosmetically, a wire ring leaves something to be desired. It's decided then! The ring shall be solid and cast. Now I need a mold for it. The type of setting doesn't require much thought—I'll use a bezel setting since it's one of the most reliable options. All that remains is to come up with the shape.

I didn't want to craft a simple band: The result would be too ordinary and commonplace. If I've decided to be creative, then I should commit all the way—without sparing myself any hardship or effort. For example, who even decided that a ring should be a ring? Who decided that it should be a closed loop? When a hulking orc removes a ring from his bratwurst finger and hands it to an elf, the game automatically adjusts the relevant dimensions, allowing the long-eared elf to slip the ring onto his refined aristocratic fingers instead of having to wear it around his neck like a yoke. I wonder—who decided that elves were aristocrats anyway? Players who played this race would behave as badly as some dwarves I'd come across...and even the NPC elves I knew weren't exactly saints! I'd need to check the library to find out how they'd earned this noble honor.

But anyway—since the ring will adapt to fit its owner, I could easily experiment with its shape. For example, instead of making it a closed circuit, I could leave it open or even...ah! That's it—I could craft it in the form of a spiral or a spring! But no—then I'd end up making a wire ring, only cast...What's the point in wasting time, when it'd be easier to braid it?

If I set an Amethyst in the center of the piece and frame it with Tourmaline, then...NO! Why didn't it occur to me right away? I urgently needed one more stone!

According to the chart of Barliona's gems, the only black stones were Onyx, which I couldn't yet work with, Melanite, which I didn't know a thing about, and Jet, which like Onyx remained off limits to me. Well, if it must be Melanite, let it be Melanite.

I left design mode and sent another request to the auctioneers. I knew I needed a black stone…

Once a black heap had joined the green and blue heaps, I returned to design mode and tried to wrap my mind around my idea.

And so!

What were the Legends of Barliona most famous for? The fact that they had three players with unique races, a myriad of First Kills, unique projections, several scenarios and a personal relationship with the Emperor. And yet, any one of Malabar's Top 10 clans could boast of these same honors—with the exception of the first. Accordingly, I decided to concentrate on the three unique races. The Siren, the Dragon and the Vampire. Green, Blue, and Black. Tourmaline, Amethyst and Melanite…

Three shapeless masses appeared before my eyes and gradually took on the forms of a Dragon, a Siren and a Vampire. It didn't matter to me that they didn't look like us in the least. The important thing is the image, not its correspondence to the original. I shaped a ring beside the figures and couldn't help but curse—the ring was almost invisible. Rather, it was a little larger than the vampire's head. I had no idea how I would position the three figures in such a small space and make the whole thing fit on a finger at the same time. Disappointed, I discarded the figures of the Vampire and the Siren and made the Dragon shapeless again. I went on working with this one piece of stone because it would be too dreary and ugly to craft the figures separately and then arrange them on a ring. My design had to be unified.

A Dragon rampant, crushing the Siren and the Vampire into the ground...

A Siren with her tail coiled around the Dragon and the Vampire—who is sinking his fangs into her throat...

A Dragon tearing the Vampire apart as the Siren impales him on her trident...

Despite all my efforts, the only thing I could come up with were scenes of violence—which would clearly end with a single victor—either the Dragon, or the Siren, or the Vampire. The scenes appeared in different variations, but the main thrust remained the same—the races were in conflict even in my thoughts...If I removed one of the trio, the composition turned out quite striking, and yet when all three were depicted together...

I must be doing something wrong...

I spent an hour in thought, trying to figure out where my error lay. If I want to craft a ring for my clan, then it should depict our legends because...Hmm...Maybe there is no 'because'...maybe my entire initial premise is wrong...I want to make a ring for my clan, proceeding from the assumption that our three unique races are what make us the Legends. But what if this isn't the case? What if the Legends of Barliona are something greater than their respective races? After all, when all is said and done, our clan's name changed not because we three were in it but because of something else...

What and who can be considered a legend anyway? Is not a legend someone who has done something that has caused the entire world to speak of them? It didn't matter whether their fame was good or bad; what mattered was that everyone knew of them. And what had I just tried to do? I had tried to fit a square peg into a round hole, forcing my opinion onto a larger system. I'm no legend. Plinto isn't a legend. Stacey might be, but most likely she is not. Then who?

How can someone even become Legendary? Take Yalininka for example—any NPC would say that she is a legend. Why and how isn't important. The important thing is that she is. Or, take for example the orcs in the Karmadont Chess Set. Every one of them committed some great deed in his life, yet could you call them Legendary? According to Prontho—you could. And the same goes for the dwarves and ogres...Which immediately raises the question of the giants that I still had to craft—what did the two giants have to do to earn their place among Karmadont's Chess pieces? And, mind you, why was it that this feat or deed fail to earn any fame among the denizens of Barliona...If I were in Karmadont's position, what would I include the giants for?

One possibility was an act of self-sacrifice. For what? To save someone's life. The next question then is why does no one know about this feat? Hmm...What if the giants themselves didn't want anyone to remember them? No, that's dumb. Wouldn't that mean that the very same people the giants saved had wanted to kill them? To scrub any mention of them from history...No, that won't work—I doubt Karmadont would add giants who had sacrificed themselves for their foes...

Unless of course these foes were children...

Even in the depths of design mode, I felt a shiver sweep across my body...That was it! I don't know the precise story that the developers had come up with, but it was clear to me that the giants had perished while saving the children of the children of their enemies...

"Darling," whispered Tigra, leaning over to her husband. "Are they going to kill us?"

"Yes," replied Ra, stroking his wife's hair. He cast a look of loathing at their guards and shivered a little—this rain was not the best weather to die in. It had been raining seven days now, and the gorge that the locals had dragged him and his wife to had already flooded up to his ankles. The water streamed from the sheer cliffs. It fell from the sky onto the earth that had become so waterlogged that the water had no place to go but seep into the dam that divided the gorge in two halves—one an enormous lake, the other a narrow passage which lay within walking distance of Zultan—the capital of the Drang people. And it would be this gorge that was to become the last resting place of Ra and Tigra...

The Drang were people, but they were people of a strange faith. They worshipped neither Eluna nor Tartarus. The supreme deity of this people was a mirror. It was an ordinary mirror, yet when the Drangians looked into it, they saw in their reflection the true vicars of the higher powers of Barliona. And seeing this, they knew that all other races had to be destroyed. Having lured the five-meter-tall Ra and Tigra into an ambush, the Drangians had bound the couple and decided to put them to death at the foot of their main sanctuary—the dam at one of the branches of the Altair River.

"Watch out—don't step on each other's feet!" came a lingering cry, forcing Ra to lift his head. Just a few meters from the giants, a huge crowd of children appeared. The Drangians had brought them to watch the execution.

"Are you sure the chains are strong enough?" asked one of the little ones, examining the fetters around the giants' arms and legs. "What if the monsters suddenly break out and attack us?"

"Do not worry," their teacher replied. "Do you see the archers?" She pointed to the guards. "Even if the impossible happens and the chains break, the giants will be shot down immediately."

"Can I have that woman's ear?" asked another girl. "I'll hang it on a thread and show it off to all my friends!"

"I want a tooth!"

"I'll take the eyes!"

"No, I already have dibs on one of the eyes!"

The kids raised such a hubbub that they drowned out the sound of falling water. They bickered amongst themselves over the gruesome souvenirs. And no wonder—it's not every day that one could watch the death of two giants—five-meter tall gargantuans that had appeared in Barliona by sheer accident. After all, whoever does not look like a Drangian must be destroyed—such was the chief commandment of Zultan.

"The poor children," whispered Tigra, moving away from her husband. "The poor, unfortunate children..."

"These poor unfortunates can't wait to see you torn asunder," barked Ra angrily, looking for the slightest opportunity to take a pair of Drangians with him. It was of no use: He no longer had the strength to break the chains.

"It's not the children's fault that they are taught to kill everything that doesn't resemble them," Tigra shook her head. "If only we could...Did you hear that?"

"What?" Ra asked surprised.

"The..." Even through the veil of rain, it was clearly visible how pale Tigra had suddenly become. The gorge resounded with the thunder of breaking logs. "The dam is failing..."

Ra raised his head—literally a few meters from the giants, the dam was beginning to creak ominously. The Drangians had constructed the base of the dam, which was about two meters tall, from stone, knowing how much pressure the river would exert on it. However, the top of the dam, which accounted for the remaining seven meters, they built from ordinary logs, assuming that the water level would never exceed two meters. After all, it never had over the entire thousand-year history of Zultan. Now the time had come to pay for their ancestors' miscalculation...

One of the logs splintered and a fountain of water spouted through the breach—the pressure was so high that the water at their feet swelled to four meters.

"Save yourself!" cried one of the guards in panic. He dropped his weapons to the earth and fled toward the exit to the gorge—a good two hundred meters away.

"A-ah-ah!" sounded the cries of twenty children, realizing that they had just been abandoned—the teacher had fled behind the guard.

"Hurry, Tigra!" yelled Ra to his wife. Seeing another log snap, the archers dropped their crossbows and also fled from the gorge—their own skins were worth more to them than some old giants. "We can get out!"

"Ra, help me!" said the giantess, pinning back two of the logs with her arms to keep them fixed in place. "Ra! I won't manage on my own!"

"Leave it!" cried Ra stunned, utterly unable to understand why his wife was doing this. "We'll drown if we don't get out of here now! We do not know how to swim!"

"If we go, the children will die!" wheezed Tigra. She was under such strain that blood had begun to flow from her nose. "I won't be able to live knowing that they died because I failed...Raaaa!"

A beam beside Tigra cracked, sending splinters flying into the giantess's shoulder.

"Run for it!" Ra barked at the children, who remained standing paralyzed, awaiting their deaths in a stupor. The adults had all fled. "Go!"

The giant darted over to his wife and pressed himself against the dam beside her—five meters and his giant's strength gave him the hope that the little Drangians would come to and make their escape. But how difficult it was!

"Ra, I can't hold any longer," Tigra's voice was all but inaudible. The blood was now flowing not only from the giantess's nose, but from her lips too, which she had bitten into from the strain. "I love you..."

Tigra collapsed and the beams that she had been restraining, suddenly sensing their freedom, came flying out of the dam.

"I love you too," croaked Ra and glanced over his shoulder to see that the children had made it out of the gorge in time.

"We did it," he whispered as the dam collapsed upon the couple...

* * *

Two transparent giants appeared before my eyes—a man and a woman, smiling, straining to one another, dressed in ordinary clothes—two enamored sentients who had sacrificed themselves for children who had wanted to see their blood. I had no doubt that the story I invented fit the idea that the Corporation had in mind. Even if I had been mistaken in certain details—like for example, their having drowned instead of being buried—the general idea would remain the same. These were the very giants who had been included in the Chess Set and not the dozens of other heroes from that race, who had earned their renown through their strength and might.

I combined these projections with the Tanzanite and sensed a feeling of satisfaction—the giants were complete. Yet my satisfaction was partial because my clan ring remained unfinished. How oddly had things worked out—I had sat down to do one thing and ended up accomplishing something entirely different...No, this wasn't the way to get things done! I'm not going to leave design mode until I figure out how to craft those rings!

Let's return to the legends!

You can become a legend by becoming a great hero. You can become a legend by sacrificing yourself. You can become a legend by creating something great and dedicating your life to helping the sick. There really are an enormous number of options for how you could become a legendary hero. But what do they all have in common? Having a unique race as I had thought before? No. The desire to stand out? Also no...

What then?

Why, for example, had Karmadont and the developers decided that the giantess was worthy of being a legend? Because she felt sorry for the children? Well...maybe...but the dwarves had invested a piece of themselves in their creations, the orcs had proven that they were true warriors and the ogres had died to save their kin. Was it pride that united them all? No...Was it honor? No...Was it the pursuit of their ideals?

No!

It was love that united them all! Damn it—that was it! For the orcs, weapons and warfare were a natural part of their essence! The dwarves were master craftsmen: No one could deny their love of creation. The ogres loved their family. The giants loved children. And Yalininka loved all people! To be great is one thing, but to be able to love and to follow that feeling is something totally different...Jeez....

What about the Legends of Barliona then?

What did players love? Or rather, what was the object of adoration for the players? What are they willing to sacrifice themselves, their time, their *all*, for? What a silly question—why, it's Barliona itself! The players love this game. They abandon their realities to live in it. It's the game that is the legend for real people—not some contrived characters! The players love this world!

My heart skipped a beat. The true Legends of Barliona weren't a character or some group of characters from the game. They were the game itself! Its legendary mountains, vast seas, endless forests, skies, monsters, Dungeons, First Kills...These were the legends of Barliona, not the Dragon, the Siren and the Vampire! Sure, these three were part of it all, but only as parts...

And if this was the case, the next question was how I could represent all of this in one tiny ring. How could I unite all these different pieces?

Yet again a shiver coursed down my spine—why was I fixating so much on Barliona anyway? After all, there was one thing that tied it all together—the mountains, the rivers, all the pieces of this immense world! I knew what it was!

Swiping away the giants' figures, I fashioned an oblong form that resembled a table's surface. I would make the foundation blue, just like that of the original. I made additional notches around the edge of the template, since the original's edges glowed blue and stood out a little, imbuing it with volume. The last and final touch was the inscription, a specific script that every single player is intimately familiar with. An inscription of five black letters...

As my template, I used an ordinary ring. I didn't do anything special with it. I wanted everyone to see the stone set in it, or rather the three united stones, instead of the band. This was precisely the point of my idea...

I wonder how much time has passed since I began working...

Clan artifact created: 'Enter' (Ring). Description: The Legend of Barliona inscribed in a

ring. +45 to all main stats when worn by a member of the Legends of Barliona clan. (Note: This bonus is calculated differently for each wearer; the actual algorithm is hidden.) Item class: Unique. Restrictions: No more than four equipped at a time.

New Recipe for Clan artifact created: 'Enter' (Ring).

New clan sigil available. Do you wish to use it?

+1 to Crafting. Total: 11.

+5 to Jewelcrafting (primary profession). Total: 124.

You have created a Legendary item. +500 to Reputation with all previously encountered factions.

Congratulations! You have continued along the path of recreating the Legendary Chess Set of Emperor Karmadont, the founder of the Malabar Empire. Wise and just, the Emperor offered his opponents the chance to settle disputes on the chessboard instead of the battlefield. Each type of Chess Piece was made from a different stone.

Pawns: The Malachite Orc Warriors (Creator: Mahan) and Lapis Lazuli Dwarf Warriors (Creator: Mahan).

Rooks: The Alexandrite Battle Ogres (Creator: Mahan) and Tanzanite Giants (Creator: Mahan).

Knights: The Tourmaline War Lizards and Amethyst War Horses.

Bishops: The Emerald Troll Archers and

Aquamarine Elf Archers.

Queens: An Orc Shaman of Peridot and an Elemental Archmage, a Human of Sapphire.

Kings: The Leader of the White Wolf Clans, an Orc of Green Diamond, and the Emperor of the Malabar Empire, a Human of Blue Diamond.

The Chessboard: Black Onyx and White Opal, framed by White and Yellow Gold. Numbers and letters on the chessboard: Platinum.

The Chess Set was destroyed upon the death of the Emperor. Now it remains to you and your Craft whether Barliona will again behold this truly great wonder of the world—the Legendary Chess Set of Emperor Karmadont.

You have created the Tanzanite Giants from the Legendary Chess Set of Emperor Karmadont. -50% Energy loss and +1% to regeneration of Hit Points, Mana and Energy while the pieces are in your possession.

You have created a Legendary item. +500 to Reputation with all previously encountered factions.

You have crafted two Unique items during one crafting session. +1000 to Reputation with all previously encountered factions.

When I opened my eyes, the enormous amount of text was the only thing that saved me from going blind. The illumination emanating from my hands could have rivaled the sun itself in brightness and intensity. Moreover, I had two such suns—the ring and the chess figurines, one more step bringing me closer to the Tomb of the Creator.

"You could at least warn me!" I heard Fleita's indignant voice. I turned in the direction of the sound and saw the girl sliding down the wall. Apparently, she had been sitting in a chair and the blast I had triggered in my poor workshop had flung it and her against the wall. Viltrius will kill me. The workshop had been blown to smithereens.

Initially I tensed up, afraid that the system would hold me responsible for doing damage to another player; however, the seconds ticked by and no Herald appeared. And anyway, Fleita's Hit Points remained at 100% as if I'd done nothing to her but sent her for a tumble.

"I sit there waiting for him like manna from heaven and suddenly he comes back and blasts everything to hell around him..."

"How many days have I been sitting here?" I asked. "And how did you know that I'd come back now?"

"A week has passed since you accepted me as a student—check it out, I'm already at Level 12! As for knowing when you'd be back, Kornik snitched on you...Well, to be fair, he got it wrong the first time. We showed up, waited around for a few minutes, then he smirked at nothing in particular and took me with him to hunt crocolupes. Filthy creatures! By the way, Anastaria stopped by to see you."

"*Stacey?*" I immediately called out to the girl telepathically, but received an error message:

You cannot reach this character. Anastaria is not currently in Barliona.

"Will you show me what you made? Oh, why that's the Karmadont Chess Set! So that notification I just saw was about you? Then you must be the creator it mentioned? Cool! Can you teach me too?"

"Let's slow down a little, Fleita," I told the girl. "My brain can't process all this text in such a short period of time."

Although I'd become accustomed to the jolt of pleasure that accompanied progress in Barliona, a one-time boost of +10 to Jewelcrafting was too much even for a hardened pleasure-seeker like me. I got to my feet and examined the results of my labors. Oh wow! I had managed to create nothing short of perfection!

"*Mahan, is our new clan sigil your handiwork?*" Barsina wrote in the clan chat.

"*Uh-huh,*" I replied.

"*If they start laughing at us, I'll kill you!*"

"I can't believe it!" whispered Fleita, examining the ring beside me. "I know what this is!"

How could she not? There's no one in Barliona—at least among the free players—who isn't familiar with the 'Enter' button that is used to log into the game. It is this very button that transports people into the wondrous world of Barliona. It's this very button that every player wants to push, it's this button that is legendary for them and it's this very button that is set into the ring I crafted, replacing our former clan sigil.

From here on out, the Legends of Barliona would be inextricably linked with the 'Enter' button. It remained to be seen where this would lead us, but as far as I was concerned, if anyone has a problem with it, they were welcome to speak to Plinto about it...

CHAPTER THREE
THE SKROOJ DUNGEON

"MASTER," VILTRIUS SAID WITH A BOW. "What shall I tell the aldermen? They have been expecting an audience with you for six days now. They don't dare return to their villages without it."

I stared blankly at the goblin for several moments, unable to recall what he was talking about—until the proper gears clicked in my head. Oh damn! How could I forget? I had asked the goblin to assemble the aldermen in the morning and then went off crafting for an entire week! A good start to my reign indeed...

"Tell them that I'm ready to see them," I told Viltrius immediately. "And take Fleita to her room. I assume you have one prepared for her?"

"I'm not going anywhere!" The girl instantly dug her heels in. "You're planning on meeting someone here without me? That's not fair!"

"First of all, you do not know the language.

Second, the audience that's about to take place is the internal business of my clan. Third, a true Shaman doesn't show her displeasure. Work on your studies. I don't want to have to babysit you. It's my decision that until you learn Malabarian, you've got no business in Altameda. Viltrius, we have a stowaway on board."

"Yes, Master." Was that a note of pleasure that just sounded in the goblin's voice? What happened next was as much a surprise to me as to Fleita. The steward teleported over to her like a Harbinger, took the girl by the hand and disappeared with her—only to reappear alone a moment later. "Your orders have been fulfilled."

"Where'd you take her?" I asked worried.

"To the castle gates, Master. More precisely, to their other side. Shall I usher in the aldermen?"

"Bring them in," I waved my hand, reclining in my throne, an extremely uncomfortable seat, I should mention—a hard surface, no pillows, no plush. How do kings spend so much time in such discomfort? After fidgeting for a bit, I got fed up with the thing and pulled my rocking chair out of my inventory. Maybe it's not a long winter's night right now, but at least I'll be more comfortable.

As for Fleita, I had been strict with her deliberately. If she really wanted to become a Shaman—or rather, my disciple—then she'd have to get used to following certain rules. Such as doing as she was told. Especially, when we were in my castle. If I let her run amok as she pleased, it'd only cause me headaches in the future.

"Village aldermen to see the Earl!" proclaimed Viltrius, starting me from my grave contemplations. Three burly men, one of whom I'd already met, hesitantly entered the throne room and stopped before me, shifting from foot to foot.

"M-master Earl, p-per your orders..." Seeing my new rocking throne, Viltrius began to stutter, evidently unaccustomed to such eccentricity on the part of his liege. I was also perplexed—the majordomo of a Level 24 castle should probably be used to serving all kinds of strange masters. I'll need to rummage around the settings. Maybe I can gift him a brocaded gown or something to make him feel more comfortable with the high level...

"Please, have a seat." I gestured the aldermen to the empty seats at the table. My throne room, in effect, was the hybrid of an Imperial office and throne room—it consisted of a small round conference table and an open area uncluttered by furniture for people to stand around. It was practical and cost-effective.

The aldermen slumped heavily into their seats, planted their elbows on the tabletop and continued to peer at me from beneath their brows. I still wasn't quite sure whether they were afraid of me or afraid that I would start heaping various dues and taxes on them. To be perfectly frank, the governing of settlements did not evoke the same delight in me as it surely did in Ehkiller and the other players granted this privilege. Often enough, I had trouble finding time to manage my own clan. Here, I'd have to deal with a whole new can of worms. I even sort of wish that I had a...Oh! Why that's simply an ingenious idea!

"Leite, could you please teleport to Altameda right now. There's some business here for you..."

Permitting players to govern settlements was an important step on the part of the game administration. The only problem is that they had granted permission to the wrong person. I had absolutely no interest in the settlements. Yet I knew someone who would be more than happy to do some city management on my behalf! Three villages with 500 residents each—Leite would work miracles with them.

"Whatcha want?" A portal popped open a second or two later and disgorged my treasurer.

"Sit down and I'll bring you up to speed..." I turned to the waiting aldermen: "And so! Dear aldermen! I have gathered you here in order to communicate to you a most welcome piece of news—I am sending you an auditor and governor who shall rule on my behalf. The Emperor personally granted me the right to govern the settlements adjoining my castle. Accordingly, I will administer your villages from here on out. I will visit the Governor of Lestran Province this very day in order to obtain an official document to this effect. However, this is a mere formality. From now on I and not the province shall be the rightful ruler of your villages."

"Formalities we understand, of course, but without a piece of paper, how are we to believe this is true?" objected Myrrh, the alderman of Happy Moss. "We, your honor, are a simple folk. We are willing to serve, of course, but we must have assurances..."

"The confirmation document will be here today," I replied unrattled. I didn't feel like swearing an oath to the Emperor or calling a Herald over these three aldermen—if I made some error in wording, I might get penalized—and it wouldn't take much to flit on over to the Governor of the Province. "But we're not talking about that right now. As the lord of these lands, I am assigning this Warrior as my deputy. He will work together with you to administer your villages. He will guide your growth and make your most ambitious plans a reality. The objective at hand is to make our villages renowned through all of Malabar. I want all the people in the land to dream of only one thing—how they too can live in Happy Mosses, Silent Vine and Lower Creek."

"Why, who would travel to such a remote wilderness?" the alderman of Lower Creek could not refrain from asking. "We can't keep our own youth from leaving as soon as they learn to hold a slingshot. We have five hundred mouths to feed, and only 150 men to do it with—and more than a hundred of them are old men and boys. Why, we have barely any men to go hunting..."

"Three villages," Leite muttered pensively, staring away into the distance. To be honest, I had taken a great risk by thrusting Leite into this meeting without warning him beforehand. If he doesn't agree— I won't look too good in front of the aldermen. "How many people all together?" Leite looked up from 'the distance' at the elders.

"Five hundred and three," Myrrh immediately replied.

"Five hundred and forty..." "Four hundred and twenty," echoed the other elders.

"What do you do?" Leite went on with his inquest and by the light in his eyes I already knew that I had managed to shift another burden from my shoulders. Who better than a financial guru to engage in economic strategy? Definitely not me at any rate...

"We are furriers, lumberjacks, farmers," the aldermen began to enumerate, causing Leite to become more interested and move forward:

"What kind of lumber? The furs of what animals? Are there tanners among you? How do you..."

The questions came flowing in a torrent and the elders could barely keep up with their answers. Judging by the camera icon that had appeared, Leite was recording and was planning on reviewing his inquest later to determine what he would do next. I sat in on the meeting a little while longer and finally slipped out. As I reached the door to the throne room, I could hear the elders begin arguing with Leite about the best tanneries and lumber mills in the area and how many fields needed to be plowed during the planting season. I couldn't help but grin—it was looking like Leite would need me to hire him another deputy. Surely the Warrior would want to maintain the villages under his close governance, and yet he couldn't abandon his work with the auctions—it was bringing in too much money for the clan. We needed more help but lacked the manpower ...

"Here," I held out the four clan rings to the Warrior when he came in from the meeting about an hour later. I didn't dare go meet the Governor without Leite—I needed to present him as my deputy, so I occupied myself with crafting further rings. It wasn't difficult now that I had the recipe and ingredients. One ring took me about five minutes, so I made several for myself and Leite and a couple for Clutzer. Who knows? Since the stat bonus formula is hidden, perhaps he'll get more than +45 to each main stat. I absolutely had to level up to Gem Cutter third rank...only where would I find the time to do it?

"Thanks. Mahan..." Leite paused, again staring off into nowhere. "You know, as long as I've known you, you've never ceased to amaze me. You always turn up with some goodie that makes my eyes pop. Are you the only one who's been granted the right to govern villages?"

"No—there are three others. They'll be testing us for six months, evaluating to see where we take the lands that have been entrusted to us. After that they'll make the decision of whether to keep this mechanic or not. I have zero desire to play as an economist. If you do—here's your chance!"

"You know I do, very much, but...Well, hell! Where am I going to find the time for it all?!"

"We need more people..."

"That's the problem—we need people whom we

can trust with our money. If we hire some bungler, he'll buy a thousand swords when we need ploughshares and we'll spend a fortune fixing it...or worse... All right, these are all details already. To hell with it though. Even if he gums up the works, I'll be around to set it straight again—it's just a horrible idea to give the first person we come across access to the bank account! He'll make off with all the gold and then good luck trying to find him."

"Do you really not have anyone in mind? I find that hard to believe!"

"What if I invite my wife to the clan and make her my deputy? How will you feel about that?"

"I'm fine with that. As long as the result is solid. She's not an economist too by any chance, is she?"

"No, but she is one of the few people I trust. I'll teach her everything I know. She'll do no worse than me."

"Okay, agreed. Bring her on board. You've already finagled yourself a messenger boy. It's high time you got a normal assistant. The important thing is that you do a good job with the villages so that I don't have to appear empty-handed before the Emperor in six months. What kind of salary did you have in mind for your wife? How about 75% of what I pay you, plus bonuses based on performance?"

"75%? Have you lost your mind? Do you want to ruin us? Fifty will suffice! That's several times more than what she makes in reality anyway. All right— let's go visit the Governor for that document...He will give you one, right? Or am I going to have to eat all those pretty words I told the aldermen?"

"Of course he'll give me one. What choice does he have?" I reassured Leite, opened my map and relayed the coordinates for the capital of Lestran to our man in Anhurs, so he could send us a portal. "By the way, Leite, there's one more job for you. I need you to figure out how to use the castle teleport, please. My Greed Toad is starting to strangle me at the thought of all the money we're spending on teleporting around the continent..."

Chrondavir, the Governor, turned out to be a very pleasant old fogey. Leite and I were received by the Governor without any issues—my aristocratic status played its proper part here. And once I explained the reason for my visit, the Governor immediately reached for his quill and penned two letters. The first one declared me the rightful ruler of the three villages, while the second delegated authority to Leite without stripping me of responsibility for the final outcome.

Assuring the Governor of peace, friendship and other lofty aspirations, I returned to Altameda and Leite took off for Anhurs in order to take care of the business we had decided on. Lounging in my chair, I was digging around the castle's properties, trying to find something that would help Viltrius when I heard the ringing of an amulet—and not the one from my clan. Strange...who needed to talk to me all of a sudden?

"Listening," I answered cautiously.

"You are an evil, nasty, mean and selfish

moron!" came the voice in the amulet. Despite Fleita's serious tone, I couldn't help but crack a smile—she was speaking in clear Malabarian. Given that only a few hours had elapsed, I could safely reckon that the girl had bought herself a language pack from the game site, installed it and was now about to tell me everything she thought about this game and my place in it.

"I hope you're still out in front of the castle?" I asked, completely ignoring the stream of abuse. When I was a programmer, I would often have to teach others—since not everyone learns everything on their own—so to some degree I was used to this kind of reaction. It would have been much worse if Fleita had silently swallowed her expulsion from my castle. That would mean that she and I would have issues later on and she would be unlikely to become a 'true' Shaman. At least, such was my view of teaching.

"If you think I'm going to pretend like nothing has happened, you're deeply mistaken! Yes, I'm at the gates, where you dumped me like a stray dog..." Even though she still sounded irate, Fleita did reply to my question. Something tells me that the girl has a lot more brains than she wants to show with her behavior and words. She's simply too...thoughtful or something...And then there's the request to take her on as my student out of the blue...Damn—I think my paranoia is acting up again.

"Viltrius," I called my majordomo without disconnecting the amulet. I wanted the girl to hear my order. When he appeared, the goblin caused me to smile—my fiddling with the castle settings hadn't passed without effect—Viltrius now sported not only a robe, but also a huge gold chain and boots with turned up toes like that of race-walking shoes. The upgrade had cost me a mere thirty thousand gold, so I couldn't resist the temptation to make a present for the NPC—we'd be working side by side for the next seven years after all. "My student is in front of the gates. Please bring her to me. If she puts up any resistance, she'll be banned from entering Altameda for the next week."

"As you wish, master," said the goblin, bowed majestically and disappeared. Oh wow! The new outfit had even altered Viltrius' bow—it was now more noble and upstanding and less obsequious than it had been earlier. This is much better in my view...

"Your Highness! Is it your pleasure that I retire to my chamber?" The venom in Fleita's voice was so thick that I couldn't help but laugh. An irate Zombie really is a hellish sight.

"Do you know what distinguishes the Shaman from other classes?" I answered her question with one of my own. Without waiting for her answer, I went on: "Composure. A Shaman must be calm and composed inside in order to understand which Spirits he needs. Remember when you were fishing—were you angry, were you irritated? I'm willing to bet that you withdrew entirely within yourself and you had only one thing in mind—the fish. Everything else, including your emotions was secondary..."

"Kornik told me the opposite," replied the girl,

without any sarcasm, however. "He taught me to summon the spirits. Didn't I tell you that while you were working on the chess set, I was hunting crocolupes? So when I was doing that, the goblin explained to me about emotions and that I can call on the Spirits only through them. As for the lake and fish...How would you feel if you couldn't do something for two weeks and then a famous Shaman came along but instead of helping you out, he began yelling at you and ordered you to sit next to some lake? Why I was ready to slash the entire lake to pieces with my fishing rod to vent my rage. I mean, really, I think you're way off base here...The Mentor as you called him also tried to tell me about staying calm, but he didn't do much good either..."

Uh-oh!

"In that case, I have no idea how to go about teaching you," I confessed. "Initially I thought that I'd tell you some fairy tales about how you must be calm and composed, show you the Astral Plane and then...Hmm..."

"I can do my own studies by reading too," said Fleita, noting my hesitation. "As I understood it, the important thing for Shamans is to pass the first trial. I already read its walkthrough on the forums. It's not difficult. Rescue the lamb..."

"That's exactly the point—the forum users are bunglers," I said, borrowing Leite's word. "They don't understand anything about the game and yet they're also eager to offer advice...."

"Are you saying that the forums are full of

misinformation?"

"I'm saying that every Shaman has his own way to follow. It is possible that for some of them, doing the trial in the manner you read is the ideal option. But for me, for example, it isn't. And for you, it remains unknown."

"So how did you do it?" Fleita asked puzzled. "There aren't many options there after all. It seems like a standard walkthrough should be useful."

"There's a standard there, I agree, but it's a different standard for every player. For some, a gold coin is money, for others it's a piece of gold, for someone else it's just an entry in a database...All three are right in their own way and each one will follow his own truth. The Shaman's task is to determine for himself—which of these truths is important to him at the given moment."

"At the given moment?"

"Of course! For example, I'm an ordinary guy who thinks that the Earth is flat and resting on three whales. Tomorrow I might be convinced that it's not whales but an enormous space turtle. And the day after I might realize that the turtle is in actual fact a..."

"But it's round," said Fleita, looking at me like I was mad.

"The Earth here is just an example, which I'm trying to use to explain my thought to you. I'll admit it's not a very successful example, and yet still...Okay, I'll put it this way, the way I personally feel— sometimes it's like a light goes on inside of me and it tells me to ignore what everyone around me is saying. Even if they tell you that two parallel lines will never intersect—if your premonition says otherwise—listen to it! Damn...this isn't making sense, is it?"

"Parallel lines do intersect," mused Fleita. "They teach you that freshman year..."

"Again, you're missing the point...It doesn't matter whether I guessed right or not. What's important is the main principle. A Shaman must stay true to his convictions to the very end, as long as he considers them true. It's by following this principle that I ended up in those movies. Had I played by the rules, I'd still be in the Mine, hammering a pick against the rock and dreaming of escape. Oh! One day, one of my teachers—I don't remember exactly which one—said: 'Thinking is for Mages. Shamans feel.' You and I are going to proceed from this very idea."

"Incidentally, you didn't tell me how you passed your trial."

"And I never will. You need to discover that on your own—or rather, you need to choose the right path for yourself. My advice here is stay away from the guides and walkthroughs. They'll only teach you the wrong things."

"So how are you going to teach me?"

"I already told you, I have no idea. So far one thing is clear—I'm going to take you with me anywhere I go. Right now, for instance, we're going to go check out this one interesting Dungeon..."

"*Magdey, Clutzer—are you ready for our outing?*"

I wrote into the chat.

"*I was ready a week ago,*" the Rogue instantly replied. "*We've been on standby waiting for your majesty to awake from your most recent crafting session and make your will known to us, your poor subjects.*"

"Check your mail then, oh my subject," I replied, sending rings to both of my raid leaders. "You can grumble some other time."

"Mahan, how many of these rings can you craft?" Magdey immediately called me on my amulet.

"What do you need +45 to all stats for?" I asked surprised.

"Maybe it's you who gets +45...It's +250 for me! I'm not Anastaria—I don't have a rich daddy. I can't dump vast sums of money into the game. And to get bonuses that add up to an extra thousand stat points with a single ring is a very respectable upgrade even at my level. Furthermore, I need these rings for my entire raid party."

"*Mahan, why do I get busy tones when I call you? Stop chatting—I need to talk to you!*" A message from Clutzer appeared in the chat. "*I need rings! Lots of them!*"

"Okay, assemble your people. We'll deal with the rings later," I replied to Magdey and invited Clutzer to the conversation. "Guys! We need to do this Dungeon right now. It'll take anywhere between a few hours to a whole week. No one's ever entered this Dungeon before, so we're sure to get a First Kill. When will the raid parties be ready?"

"Two hours," replied Magdey quickly. "Some of my people are still out in reality. I need to invite them."

"I need a couple hours as well," Clutzer echoed.

"In that case, I'll be expecting everyone in two hours at the castle. Let's get out of here..."

"First Kill?" Fleita asked with surprise when I put away the amulet. "You're taking me to get my First Kill?"

"Why not?" I shrugged. You're of no use to Malabar or Kartoss...Hang on a second..."

I pulled out another amulet and made a call.

"Speaking!" answered a serious, self-assured voice. The best clan of Kartoss deserved no less.

"What's up, Evolett? This is Mahan speaking. I have some business for you worth a million gold..."

A First Kill for completing a Dungeon is a very respectable reward, but I didn't want to invite anyone from Malabar—there wouldn't be enough for the rest of us. Evolett, however, was a different matter. I wouldn't have to split my spoils with Kartoss...

Message for the player! A new territory has been discovered: Glarnis Dungeon. +50% chance that an ordinary mob drops a Unique item and +20% to Experience earned.

"I gather you've never heard of the proper way to assemble a raid party?" Clutzer quipped as soon as we teleported to the Dungeon. Frankly, when I made my deal with Evolett, I was worried that he would teleport to the coordinates I sent him without us. However, ever mindful of the agreed upon terms, the Priest was awaiting us at the entrance. As for Clutzer's barb, I had to confess that our gang really was a mangy bunch: Magdey's Raid Party with an average Level of 240, Clutzer's boys with an average of 190 and Evolett with two dozen 300+ players and two minnows. Meanwhile, I was at Level 116, while Fleita was Level 12! In effect we may as well have been a mob of Level 100s, since this what our average came out to.

Unlike all the Dungeons I'd seen, it was difficult to call this place a Dungeon. The portal took us to an enormous plateau with a stone labyrinth located about a kilometer from the entrance. Several packs of strange creatures, twenty or so per pack, were running around together in the stretch of ground between us and the labyrinth. They resembled slightly greenish wolves—or else very nimble crocodiles—it was difficult to describe these mobs accurately. Yet the average level of these reptilian dogs, which turned out to be the same crocolupes Fleita had mentioned, came as an unpleasant shock for me: Crocolupe is too cute a name for a 300 Level monster...

"Ahem," Clutzer cleared his throat when he realized the futility of participating in this venture. His Level 190 fighters wouldn't be able to do much against a 300 Level horde of crocolupes, aside from maybe distracting them for a bit. And by 'bit' I mean the 2–3 seconds it would take these underdeveloped wolves or overdeveloped crocodiles to send them to respawn.

"Ahem indeed," muttered Magdey with concern. "Evolett, do your guys speak Malabarian or are you the only one?"

"Unfortunately, only I do," the Priest replied, peering at the menacing mobs teeming ahead of us. "I'll take care of that problem shortly, but...Hmm, I don't even know...One pack of those guys won't do much to my boys, but crocolupes have a very large aggro zone...If we attack one pack, a second one will show up immediately—and it'll fall to you to deal with it..."

"That works. Here's what we can do," Magdey jumped at the idea and immediately began to plan the tactics for the coming battle: a battle in which Clutzer, Fleita and I would play perhaps the most important role of all—that of extras.

"I'm reeling in the first group!" said Evolett's tank once everyone was ready for battle. Despite the fact that he spoke in Kartossian and only his clan mates could understand him, the habit of reporting his actions remained. "Attention! We have a second pack aggroing!"

"Bunch of bunglers," Clutzer muttered, watching helplessly as the first pack of five crocolupes was joined by two others—of four and seven monsters respectively. I wonder, whose term is 'bungler' anyway? Leite's or Clutzer's?

"We'll take the newcomers!" Magdey commanded and his tank immediately began to throw something shiny at the third wave of crocolupes. The doggies, which weren't especially intelligent, immediately surrounded the tank from all sides, trying to tear their current target to pieces so they could pass on to their next quarry as soon as possible. They didn't even notice the other players! This at least was some relief. I had been afraid that these ordinary mobs had been imbued with advanced Imitators and that we'd have to respawn several times—yet here it turned out that everything was business as usual. If it wasn't for their high level, we'd probably hardly notice these mobs at all.

"Are these the same puppies that you and Kornik were hunting?" About thirty seconds into the battle—when it became clear as day that the crocolupes posed no threat to us—I decided to prod Fleita, who stood frozen beside me, into some semblance of activity. Judging by the wide-eyed look on her face, watching a raid battle on TV is one thing, and taking part in it yourself is something entirely different. Halos of light constantly flashed around the girl, informing everyone around her that the Zombie had received that which players hold most dear—a new level. Fleita was in our party and therefore received a very small but steady percentage of the XP from the Level 300 crocolupes we killed. And at Level 12, you didn't need much to level up...

"Y-yes..."

"So what are you standing there for? On your mark, get set, go! You didn't come here to enjoy the pleasant weather. Help us out..."

At the ninth wave of mobs, I received a blessing

of my own in the form of a new level. Now, I am a Level 117 Shaman. I'm pretty scary—as long as I don't take a hit or two...

"Goddamn!" cried one of Clutzer's raiders who had been designated to collect the loot. Evolett had tried to bargain for a share of the profits, but I dug my heels in and insisted that my clan would get all the spoils from this dungeon. I'd gifted Evolett a ticket to a Fist Kill—no one had said a word about him getting the loot too. And as practice showed, this was absolutely the right decision... "What're the chances that they'd drop this kind of thing?"

"This would be for you, Mahan," smirked Clutzer, offering me a crocolupe paw. "You showed me something similar one time...What do you think, shall we go?"

Fleet Hound Paw. Description: A hundred millennia ago, before humans appeared in Barliona, the world was ruled by cruel and capricious Tarantula Lords, who subdued all other races with their power. The slavish crocolupes served the Tarantulas, bringing them the prey they caught or sacrificing their souls to their masters. The Tarantulas passed into oblivion, yet to this day, the leader of the crocolupes remembers his former rulers and wants nothing but to return the Tarantulas to this world to sink it back into the gloom of fear and pain. Stop him or it will be too late. Go to the Emperor for further instructions. Quest type: Legendary. Level

restrictions: Must be at least Level 100. Party restrictions: at least 20 members. Reward: hidden.

Warning: This item will be lost if you do not complete the Skrooj Dungeon during this attempt. The item will be lost if...

"Would you believe it? We just received a restriction," Evolett said pensively, gazing at the properties of my new acquisition. It would be silly to keep anything from the very player I'd invited into my raid party, so I kept the Paw visible to everyone around me. "Now we'll have complete this Dungeon in one go. We can't afford to lose this thing. You know, Mahan, you're quickly becoming a prohibitively desirable member of any clan!"

"My own is enough for me, thank you very much. If anyone has need of me, they're welcome to pay me a visit. I haven't turned anyone away yet. Besides, I was planning on doing this Dungeon in one go anyway, so this paw doesn't change anything for us. As for the quest," I turned to Clutzer, "no one's going anywhere until our raiders reach an average Level of 200. The quest's non-recurring. We'll only have one crack at it. As soon as you feel like both raid parties can work together fluently, we'll activate the Eye or the Paw. Until that point, though, you may as well forget about this item. And in general—let's focus on the task at hand..."

"The crocolupes are starting to respawn," one of the fighters informed us. "Judging by the timer, it looks like the respawn time is one hour."

"In that case, the smoke break is over!" I declared, prodding the players back to work. "Evolett, Magdey—we need to reach those cliffs in the next thirty minutes. Let's go!"

What followed was routine—Evolett's fighters would draw a pack of crocolupes, Magdey and his men would take the reinforcements, both packs would be cut down in short order, we'd pick up our loot and move onward. Another pack, another set of reinforcements and more loot. Mobs, mob reinforcements, loot. Mobs, mob reinforcements, more mob reinforcements, loot. And another Level...

"There's three paths here. Which one shall we take?" said one of the Rogues, whose role as I understood it was to play the scout. Despite my orders to move forward as fast as possible, it took us another hour-and-a-half to reach the large mountain of stone which the devs had formed into a labyrinth— at one point we drew in four packs of crocolupes at once and in the course of dealing with them, lost half our raiders. So much time passed while we were finishing off the mobs, reviving the fallen and re-casting buffs, that the pack of crocolupes we'd killed earlier began to respawn. Then we had to deal with them again, since these beasts had an enormous aggro radius and no one wanted to move on with ravenous packs of crocodile-dogs nipping at our heels.

"We'll take the middle one," I made my decision immediately, since Magdey and Evolett were looking in my direction expectantly—as if I had a map of the area in my hand!

"Drang, Ustar," Magdey commanded, "scout ahead."

"Mahan," Fleita, who had by now reached Level 67, approached me haltingly. "Maybe..."

"Hold on, Magdey!" I said, looking at the girl who became even more embarrassed. "Fleita, do you sense something?"

"I...Yes...No...Well, basically, the right passage..."

"What about it?" I pressed her. Unfortunately, I felt absolutely nothing myself—it seems that my capsule had somehow blocked my premonition. Or else I had become so numb that I had ceased to be the Shaman I had once been, and my premonition had withered away...

"It's just that when I look at the middle and left entrances, I get nothing but a vague urge to yawn. But as soon as I glance at the right one...I get this feeling as if something is turning over in my chest and I have to catch my breath...Is this normal? Should I go see a doctor?"

"No, it's fine. That's what we call a premonition. The only thing that's unclear is whether it's cautioning you away from this path or telling you that it's the right one..."

"Why is this happening?"

"Because you chose a class that operates at the level of feelings and emotions. The developers have coded in various mechanics that allow us to make decisions about how to act in certain situations. However, this works only in respect to the game world. Our premonitions are utterly useless when it comes to other players. And on top of that, one of the other Shamans told me that once you pass Level 100, the system begins to generate false sensations that mislead you."

"Is that happening to you now?"

"Well, you know that I can't do anything for the next two months. All my Shamanic skills have been blocked. But forget that. Let's test your premonition—we'll take the right passage!"

Fleita's premonitions did not disappoint—what did disappoint was our misinterpretation of them. When the girl said that she had to catch her breath when she looked at the entrance—you really needed to be a true, ahem, Shaman to send the entire party that way.

The passage was winding but did not resemble a labyrinth. It was more like a cave without a roof, or a canyon. Yes, the road was a winding serpentine, but we never once encountered a branching path. Everything was linear and very laid back until...until it occurred to me that my student's premonitions had augured peril after all.

Ten players from Clutzer's raid party were walking ahead of us. We had decided that if there were monsters in these stone jungles, then they would surely attack the low-level, defenseless players, whereas they may not even notice Evolett's high-level fighters. The idea was logical enough, so no one questioned it until the worst happened.

In Barliona, a player can be incapacitated for up

to one hour. More specifically, a player may be frozen, blinded or paralyzed—in short, he may be variously deprived of the pleasure of moving freely around the game world. If the period of such incapacitation exceeds one hour, then the player receives a temporary immunity to all kinds of status effects, just so he can extricate himself from the given situation. But there are exceptions. Take for example a player who goes for a walk, slips, falls and, when he wakes up, finds himself in a crevice. There are sheer cliffs all around him; he has no scrolls of teleport on him; no one answers his messages. What can he do? Sit and wait for his friends to enter the game so they can bring him a teleport scroll to the nearest town? And what if he doesn't have any friends? Will he have to beg on the forums for someone to buy him a scroll? Why, they could quote him such a price for it that he'll be left penniless...So in this situation our unfortunate player may do the following: He can stay in place for eight hours, not budging an inch, until the 'Character Stuck' button appears. Once you push this button, you'll be sent to the nearest respawn point without having to pay anyone any money.

And so now...

It was a good thing that our raid party was large and we could stretch out in a long file. It was a bad thing that Evolett's high-level warriors were following right behind Clutzer's low-level vanguard.

With each step forward, a greater heaviness descended on my soul. On the one hand, I knew very well that my Shamanic skills were blocked and this included my premonition—so technically, I shouldn't be feeling anything right now. On the other hand...Several moments before the catastrophe, I stopped as if rooted in place, suddenly realizing that a big boom was imminent...

"Everyone back!" I yelled and repeated the warning in the chat. I turned, grabbed Fleita by the hand and yanked her back in the direction we had come from. Ten seconds—that was exactly how long I gave myself to get out...If only I had listened to myself earlier...

I rushed forward, pushing through the bewildered players as a deafening roar came sounding from behind me. An enormous cloud of dust—which didn't occur in Barliona naturally—now surrounded me, covering the players from head to toe and making it difficult to see anything, but I kept running without stopping for a second. I had fully surrendered to my feelings which screamed at me to keep running...

The roar behind me continued to grow and the raid party chat erupted with curses. I sensed that someone was with me, running beside me, but in the cloud of dust it was difficult to tell who it was. The one thing I knew for sure was that I needed to sprint the three hundred meters we had managed to travel from the entrance without pausing for a single breath...

"What was that?" Fleita murmured when I poured an elixir of Energy down her throat. I had had to carry the girl on my shoulders the last hundred meters, since she had become little more than dead weight—the girl's recent, abrupt jump in levels hadn't allowed her to increase her Stamina and her Energy plummeted almost instantly.

"A trap," I muttered angrily, peering into the frames and barely refraining from swearing. The raid party was still alive. All of it. Of the 93 players who had entered the Dungeon, all 93 were still alive—the only problem was that a mere 32 had managed to escape the canyon. The rest were buried under the rubble—the first three hundred meters of the right passage no longer existed. The walls had collapsed like a house of cards, trapping without killing the majority of our players.

"*We can't cast a portal—there's no space to cast it in,*" the trapped players began to complain in the chat almost immediately. "*Teleport us out with the Mages.*"

"Clutzer," I said to the only surviving raid leader—Magdey and Evolett had been caught with the others. "Pull them out."

"Form a circle!" The Rogue didn't have to be asked twice and instantly began to organize his men. There were four Mages among the thirty-two players who managed to escape, so we could build an adequate teleport circle. Generally, you only need three Mages for this spell anyway.

"We can't cast a teleport in this Dungeon!" the only survivor of Evolett's group reported.

"What's he on about?" Clutzer glanced from me to his Mages and then smiled and added: "We shouldn't have taken the right passage, eh?"

I nodded vaguely, took out an amulet and called

Barsina:

"Barsa, I need your help. You need to find me three 'adult' Mages this instant. I need them to teleport a player to their location."

"Whom are they going to teleport?"

"We'll start with Mag...actually, never mind. Let's start with Drangardir the Observant," I named one of our scouts, who typically went by Drang for the sake of brevity. There weren't any objective reasons to be worried—the Mages would haul the player out of the Dungeon, he'd teleport back to the entrance and rejoin us—however, I decided to play it safe. Something else was stirring deep within me and this time around I decided to heed it right away.

"Roger that. I need five minutes."

Player Drangardir has left the raid party. To have the player rejoin the raid party, please assemble the party again.

"What the hell!" Drang cursed in the clan chat. *"It's not letting me back into the Dungeon!"*

"Abort, Barsa, abort!" I instantly called the Druid. "If a player leaves the Dungeon, he leaves it for good. I need to think things over."

"Twenty minutes before the crocolupes appear again," injected Clutzer, peering into the collapsed right passage. "What are we going to do then?"

"We can summon Anastaria to our location," I replied, already knowing what the Mages would say: Summoning was no doubt blocked in this Dungeon too.

"The summons isn't working!" the players confirmed my premonition. Now things really were looking grim…

* * *

"…So that's the situation as it stands," I finished my quick briefing, putting down the amulet. I called Stacey, added the still-buried Evolett and Magdey to the call and had Clutzer sit in as well. This small meeting was now mulling how to proceed. I reviewed the state of affairs and fell silent, having nothing to add. To continue our conquest of this Dungeon, we would have to first rescue our people from under the rubble. We had to keep in mind, however, that leaving the Dungeon automatically excluded the player from the raid party and we'd have to restart from scratch to bring him in. Actually, this was utterly normal for a first attempt at a Dungeon, yet at the moment we had a limiting factor—the Paw of the Fleet Hound we had found. If I start rebuilding the raid party—this item would vanish and that was the last thing I wanted.

"And you can't invite a new player into the party either?" Anastaria clarified.

"The summons doesn't work," replied Restan, one of our Mages. "When we try, we get a message that summoning is blocked because this is a first attempt and because we have the Paw…"

"And how many of you managed to escape again?"

"Thirty-two, most of them under Level 180."

"You have no choice then, Mahan. You need to reassemble the raid party," Anastaria offered. "I realize you want that Paw badly, but...Well, this is precisely why Phoenix has a rule that loot from mobs is examined only after the Dungeon's been completed. Knowing that a valuable item is at stake has too much of a psychological impact otherwise."

"I would risk it and try to go further," Clutzer proposed. "We can restart the raid whenever we like. We've gotten this far and we may as well check out what lies in the other two passages."

"That's pointless," Anastaria immediately interrupted the Rogue. "As soon as we reassemble the raid party, the Dungeon will regenerate anew and this same trap could end up in one of the other passages."

"I agree with Anastaria," said Evolett. "Moving onward with thirty weak players doesn't make sense. Mahan—I would like it very much if you invited me to the Paw quest, but you'll have to sacrifice it in this case. Leaving the Dungeon is the same as leaving the raid party, and you..."

"Why'd you hang up on everyone?" Clutzer asked with surprise beside me.

"Because they were talking gibberish. I'm not going to restart the raid. We're keeping that Paw."

"*Dan, what happened?*" Stacey's thought immediately appeared in my mind.

"*I'm going to try and keep the Paw...I have this one idea; I just need to consider it some more.*"

"*This is exactly why I love you—you never give*

up! Good luck!"

After a little thought, I clenched my fists and sent a message to the raid party:

"Raiders, we can all see what's happened. We have no choice but to either dig out those who are trapped beneath the rubble or burry them completely. Either we will rescue them or kill and revive them. I need a player who can resurrect others, as well as anyone who knows how to hold a pick. Everyone else can take a break—our raid will continue again tomorrow at nine in the morning. Those who are under the rubble have to remain in place; otherwise, our efforts will be in vain..."

"Dig them out?" Clutzer asked, watching me produce my long-forgotten pickaxe from my bag.

"Or bury them until they die," I confirmed and stepped up to the rocks. "Let's hope that these stones are destructible terrain."

Swing, strike...Swing, strike...

Each stroke of the pickaxe sent such a shower of sparks cascading from the rocks that I couldn't help but close my eyes. The sparks did 5% damage but thankfully, Kalmira—our only surviving healer—was on hand to heal me as I worked. Of course, there was also Fleita, but her Spirits hardly had an effect on me—how much healing can a Level 67 player wearing Level 12 clothes do? And that's not mentioning that she had nothing but a Minor Healing Spirit available to her...

Swing, strike...Swing, strike...

Aside from me, only one other survivor had a

pickaxe with him—as well as, thankfully, Mining as his character profession. This was none other than Clutzer, and as he explained, he had kept the tool as a memento of his past hardships. The other survivors could do nothing but spread their arms in futility— they had no way of helping. Experience showed that Mining was not a very popular profession among players who had dedicated themselves to raiding dungeons. I'd need to ask Anastaria to share her stats with our clan as a lesson—in addition to her many raids, Stacey had leveled up her Herbalism almost to Level 400. You'd think this was a useless specialty for a raider, but when you encounter some rare plant in the Dungeon that you can sell at auction for 10–20 thousand gold (as sometimes happens), you'll learn a valuable lesson about how useful typically-neglected skills can be. You never know what may come in handy...

Swing, strike...Swing, strike...

My Mining was at Level 65, and the pickaxe I'd received from Rine back in the day granted me +1, which meant a total of Level 66...Man, I really liked that gnome. I should visit him or something. I think Pryke Mine has a visitors' day coming up if I'm not mistaken. No doubt the gnome doesn't remember me anymore (why would an Imitator retain memories of convicts that had long since left the mine?) and yet I wouldn't mind paying the place a visit. I could use the opportunity to show Fleita where I began my difficult path as a Shaman...

Swing, strike...Swing, strike...

And right after Pryke, I'll go visit the wolves...Who cares if I have a ton of unfinished business—I want to complete that particular quest chain. The Gray Death and her wolf cubs were the first serious quest that I received in Barliona, so I couldn't put it off further. What if some crazy player decided to kill the wolves again? I'd have to wait again...I don't think so!

Swing, strike...Swing, strike...

And in general, I should just take that damn list and...

Player Kalmira wishes to revive you. Do you accept?

"Three have been dug up and another twelve have been buried," Fleita announced the welcome news. "The buried are being revived and...Hey Teacher, why are you resting? What was it you told me? Do you remember? I don't know why, but your phrase won't leave my head: 'On your mark, get set, go! You didn't come here to enjoy the pleasant weather.'"

"Little bore," I muttered, getting up from the ground and heading back to the rocks. My last blow from the pickaxe had caused a cave-in, which finished off the players below and also gave me a nice knock on the head, forcing me to take a rest. I looked around and saw that all the players were already gathering inside the collapsed passage, since the crocolupes we had killed had respawned by now. "And how am I supposed to continue being your teacher after this? Kornik would have me whipped and expelled for speaking to him like that."

"That's why I chose you," the girl smiled. "Besides, you're not a goblin…"

Frankly, I had taken a great risk in deciding to bury the players. Despite the fact that we were in the same raid party and therefore I couldn't technically do damage to them, the collapsing rubble could count as doing damage to other players and send me back to the mines for a more permanent 'rest.' We got lucky though—the game decided that Clutzer and I were acting within the permitted boundaries. And yet if it weren't for that Paw, I'd never decide on such a risky step—in the end, my own skin is more valuable to me…

Adjusting my grip on the pickaxe, I approached the rocks again—there was still a lot of work to do and we had plenty of people left to rescue.

The excavations continued for about twelve hours, so we were forced to delay the resumption of the raid for sixteen hours all together. Clutzer and I were falling asleep on our feet. No, I don't think I want to go back to the mines one bit—the sheer monotony of this will kill me.

"What about now? Shall we go down the middle maybe?" Clutzer cast me a caustic glance. "Or do you have some other ideas?"

"Actually, I do," I replied. "We'll continue with the right passage…"

"What do you mean?" All three raid leaders

looked at me puzzled.

"The right passage is almost completely destroyed. We could even say there no longer is a right passage. And there's good reason to suspect that whatever of it remains is also a trap. Therefore, here's what we'll do—we send in another squad of victims, have them trigger the collapse and then dig them out and see where this passage leads. It's not like we have any guarantees that the other two passages are full of roses and chocolate. Let's finish with this one..."

As I predicted, the remaining part of the right passage turned out to contain the exact same trap. What was more was that the trap only activated after more than half of the raid party had entered its area of effect, while the range of the collapse equaled the maximum distance that the leading player had traveled—as we discovered after the first test. Since during the first test, we had been at the very border of the rock jungle, only several dozen meters of the passage had collapsed.

"Now we know what we need to do." Right after the first test which failed to bury a single player, I gathered my raid leaders and explained my hunch. "Which one of us is the fastest?"

"Drang was, but he's out...Ustar is the second fastest, but he's quite a bit slower."

"Doesn't matter. The main thing is that he makes it to the end of the passage but doesn't actually leave it."

"What if that blocks the trap?" Clutzer instantly asked.

"Or triggers another one," I parried. "We'll do as we did before. First we trigger the collapse and then see what comes out. Tell Ustar to make the dash..."

Our second attempt at passing through the stone labyrinth really did turn out to be more effective—the only catch was that everyone had to enter. The walls simply refused to collapse. I flirted with the idea of shuttling everyone one at a time across the remaining 700 meters (as Ustar reported), but then immediately rejected it—who knew what other traps those developers had laid in store for us. If we break the walls, then we might simply destroy everything they had prepared. Sometimes destroying everything just works better.

"*Dig us out.*" As soon as the dust settled, the raid chat came alive with messages that grew steadily happier and happier—before the walls had collapsed, the players had noticed that the right passage had been utterly destroyed. We were now free to move forward, but first Clutzer and I would have to put in some work again, while the raid as a whole was delayed for another day...

+5 Strength, +21 Mining, +3, Dexterity and +3 Stamina—such were the returns from waving my pickaxe for two days. Several times my Energy decreased to zero and I had to take a break to drink an elixir, and several times, my healers had to revive me when a strike from the pickaxe caused a cave-in onto my head. One time, we were visited by a pack of seven Level 300 crocolupes that Ustar had aggroed. The Rogue had decided to see what was in the neighboring passages, but overestimated his stealth stat. Instead of dying peacefully and waiting for us to revive him, this, uh, nearsighted player led the crocolupes straight back to the raid party. It was only because I had decided to unearth Evolett's healers and warriors first, that we managed to lose half of our party including myself. But it worked out in the end, although Magdey pledged to strip Ustar of any loot not only from the current raid but from several forthcoming ones as well. All in all, it was a difficult two days. The only nice thing was that my Altameda timer had stopped in the Dungeon—the game had graciously decided to allow me to enjoy the current quest...

"As I understand it, we need to reach that island?" Clutzer asked, making himself comfortable on the boulder beside me. We had just freed the last player from his stony prison and scheduled a new time for when we would resume our conquest of the Dungeon—tomorrow at nine in the morning. "And is that work of beauty there our final objective?"

Just beyond the rock trap, which we so ruthlessly destroyed, lay a huge lake—you could even say, a sea. Blue, wavering...Along with the sands that formed a beach, this would make an ideal vacation spot. About five hundred meters from the shore was a small island with a tower occupying the majority of it. Though, perhaps the word 'tower' doesn't do it justice—this epic work of construction rose five hundred meters into the sky. If it were to fall suddenly, it could easily form a bridge between the island and the shore we were on. The crown of this majestic tower was obscured by a constantly swirling blot of strange matter, very reminiscent of Geranika's shadows. Or a dark storm cloud, depending on how you wanted to see it.

"Yup," I confirmed Clutzer's guess.

"The sky is full of birds. The water is full of some kind of flickering shades...Maybe the aqueous relatives of our dear crocolupes? What do you think— how many of us will make the swim? For the record, I don't have a Diver skill."

"Mine lasts only about 18 minutes...Let's see what our options are tomorrow after everyone returns."

"Okay, until tomorrow then," said Clutzer. He gazed out at the lake with me for a little while, then sighed, grew transparent and dissolved right before my eyes.

All I could do was gasp for breath and struggle with the sudden flood of panic that washed over me— a prisoner had just signed out to reality. He had signed out like any ordinary player, who had had his fill of Barliona and decided to rest a little at home...

What the hell had just happened?!

CHAPTER FOUR
RETURN TO FARSTEAD

*M*AHAN, I HAVE A REQUEST: *Please don't say a word to anyone about what you just saw—no one, not Eric, not Leite, not Plinto, nor even Anastaria. I'm risking a lot as it is by logging out in front of you. When I return, please don't even hint that you know I've been released. Everyone else has to believe that I'm still incarcerated, the same as you. Sorry, but I can't tell you anything else. I've got so many non-disclosure agreements hanging over my head that I'm ready to lose my mind. Signing out in front of you and this letter "about nothing" is the only loophole I found to tell you about "the situation back home." Think...think very carefully about why I did this...One slip of the tongue, one wrong move that suggests you know about me and I'll be done for...*

Clutzer's letter arrived exactly a minute after he signed out into reality. I re-read it several times, looking for the slightest clue but failed to make any sense of what was going on. This was simply not possible. I must be dreaming. I'm about to wake up, tell the Rogue about my crazy dream and we'll share a nice laugh about it. I had no other way of describing what just happened. Prisoners aren't allowed to sign out into reality—it's as simple as that, and what I'd seen had to be nonsense.

Frantically, I tried to recall everything I knew about the Rogue. He was a thief who had been sent to prison for stealing the 'Mona Lisa,' as he put it. The amount he had to pay to go free was twenty-two million gold...Even if he were the most brilliant raid leader in Barliona, he couldn't have earned this amount in the three months since I'd left Beatwick. But even if he did manage to amass such a fortune— how'd he get out of the rehabilitation center? According to Nurris's letter, after serving the lengthy sentence in Barliona, there's still the rehabilitation phase! When had Clutzer found the time to complete it? He was right here with me the entire time! I really was at a loss. We had met a little over three months ago and I had paid for all three to have the headbands removed. At that point in time, Clutzer was definitely a prisoner—otherwise the Herald would have accused me of a making an improper summons. And now, suddenly, here was Clutzer telling me that he's a free man and that he doesn't have to live with the burden of a debt of twenty-two million...

"*Stacey?*" Unable to resist, I called Anastaria. I needed an answer, and, no one but her could give it to me.

You cannot reach this character. Anastaria is not currently in Barliona.

Damn it! Double damn it!

"That's the situation then," said the Rogue's voice behind me, making me start. "Got to get up early tomorrow. I'll go hit the hay. By the way, you should get some rest too, wash up, clean the dust off. Taking on a bunch of water mobs after several days of waving the pickaxe probably deserves a good rest first."

Clutzer was behaving as if nothing had happened. However, the dead earnest look in his eyes let me know that he was under immense stress. He was watching to see whether I'd keep his secret or not.

"You're right. A rest would be best," I replied carefully, and took the tent from my inventory. "Help me set it up?"

Whoever Clutzer was, he had revealed something I would never have guessed on my own. Had the Rogue returned in the morning, I could have begun asking around about his absence, but he left the game for exactly as long as it took me to read the letter and consider how to react. Now, my second raid leader was helping me set up the tent as if nothing had happened, whistling some tune under his breath. I need to do some thinking, a lot of thinking. It's a good thing that Anastaria hadn't been in the game—

since Clutzer had asked me not to tell anyone, including her, I guess I'll forget what I saw for the time being.

But who is he?

I could not fall asleep that night. No matter how I tossed and turned, no matter how much I prayed to the medical equipment that should have turned me off—sleep just wouldn't come to me. Clutzer's secret ran circles in my head, gradually forming the following picture:

Clutzer was an employee of the Barliona Corporation. More accurately, a contractor hired by them to...to do what? Whatever it was had something to do with me. Otherwise the Rogue would never have taken such a huge risk. Damn...I needed more information...What if I'm mistaken and Clutzer has nothing to do with the Corporation? In that case, how did he come up with the 22 million? And why is he so secretive about the whole thing?

The clock read two in the morning and I wasn't tired in the slightest. When at last I got sick of looking at the tent's walls and ceiling, I stepped out into the night to the dark lake. The two moons were in the sky, illuminating the surroundings, and in the dusk that had descended on the lake, there was no sight of the pterodactyls that had teemed above it all afternoon. But the sky hardly seemed interesting to me at the moment because the depths of the lake glowed with a stunning light show—either all or some of the aquatic mobs were luminescent. Huge sparkling sharks swam slowly and majestically along the shore, smaller creatures that resembled octopuses rushed between them at high speed, and schools of small fry huddled near the shore, no doubt to avoid the sharks. The beauty of all this was so indescribable that I could not resist. I turned into my Dragon Form and soared up high over the lake, wanting to take some pictures for memory.

As soon as my wings felt the first gusts of wind, all my thoughts of Clutzer evaporated—the act of flying always captivated my mind. A dark sky, dark waters, glowing monsters—what could be better?

Damage taken: Bluewing Bite

Out of nowhere, my pleasure of flight was rudely interrupted, and I felt an invisible force dragging me to the water's surface. Or rather not a force—I just suddenly for no reason at all had become much heavier than I was a few moments before. Given the system message that some beast was gnawing at me, I began to flap my wings with more force and managed to twist my neck so as to get a look at my back. Better I hadn't done so—as soon as my head turned, a furry, blue monster flashed past my eyes with tremendous speed and cast the "Blindness" debuff on me. It only blinded one eye, but that was enough to confuse me entirely—the pain was so intense that I roared and jerked forward and began to spin around my axis of flight. It was very difficult, since my wings kept buckling, but I was rushing forward at a breakneck pace, understanding perfectly well that if I don't shake the bluewing from my back, he'd eat me alive and all my plans of keeping the Paw would vanish in the oblivion of Lethe. A Paw into Lethe...what a way to put it.

Damage taken: Physical blow...

I really did the right thing by adjusting the notification settings. What does it really matter how much damage I've taken? I'm alive so who cares? As long as my frame isn't gray, I'm good. That was why a short while back I had adjusted my settings so that notifications would only report what was happening. This way there was less clutter. One should never forget about ergonomics!

The hit had been a mighty one. It was so intense that all I could do for the first several seconds was stare at the notification and contemplate my settings, as if nothing else was even happening. The debuffs 'Stun,' 'Deafen,' 'Vertigo' and another five similar status effects completely interrupted any sense of objectivity I had. If I were a functional Shaman, I would have summoned some Spirit of Cleansing and dealt with this bastard in short order. As things stood, however, I'd have to wait five minutes until the debuffs expired.

Although...I don't much feel like waiting around either...

The Shaman has three hands...
... and behind his back a wing...

... from the heat upon his breath...
Shining candle-fire springs...

Returning to my normal state was like an electric shock—such a wave of either pleasure or pain passed all over my body that I arched, my appendages shaking—yet literally a second later, the transparent veil that separated me from the world popped. Smells, sounds and the realization that I was right beside the tower on the island came to me. Next to me lay the corpse of a Level 300 bluewing.

My Hit Points were deep in the red, so I reflexively summoned a Spirit of Healing and looked around. The lake shore was only ten meters from the tower so it was simply a miracle that we hadn't missed the...

I summoned a Spirit of Healing?!

The news was so overwhelming that I sat right down on my tail and propped up my head with my wing. That's not supposed to happen. My Shamanic powers are supposed to be blocked at the program level—and it's not like whatever just happened could be called a 'hack.' No one was attacking me anymore, so I opened my log and began to study what just took place...

3:24:01 Used spell 'Cleansing Fire.'
3:24:01 Removed debuffs 'Stun,' 'Deafen...'
3:24:12 Used spell 'Healing Fire'
3:24:12 Dragon Rank promotion ...
3:24:12 Dragon Rank has reached current level

cap...

Fire...the Fire Spells...I opened my character properties and looked at the Dragon Rank entry—I had just reached Rank 10 and needed to go see Renox if I wanted to level up further. All well and good, but I still don't understand how I cast those spells! They're not Spirits after all!

"Mahan, where are you?" Clutzer said in the chat. Whoever he was, he was worried about me. On the other hand, maybe he's just worried that I'm telling someone about his secret...Well, I will leave it for now. When I have more time, I'll deal with the situation and punish whoever's responsible. For now I'm grateful to the Rogue for helping me gather my thoughts. I am on the island that our party will need to reach tomorrow. If I deal with the bluewings, we won't have to worry about the aquatic monsters and I'll be able to ferry everyone over by air. At Rank 10, I could remain in Dragon Form for 100 minutes. That should be enough to transport half our party, so we'd all be on the island in two days.

"On the island, doing recon," I wrote back in the raid chat. *"Pack up the tent, Clutzer, please. I don't want to waste time in the morning with it."*

"Okay, but how did you get there?"

"By air. You're forgetting, I'm, like, a Dragon and so on. I'm going to have a look around. Maybe there's something useful here."

Fifteen minutes later, I concluded that the tower had no door. Turning back to my human form and muttering over the fact that the XP from the bluewing I'd killed had gone to my Dragon self, I walked several times around the perimeter of the tower, but did not notice any entrance—no doors, no windows, no embrasures. It was a simple circular wall of stone, about seventy meters in diameter. It's worth also remembering the swirling fog up at its top—the fog hadn't responded to my presence on the island, but it was still a good idea to keep an eye on it just in case...

"What do you have?" Clutzer inquired again. It so happened that of all the Raiders, only the two of us had remained in Barliona. The rest had signed out to reality, so we could safely talk in the raid chat as if it was our own private channel.

"Nothing. A tower with no entrance, no windows, tall as hell and that's it."

"Have you tried to fly up to the top? What if you simply can't see the entrance from the ground?"

Hmm...Why that's an idea! Once again turning into my Dragon Form and trying to stay as close to the tower as possible, I started to spiral around it in tight circles, with each turn climbing higher and higher...

I almost missed the window. After rising almost three hundred meters above the ground without finding anything, I began to look askance at the fog I was approaching. It continued to act as if I weren't there, but I was getting the ominous feeling that if I touched it, I'd discover out that this was no friendly fog at all.

Gently landing on the window's sill and mentally

thanking the Patriarch for teaching me how to fly, I slashed the shutters with my wing—not giving much thought to the possible consequences. There was the noise of breaking glass and the window, along with the beams holding it in place, collapsed inward to reveal a spiral staircase on the inner walls of the tower's perimeter—and another tower inside. This internal tower was so narrow that it was more of a spire. It was only about thirty meters in diameter, but it was covered with windows and doors that were located in places that seemed pretty difficult to get to, since...Okay...I could be getting ahead of myself here...

Several suspended bridges led from the outside wall to the internal spire. They were located at varying heights—and meanwhile, this internal spire was rotating around its axis, periodically connecting its doors to the bridges. A pretty little piece of architecture, what can you say...

"Mahan, the fog is beginning to descend. Try to be careful..."

Sticking my head out and looking up, it only took a moment to make a decision, jump out the window and plummet like a stone. The distance between the fog and the window where I had been was a little more than ten meters—despite the fact that before I broke the window it had been an entire hundred. The fog really had tried to sneak up on me quickly—but Eluna had watched over me. I had three hundred meters between the earth and the window, so I decided not to unfurl my wings and enjoy the free fall.

"If that tiny falling speck is you, then you should probably flap your wings a little faster. It's looking like you've woken someone!"

I looked up, cursed, paused and cursed again. The wind was rushing past me with a terrible whistling and even folded, my wings were fluttering, but the fog wasn't lagging behind even a bit. The incomprehensible substance continued to chase me at the same speed, maintaining the twenty meters distance on my tail. I felt no desire to become better acquainted, so I began to gently open my wings and come out of my free fall. I didn't feel like crashing into the ground either. (What a lazy dragon I am! I don't feel like doing anything!)

About fifty meters from the ground, I finally spread my wings and abruptly changed direction, flying away from the tower. All that I could rely on now was my +30% flight speed from my upgraded armor. The system stayed treacherously silent about the option of using Dragon Breath, so I had no weapon to fight the fog with. I hoped only that it was somehow bound to the tower and wouldn't chase me away from it. Otherwise, I'd be helpless.

"Mahan, the fog is following you. Heads up— there's another speck approaching you from your right—five o'clock. And don't pull an Ustar—I don't want to respawn..."

The fog is following me? Damn! Double damn it all! Glancing in the direction Clutzer indicated, I cursed yet again—ears plastered back, another bluewing was rocketing in my direction! He was Level 300 just like his brother, and he was just as blue and furry, though it was harder to tell in the darkness.

The fog did not lag behind. Moreover, I got the feeling that it was coming unacceptably close to me and was about to devour me. Something clicked in my head, giving rise to a plan. It was so extravagant that I was sure it would not work, but I had no other choice—I couldn't lead the fog and the bluewing to Clutzer. If I died, the raid could go on without me. If both of us died, however, the players returning in the morning would find themselves at the entrance to the Dungeon and the first attempt would be history. Like hell! If someone must die here, let it be me. Cue the dramatic music!

Using my tail to adjust my bearing, I turned straight for the bluewing. A joyous squeak pierced my ears and saddled me with several debuffs, but gritting my teeth, I ignored the pain and disorientation and went on flapping my wings. Forty meters...the bluewing had already spread his claws, preparing to land on me, his red eyes following my tiniest motion, and I realized that in the eyes of this Imitator, I was as good as dead. The desire to tear apart his hated enemy was so evident in this mob that I had to make a great effort to keep flying straight. I'm going to ram him! Twenty meters...I could see the slobber dripping from the mouth of the monster flying towards me. It seemed that this mob's Imitator had already eaten me in his processor and was now trying to turn his dreams into reality. Five meters...The speed at which we were approaching each other was so huge that we were covering tens of meters in mere moments. When the distance between us was very small, the bluewing flared its wings like a parachute, wanting to slow down and latch onto me with greater efficiency. The mob didn't want to lose such a piece of prey. Just as I expected...

I all but wrenched my wing as I went into a steep bank and dropped like a stone to the lake's surface. All kinds of welcome messages about overloading my wings and new debuffs flashed before my eyes, I passed out for a moment, but came to in time and was able to level off right over the surface.

"*Clutzer?*" I managed ask in the chat. I didn't have the time to turn and see what was going on behind my back.

"*The fog swallowed the mob, slowed down a little, absorbing it, but is once again after you. I could be wrong, but it doesn't seem to be moving as quickly as before. At any rate, it's definitely no longer gaining on you.*"

I will never know by what miracle I escaped the jaws of the shark that jumped out of the lake. I simply sensed at one moment that I was about to be done for and banked aside, figuring that the fog had crept right up to me. Right in the path of my former trajectory, an enormous pair of toothy jaws appeared, wishing like Charybdis to devour another victim. If I had gone on flying straight, I would never have avoided those teeth...At the same time, the amazing thing was that this lake-dwelling doggy was not sparkling like the others, as if it was designed to hunt the flying bluewings and players. By the way, I wonder whether you can fly on griffins around here...

"*Minus one fishy,*" Clutzer immediately replied. "*The fog ate him too. By the way, the fog's gotten bigger...Heads up: Bogey at your ten o'clock!*"

At the whim of the developers, another bluewing had decided to cruise around its surroundings this fine night and maybe check out the mysterious creature zooming around the Dungeon's dusky sky. All right, we'll resort to our tried and true plan one more time...

I ended up feeding another seven bluewings to the fog, as well as three sharks who came jumping ten meters out of the water. My Dragon Form timer was approaching its last ten minutes when Clutzer sent me another message:

"*Just now, another fishy jumped into the fog, trying to eat it. Now the fog's stopped in place. It looks like it's had its fill...Mahan, if there's no one else guarding the tower, maybe you'll go see what's inside of it?*"

The island was only a hundred meters away from me, so I flapped my wings several more times and fell to the sand, turning back into my human form. My Energy had dropped almost to zero, my whole body ached, I had trouble breathing, and at the moment I had only one wish—to get some sleep. Pulling out an Elixir of Energy, I poured it down my throat without swallowing—the fluid knew where to go and I didn't have the strength for such mundanities.

The elixir replenished all of my physical stats, yet it was incapable of restoring my mental fatigue— the last thing I wanted was to turn back into a Dragon and crawl back into the tower. I'd need an entirely different kind of elixir to go on—not that it would help much, since booze doesn't work properly in Barliona anyway, the desire being to promote a healthy lifestyle among the players. For all that, I understood Clutzer perfectly well. He was now acting like a true raid leader—while the Dungeon boss is busy digesting, it's not a bad idea to dig around his coffers to see what's what. You never know when the next opportunity will show up. If it weren't for the jewels that I needed for my Chess Set, I wouldn't lift a finger right now—however...I'm starting to get the impression that Clutzer is manipulating me, making me do things that he needs done.

As soon as I reached the window, I turned back into my human form again. It wasn't a great idea to waste what few minutes of Dragon Form I had to check out what was inside the tower. The internal spire was still rotating, though now I could make out a spiral staircase that ran along the inside perimeter of the outer tower. In actual fact, this staircase led to two bridges, which were located at different levels and led to the center. I began to grasp the overall design of this obstacle: Somewhere down there, there was an entrance after all, by which we could reach the spire, go up several floors, emerge through a door to a bridge, ascend the spiral staircase to the next bridge and re-enter the rotating spire. Then we'd just repeat this operation until we reached the very top of the spire. I couldn't see what was up there from where I was sitting, but I did notice several more windows on the same level as me. This meant that someone in the spire needed light from this level in order to....Yeah, okay! It wouldn't be a good idea to break into someone's place for a visit, so I turned into a Dragon again and soared up between the two towers. Every single manual and guide for Barliona claims that players aren't allowed to fly on their own—that they must use pets to do so, but the manuals don't mention Dragons, so we'll just assume that I'm not breaking any rules. In the end, this is my Dungeon and I can behave however I like...

I crossed the fifty meters that separated me from the top in a minute. All I really had to do was jump from bridge to bridge and perch to perch, since there wasn't any space to flap my wings freely. And when I reached the top, I was rewarded with the sight of three open chests...

Achievement unlocked: 'Bah! Humbug!' First completion of the Skrooj Dungeon.

Achievement reward: +20% to all resources mined.

Message for the player: In five months' time you will be teleported to an audience with the Emperor of Malabar. You may take two companions with you; for this you will have to give them the invitation letter in the course of five months. You may obtain the invitations in

any branch office of Barliona Bank.
Level gained...

Twelve notifications about new levels that I'd gained flashed before my eyes as quickly as a passing express train, but I did not pay any attention to them. My entire being was concentrated on these three chests—which were filled to the brim with precious stones, gold bullion, platinum and several diadems. As Ishni had told me, a complete set of ingredients for the Chess Set was waiting for me in the Dungeon, but he'd never mentioned the additional loot. What had I just stumbled on?

"Do you understand that if the boys return right now and don't receive an achievement of their own, they'll have our scalps? By the way, I just gained 10 levels, so thank you! Did you find your gems?"

"Yeah," I replied and, dismissing the chat, began to empty the contents of the coffers. At the moment, my inventory bag had 260 slots, each of which could hold a stack of 40 items. In this sense at least, the developers had departed from reality to do the players a favor. Even though my bag was more than half full, I should still be able to fit everything in it. Otherwise my menagerie, which was currently swimming in the coffers before me like the Dungeon's duck-namesake, would get completely out of hand and start a riot. By the way! Stacks of Malachite, Lapis Lazuli, Marble and other low-level gems can be sent immediately to Leite for storage in the castle warehouse. I'd sort everything else myself...

When I finished stuffing my bag (without even bothering to check the diadems' properties), I took out my mailbox, wrote a letter to my treasurer and attached twelve stacks of stones. You can't store more than 60 items in your mail—a limitation of the game world—but the system treats one stack as one item. Very convenient arithmetic...

This player is not currently in the game. The letter will be delivered later.

This message was so unexpected and simultaneously shocking, that I didn't even react as three black, red-eyed humanoids appeared on the tower's roof. Shrieking wildly and utterly ignoring me, they rushed to the empty chests, paused above them, bellowed like mad buffaloes, turned to me, bared their sharp teeth...and Barliona ceased to exist for me for twelve hours as I was sent to the nearest respawn point.

The last thought that flickered across my fading consciousness was, "*Et tu Brute!*"

* * *

"*Welcome back from the dead!*" As soon as I reappeared in Barliona, Anastaria's voice immediately appeared in my head. "*Evolett is super pissed at you for stealing the Dungeon loot from him!*"

"*Stacey! Leite is free!*" I blurted out my thought, deciding to stay silent about Clutzer. Since he made it known to me that he's no longer a prisoner, I'll deal with his case separately. But Leite was another matter—he was the treasurer, had full access to the clan coffers, and now it turned out that he was not who he claimed to be...Personally, I don't like this bit of news one bit—what if it turns out that all the money is gone?...Of course there'll be the contract, but it was a cinch for a capable manager to find a loophole! Now more than ever, I needed Stacey's help. She was smart as hell, while I was utterly confused and did not know what to do. I had finally decided that if there was anyone I could trust in this world it would be Anastaria.

"What do you mean? Hang on, I'll summon you to Altameda in a second and we'll talk normally! Also, Leite is right here. I suggest we let him join our conversation. Give me five minutes—I'll go get the Mages..."

I sat down on the boulders of the respawn point and tried once again to think through all these goings on. All the other players had had twelve game hours to make their decisions, but my respawn had passed in a flash.

And so!

Clutzer and Leite are free people. It stood to reason that Eric was free too. Why not? The buyout amount for Leite and Eric was fifteen and ten million, respectively, so ...

Stop!

Leite's buyout was only 15 million! What if...No, no...the clan's budget remained at its previous level...Although, my treasurer earned a salary of about one million per month...Stacey where are you and your Mages?

"*Dan, you threw me off!*" Anastaria's thought occurred to me as if she'd heard me. "*I can just summon you myself! Hang on. I'll teleport to Altameda and bring you over. Leite is already there...Ten seconds...*"

Your other half wishes to summon you to her location. Do you accept?

"...And that's how things stand," Leite said, finishing his confession and staring at me guiltily. I didn't know whether I should laugh or rejoice at what I'd just heard. The one good thing was that the treasurer had not betrayed me. Moreover, he had put himself in such a position that he was now iron-bound to our clan. But still—I hated the fact that he'd pulled off such a maneuver on his own, without asking for my help...

When I allowed the Warrior to hire his wife—he was still a prisoner. By that point, as I had reckoned correctly, Leite was earning about a million gold per month. In addition to his wife's contribution, the total income of his household was around 1.5 million. And then Leite decided to take a loan from the Bank of Barliona to finally secure his freedom. He simply wanted to go for a walk with his wife once in a while, under a real sky—plus it turned out that my treasurer's child had grown up quite a bit too. He received approval for the loan and he paid for his release from Barliona just three days ago. Every day now, according to the agreed upon schedule with the rehabilitation center, he was attending his rehabilitation class. Given that the Warrior had been in Barliona for a mere 18 months, his rehabilitation period was only two weeks. It was just yesterday that he was at his last therapy session and...When I asked him why he hadn't borrowed the money from the clan or from me, Leite merely shook his head and mumbled something about wanting it to be a surprise. It's no good, he explained, when the treasurer is a convict and is in danger of being sent back to the mines at any moment. Now that the monthly payment on his loan was about 1.5 million— such is the draconian interest for in-game credit—he would do everything in his power to improve the clan's financial condition. You could say that now, he was motivated up to his tonsils...End quote...

"We better warn Eric and Clutzer to speak to us before they try to do something similar," I told Stacey, nodding in the direction of the door that Leite had just departed through. "That was a pretty shocking piece of news..."

"I'd say so...A desperate step...A loan, rehab therapy, your distrust...Did you see the giants' quest?"

"Eh...Not yet. I guess I've been occupied. Shall we take a glance? Although...You were right when you said that we already know the next letters in the verses. Have you sent anyone to check the coordinates yet?"

"Not only did I send someone, but I already found the entrance," smiled the girl, relishing the wide-eyed astonishment on my face. "All that's left is to craft the green and blue knights and that's it—the key to the Tomb will be ready..."

"You found it?" I cried, completely losing my head. "And you waited to tell me?"

"I asked you about the giants for a reason—I only received the exact coordinates of the entrance six hours ago. When you respawned—I was actually there, checking that it was indeed the place. I'm sending you the coordinates, a video and a portion of the updated map—the entrance is right here..."

About two hundred kilometers from Sintana and almost on the border between Kartoss and Malabar, a small plateau was located deep in the Elma Mountains. Covered in a permanent fog, it was safely hidden from view—unless you knew that the slope of the mountain with the proud name of Kaltarnix jutted out to form a field, you'd never stumble on it by accident. You couldn't call the plateau large—it was no more than a flat, round field about fifty meters in diameter, lying flush against the mountain. As the camera filming shifted a little and floated over to the mountain, the outlines of a door came into focus. An inscription was carved upon it: 'Karmadont.'

"I spent three hours trying to get inside of it by every means possible—I had high-level miners try to demolish the door, the walls beside it, the stone floor of the field. I tried to blow up the door with the help of

Mages—all in vain. We couldn't even break off a tiny piece. This area is blocked at the system level and can be opened only with a key which is the six different figurines of the Karmadont Chess Set...That's my spousal report then. Wait, that's a lie. Also, I was with Nashlazar and she taught me to fight in the form of a Siren—check it out...what do you think?"

Anastaria turned into her Siren Form and I couldn't help but gasp—the girl's entire body...um...the Siren's entire body was covered in glittering armor which reduced all damage taken by 40%.

"Whoa," I managed.

"You bet! I am now...But wait, Dan, let me get back to the door, okay? The key is the key, but I can't help but try a couple more tricks. I have this Thief friend, who has an incredibly high Lockpicking skill. I want him to have a go at the place. Who knows, maybe it'll pan out..."

"Yes, of course," I managed again. I don't know why but lately I'm having trouble coming up with something to say. I should probably deal with this habit.

"In that case, see you later," Anastaria kissed me, activated the portal and, before departing reminded me: "Tomorrow, I'll sign out to reality for about a week. Try not to break Barliona while I'm gone—I'm quite fond of it."

Ding! You've received 433 new messages. Would you like to read them?

Collapsing in my rocking throne, I shut my eyes

and snarled—how was one supposed to live with all these people bothering me constantly? Who needed me now? For what?

"*Can you introduce me...,*" "*Can you give me...,*" "*Can you lend me...,*" "*Can you introduce me...,*" "*Can you invite me...*"—right...and then how did this last letter squeeze through all my inbox filters? I looked over it once again and grinned: "*Inveite me unto ur clan. I will be the stongest player you have. I'll wipe out all the...*" So it looks like the mail filters don't account for spelling mistakes. And these are surely purposeful typos too—calculated to sneak the letter past my filters and stand out among the remaining mass of players. Barliona doesn't allow grammatical errors by default—when all is said and done, we don't write the text ourselves: We think the thought and the system extracts the words and formats them into text. You really do need to go through a lot of trouble to write poorly in this game. You have to buy a fairly expensive piece of paper, write the text by hand using your calligraphy skill, confirm that the errors are acceptable...It's a good thing that Barsa explained all the finer subtleties of the Barliona playerbase to me. Otherwise, I'd delete this letter without a second thought. Forwarding this little marvel to Barsa, I had almost finished sorting through the remaining avalanche of mail when I came across a letter with a rather grandiloquent subject line: "In Private Confidence—To the Head of the Legends of Barliona from the Head of the Nav Clan..."

Why look at that! 'In Private Confidence' and to

the 'Head'! I wonder what this Spiteful Gnum wants from me? The name sounds familiar…

Hey Mahan! Sorry for such a pompous subject line but otherwise the Imitator might reject this. You probably don't remember, but we met recently. Rumor has it that you need craftsmen who can work with Imperial-level resources. I'll mention right off that I'm not trying to join your clan. I'm not interested. But I am interested in offering you a deal: You send me a stack of Imperial Steel and the reagents in the list attached to this letter, and I, in turn, will craft something useful for your castle from them. My only condition is no contracts. We do it all only on trust. If I'm a crook, you lose some valuable resources. If not, you'll receive the product without paying a penny for the work. Make your decision, Shaman!

We met recently? I honestly spent some time going over the people whom I'd seen or spoken with the last, say, couple of days, but Spiteful Gnum did not show up among them. An open and shut case then—yet another conman, trying to pull off the big con. Why test the waters with ordinary ingots of gold or steel? This one goes straight for the Imperial Steel! Who cares that you need to be at least at Level 400 in your profession to work with that material—just send it over and that's it! I'm so tired of these players…

And yet, well aware that I shouldn't bother, I wrote Gnum a reply:

Greetings! Losing so many resources over some harebrained proposal from a person I don't remember meeting is overkill. Prove to me that you are worthy of such trust...

In the beginning, when the letters asking for resources began to roll in, I would honestly ask people what they needed them for and what I'd receive in return. Ninety-nine-point-nine percent of the beggars immediately vanished at that juncture, and only one out of a thousand was offering something that could be of use to the clan. Eventually, I stopped responding to such messages by configuring the spam filter accordingly, but Spiteful Gnum managed to sneak by. Okay, let's see what he's got...

"Fleita, where you at?" Having finished with my mail, I immediately called my pupil. I didn't feel like staying in the castle—or starting to craft the War Lizards, despite the fact that the entrance to the Tomb had already been discovered—so I decided to travel to Pryke Mine and then to Farstead.

"Me? I'm at a party—Evolett invited me to his castle. You'll never believe it—I've been invited to join the Dark Legion! And not just as a Recruit—they're going to make me a Raider! I'm now a Raider of the Dark Legion! No one will believe me when I tell them!"

"I see...Is, uh, Evolett there by any chance?" When I brought Fleita with us on the Dungeon raid, I never for a moment doubted that the Priest would chat her up in his spare time to find out who she is, figure out what her relationship to me is and invite her to join his clan. After Anastaria, Evolett was the second person whom I was willing to trust (at 60% confidence), and that trust was based on mutually beneficial cooperation, so I saw nothing wrong with Fleita joining the Dark Legion. The only surprising thing was the rank of Raider they'd assigned the Level 67 Shaman. As far as I recall, Evolett pays the Raiders a salary even if they don't go to the Dungeon. In my view, 'buying' the girl this way was too much. She is still a student after all. What if she gets sucked into the game, quits her studies and real life, and plunges headlong into Barliona? The youth are the youth...I really hope that her parents are watching after her, but it wouldn't do any harm if I spoke with her either...

"No, I'm at the training ground at the moment. As the local trainers explained to me—I need to catch up to all the levels I gained recently. Why didn't you warn me that I need to focus on skills first and levels later? And in general—this is all your fault for taking me on that raid!"

"If you keep whining," I snapped, "I won't take you anywhere anymore."

"Actually, what I meant to say, was thank you," came the astonishing response, utterly unrelated to the earlier direction of our conversation. "Are you calling me for something? Are we going somewhere?"

"Yes, I wanted to propose we visit this one place," I drawled, deciding to myself that Pryke Mine was out of the question—at the moment, at any rate. "But since you seem so busy, we'll put off our travels."

"I'm not busy!" the girl yelped immediately.

"In that case, I'll be waiting for you in Altameda in an hour."

"But...I don't have the money for a Portal Scroll..."

"I'll have you summoned in an hour, just be ready," I replied wearily, hung up, took out another amulet and stared at it for a minute, trying to decide what to say to Evolett. In essence, I need to give him the money I owe him, apologize, and...That's it! That's what I'd do...

"Speaking!"

"Evolett, this is Mahan...I'm calling to apologize for the Skrooj affair and to tell you to check your mail. We can talk about the whole deal in detail later."

"Hmm..." the Priest replied expressively after a moment, causing me to smile and continue:

"What I want from you remains the same—I want us to continue our partnership. I really am sorry that things worked out the way they did. All I did was go for a flight to see the Dungeon at night. I wasn't planning on...Well, please accept my apologies. I hope that this incident will not affect our future cooperation."

"Hmm..." came the meaningful reply once again, indicating that Evolett was thinking. And there really was something to think about. The letter I sent contained the Fleet Hound Paw—and without any kind of strings attached. I had gifted an item that I could have sold to Phoenix for 10–15 million to a stranger just like that. What an unpredictable

Shaman I was...

"I hope we can consider this incident behind us. What do you say?"

"Yeah," Evolett came to at last. "I didn't expect this...Frankly, I never for a moment doubted that you'd call me, but this...You continue to amaze me, Shaman...I would love to see you in my clan..."

"I have one more selfish question—it's about Fleita," I continued, ignoring the Priest's offer. "Did you have some ulterior motive in mind when you invited her to your clan? Because, unofficially at least, she is my student and I would prefer her to be available. But as I understand it, Dark Legion Raiders are extremely busy people..."

"Sure—she must become as great of a Shaman as her teacher—even greater, although I'm afraid that greater is hardly possible. I don't intend on taking her on raids—let her focus on her studies. That's stipulated in our contract, by the way. She must attain her higher education degree. I have no intention of ruining a girl's life, so please make sure to plan your teaching activities with her with that in mind. To be honest, I'm surprised that the Corporation has permitted a player to teach another player..."

"No one gave permission, since Fleita never asked for it. She just showed up and told me she wanted to study with me. I could not say no."

"What did the check uncover?"

"We never did a check on her." At first I didn't understand what Evolett was talking about, but when at last it got through my thick skull, I added: "I relied on my premonition."

"Got it. I'll get someone on it and send you the report when I have it. Premonition is good and all, but when there's a person constantly with you who has access to all the locations you have access to, you'd better be sure of them."

"Thank you, I'll be waiting for that report. All right, I bow humbly before you and bid my farewell. If something comes up, give me a call..."

The old guys really do have their heads screwed on tight. I never even thought of checking to see whether Fleita had been in any other clans—like, say, the Heirs of the Titans or the Azure Dragons. The fact that she's not 18 years old yet, doesn't mean she's automatically clean.

"Viltrius," I summoned my majordomo. "What's the current status of the castle portal?"

"The portal was activated at the order of Master Leite. The same also hired a demon for ensuring that..."

"A demon?" I interrupted a goblin. As far as I know, demons in Barliona were something like flying pigs—everyone's heard of them, but no one's seen one—so it was a surprise to learn that we had one working in my castle.

"That's right—a demonic being that assists the process of teleportation. In this manner, castle resources are used more efficiently."

"And what does this demon want in return?"

"Ordinary gold, since providing this service does

not require any extra costs on his part. I can assure you that as long as the number of outbound teleports will be fewer than ten per minute, it makes more fiscal sense to pay the demon than the Mages, since we have to pay them every time they do the work..."

"I see...Please arrange for my student to be summoned and for the two of us to be sent to these coordinates." I sent the goblin the coordinates for Beatwick.

"I'm sorry, a small clarification. Your student is Zombie Shaman Fleita the Decembrist?"

"That's correct. Make it happen!"

The goblin disappeared, while I looked bitterly at the mail icon, indicating that someone new wanted something else from me. Well okay, I have some time to kill anyway. May as well take a look...

"In Private Confidence—To the Head of the Legends of Barliona from the Head of the Nav Clan..."

Spiteful Gnum again? What a stubborn young man...What kind of a story has he invented now to defraud me of my resources?

*So you've assumed fraud right off? You're that certain I'm a crook? Lol...What a greedy Shaman you are...Where's your sense of adventure and daring? Oh well—in that case you can forward my letter to your personnel manager. I'm too lazy to go proving myself to someone who won't give me the benefit of the doubt. I am willing to offer my—naturally, not inexpensive— services in several professions...As an example, here is a description of one of my latest creations: "**Onyx**

Gargoyle (Castle Ornament). Description: By means of a demonic essence, this ordinary sculpture has become a stone guardian..." *Apologies, I won't send you the full description but rest assured, the critters turned out pretty well. Until they're activated, they're utterly indistinguishable from ordinary statues. And they don't have to come alive immediately if you don't want them—they can for example wait until some healers pass by...But those are just the highlights, let's say. If you could only see them play dice at night...Rumor has it that one of their owners from the Azure Dragons almost had a heart attack when he saw it. Good luck to you, Shaman!*

Here at last, Gnum managed to pique my curiosity and pique it quite intensely...Gargoyle sentries would look very good in my castle, even without any kind of defensive functions. Who wouldn't want to improve their castle? To reach Level 25, my castle needed some serious decorations, since all the major facilities had already been built. This fellow wants a stack of Imperial steel, so is the gargoyle going to be made of metal? Aren't they supposed to be stone sculptures...or is he going to use the steel for the frame? Hmm...I have to say that this guy has me curious. What do I have to lose anyway? Forty units of Imperial Steel? Considering how much of it I have in our vaults—losing that much won't be a big deal...

"Your pupil, Master," Viltrius appeared beside me, holding Fleita by the hand. The girl was quite the sight—it seems that the boys of the Dark Legion had issued her a special set of equipment designed for a Zombie because my pupil now looked simultaneously extravagant, beautiful and repellent. The bloody bones that made up her pauldrons alone must have cost a fortune...

"Thank you. Could you bring me three stacks of Imperial Steel please?" I asked the goblin.

"What do you need steel for?" Fleita asked when Viltrius disappeared without any further questions. "Are you about to start crafting again?"

"It's not for me," I replied, trying to maintain my temper. Evolett is right—trusting people is okay as long as you check them too. Who could tell me, for instance, why this girl is so nosy?

"Then who?"

"What's it to you? Stop asking dumb questions, Fleita! You're my student, not a member of my clan! Why don't you ask something about summoning Spirits, for example?"

"Whatever. What's the big deal!" scoffed the girl and began examining the ceiling demonstratively. Shaking my head and contemplating that talking to seventeen-year-olds who consider themselves mature is very difficult indeed, I wrote a reply to Spiteful Gnum:

That's exactly what I was talking about—I wanted at least a description of what you do. You cannot imagine how many such letters I receive, and every single one needs something—timber or stone or ore or ingots. Then when I start asking them what they need it for, they simply vanish. Attached, please find three stacks of Imperial Steel. If your gargoyles are as good as you say they are, I'll be happy to see you in my castle. As I understand it, you're looking to level up in your profession—my castle is completely in your hands if you want to work on it.

Like that! Let's see what this Spiteful Gnum is made of! I effectively just gave him extra stacks for extra work—I'm sad to see them go of course, but it's worth a shot—plus, I hinted at the opportunity of leveling up in my castle. I need to develop Altameda further. Stagnation is no good, but hiring players or NPCs to do this kind of work will cost me an arm and a leg. Since Gnum is offering to help, it's worth risking it. By the way—I haven't heard from Sakas yet...Is he still in the Mine after all this time?

"The portal is ready," Viltrius appeared beside me. "Will you be departing this instant?"

"Yes. Fleita, how much time do you have left today?"

"I didn't have any special plans, so...Let's play until midnight and then see."

"Great. Then we're heading out without any further ado—here's the quest."

I opened my quest list and scrolled down to the bottom where the 'Last Hope' quest chain (which I still hadn't technically received) had been lingering for several months now.

"Quest canceled," I smirked when the system informed me that I couldn't share a quest that I didn't yet have myself. "Viltrius, take us to the teleport."

"Here's a quest, there's a quest...I wish you'd make up your mind," Fleita couldn't keep from sniping, offering her hand to the majordomo. There was a bright flash and for the first time in my time in Barliona, I beheld a real—that is, a living—demon.

Smallish and red, the demon was as wrinkled as an old man. On his head he bore two smooth horns and a carefully trimmed goatee, and he was dressed in a fairly respectable-looking waistcoat which gave him the resemblance of a pirate. To my immense disappointment, he had no trident—otherwise, the image would've been complete.

"And so where's the trident then?" Unlike me, Fleita was not too embarrassed to express her true feelings. If her brain thinks something, then that something instantly appears on her tongue...Hmm...I wonder why she ever stays silent? Could it be that there's utter silence 'up there' in those moments? But okay—I shouldn't make fun of the girl.

"Only Archdemons may carry a trident, as well as creatures of a higher order," the demon replied and offered his open hand to Fleita. The creature's voice was so high-pitched that I got the impression that I was speaking with a lady who had decided to yell a little.

"What?! A hundred of what? For what?" screamed the girl, who had it seems just received a bill from the demon.

"Gold—the round, metallic kind. For answering your question. I just set this new rule," said the demon, his paw steadily awaiting its fee.

"Three hundred? One hundred per question?"

"Absolutely correct—three hundred. Such is the price of three answers."

"Fleita, kindly quit haggling with our esteemed demon," I cut off the girl who, judging by her appearance, was about to become outraged about the five hundred gold. Leite sure did hire a curious fellow to manage the portal... "I will pay the girl's fee. But before I do so," I was forced to add as the demon's paw shifted in my direction, "I would like the esteemed demon to pay a fine of five thousand gold for conducting entrepreneurial activities on the premises of Altameda without prior approval or permission from the castle's owner. Viltrius—I assume that we have a castle code? Please add this clause to it."

"Hang on just a minute!" Judging by his mug, the demon was quite taken aback. "This clause was not in the code earlier. Therefore, I did not violate any law!"

"Ah, but now it is! Let's add a fine of two thousand for a demonic creature arguing with the castle's owner. Viltrius—add this clause. That will come out to a total of seven thousand gold."

"I object! This is extortion!" The demon became completely outraged. As if outrage would change my mind!

"Demonic outrage on the premises of Altameda—another three thousand gold. If you are unsatisfied with the terms of your contract, you are free to leave your job, but there's no need to be outraged here. We can find someone who won't be outraged! That will be ten thousand. Shall we go on or shall we pay?"

"Ahem," sounded a cough behind my back, causing me to turn and regard the short owner of this low-timbered and pleasant voice. I almost jumped— right beside me stood a creature whose properties indicated only its occupation: Archdemon. The creature's appearance very much resembled the classic demon from old computer games—it had enormous wings, a proud look, and a trident (Fleita must be pleased).

"The esteemed Dragon wishes to violate the rules of exchange between our two worlds?" the newcomer began without bothering to introduce himself. Although, if I recall the fairy tales correctly, he who knows a demon's name can control him, so I doubt that such a respectable Archdemon would bother to introduce himself to a Free Player.

"I don't understand the gist of your question," I went on the counteroffensive. I mean, give me a break—it takes more than a trident to scare me. "This esteemed demon, whom we employ as a teleport conductor, without announcing the costs of his services, or the terms of their use, began to issue my pupil invoices for payment, without bothering to inquire about her opinion on this matter. Consequently, he was engaging in unsanctioned entrepreneurial activity on the premises of my castle, and I, as the castle owner, am allowed to demand damages. If the law applies equally to the esteemed demon, why isn't he subject to similar sanctions? I believe that I acted justly and according to the letter of the law..."

"I have no complaints against the first and third fine. I am here to establish the grounds for the fine of two thousand gold for arguing with the owner," the Archdemon lost some of his stature but went on plying his line. "How can we have any further agreements whatsoever if it's impossible to argue with the owner? This contravenes the legal norms governing the relations between our worlds—and does so flagrantly, I might add."

"I concede that I went too far with the second clause. I admit my guilt and void the fine of two thousand gold on the grounds that it was levied without justification. I also void a further thousand worth of fines as compensation for emotional distress. However, I consider seven thousand gold a fair fine and am prepared to argue my case before any court..."

"There is no need. I have no objections to the other points. It was nice to meet you. All the best," the Archdemon nodded and vanished without casting a portal. What kind of security do I have in my castle that all kinds of strange creatures can wander in and out as they please? I wonder—are demons unique in this regard or can Rogues and Assassins do the exact same thing? As it stands, they won't have to even bother sneaking through the darker corners of my castle. I'll need to ask Viltrius about this...

"I'm waiting," I said, mimicking the wrinkly demon's gesture and stretching out my hand for the gold. "Where are my seven thousand?"

+10 to Trade. Total: 19.
+5 to Charisma. Total: 80.

"It's a pleasure to deal with business-minded people," smiled the demon as the system notified me that I had just received my seven thousand gold. "In that case, I request that you pay me what Fleita the Decembrist owes and we can consider the matter closed. It's looking like running my own little travel agency in Altameda will cost me a bit too much in regulatory fines..."

I gave him the amount he demanded without saying anything, took Fleita—who was standing there gaping—by the hand and stepped into the open portal. I really need to do something about the girl's perpetually open mouth and bulging eyes—who knows what scrape we find ourselves in...This is a game after all!

Quest available: 'Last Hope.
Step 3. Demolish the Transformers.'
Description: The Gray Death and her pack have been driven mad by the Transformers of Kartoss—the same devices that blackened the lands of Farstead. They have transformed the wolves into terrible monsters who now terrorize the backwoods of the province.
Rid the lands of Kartoss of this scourge
Quest chain class: Rare.

Reward: +50% Experience towards next level.

Reward for completing quest chain: Hidden.

Penalty for failing/refusing the quest: Hidden.

CHAPTER FIVE
THE GRAY DEATH

"SO THIS IS BEATWICK THEN?" asked Fleita, staring at the remains of the village. "In the movie it looked...a little more...in one piece..."

I sighed bitterly, agreeing with the girl—Beatwick no longer appeared as a settlement on the map of Barliona.

All that remained of the houses was scorched earth and half-ruined, soot-covered chimney stacks. There were neither fences nor barns...Nothing at all. Only a slumped stockade around the village, burned and broken in several places, survived the recent disaster. Beatwick had become a monument to itself...It's a good thing that we had managed to evacuate all the residents in time...

"What a terrible sight," shuddered Fleita, pressing herself to me unconsciously, as if seeking support. "I don't understand why they left all this? Why not simply raze it all to the ground."

"Let's go," I said dully, having seen my fill. Formally speaking, Beatwick was but one of hundreds of thousands of virtual villages, but it was still upsetting that it had been 'excluded' from the future lore of this world.

"You wanted to give me some kind of quest," Fleita reminded me as soon as we left the ruins. "Or is this 'official clan business' again?'"

"Don't be a smart aleck," I grumbled. I opened my quest list, found the quest I needed and tried to send it to the Zombie...and I do mean 'try' because the system glibly replied that I couldn't share a quest chain that I'd already completed more than 25% of.

"You really are terribly greedy," the girl concluded and asked: "Where to next? By the way, why haven't you said anything about my new appearance? The Dark Legion outfitted me with some really cool stuff, but you act like you didn't notice a thing! Some teacher you are!"

"We're going to the forest." I did my best not to lose my temper with the girl—the grim impression that Beatwick had made on me was still vivid in my mind. I walked another hundred meters or so before my distracted and foggy consciousness noticed an odd fact—there was a number '1' glowing over Fleita's head. The girl had received her First Kill...

"*Stacey, when you mentioned Evolett recently, what were you talking about?*" I asked my virtual wife telepathically, a feeling of dread surging inside of me.

"*That he's very upset that all the experience for completing the Dungeon went to you and Clutzer. That you two are welcome in any clan for doing what a hundred other players couldn't do...Dan, I have a question of my own—what prompted you to hand over the Paw to Evolett? And for free? My uncle is still in shock—he's obsessed with finding some ulterior motive to your gift. He's even contacted Corporation officials to have them make sure that the transfer of the Paw was legit. People don't just make presents like that, especially over several percentage points of Experience...What do you really want from him, Dan?"*

The news struck me like a ton of bricks—so hard that I barely kept my balance. I immediately recalled my conversations with Stacey and Evolett—no one had mentioned the loss of the First Kill...This meant that with my own two hands I had handed the Paw over for nothing...Damn it!

"Dan? Is something wrong?"

"Stacey, I thought that only Clutzer and I had received the First Kill! And that Evolett was pissed at me because he'd missed out on it...I am such a moron!"

"You gave him the Paw as compensation for the First Kill?" Even through our telepathic link I could tell that Anastaria was laughing. *"My poor uncle! He's been fretting about all the various schemes that you're plotting to pull on him and arranging all kinds of defenses against your exorbitant demands. And it turns out that you simply misunderstood things and made a knee-jerk decision...Daniel, oh Daniel...It's like having a child of my own with you! I'll have a chat with him..."*

"Is everything all right with you, Mahan?" Fleita

asked worriedly, as I had completely clicked out of her world.

"Yes...Fleita. I just...Oh, never mind. Let's go. We need to find the den of the Gray Death."

"Tell me, why did the wolves show up in the Beatwick film anyway?" the girl began to interrogate me as soon as we entered the forest. The paths that I had run back and forth along 3–4 months ago hadn't changed, so I felt quite at home here. "I thought they weren't part of the scenario..."

"If I only knew." I really had no good answer for the girl.

"Mahan, when are you going to start teaching me how to be a Shaman? Kornik said that in five months I'll have to do my initiation trial, but you've only taught me a thing or two and even those turned out incorrect...Am I your student or what?"

"You're not a student—you're a pain in the neck! If you keep whining, I'll send you back to Evolett and ask him to lock you in the training ground until you reach Level 200. If you hadn't noticed, your education is going at full steam. You've at least learned how to use your Spirits."

"But Kornik taught me that, not you," Fleita parried.

"But I'm the one who asked him to do it. He wasn't going to teach you himself, if you recall. Can't you tell the difference? So stop moaning and walk on in silence. Oh, what a familiar glade! There used to be a mine here in which..."

"A-ah-ah!" The girl's piercing scream resounded

throughout the entire forest no doubt—after which, I was left all alone. Fleita had signed out of the game.

"Shamana Mahana, speak the password, eh?" A hushed whisper sounded from somewhere beside me. I turned and almost jumped—a disfigured goblin stood next to me. He was missing an arm, a leg, a part of his face, and he was transparent like a ghost. The creature before me was buried to his knee in the ground, giving me the impression that even his one remaining leg had been lopped off.

"Password?" I asked befuddled, trying to still my trembling and not sure what this ghost wanted from me. And—what was more interesting—what was this goblin doing here?

"The new bossa said that Shamana Mahana will come and speak the password. The bossa said that I have to listen to Shamana Mahana like the bossa. That Shamana Mahana will speak the password...Shamana is here—what's the password, eh?"

Why this is the very same goblin that Hellfire killed! But how?!

"Blah-Boom," I said, remembering the secret words. Once upon a time, I was fortunate enough to become the owner of a goblin work gang. They mined Tin Ore for me—which turned out to be Cursed later on—but then Hellfire and Anastaria showed up and killed them. They killed them in passing without bothering to find out by what miracle a gang of goblins were working in Malabarian mines...Of course they compensated this loss for me, but still, I was sorry to see the goblins go. Now, the glib and grinning goblin ghost began to report on the work they had done:

"We are producing two stacks of Spectral Ore a day and storing it under a bush. But, Shamana Mahana, the stacks, they are a-vanishing! We cover it with leaves and guard it—still they disappeara! The bossa, he ordered a resta, so..."

"Do you know him, Mahan?" I heard Fleita's stunned exclamation. She had found the courage to re-enter the game.

"What's with the screaming, Fleita?" I asked the girl. "You scared one half of the forest and cracked up the other half—a player terrified of an ordinary goblin!"

"But just look at him!" the girl flushed.

"Have you looked in the mirror lately? Imagine— a hideous Zombie criticizing a ghost's appearance."

"I'm not hideous!" Fleita protested.

"Okay, pupil! Here's a job for you—take your fear by the scruff and toss it out the window. Then, step up to our esteemed goblin friend and shake his paw! If you're going to act like that anytime someone odd shows up, maybe, it's a bit early for you to be playing in Barliona? Maybe, dolls and cross-stitching is more your line?"

"I was behaving myself!" objected Fleita. However, she took several shuffling steps to the ghost who had frozen in place as soon as he'd been interrupted. The Zombie offered her hand to the goblin and started noticeably when the ghost took it.

"Oh!"

At first I imagined that the girl hadn't overcome her fear and cried out again, yet what followed was difficult to explain. My student squatted down before the poor goblin, muttered something, and then took a handful of earth, kneaded it like playdough and began to attach it to his stump. At first I wanted to stop Fleita, since the earth is substantial while the ghost is not...but when I saw that the earth attached to the disfigured goblin was beginning to fade and become transparent, I stopped in my tracks. The spectacle I was witnessing with my own eyes simply didn't square with my understanding of how ghosts worked. Fleita was using ordinary earth to heal this creature...Was this possible?

"Thanksa," said the goblin when Fleita finished treating him and a halo appeared around her indicating that my student had gained three levels at once. The girl completely mended the goblin—she had even fashioned eyes for the now happy face of the creature before us. "Bossa, it'd be good to fix all our workers. Even if we're bound, it's easier to work in one piecea."

"Bound?" I zeroed in on the word that would explain to me how these ghosts had managed to linger in this plane of existence.

"The Transformer," the goblin answered curtly, pointing with a fixed arm off to the side. I looked in the indicated direction and swore—a mere twenty meters from us, several steel antennae protruded from the ground. A Kartossian Transformer...one of the devices that spread darkness through the hallowed lands.

"Is that like the one that was in the temple?" Even Fleita caught on to what the goblin was talking about. "So the goblins were killed, but they couldn't leave this world because they became cursed?"

"Plus one Intellect to Fleita," I quipped sarcastically and grinned—the girl's attitude was beginning to rub off on me. I was picking up her sarcasm. "Tell me, though, what just happened? Why'd you heal this goblin like some Mother Teresa and, more importantly, how did you manage to do it?"

"I...As soon as I touched him—at your orders, I'll remind you, so give me a break—as soon as I touched him, I received a notification about a unique quest. Zombies have restorative powers, though only for themselves. The quest allowed me the opportunity to restore the ghost...So I combined my powers of restoration with a Spirit of Healing and cast it into the ghost. It didn't work...So then I...Well what else could I do? Turn to you and say, 'Oh, great teacher, please help me...'? So I did whatever came to mind...I fashioned him an arm, imbued it with a Healing Spirit and activated my restoration...And don't even ask me how come it worked...I have no idea. Are you about to scold me again for being a hideous Zombie instead of a Shaman?"

"No," I smiled at the girl's vicious reaction. "You asked me when I'd start teaching you how to be a Shaman...So here you go...I don't even have to teach you anything—you're headed in the right direction.

What you did just now—this is the Way of the Shaman. Your personal Way of the Zombie-Shaman..."

"Does that mean that I'm a Shaman?" the girl's eyebrows jumped, transforming her already blank eyes into saucers. Two terrible, pupil-less saucers. She really was hideous!

"What are you doing with the ore?" I returned to the goblin, leaving Fleita without an answer to her question.

"Putting it in our pocketsa. We can't drop it to the grounda—it disappears right away. Our pockets are little, they fit only five stacks...Afterwards, we place them under the bush, but they always vanish in the end..."

"Carrying the ore in your pockets is no good," I shook my head. "Let me have it."

Spectral Ore...Looking at the five clods of swirling fog, I had no idea how to use it. You can't cast ingots out of it, which means that you can't forge swords out of it...What is it for anyway?

"Let's go to the mine. Fleita will fix up the rest of you and then we'll decide what to do with you," I said, placing the ore in my bag.

Upon seeing the six other disfigured goblins, Fleita did not leave the game. After spending several dozen minutes on each one, she stepped aside satisfied and asked:

"Tell me, Mahan, does it make any sense to adopt Architecture as my main profession?"

"Well...You'll have to decide everything related to

choosing your profession on your own. Did you like molding the earth? If doing it didn't bring you any pleasure, then there's no point in choosing Architecture. And if you did like it, then why not? Architects are in high demand in Barliona. For instance, I definitely need people to work on my castle. You can work for me…"

"To hell with him," said the girl and her character vanished for a moment. It seemed that she'd lost her temper again.

"Why'd you say 'to hell with him?'" I asked the girl when she returned.

"Because I wanted to become like you. I wanted to be a Jeweler…"

"Each player has his own Way," I smiled. "If you want to be an Architect, then be an Architect…What's being a Jeweler have to do with it?"

"Bossa, here's some more ore." The fully restored goblins dumped another thirty or so stacks of Spectral Ore at my feet with the satisfied air of sentients who had completed their tasks.

"What am I going to do with you boys?" I thought aloud, staring at the ghostly gang.

"Maybe you can release them?" Fleita suggested, but I shook my head:

"It won't work. They're not listed in my work gangs…They effectively don't exist for me, but at the same time, somehow they're still here…And, to be honest, I really don't understand why the developers kept them around. Maybe as a source of Spectral Ore?"

"Have you seen the Gray Death?" Fleita asked the goblins, while I was contemplating being and nothingness.

"The enormous Level 150 she-wolf with broken ribs, a half-split head and a missing eye? There's a pack of twenty similar-looking wolves with her?" ascertained one of the goblins, speaking clearly and properly. Listening to the ghost, I was becoming more and more upset—according to the quest description, you could assume that the Gray Death was attacking all the residents of Kartoss and all I had to do was lead her to some other location. After all, the quest made no mention of killing her. And yet if the Transformers had changed the essence of the Gray Death so much, then she was already beyond any help....Damn! She had been such a cool wolf!

"The same," Fleita confirmed.

"They come running past our mine every seven days," the ghost replied. "The last time was five days ago, so she should show up in two days. They tried to attack us several times, but we belong to different planes of existence, so the wolves couldn't do anything to us..."

"*Clutzer, hello! Assemble your party and teleport to these coordinates,*" I indicated our location. "*We are in Kartoss, so make sure to travel through Altameda. We need you as soon as possible...*"

"*Be there in 10 minutes,*" the Rogue wrote back.

"Mahan, we have to do something!" said Fleita, who couldn't see my exchange with my raid leader.

"*Dan, what are you up to?*" Anastaria didn't

waste time checking in on me.

"*I'm going to try to destroy a Kartossian Transformer...*"

"*They're unbreakable—they're the source of the darkness spreading across Kartoss. Clutzer won't be able to do anything to it. Hmm...Didn't we decide to put off the wolf quest for later...?*"

"*Plans changed...If we don't manage to break it, we'll at least scratch it up real good. Stacey—you are the coolest girl in the world!*"

"*I know!*" came the response, and our telepathic link went silent.

"We'll do something, don't worry," I replied to Fleita and briefly described what I had just done. "The Transformer is keeping the goblins here, so we'll take it offline. Guys!" I turned to the gang of workers waiting for us. "Tell me, what do you have against the landlady? Why steal her ore?"

The speed with which the ghosts tore back to the mine would even make Plinto's phoenix jealous.

"The landlady?" Fleita asked, surprised.

"It's a long story," I waved her off, not wishing to delve into the topic. I couldn't well tell the girl about how I tried to seduce the miners in the form of an orcish maiden. I'd never hear the end of her laughter...

"We got zilch," Clutzer shook his head sadly, after several hours of struggling with the Transformer. "It doesn't even have a Durability bar. It's as if the thing is indestructible...Mahan, either I'm an utter newb or this hunk of junk can't be destroyed."

"Got it...Okay, a pack of cursed wolves is due to come running through here in two days. It needs to be destroyed. But it's vital that I'm present when that happens...Tell Leite to summon you back to Altameda—there's no point in paying for your own portals..."

Anastaria was right after all—the Transformer could not be destroyed. Clutzer and his raid party tried so hard that not a single tree remained standing within twenty meters of the Transformer, while the ground around was scorched and dead. Yet the Transformer remained, whole and undamaged.

"What are we going to do now?" Fleita asked almost melancholically. "We can't just leave them here—they're suffering..."

"Fleita, they're only software..."

"I get that obviously! But even if they're software, then the software's suffering! You have to think of something, Mahan!"

An idea was beginning to form in my head, but I couldn't quite grab a hold of it. The goblins were still alive because they were cursed at the moment of the explosion...They had gone on working because of my earlier order...By the way, I forgot—the goblins were cursed because of the Transformer that couldn't be destroyed...

But we could fence it in and block its effects! The idea finally reached me, evoking the image of the Imperial Throne with Geranika's Dagger stuck in it and the Stones of Light situated around it. We needed to create a barrier around the Transformer!

Digging around my bag, I found a piece of Blessed Ore. I did the right thing by stopping by Elizabeth's and buying the ore from her—now I know what I have to do. I'll need to craft a Blessed Rose of Eluna and put it on the ghosts. Then, according to precedent, they should stop experiencing the effects of the Transformer.

"What do you have in mind, Mahan?" asked Fleita with surprise when I produced my Smithing Tools and began to smelt the ingots. I didn't feel like answering the girl—first I had to prepare the ingredients, do the business at hand, and then I could explain my plan...

Creating the ingot and fashioning it into a Rose only took me ten minutes. I called over the nearest goblin and with a satisfied expression clasped the amulet around his neck. What a resourceful and intelligent player I am—whatever the developers come up with, I'm right there to thwart their plans...

"Stop bossa! Take it off, bossa! It hurts! Ow ow owa!" Not a second passed before the ghost began to holler in an inhuman voice, collapsed to the ground and began to roll around it, periodically passing through the tree trunks and flat-out refusing to leave this world.

"What are you doing, Mahan?" yelled Fleita, when I dashed towards the goblin to rip the amulet from his neck. It took me several attempts, since the goblin wouldn't hold still but kept rolling on the ground, screaming his head off across the entire forest. The other goblins were looking at this spectacle with terror, rubbing their necks. When at last I managed to tear off the amulet, I could clearly see a burn that the chain had left. The ghost's chest was an even more terrible sight. My amulet had scarred this otherworldly being.

"Why you are just a..." Fleita couldn't come up with the right word. She sat down before the ghost and healed him in several seconds by again mixing some earth with her Spirits.

"Are you alive?" I asked the goblin who had finally stopped whimpering and was slowly edging his way to his fellows while casting glances at me from the corner of his eyes. Prudently storing the amulet in my bag and deciding that I knew now how to kill the Gray Death, I approached the goblins. The poor darlings pressed their ears to their heads like scolded cats, but didn't try to run—I was the bossa and could do whatever I wanted. Even if it was burning them alive in holy water...

"Y-yes, bossa... It doesn't hurt anymore..."

"Go on with your work," I finally decided the goblins' fate. "I will return tomorrow and we'll see what we can do to release you. Fleita, we're going back to Altameda...Leite," I instantly called my treasurer in the castle on the amulet, "tell Viltrius to summon us. I need to mull things over..."

The first thing I did upon returning to the castle was call my majordomo and hand him an amulet. I was sick of asking people to ask him to summon me every time, so from now on I would communicate with Viltrius directly. After that, I sat down in my rocking chair and sank deep in thought—what could I do about the goblins?

The only thought that came to mind was to surround the Transformer with Stones of Light, the same way as had been done with Geranika's Dagger. The holy stones should be powerful enough to neutralize the Kartossian Transformer without doing any harm to the ghosts in the process. No, I could of course also hand the Stone to the ghost and watch on as he burned, but I have no way to be certain that the goblins wouldn't simply respawn later. After all, they had returned after being killed by Hellfire. And anyway, if I do that, Fleita will leave me and I'll have to take on some NPC as a student...So all in all I'll need to obtain the Stones—which belong to a single sentient in Malabar—the High Priestess of Eluna.

But will she give them to me? That is the question...

"Fleita, I'm leaving you in charge," I said, deciding to pay Elizabeth a visit. It didn't seem very appropriate to take the Zombie with me to the High Priestess. "Viltrius, I need a portal to the Anhurs Central Square."

The girl tried to object that she needed to be with me the entire time, but I didn't listen to her—a new idea was slowly forming in my mind.

"Hey Svard!" Prior to teleporting to the capital, I called one of my craftsman acquaintances. Since the thought occurred to me, I should take it to its logical conclusion—otherwise I'll hurt its feelings and it'll refuse to occur to me anymore. "You asked me to get in touch with you the next time I had a crazy idea...I just had one that isn't simply crazy, but straight out unbelievable! What would you say to crafting a Stone of Light? Oh, you don't know what that is? Then you should look it up. I'll be waiting for you in ten minutes at the High Priestess's place. Tell the doorman that you're expected..."

"But that's not possible!" Elizabeth continued to insist. Long ago, the Priests lost their recipe for the Stones of Light and now that I had proposed to craft one, Elsa refused to show me the research her Priests had done on this question. According to the High Priestess, the very thought that a Free Citizen could create it was heresy. All that was left were several bas reliefs that depicted the process of crafting the Stone, but they depicted not only Priests conducting the ritual, but also Paladins as warriors of Eluna.

"It'll be difficult," agreed Svard, who had by now managed to read up on the topic. To my surprise, he was well acquainted with the High Priestess and she knew him as well, so our conversation resembled that of partners if not outright friends.

"Elsa, I understand that my proposal seems very...how do I say this...strange. But I believe that if you show me the research you have done, we will be able to come up with the recipe. I can't explain this with anything other than my premonition...As you see, I even invited Svard to our meeting, since I understand that I won't be able to do this on my own. Now at least I know that to create a Stone we'll need two circles—Paladins and Priests. Accordingly we'll need you to put out a call to your highest-ranked Free Citizen Priests. We'll form one circle with them. We'll have lots to do, including meeting with the Emperor to get the Sphere of Abnegation to form the unity. But Elsa—you simply have to trust me."

"I wouldn't even bother listening to anyone else. I'd have them escorted straight out of the temple," the High Priestess replied slowly, as if having trouble believing her own words. "Mahan, I am ready to trust you, but I warn you—no one, I repeat, no one can know how we lost the recipe and what has been accomplished to restore it. If information about this leaks to the world, the doors to the temple will be shut to you forever. Do you accept this condition?"

"Yes," I didn't look away, despite the immense drama of Elsa's speech. 'Only you,' 'doors will be shut'...in my view, this is all a bit over the top.

But I was mistaken for thinking so.

The recipe for the Stone of Light was invented by a Necromancer named Carliori many millennia ago. Despite the fact that, in effect, the Stone was the distillation of Light, it had been invented by a sentient who had dedicated his life to pain and suffering—and not his own pain and suffering at that...

Carliori was mad and used his madness to create. It turned out that each Stone of Light consisted of hundreds of lost and ended lives. One day Carliori was conducting a ritual sacrifice, while distilling the souls that were 'released' in a particular way. When the concentration of souls became critical, Eluna descended from the heavens and did something to it—forming a small statue. That was how the first Stone of Light was born. Carliori was surprised and repeated this procedure thirty more times, obtaining each time one more Stone. Since he couldn't find a use for these Stones in his tortures, the Necromancer gave them to the Priests. Of the thirty-three initial Stones, the Priests had seventeen remaining. The rest had been lost in the millennia past.

And now the most interesting part...

The Priests tried, are trying and will keep trying to make the Stones on their own. According to Elsa, every year one attempt is made to create a Stone, but the very fact that the Priests of Light—the followers and adherents of Eluna are conducting dark sacrifices...

"What does the bas relief show then?" I asked Elsa in shock and received the reply that it was merely an uninformed artist's view of the Stones' creation. After all, if the public discovered what the Priests were really up to, Eluna would quickly lose her followers.

"Now do you understand why no one can know about this?" the High Priestess asked.

"I understand now. What did you manage to learn during your attempts?"

"We are having trouble concentrating the souls. That's the most important step in creating the Stone, and it's been thousands of years now but we just can't get past it. Carliori was insane, but he was also a true genius...Unfortunately, he left no notes, and when we ask Eluna for help, she just shakes her head and begs us tearfully to stop our experiments."

"Eluna is okay with her priests taking hundreds of lives every year?" My shock was starting to resemble a stupor.

"Of course! The mother is burdened by her divine obligations and cannot manage the process directly, but she accepts all the souls we release into her embrace...I'm afraid I have nothing to help you with, Shaman. I can give you a Stone to free your ghosts, but I cannot permit you to take a hundred lives. We already made one unsuccessful attempt this year."

"I understand you, but...Look, Elsa, giving up at the very beginning after learning some shocking information isn't how I like to play this game. That's exactly how I beat Geranika...Assemble your Free Citizens of High Priest level or greater...We'll craft the Stone!"

"I believe you, Great Shaman," Eluna's High Priestess addressed me in a formal tone. "What further assistance will you require of me?"

"I need Paladins as well. Rank Lieutenant or higher...Will you be able to speak to their leadership?"

"Yes. What else?"

"The most interesting bit—I need the whole lot of them brought to my castle. We'll travel to Beatwick from there..."

"Beatwick?" A crack showed in the High Priestess's mask.

"Uh-huh. You have two days. I want everyone ready to go the day after tomorrow at 9 in the morning. Can you do it?"

"I will do everything in my power to make sure you get what you need. If there won't be enough Priests, I'll go myself! I beg you, however, don't follow in the steps of Carliori..."

"Dan, is this your doing?" As soon as I emerged from the temple, Anastaria's thought popped into my head. *"You've reached the point of issuing quests to other players?"*

"Huh? What happened?"

"All the Paladins of Rank Lieutenant or higher are being asked to report to Eluna's temple tomorrow in order to travel to Altameda—the castle of the Great Shaman—and to Beatwick from there. Supposedly this quest is highly important for our order and all that...Dan, have you lost your mind?"

"Excuse me?"

"There are about twenty thousand players who are Lieutenant Paladins or higher! They're all going to visit our castle! Are you trying to cause another siege of Altameda? The Azures and the Heirs are still waiting for their chance to get revenge. We're still at Level 24 exclusively thanks to the castle teleporting to a location they don't know. Dan! This is a disaster! Activate the teleport protection!"

Blast! Why hadn't I thought about this earlier?

"Yes, Master," the majordomo answered my call.

"Viltrius, in two days, several thousand Free Citizens will begin streaming into the castle and taking the teleport from there to Beatwick. Tell me—can we do something to ensure that they don't learn the coordinates of the castle?"

"We can activate the castle security function that will block the coordinates' reading inside Altameda. This function costs a hundred thousand a month. Shall I activate it?"

"Do it," I agreed.

Then, deciding that I should pay for my mistake, I added: "Withdraw the money for this expenditure from my personal account."

"That's it, I've activated the security system," I assured Stacey. *"What're you up to? I really need you here in Anhurs. I need to speak with the Emperor..."*

"Are you having a laugh?" Anastaria scoffed. *"I'll see you in the Central Square in five minutes..."*

"Am I correct in assuming that I shouldn't ask you about what the High Priestess told you?" Svard approached me.

"Uh-huh...Listen, I have a favor to ask of you too—I need every craftsman who can enter into a unity. And I mean every single one—not just one or two...I need like a hundred or two hundred...Sorry that I'm asking you to do this. I don't know the community myself..."

Ding! You have received a message from your private circle. Do you wish to read it?

"Svard, forgive me, I need to check my mail..." I apologized again before the pensive Mage and retrieved my mailbox. The letter was from my private whitelist—in other words, someone I'd written to before and not somcone from my clan. My own people would simply call me...

In Private Confidence—To the Head of the Legends of Barliona from the Head of the Nav Clan. Hi! Looks like you've had time to reconsider your initial response...I'm writing to remind you of the list of reagents that you forgot about. But there's no rush there. Besides the list, I'll need two pieces of Epherite and a group of players of Level 300+: Two tanks, at least three healers and as many long-range fighters as you can muster. Can you do it? Technically, I can get by without the players, but the result won't be the same...

"Is there something funny in there?" inquired Svard, when I began to giggle at Gnum's letter. Not only had he nothing to show, but my new partner now also wanted a group of Level 300 players! I think the boy has lost the plot in his attempt to con me.

"This guy is asking me for two pieces of Epherite, whatever that is. And he wants me to provide him with a high-level raid party," I replied after I finished laughing. It's not enough that I already gave him three stacks of Imperial Steel—he wants to milk me for more! Where do people learn such temerity?!

"Epherite?" Svard echoed in surprise. "Who would need that?"

"You know what that is?" It was my turn to be surprised.

"Yes, it's incredibly rare and seldom used. Out of all the craftsmen I know, only perhaps Gnum could use it..."

"Spiteful Gnum?" I asked.

"You know him?"

"Well, the letter is from him. There's nothing particularly confidential in it so—here..."

"You sent him three stacks of Imperial Steel just like that?!" Svard exclaimed after reading our exchange. "I mean—I know Alex—he's a man of his word, but you! Do you really trust people that much?"

"War is easy, logistics is hard," I replied philosophically and shrugged my shoulders. "Tell me, would it be a bad idea to send him everything he's asking for? Your Alex, he won't run off with it, will he?"

"Oh no," smiled Svard. "Out of everyone I know, Gnum is the oddest person by far. He's weirder than you. But the one thing you can't accuse him of is not keeping his word. He's got like some principle about that or something. So, if you're ready to risk it—go right ahead and send him whatever he needs. You'll get the result, don't worry."

"Thanks. By the way, do you happen to know how he's able to work with Imperial Steel? Don't you need an incredibly high profession rank to do that?"

"Tell me about it. He's such a good Architect that Chirona herself is dead jealous of him. And he's a good Tailor. The clothes he sews will make you swoon. Why do you think my outfit looks the way it does? Because Gnum, in his immense generosity, made me a present of a cape with +20 to Enchantment."

"Uh-huh..." I remarked thoughtfully and instantly sent Leite a letter asking him to find the things Gnum required. And in threes—I had sent three times as many ingots than he asked for, so I'd need to send him the same amount of ingredients. You really do come across all kinds of players in Barliona. "Don't forget to invite him to the unity."

"He won't come, I won't even bother asking him. Gnum is a terrible misanthrope. It's his thing. He'd never let anyone enter his mind. However, I can promise you a group of about fifty craftsmen the day after tomorrow."

"Nine in the morning," I clarified just in case. "The day after tomorrow is a bit too indefinite."

"Mahan, Svard," Anastaria greeted us. "Do you want me to guess what you two are up to? Another unity!"

"You have to think bigger," I replied. "We are planning a large-scale event, in which you are destined to play a pivotal role."

"What's that?"

"You will need to coordinate two defensive circles—of Priests and Paladins—while the craftsmen engage in a unity."

"How many players will it be all together?"

"Svard says about fifty, so I'll have a favor to ask of you—go through your channels and tap anyone who has Craftsmanship. We need any profession we can get."

"Okay, but what are you trying to create?"

"A Stone of Light," I blurted out.

"You...Dan...But that's..." Anastaria froze, staring at me wide-eyed. It was unbelievable! I had managed to astonish the unshakable Anastaria!

Surely I deserve an Achievement? And, what I liked most of all was that Anastaria knew how the Stones were made—there was no other way to explain her reaction.

"I just got out of a meeting with the High Priestess. She told me everything," I answered her unasked question. "I see no reason I shouldn't try to do what the bas relief depicts. Who knows? Maybe he who created it was a genius..."

"I understand...hmm...but why Beatwick?"

"Because the Transformer I want to experiment on is located there. My wolves are there—as are the ghosts of the goblins you killed."

"They can't leave?" Anastaria started catching on. "Have you tried ordinary amulets?"

"Like you need to ask! I almost burned one alive—err, dead—err, well, mostly ghostly."

"I assume then that you want the Emperor to give you the Sphere? For personal use for two days?"

"Uh-huh..."

"It's unrealistic, but I'll help you see him...Mahan—I'm with you!"

As I reckoned, we had no trouble gaining an audience with the Emperor with Anastaria's pass. Svard refused to go with us, explaining that he had to corral his craftsmen colleagues for the ritual. His only request was that I warn him in advance if we didn't manage to obtain the Sphere.

"The Sphere of Abnegation," Naahti said pensively when I explained the reason for my visit. "Judging by the high-level Paladins and Priests already gathering across Malabar, you are confident that I will give you the Sphere. What is the reason for such confidence?"

"The battle against Geranika is imminent," was my simple reply. "Whether the Free Citizens manage to win the Heart of Chaos or not, Geranika will remain and he will be as powerful as before. If our plan succeeds, the Empire will acquire one more weapon against the Lord of Shadow. If not, we will simply waste our time and return the Sphere to you. The Empire has nothing to lose and everything to gain..."

"Throughout the entire history of Anhurs, the Sphere of Abnegation has never once left the confines of the palace," the Emperor said, but I had an answer ready. I knew what Naahti was going to say!

"Throughout the entire history of Anhurs, never once has a Master of Kartoss become the Emperor of Malabar. Everything flows with time, everything changes."

The Emperor fell silent in thought. Judging by the way his eyes had fogged over, the Imitator was currently updating as fast as possible, while the developers in charge of game scenarios and items were cursing me with their worst expletives and preparing the ritual for creating the Stones. I hadn't any doubts left about what this ritual entailed, but I did wonder what I needed the Paladins for.

"I have one condition that you must agree to before I give you the Sphere," the Emperor said at long last. "You shall not follow in the steps of Carliori."

"I have no desire to kill hundreds of sentients to get what I am looking for," I replied immediately. "I don't want to go down in history as yet another mad genius."

"I will have a Herald deliver the Sphere to your castle the day after tomorrow at eight in the morning," the Emperor said decisively and turned to Anastaria: "My condolences—this meeting is more useful to you than to me, so I am hereby revoking your right to receive an audience from me whenever you like. If Mahan succeeds in crafting the Stone, you will both receive this privilege. If not, you will have to go through the regular channels in the future. My friends, I dare not take up any more of your time!"

Anastaria returned to Nashlazar, promising to kill me if I didn't manage to create the Stone, while I headed back to Altameda. I had received a notification about a letter that had arrived from a 'trusted' source—I knew very well which one. Leite had managed to call and inform me that he'd sent three hundred thousand gold, of which two hundred and fifty were for the two pieces of Epherite—an incredibly rare stone.

"Come here, Viltrius," I summoned my majordomo. "Take off your robe."

The goblin stared at me shocked, but at last began to remove the item he had grown so attached to. His eyes looked like he was removing a part of his soul along with his robe, so I felt like I needed to explain to the poor NPC what I had in mind:

"I have a Tailor acquaintance. I want to send

your robe to him so that he can do some work on it and make it more presentable. I think it unfitting of a majordomo of a Level 24 castle to go around in an admittedly expensive yet fairly ordinary robe. I want to ask my friend to work his magic on it. He's sure to do something wonderful with it. You don't mind, do you?"

Viltrius began to shake his head so violently that his large ears began to slap against each other. As if he could have minded! As I had discovered, the majordomos of Malabar had their own tacit hierarchy along with their own meetings at which they would share experience. My goblin also attended these and I didn't want to impair his standing...

Opening my mailbox, I penned an answer to Spiteful Gnum:

On the subject of reagents—sorry, I've been very busy and simply forgot. Attached, please find all the contents of your list—and in triple quantity to match the Imperial Steel I sent you. Hmm...Hang on, my majordomo here has fainted from hearing how much money I'm about to send you...Okay, I'm back. Getting the players you need is a bit harder. I don't have anyone who's Level 300+. I can scrounge up some people from Kartoss—where do you stand on the question of alignment? I don't have any others. An enormous request—a favor—could you please embroider some ornament on this robe (attached)? It's for my majordomo. The goblin keeps complaining that he can't go out like this, that I've put him in an awkward position before his friends. I'd like to make him a present. We can figure out what I owe you for resources later. Mahan.

Well, let's see how quick Gnum is on the uptake. I just let him know that I know more about him than he thinks. Now we'll see what his reaction'll be. By the way, I'm interested to see what he's decided to create if the reagents alone cost so much money. Including the Imperial Steel, this whole thing has cost me three-and-a-half hundred thousand so far...The product better astonish me, or I don't know what I'll do.

The entire next day turned into one enormous conflagration...I would have never thought that we had so many Priests and Paladins. The players began arriving in Altameda in the early morning and were immediately relayed to Beatwick. First dozens, then hundreds, then thousands, the tens of thousands...By day's end I was squeezed as dry as a lemon and incapable of doing anything else. I was more exhausted than I had been after a day's worth of swinging the pickaxe at the mine. In the evening, having collapsed in my rocking chair and nodded in the direction of yet another group of players who wanted their pay and permission to take a stroll around the castle, I began to go through my mail. I was curious to see what Gnum would do with the robe. Evidently to remind me of his loss, Viltrius kept sighing deeply, shivering demonstratively and trying to get closer to the fire, even though it was fairly hot out.

I went through the chaff quickly, filtering out two unread letters. And while Gnum's was expected, the letter from Kreel was about as expected as a draft notice to a septuagenarian. Unexpected and entirely unprompted...

Dear Mahan! Some circumstances surrounding a quest that I received and accepted as head of the Stepsons of the Abyss Clan compel me to invite you to participate. In issuing me the quest, a mutual acquaintance of ours has set the mandatory condition that 'his children' participate in this adventure. Enclosed, I am sending you a recording of my conversation with my employer. I invite you to meet with me at The Cross-Eyed Angler tavern outside Anhurs to discuss your clan's participation in this event. Please let me know when you will have the time to do so. Sometime within the coming week would be best. Kreel. Head of the Stepsons of the Abyss.

The clan heads—they're multiplying.

* * *

"Greetings, Kreel. My name is Aarenoxitolikus," boomed the green Dragon. "You may call me Renox for short."

"Greetings to you, oh Ancient Foe," replied an enormous player who was about two-and-a-half meters tall. He began to make passes with his arms as if preparing a spell and something dark and foggy started to form behind Kreel, resembling Geranika's Shadows. Gradually the effect changed and the darkness came to resemble a cape.

"Why such hostility?" Renox replied, paying no attention to the preparations Kreel was making to attack him. "I admit that Dragons were involved in your demise, but there's no longer a conflict between us. We too have departed Barliona...Hmm, I think it would be best if your minions there take a smoke break while we chat," the Dragon breathed a green flame in Kreel's direction. It flashed brightly about halfway as if it had encountered a protective barrier, but didn't stop and continued on its way, completely destroying Kreel's dark cape. The player began to cast various spells at the Dragon, but they caused Renox no harm at all. In fact, Renox swallowed a lightning bolt that Kreel cast at him and even closed his eyes as if savoring it.

"A chat then?" said Kreel, having expended his Mana pool.

"A chat it is," hummed Renox and smiled a toothy grin.

"What do you need from me, Dragon?"

"I want to hire you to do this one delicate thing for me..."

* * *

The video ended, but I remained sitting, staring into nowhere. The footage had been shot in Barliona, yet Renox was not allowed to enter this world...Or is there something I don't know? Why the hell would he get in touch with the inexperienced Kreel and not with me? What the hell is going on?!

Besides the video, the letter had one other attachment. Opening it, I saw the description of the quest that Renox had issued to Kreel:

Assassinate the Dragon Aquarizamax. Type: Unique. Description: Dragons are both wondrous creatures and the perfect killing machines. Geranika managed to discover the lair of one of the few Dragons remaining in Barliona. He corrupted his spirit, filling it with Darkness. And so the once proud Dragon began to transform into a Cursed Dragon of Shadow. Kill him before it's too late...

Kreel didn't include the rewards for this quest, but the description was enough to let me know that I needed to be involved. As soon as I finish with the Stone of Light, I'll meet with Kreel. Plus I need to find out how he managed to bring Rogzar's Crystal to Altameda...But first:

"Stacey, I need you. Urgently and in person..."

"Twenty minutes, no sooner..."

One head is good, but two—considering that the second one is very pleasant to look at and kiss—is better. We're going to do this quest together—that's for sure. I couldn't care less what Nashlazar thinks about it.

Hello again! As far as alignment is concerned, I don't care. The players could be from Shadow for all it matters. Believe me, in comparison to some of my critters, the Kartossian race are real beauties. Enclosed, please find your favor. Don't worry about the resources I used—you don't have them anyway. By the way—if you show this robe to Rick, you can forget that we know each other. I can say the same thing about the castle. I watched the video of the Azures' assault—I can fix your gates. But I'll warn you right off that it'll take more than one oak. And that blathering dimwit needs to be kept as far away from me as possible—he drives me nuts! Forgive my sincerity in the matter. I'll be waiting for the warriors at the coordinates below, tomorrow around two.

What a day! What did I do to deserve all these intrigues with Kreel and Gnum?

Getting my amulet and clenching my fists in the hopes that Evolett was still online, I made a call:

"Greetings! Sorry for such a tardy question, but I need your help again—I need people..."

"Ahem, Master?" Viltrius politely reminded me of his presence. He could see the glimmering item of textile in my hands. Evolett agreed to send me some people at the indicated time, so I managed to accomplish at least something today. I opened the item properties for the robe and couldn't help but grin—Gnum had really put in the effort. If he makes the gargoyles with the same spirit, I'll have to admit that he is worth the money I spent on him. The only thing I didn't understand was why he thought that I found out about him from Rick and why he disliked him so much...

Parade robe of Bargo-Khan. Class: Epic. +20 Attractiveness. Restrictions: Only for goblins.

You should've seen Viltrius's eyes when he took the robe in his hands. There was so much devotion in them and such a readiness to die for his master that I even shivered a little—I had become something like a father, brother and god all rolled into one for my majordomo. Gnum encrusted the robe with small gems, added a drawing on the back that was stylized to resemble a goblin's face, cuff links, a collar and a fringe of fur. He also added a hood and some kind of tassels...He even dyed it into a different color!

Anastaria had not yet shown up and I was getting sick of writing all this correspondence, so I wrote one more letter to Gnum, enclosing in it an amulet of communication. If anything, he may as well just call me...

The people will be there tomorrow. Make sure to meet them. The player in charge is named Clutzer. As for Rick, don't worry—he and I don't speak much after I stole this belt from him (link to belt). As for the gates—I'm already curious how long you've been playing this game? You're an Architect, a Tailor and a Carpenter. And all three of those professions allow you to work with high-level resources. That's pretty impressive...As for the blathering dimwit—why would you speak so poorly of Svard? I have a good working relationship with him, and he found nothing shameful about sharing information about a player who like us has stepped on the path of craftsmanship.

That's it! Now no one will make lift a finger until tomorrow morning! I'm sick of it all!

"Dan, what happened?" instantly, as if following Murphy's Law, sounded Anastaria's voice.

"I'm sending you the quest description along with a video clip. Stacey, I need to know everything there is to know about this guy...Can you do it?"

It took the girl several minutes to figure out what had happened, so I wasn't surprised by her answer: "I'll figure it out...You know, Dan, since I'm here, we may as well...Are you going to perform your spousal duties or what?"

At least there was something I managed to accomplish all the way that day...

"The Emperor has sent you the Sphere." The Herald's bell tinkled halfway through my dreams, tearing me from Morpheus' embrace. Without opening an eye, I reached out my hand and felt as something large and heavy was placed into it. Then came the clap of the portal, informing me that the Herald had vanished, so I made an inhuman effort and opened my eyes. Anastaria was already gone—I guess she'd fled back to Nashlazar or signed out to reality. Or perhaps she's off wandering around the castle—a large-scale operation was due to begin in an hour and it was unlikely that the girl would miss such an event.

"Master," Viltrius appeared right beside me.

"Twenty-two thousand, three hundred and five Free Paladins and Priests have been shuttled to Beatwick during the past day. According to the inimitable High Priestess, there are another three hundred and forty Priests left, as well as seven hundred and twenty-three Paladins. Their teleportation is currently underway. As per your orders, none of the visitors were allowed to leave the castle, although 32 Free Citizens began to demand that we respect their right to free movement throughout Barliona, wishing to leave the castle. Four even attempted to break through by force, but Vimes and his guards promptly sent them back to Anhurs. There were no other incidents..."

"Thank you."

"Master..." The goblin shifted in place, as if wishing to say something but not finding the courage to do so.

"Yes Viltrius?" I prodded the goblin to get on with it.

"Master, I have had the pleasure of serving in seven castles, but this is the only one in which I am treated like an equal. I have nothing to repay you with, except that you may withhold the second half of my annual salary if you wish. I am happy to work in Altameda, and 50% of my current salary will suffice."

The goblin bowed and instantly vanished—no doubt something new had happened demanding his attention. It looked like I'd need Spiteful Gnum to do some more work. Vimes and his band hand been working up a sweat, dashing around my castle and working hard for their paychecks. It might be a good idea to gift them some new capes too.

"*Dan, everyone's in position,*" came a message from Anastaria. "*I can summon you.*"

"*Do it. It's time to get this show on the road.*"

The bas relief that Elsa had shown me, didn't depict anything very complicated. The ritual for creating the Stone of Light required us to form three circles: The Paladins would stand shoulder to shoulder with their backs to the center. The circle of Priests facing the center would stand within the Paladin circle and the Craftsmen would do the main deed in the very center. Why we had to form circles and what their purpose was remained a riddle clad in darkness. I guess we were about to solve it...

"Bossa!" shouted the goblin ghosts as soon as I appeared in the forest. My ghosts came dashing out from the nearby trees. "Bossa the mine is brokena! There's no more ore!"

I was forced to snarl when I realized what had happened. It looked like the Priests and Paladins hadn't succeeded in killing my workers, so they decided to turn their attention to the mine and see who could do more damage and cause more ruin.

"Stacey you have to stop those idiots. Kick anyone who resists out of the raid party!" I said and turned to Svard: "Here, take the Sphere. Start bringing the players into the unity. I'll join you last."

"Okay," replied the Mage and stepped over to a separate crowd of players among which I had already noticed Chirona and Rick. I have to admit that however I felt about Rick, I couldn't deny his mastery as a craftsman, so I was happy to see him there. It remained to be seen how he would do...

"Stacey, you have the most important task—I'm going to enter the unity and manage the players from there through you. I don't know how to make a mob of that size do what I tell them, but I trust you can. Keep in mind that I need two circles..."

Stacey made a call on her amulet and in literally a minute four High Priests and three Paladin Generals approached us. Odd, I figured that Stacey was the most senior officer in her order...I explained the objective of the two circles surrounding the craftsmen and, to my deepest astonishment, the players which I had figured for an unmanageable mob of bunglers began to take their positions as if they had spent their entire lives practicing for just this maneuver. In less than ten minutes, the Paladins formed the outside circle about a hundred meters in diameter. The Priests needed more time, but they managed to do it in half an hour. I would've never imagined that players could be this orderly.

"Clutzer, Magdey," I called my two raid leaders while the circles were forming. "You will have the main task—in about an hour, a pack of wolves should come running through this place. You need to freeze them and keep them frozen until we craft the Stone. Under no conditions should they be killed—that's critical!"

My warriors nodded and left the circle, while I sighed deeply and looked around one more time—the gigantic army of players had arranged itself in the required pattern and was prepared to start acting in unison. They weren't about to attack each other or kill some mobs—they were going to work together, an endeavor in which the actions of one individual would determine the success of his neighbor. It was simply impossible to compare the inspiration I felt at this moment with anything else. Even in reality nothing was ever so immense, epic, captivating and simultaneously impossible. I was anxiously rubbing my palms against my jacket, despite the fact that they were physically incapable of sweating—my brain had begun to perceive the current events not as a part of a game, but as a part of reality in which I was to live and do battle. A mesmerizing sensation.

You have entered the unity.

One hundred seventy-three versions of myself stood facing me, awaiting my orders. One hundred seventy-three players had united their consciousnesses into one whole in order to create the Stone of Light...I was a genius Scribe, Sculptor, Tanner, Carpenter, Glazier...I was at once everyone and myself, floating above the other consciousnesses.

"*Let us begin,*" said I-Svard.

"*We need a plinth. We are crafting the Stone of Light—we need something bright and small in order to concentrate our professions on it...*"

"*I have something,*" said I-Kimrat, an Herbalist. "*There is nothing brighter than the essence of the sun...*"

"*Very well but it needs to be improved,*" said I-Svard. "*I will strengthen it...*"

"*I will add light...*"

"*I will add power...*"

"*I will add steel...*"

The good thing about working in a unity was that the players could sense what they needed to do next at the level of premonition.

"*The essence of the sun is not bright enough. Look—there is some dark fissure forming there...*"

A wisp of smoke began to stream from our masterwork and gradually went from being light and almost invisible to thick and black as if a tire was burning.

"*Stacey, activate the Priests! We have to be surrounded by blessed ground!*" As soon as the smoke from our Stone began to cover everything around us, I brought in the Priests.

"*On it!*" the girl replied and the smoke instantly ceased as if it had encountered some invisible and impenetrable bubble. The outcome of all this was a strange kind of sun—a bright smoky center, then the bulk of the smoke, growing thicker and thicker, and above it all the bubble that the Priests had created.

"*Dan, we're being attacked by some kind of Shadow creatures!*" Stacey suddenly warned me with urgency. "*They're coming at us from all directions! It's as if the entire forest's lost its mind and is trying to stop the ritual!*"

"*Tell the Paladins to hold their ground! The*

Priests can't be distracted even for a second!"

"I will add the scent of the sea..."

"I will install Imperial Glass..."

"Dan, we're in the bubble. About a thousand players have fled—they were too scared...No, it's up to two thousand now..."

"It's not working," concluded I-Svard, adding another piece to the Stone. *"We made some mistake when crafting the plinth!"*

As if it had been waiting for just these words, the core we had made exploded, casting smoke across the entire unity like black ink. As the unity broke, expelling us into the main game world, I caught a glimpse of the bubble that Stacey had mentioned, right before it vanished. Dark and enormous it cast lightning and wind at our Paladins who took the blows on their shields. It looked like everyone outside of the unity had been working hard as well.

But that wasn't the main thing. The main thing was that our first attempt had been unsuccessful...We had chosen the wrong plinth for the Stone...

"Raid Party, 10 minute break!" I wrote into the chat and took a seat on the ground. I needed to do some thinking.

And so!

We took the brightest thing we had available to us for the plinth—the essence of the sun. However, this turned out to be insufficient—as soon as we began to work with it further, a thick smoke began to billow forth, which the Priests confined to a sphere.

And at that point the attack began...

"Stacey, who was attacking us?"

"Look for yourself." I instantly received a video which showed shadow creatures rising from the earth and heading in the direction of our raid group. Rabbits, wolves, foxes—all the creatures that had once lived and run through this forest and later died, were now rising from the dead and setting out in our direction. At the same time, birds came flying from the sky spurred on by lightning and wind. The Paladins swayed and held onto each other, but stood their ground. Unfortunately, not all of them—a thousand players cast their portals and left the raid. Roughly the same thing happened with the Priests— when the dark bubble formed, a portion of the players grew afraid and ran away.

"Mahan," Clutzer called me on the amulet. "The wolves have been trapped and frozen in place. What should we do next? By the way, what a scary bunch they are! Pure horror! It's hard not to cast every fire spell I have at them! I haven't seen so much anger, hate and bloodthirst in a long time!"

It was like I had been struck by a lightning bolt—that was it! This is what that mad Carliori had done in his experiments—he was trying to distill pure hatred! This is why he needed so many sacrifices— one human soul is incapable of generating so much hate—hell, not even a dozen could! After all, people harbor hope even on the brink of death. But if we use the Gray Death as the foundation for the Stone and all her hate...Eluna! I understood now why she had descended from the skies—the Stone of Light was her way of confining pure hatred! This is precisely why it's a concentrate of divine light! Because that concentrate encircles and contains an utterly other kind of concentrate! This is also why no two Stones of Light are the same—the level of hate and evil varies every time!

"All right people, we're about to witness a hell of a light show! Paladins—this isn't any ordinary security operation. We're about to be assaulted by the most evil creatures that have ever lived in this forest! You won't hold out just like that—you have to use your holy powers! Priests—I need a blessing so powerful that it'll hold even if Armageddon goes off in our midst and tears all of you to little pieces! People—if someone doesn't feel like putting in some work, better leave now! Abandoning your fellows once the process is underway is out of the question—whether this works depends on each and every one of you. Svard—bring us in!"

"Clutzer, bring the wolves over here!" I called my Rogue on the amulet before Svard brought me into the unity.

"What do you have in mind?"

"Svard, we're in your design mode right now, right? There should be a pack of wolves nearby. Materialize them..."

"Whoa," thought I-Chirona. "They're dark through and through!"

"The poor creatures," said I-Lastrix. "Sorry, but I can't watch this—they need to be cleansed first!"

"*Hold on! Let's confine the darkness to a cage!*" said I-Zarlatan.

"*The cage has to be reinforced,*" said I-Svard.

"*Remove the darkness from them and I'll repair their furs,*" said I-Rick.

"*Bring the darkness over here and put it in the cage. Nice punishment for it, eh? I suggest we reinforce the cage...*"

"*And then tear it asunder...*"

"*Dan, we're under attack again. It looks like the forest sent the kids the first time...It's the adults' turn now.*"

"*The darkness has been separated from the wolves! How is this possible? It's—it's alive! Don't let it escape the cage!*"

"*It won't pass! I enchanted the cage myself! No! It's seeping through!*"

"*Stacey, tell the Priests to act!*"

"*It's stopped!*"

"*Svard! Try to make the cage smaller! We need to compress the darkness to a point!*"

"*Got it—I'm shrinking the cage,*" I-Zarlatan replied in I-Svard's place.

"*Dan? I'm coming to help! It's unreal! We're being attacked by the darkness itself!*"

"*Everyone—the cage has to be smaller still!*"

"*It can't get any smaller! The material has reached its limits!*"

"*Stacey, tell the Priests to increase their power! We need just a little more! A mere drop!*"

"*Hurry, Daniel! Half of us have been sent to*

respawn already! The Priests are falling with zero Energy!"

We had forced the darkness into all but a point, and still Eluna refused to appear. As far as I was concerned, the concentration of hate was already so dense that the darkness was as hard as a stone— more so than smoke or fog...a Stone!

Tanzanite, Tourmaline, Amethyst, Emerald, Aquamarine, Sapphire, Opal—all shattered to dust when I tried to combine them with the concentrated darkness. My Greed Toad was beginning to strangle me, but I refused to stop—the Skrooj Dungeon had earned me stacks of basically every gem in the game, so I could afford to try one of each.

Ruby...

"The Paladins are gone," flashed a thought from Anastaria when the world stopped.

"Hello, Shaman." Eluna was so divinely beautiful, as usual, that I looked away. The other hundred and seventy me's stared at the goddess like god himself had appeared...which, err, effectively is what had happened. The goddess had descended to her children.

"Eluna," I replied, feeling my consciousness fill with love towards the goddess. Perhaps, it wasn't mine, but that of the craftsmen who were in the unity with me.

"I already told the High Priestess about your success and the sequence of actions that leads to the creation of the Stone. Don't bother my daughter right now—she will be busy for the next several weeks. As soon as she manages to create the Stone using the method you discovered here, Elizabeth will get in touch with you."

"Forgive me goddess, but I wasn't the only one crafting the Stone." I nodded in the direction of the heart-shaped, blood-red Ruby that was changing colors. "If it hadn't been for the craftsmen, I would not have succeeded. If it weren't for the Paladins, then..."

"I will appraise each member's contribution personally," Eluna interrupted. "I am speaking to everyone at the moment, not just with you, although most of myself is right here beside you. Are you still afraid to look at me?"

"You haven't changed," I shrugged, only now noticing that every player in the unity was moving his lips. I guess they were all answering their own instance of the goddess. "So I do not wish to traumatize myself. Judge for yourself—it would be blasphemy if I begin to desire a goddess."

"Who knows, Shaman, who knows," Eluna replied enigmatically. "I don't even know how to thank you for discovering the algorithm for creating the Stone...Do you wish to receive a unique Item? That's too easy though...Perhaps another buff? But that's too ordinary and it won't reflect what you have accomplished...Shaman—you are forcing me to think hard!"

"If the goddess permits, I know what I want," I said, shocked by my own temerity. "Send me to Renox. I need to discover the truth about the Dragons, increase my Dragon Rank and, well, just chat with him in general. I don't want to ask Kornik to do it—I get the impression that Renox asked him not to bring me there anymore. And I really need to find out why he sacrificed Draco to the Tarantulas..."

"Renox didn't sacrifice Draco to them," said Eluna pensively. "Draco appeared much later..."

"But..."

"I will do as you ask, Dragon," Eluna cut me off. "You are correct—Renox is afraid of meeting you. He knows that you spoke with Nashlazar and is worried that you won't accept his past. I must admit—his was quite a horrible past. I will come for you in twenty-four hours. Until we meet again—I expect it will be soon..."

Scenario completed: 'Stone of Light.' The Malabar Empire can now create Stones of Light. All players who took part in the scenario are granted a reward commensurate to their involvement.

+1 to Crafting. Total: 13.

+5 to Jewelcrafting (primary profession). Total: 134.

Your Reputation with the goddess Eluna has reached the status of Esteem. You are 12000 points away from the status of Exaltation.

Your Reputation with the Priests of the goddess Eluna has reached the status of Esteem. You are 12000 points away from the status of Exaltation.

The Stone of Light has blocked the

Transformer and the goblin ghosts have departed this plane of existence.

The unity ended and light auras began to flash around the players—Eluna resurrected everyone who had died and had not signed out and began granting various bonuses to them. As I watched the players around me, I couldn't help but smile—the players were celebrating like children: Today, the Paladins and Priests had personally seen the one for whom the fought, the one for whom they carried the light to the masses.

Something soft and wet touched my hand. I barely contained a joyous exclamation when I turned—the Gray Death was standing beside me with her pack.

They were all in one piece, just as I remembered them after I helped them with the arrows way back when. The she-wolf was staring into my eyes, her ears flattened as if in an admission of guilt. I could read so much in her eyes—a recognition of her guilt, an attempt to explain herself, a request and prayer that I help her or at least refuse to abandon her in this location.

It took me a moment to make my decision, so I got out an amulet:

"Viltrius, arrange for a portal to these coordinates," I dictated my current coordinates, looked the Gray Death in her eyes again, and added: "I won't be alone. There's a whole pack coming with me..."

Quest chain completed: 'Last Hope.' Reward: A wolf pack (Level 150) has joined your party! Maintenance cost: The pack must be fed twice a day...

CHAPTER SIX

THE DRAGONS CHRONICLE

"OKAY DAN, HERE'S THE DEAL with Kreel," said Anastaria, sitting down across from me. "We can't ignore him. According to the information I have, this person is untouchable. Of course he can be killed, tricked, bargained with—but we cannot ignore him or blacklist him. That would be a bad idea."

"Why?" I asked surprised. That's the first time I've heard of a player whom you have to handle with kid gloves.

"My source doesn't have all the info, but the gist is clear as day—this guy is with the Corporation. Either he used to be with them, or he is currently—it doesn't matter. The important thing is he's one of their creatures."

"But I would still like to meet with him. And as soon as today—several hours ago I sent him confirmation that we could meet in the Cross-eyed Angler, today at noon. He even responded already..."

"At noon huh?" Anastaria said pensively. "That's nice, considering it's five minutes till noon right now..."

"Yeah, that's the point," I grinned at the girl and summon Viltrius to make us a portal. After she had read all there was to read on the forums about the creation of the Stone of Light, Fleita made me promise that I would take her with me wherever I went. She didn't want to miss another fascinating event like that one, so now we had to act quickly and surreptitiously. I didn't want to take Fleita with me to meet Kreel...

The portal dropped us off right in front of the doors to the Cross-eyed Angler. Located beyond the Anhurs city limits, you couldn't call this tavern a popular spot. It distinguished itself neither in terms of its prices, nor its quality of food. It was like a hundred other similar establishments, so when I opened the front door, I had no trouble spotting the table we needed with the two players sitting at it. I couldn't read Kreel's class as it was blocked, but he was with Alisa Reyx, a Level 238 Dark Elf Mage. Unlike the giant who had arranged himself at the table with difficulty, the girl's properties were readily available to be read, which gave rise to certain conclusions. The nice thing about the Cross-eyed Angler was the all but utter absence of any other players. In addition to the couple we were meeting, there were only seven low-level players in the tavern. As per habit, they began recording as soon as we appeared. As long as no new ones showed up, though, we'd find a way to convince these guys to mind their business.

"Greetings Earl and Duchess," said Kreel, getting up from the table and making a humble bow. Considering that this monster was over two meters tall, I felt like a dwarf looking up at him. An unpleasant sensation and an unpleasant beginning to our conversation—if Kreel had done this on purpose, then he was letting us know that he was the big fish here and prepared to kill anyone who objected. Of course, maybe I was just being paranoid and this player was simply saying hi to me and my wife. "Please have a seat. Shall we order some beer? Despite the condition of this place, the beer here is very tasty."

"Top of the morning to you too," I greeted Kreel, trying my best to sound carefree. Sitting down at the table, I added, "I think beer's a wonderful idea. I never seem to have the time for one. Is there a particular type here you recommend or are they all good?"

Judging by Kreel's smile, he approved of my response, so he waited long enough for the girls to sit down, lowered his enormous torso onto the chair, and said: "Any one is good, but I recommend the lager. I like it best of all, but as they say, there's no disputing about matters of taste. Since we know who you are, but you don't know us, allow me to introduce ourselves. I am Kreel, the Earl of Grotfeld and head of the Stepsons of the Abyss. My companion here is Baroness Alisa Reyx."

"I have a question, if you don't mind," Anastaria said in a voice so odd that I knew instinctually that she was using some kind of Siren ability. I had heard such a sweet, gentle, evocative and pleasant voice only once before—when I had been asked to give up the Chess Set. "I did not know that the Emperor or the Dark Lord granted anyone a title as high-placed as ours. It follows that you are playing for the Free Lands...Where are you from, if it's not a secret?"

"As Anastaria is right to point out, Barliona is vast and there is plenty of room in it for everything and everyone," replied Kreel, passing a flagon to Alisa and all but pouring it down her throat. Unlike me or Kreel, Alisa fully succumbed to Anastaria's charms and began regarding my wife with love-struck eyes. Making sure that his partner had come to her senses and tossing his head several times, Kreel went on as if nothing had happened: "For example, oh daughter of Sirens, my suzerain is Mark I the King of Skyfoal, may he dwell in everlasting health."

Kreel knows who Anastaria is and judging by Anastaria's narrowed eyes, she's not too happy about it. I wonder whether this is Stacey's way of getting to know people—try out the Siren's charms on the player and see if it works? She said herself that Kreel is untouchable...

"Okay, let's hold off on the beer for now. I think we're getting off on the wrong foot," I decided to steer the conversation in the necessary direction. "Kreel, you almost ruined my castle for me. Are you aware of this? When I saw that Crystal, I had a real shock—in a place that no one should be able to enter, stands a rock that you had brought there. Are you aware of what followed?"

"The Heart of Chaos?"

"The very one. Geranika needed to incapacitate Altameda's guards, and he accomplished this. By the way—how? That question is still bothering me. Although, no—now I have a more interesting one. Tell me, who are you anyway? I've never seen such an enormous player before—particularly one who's immune to the Siren's charms."

"A Titan," Anastaria replied for Kreel. "He's a Titan. The only thing I don't understand is how this race even appeared in Barliona."

"A Titan?" I asked baffled. "I thought your race was exterminated or something?"

"By your ancestors—that is true. Only, one of us survived, as you see," Kreel said with another smirk as if he was relishing the fact that our conversation was following the script he had imagined for it. Me being a Dragon is no great secret. And Anastaria being a Siren is no secret either. And yet to find this information you do have to search for it. Kreel knew, so consequently he had researched us and is letting us know as much at the moment. I wonder why he wants to kill that Dragon. Hmm...If the Titans and Dragons were enemies...Does Kreel know the history of his race? What would happen if I improvise a little here?

"Stacey, do you know anything about the Titans?"

"Very little...I was never interested in them...We need to buy time..."

"Ancestors come in all kinds of shapes and

colors," I shrugged to Kreel. "Some are good, some not so much. For instance, I don't blame you for that time eons ago when Chronocide—someone's son I believe—almost wiped out Barliona. He got bored and wanted to have some fun. So the gods had to get involved to stop the Titan...so, well, why dredge up the past?"

"Chronocide?" Kreel asked once again, clearly puzzled by the name. No wonder that—I'd just made it up. I knew there was a Chronos, so why not someone with a similar name?

"*Dan?*" Anastaria immediately asked. "*Where are you getting this from?*"

"*I just made it up! If he wants to lecture me on history, I'll do the same. Hah!*"

"Maybe we'll get down to business, Kreel?" Alisa interrupted our argument about nothing.

"Why Baroness—what's the rush?" smiled Kreel, spreading his arms in a gesture of peace. "For the first time in ages we've encountered a pair of players who have reached high levels on their own merits, and you don't seem interested in them one bit. But all right, let's talk shop."

"Let's," I replied. "Tell us, Earl, what is the problem with your quest?"

"You said yourself you wanted to know how I delivered the Crystal to Altameda," smirked Kreel, ordering another round.

"Well—go on then," I admitted and leaned back in my chair. "The Crystal really is more interesting to me."

"I reckoned as much, and so I went out on a

limb and prepared a video for you. It details everything related to the Crystal—both how I got that quest and how I did it. For me, at the moment, it's more interesting to discuss the Dragon quest...I hope no one's opposed?"

"*Stacey, I could be wrong but are they one step ahead of us?*" I said aside to Anastaria telepathically. "*I get the impression like they know what we're going to say in advance and have a response prepared...*"

"*Yes, this is called 'doing your homework.' It works better than your preferred approach of 'we've got five minutes, let's wing it!' If only I had had a little more time...Oh well, it's too late now. Just keep in mind that Kreel is a very dangerous opponent...*"

* * *

"What do you think?" Anastaria inquired once we had returned to Altameda.

"I think that Renox owes me yet another explanation," I shrugged, getting comfortable in my rocking throne. A strange item by the way—it was like it didn't even exist for other players. I mean, they could see it, but even Anastaria who had my permission, couldn't actually use this peculiar piece of furniture.

"Dan, I'm interested in Kreel..."

"Stacey, it's already clear as day that we'll take the quest. Kreel needs three weeks to get ready. It's not a big deal, we can wait. I'll go see Renox in the meantime. Better tell me—how did a player manage to select a Titan as his character?"

"The same way you selected a Dragon, I a Siren and Plinto a Vampire. Simply lucky enough to be in the right place at the right time."

"I have my doubts for some reason...That Kreel seemed a little too...I don't even know...He's almost like you but wearing pants. That would be the best way to put it. He's too smart to simply be lucky enough to be in the right place at the right time. There's something else here..."

"I can see that you've begun to strike off the quests from your quest list at a faster pace," Anastaria changed topics. I couldn't say I envied Kreel—there aren't many who could blindside Anastaria, but the guy had managed it. Now Anastaria would bend over backwards to discover everything she needed to know about the Titan. I was curious about Kreel. I wanted to find out some more about him too.

The quest in the video that he had sent me wasn't any different than any other 'take this thing there' type quests—with the exception that the Titan had received the quest from Geranika himself. Kreel had activated the Crystal right before he teleported to Altameda, blocking Urusai's abilities, but Anastaria and I were much more interested in the players who went with him than the actual quest itself. Alisa was there—evidently she was the Titan's companion outside of the game—as well as a certain Feanor the Merciful. I'd wager my head that Stacey would begin her investigation with him.

Anastaria kissed me in her customary manner and flitted off back to Nashlazar. She had to continue her training. Fleita wasn't in-game, there were no imminent adventures to be had, everyone seemed happy and content, and for the first time in several months I found myself in possession of the thing I had only dreamed about recently—free time. Free time that I could spend on myself in order to...

"Greetings, as they say!" Pursuant to Murphy's Law my amulet began to vibrate and when I answered it, I heard a male voice suffused with unheard of optimism. "What are your coordinates? I've got a present to deliver you! Ah! It'd be nice if there weren't any other players around. I don't care if there's an army of NPCs there, but players are out of the question. Then again, it's up to you...Hey! Mahan! Can you even hear me?"

"Gnum?" Even though I was pretty certain who this was, I decided to make sure.

"Well, yeah. Why? Do you frequently get calls from your own amulet?"

"No caller ID in Barliona," I grunted. "I won't send you the coordinates, but I'll have you summoned. Are you ready to go now?"

"Why not? Summon away! Although wait—I'll throw a shroud over my creation. More suspense that way...something like that anyway. Give me a minute, then summon me."

Spiteful Gnum was in his element: 'Hi, I'm ready! Let's blow up the world! You don't want to blow it up? Then I have this cookie here—eat it and you'll change your mind.'

"Viltrius, activate the portal and summon Spiteful Gnum. And by the way, bring me to the teleportation room," I told my majordomo, getting up from my rocking throne. There goes my free time. It had barely begun. Welp, no point getting complacent.

"Ta-dah!" Spiteful Gnum grinned and pointed at two enormous statues. To my surprise, he really was a Gnome—small, giddy, with violet hair coiffed in such an elaborate modern fashion that a less-discriminating person might have imagined that Gnum hadn't combed his hair in a week. But I knew that the default styles in Barliona were cool and neat, and if someone wanted to do something out of the ordinary with one's appearance, one would have to put in the effort. Gnum had put in the effort.

"I take it you haven't brought a bottle of Champagne? You clients are always like that—you make them something special and they just show up empty-handed."

"You want to smash a bottle of Champagne against the statues?" I echoed surprised. As I recalled, this was a maritime tradition reserved for ships, not statutes.

"The hell for? I was going to drink it for, uh, moral as well as chemical fortification."

"If you manage to surprise me, I'll take you to the Golden Horseshoe," I promised Gnum who had in the meantime begun to sound a fanfare...Oh but really—if you don't have an ear or a voice, but you do have an extraordinary desire to sing, then the sanity of those around you becomes their problem, I guess.

"Ta-da!" Gnum finally finished his song and whipped off the shroud.

"Tiamat the Great," whispered the portal demon, who was staring at the two two-meter-tall demonesses beside me.

The six-armed ladies, Ashen Elves by their appearance, resembled each other like two drops of water. Gnum had managed not only to imbue the figures with beauty, but also render the statues as if they were in motion. Examined separately, each statue was performing some kind of complex dance, emphasizing the motions with the twists of her body and the gestures of her hands. Together, however, the ladies gave the impression of utter completeness and harmony.

The Shi Twins: A castle security system. Description: Shi'Li and Shi'La are demoness twins who distinguished themselves from birth with their immense proclivity for weapons and dance— and in the end found a way to combine these two desires. The dance of arms integrates 12 melee weapons to up to Level (18 x Castle Level). Restrictions: The twins may be activated only in a castle of Level 20 or higher. The system may be activated only after all 12 weapon slots have been filled. Further functions of Arch-essence: Hidden until activated.

"A pair of beauties, wouldn't you say?" Gnum

was relishing my reaction to the statues, or that is, the castle security system.

"I'm speechless," I exhaled, coming to my senses and sending Viltrius to the vaults to get some weapons. It didn't matter which ones as long as they were melee and the highest level possible.

"One, uh, thing...They come with two dongles," Gnum added, producing two shining wedges. "You could get by without them too, but the result will be worse...The wedges should be inserted last—the red one is for Li, the blue one for La."

"Gnum, I can't help but ask—what's the catch?"

"What do you mean?" The gnome was taken aback by my question.

"You just gifted me an insanely expensive security system for my castle. It's true it has several drawbacks—there's no long-range effect—yet inside the castle, the twins will be a nightmare to any trespasser. This immediately begs the question—if such an expensive item is given for free, then there must be some mousetrap somewhere. I'd like to know this—where? Do I need to make sacrifices to them once a week or something?"

"Bah! What a thought. The girls require no sacrifices—they are self-sufficient. As for 'why all of a sudden'—by creating the twins, I increased my Craftsmanship, and did it at your expense. The idea of selling them...Well, what kind of moron would spend so much money on a security system? And anyway, I promised to give you the result if you gave me the resources without any strings attached. I was curious to see if you'd trust me or not...Here, let me help you activate them. I'm interested to see myself what they'll do."

"Interested?" I echoed, beginning to smell where the cheese lay, as it were. "Should I call the guards? Am I to understand that you can't guarantee they'll, uh, be on our side?"

"Ah it'll be all right!" Gnum said, not quite as confidently. "But yeah call the guards—who knows..."

"*Security system activated.*" As soon as the 12 blades were handed to the twins, the castle resounded with a metallic, female voice. "*Castle assignment completed. Current castle—Altameda. Current owner...Error—the castle has three owners...Determining ranking owner...Owner identified—Anastaria. Please confirm the owner identification.*"

"The ranking owner is Mahan!" I almost lost my voice from this humiliation on the part of the system—yet I found the strength to express my disagreement.

"*Desired owner is Mahan. Warning—in terms of seniority, Mahan is the least desirable of the owners. Please confirm the selection.*"

"Confirmed!" I didn't yell or anything but certainly raised my voice because, beside me, Gnum began to giggle.

"*The current owner is Mahan. Security system initializing...Arch-demonic essence identified...Do you wish to upgrade auxiliary security system functions?*"

"Yes!"

"The following auxiliary functions are available: Improved magic resistance, improved poison resistance, improved fire..."

"Magic resistance!" I selected right away, doing away with this one Achilles' heel of the twins.

"Improved magic resistance added. Arch-demonic essence identified...Do you wish to upgrade auxiliary security system functions?"

"Yes!" I cast a puzzled glance at Gnum, who was beginning to rub his chin with a pensive look on his face. Two essences?

"The following auxiliary functions are available..."

"Improved Durability!" My second selection granted my security system more Hit Points. If we were attacked, the extra 5–10 points of Durability would come in handy.

"Security system activation complete. The security system is now in operation."

The twins' eyes came alive with a red and blue flame respectively. The demonesses spent several minutes coming to, stretching their muscles as if they were ordinary players. Then, gracefully, silently and to some degree charmingly, the two left the chamber.

"I will offer a discount on my services if those two can come visit me once a day. Simply as guests, without any strings attached," the portal demon immediately spoke up, watching with love-struck eyes the door that the twins had passed through. "I'll take care of everything myself, let them just show up."

"If the discount we're talking about is 50%, I'll give the order." I couldn't pass up another chance to save some money.

"That works!" The demon agreed a little too quickly, causing me to feel like I hadn't bartered as hard as I should have. I should've begun at 90%...

"What else do you know how to craft?" I asked Gnum, after the demon departed back to his demonic plane to brag about his new neighbors.

"I can forge. I can not forge. I can make the hammer sing lullabies or roar death metal."

"And if we're being serious?" I asked when I finished laughing. It was looking like Gnum was my type of people. I wasn't sure why Svard had pegged him as a misanthrope.

"If I'm being serious—do you remember when you asked me how long I've been playing? Well, back when I started, Barliona didn't have prisoners. Listen, Mahan, I don't feel like beating around the bush, so let me tell you right away what I want, and you can make up your mind as you see fit. I really could not care one iota less about all the clan drama—I have my own clan, but I'm much more interested in growing as a craftsman. To do that, I need resources and I need work. A lot of work and a lot of resources. You, as I understand it, have a castle that needs—A) to be fixed and B) to be upgraded. I'm ready to do both, but I won't spend my own resources on it. If you are interested, let's work together. If you're not, there are other castles. Oh yeah! Another thing I need is a humble salary of a hundred thousand gold a month. If that's on the table, then I think I'll spend several months here...What do you say?"

There wasn't much I could say, except agree and glance at the castle's experience bar. As soon as the demonesses had been activated, it had jumped by 10%, telling me quite clearly that I couldn't let Gnum go—he was too valuable to ignore.

* * *

"Dragon, I have been sent to you by Eluna in order to bring you to Vilterax." As soon as the last second of the 24 hours the goddess had given me elapsed, an Angel appeared beside me. Snow white and shimmering like Urusai, he offered me his hand without bothering to find out whether I could fly or not, or whether I wanted to go or not—and in the blink of an eye I was transported to the frozen peaks of the Dragon world. "Eluna said that you shall return on your own," the Angel added and vanished.

"You have found a way to come here, after all," came Renox's familiar voice, full of sadness and pain. Noting that Draco was not around, which meant he was back in the Anhurs library, I transformed into my Dragon Form, soared up and met my virtual father eye to eye.

"Hello, father. I have accumulated several questions concerning the history of our race, will you answer them?" I said, burning all the various, politic bridges available to me. I could have said that I had stopped by for a visit or that I was curious about the bluewing populations in the headwaters of the Altair, but I didn't feel like dissembling. I had come to

Vilterax with a concrete goal and I wanted answers to the questions I had.

Listening to Renox's tale, I couldn't help but slump where I sat further and further. No, I had suspected that the Dragons weren't white, fluffy bunnies, but this...

In a fit of hatred towards Barliona, Harrashess—the youngest son of the Creator—begat the Tarantulas, who were destined to become the evil rulers of the world and drag it into chaos. However, when the other races of Barliona began to kill the Tarantulas, Harrashess was compelled to create the defenders and servants of the Tarantulas—the Dragons. Since he had already poured his utter loathing and hatred of the world into the Tarantulas, Harrashess could only imbue the Dragons with envy, scorn, conceit and arrogance. Having granted the Dragons the power of flight, which no other race enjoyed at that moment, the Creator's youngest son calmed down, forgetting both the Tarantulas and the Dragons once and for all. He had lost all interest in them...

Several thousand Dragons served the Tarantulas, destroying all living things at their masters' behest. Renox had been created as the head of the Dragons, so he was the one who made the decisions about who had to be killed and when. This went on until the time that humans first appeared in Barliona...

Humans were not born in Barliona—they came as refugees from another world, through a portal opened by Eluna. Calaan—the homeland of the humans—was destroyed in a war between the gods for absolute power. Besides humans, Tartarus also brought Orcs, Darkbloods, and Goblins from Calaan—this was the time of the other races' great migration to Barliona. Naturally the newcomers immediately began to fight for their place under the sun.

Having attained a quick victory and secured some land for themselves, the humans grew peaceful and turned their attention to building their world. The neighboring Dragons, Tarantulas, Titans and other races did not bother them—the refugees from Calaan were tolerant towards all. The thing that occupied the humans was internal struggle—the desire to be better than their peers and subjugate those who were like them. The Tarantulas ordered the Dragons to leave the new settlers in peace and concentrate on the chief enemies—the Titans and Sirens. It was these progenies of Harrashess's first creations that were the chief enemies of the Dragons, fighting them with armies of Cyclopses, Minotaurs and Almageryians.

"Nashlazar said that Shaldange approached you with an offer to ally with the Sirens," I recalled the Siren's words.

"That is correct. The terrifying thing about the Tarantulas was that they could mind control any creature, apart from Dragons. None of the initial denizens of Barliona could oppose the dark creations of Harrashess, so Shaldange decided to take a risk and approach me. As head of my tribe, I did not take part in the battles, guiding the Dragons from afar, so the Siren got the impression that I could be negotiated with...Silly little hussy...Drawing her armies into my trap, I turned them over to the ravishment of my masters...The Dragons had been created to obey and I did my duty to the very end...It was then that I encountered Eluna..."

The goddess was enraged—the bloodbath the Tarantulas had caused had released so much dark energy that the Lord of Chaos could enter Barliona. Despite the fact that the Lord of Chaos was on his deathbed, he had managed to hide himself from the gaze of the gods and corrupt an ordinary human to serve him. The subsequent fate of this sentient was already known to me—he founded Glarnis, in the depths of which the Heart of Chaos was secreted.

Managing to bridle the unruly energy, the goddess found the strength to rein in her wrath and met with Renox. She gave the Dragon that which he desired most of all in the world—the chance to have another child.

Yet another piece of news came as a surprise to me—the Dragons had no castle. They had no males either in actual fact—each Dragon could lay one egg in the course of his life and receive his breed, calling him son as per custom.

"Another child?" I asked surprised. "So it follows that you already had a son?"

"Yes." Judging by is eyes, this was the most difficult topic for Renox. "The Tarantulas decided to have some fun with me and breathed all of their hate into my egg. My first son was not simply a true Dragon—he was the first Dark Dragon. A primordial darkness, terrifying, one that forced you to tuck your tail between your legs and run and run and run without turning to look back. It was only when my son cracked his shell that I realized the full injustice of our servitude. The Tarantulas had to be destroyed..."

"Nashlazar said that you watched as they killed your son..."

"Yes. Having reaped their blood harvest during the massacre, the Tarantulas thirsted for more. They now set their myriad eyes on the refugees from Calaan—and in enormous quantities. We gave them one city, then a second, then a third—no one bothered to count the humans and orcs; there were so many of them. But my former masters were not satiated. They desired to taste the body of Tartarus himself—the dark god of Barliona...This was when my first son was born and I decided to give him to the Tarantulas, under the guise that he was a piece of Tartarus..."

"Hang on, you skipped something. Did Eluna visit you after you sacrificed the Dark Dragon or before? Because at first you said that she found the strength to go see you..."

"It took over a hundred years for Eluna to summon her energy. It's not a simple matter to calm an energy storm and it took the gods a long time to do it. So the goddess came to me after I had destroyed the Dark Dragon..."

"Did the Tarantulas really not notice anything?"

"By that point in time they were chock full from consuming beings of light, and true Darkness was precisely what they wanted. They didn't inquire into what they had eaten. That it tasted good was enough for them...And then Eluna appeared. She offered me a deal I could never have imagined—the chance to have another child. But the goddess had her own conditions—I had to help Karmadont destroy the Tarantulas and afterwards depart this world."

"Karmadont? You knew the first Emperor of Malabar?"

"It was I who brought him to the Tomb of the Creator, and it was I who explained how he could pass through its perils. It was I who helped him unite the peoples and create the Chess Set. Why Eluna chose an ordinary warrior, I do not know. But yes, I knew this sentient personally."

"You oversaw the destruction of entire cities," I recalled the Plague's account.

"I had to teach the younger Dragons. When I was the head of the Blue Flame, we saw everyone as mere food for our masters. After Karmadont set in motion the cataclysm that destroyed the Tarantulas, my followers and I departed Barliona. But before we did this, Karmadont decided to cast us into the image of wise and just guardians of this world. He needed an ideal for people to look up to and emulate. Over the course of almost a century, practically all the Dragons were killed. You could count the few that remained in Barliona on one hand—and even those were languishing in a deep slumber. This was when the process of idealizing the Dragons commenced."

"And yet here you are doing everything you can to kill the few survivors. Like for instance hiring a Titan..."

"I cannot allow Geranika to create a Dragon of Shadow. Even if he won't be as powerful as a Dark Dragon, he will still be capable of destroying the world."

"Why the Titan instead of me then?"

"Because I need to correct my own mistakes. I personally destroyed the beautiful city of Olympikos—the capital of the Titans. I personally killed Chronos and Uranus, tearing them asunder and sending their souls to the Tarantulas. I must pay for all of this...The Titan must pass his initiation. To do so he must kill the Dragon. I granted this opportunity to the sentient, but I also wanted him to request your assistance. I need you to see the way we were in the past. Words do not suffice to describe it—you must see it with your own eyes."

"You know, father, what you were like in the past, doesn't matter. What's important is how you are now. If you had killed Draco and then...Wait...So that's why the Guardian sent us to see you about Draco—he considers Draco to be the Dark Dragon! Since you can only lay one egg!"

"That is correct. According to my agreement with Eluna, I can enter Barliona once a millennium. I used this chance to make a deal with the Shamans about my son. He really did die at the hands of the Ice

Giants. When the Beatwick tragedy was underway, Eluna granted me one more chance to appear in Barliona, so that I could stop Geranika and act as a judge. The legend of the Dragons' majesty and wisdom had to be maintained."

"If the Free Citizens fail to destroy the Heart of Darkness, Eluna won't go after them." It suddenly dawned on me what Renox wanted to say. "She has you..."

"If the Free Citizens fail, I have one-and-a-half months to live. As soon as I take the Heart, it will kill me in a matter of minutes. But before that happens, I will return to Vilterax and prevent Geranika from completing his ritual. One must pay for everything..."

"So then in a month and a half I won't have a teacher any longer?"

I smiled bitterly. It was silly to try to persuade a program to take a different course—it was written to fulfill its function.

And yet getting the most out of any situation is the one true calling of any player.

"Before setting out after the Heart, I will transfer my power to promote you to the Patriarch. Your training shall not be impeded, oh my son."

What a disaster!

"I will miss you very much, father. But I understand your motives and haven't the right to dissuade you. I do have one more favor to ask—unlock my rank so I can keep leveling up. I have earned Dragon Rank 10 and stopped. I can't go any further without your aid."

**Quest completed: 'A Heartfelt Conversation.'
Reward: You may open a portal to Vilterax once a
week.**

Dragon Rank promoted. Current Rank: 11.
New ability unlocked: 'Thunderclap.'

"Listen, Renox, I have several more questions—
the Guardian said that Draco's name is Nilirgnis. This
name seemed familiar to him. Learning it even made
him level up. But he reacted to it in an odd way. It's
like it isn't his name after all..."

"Nilirgnis is the name of my first son...He whom
you call Draco is named Shiel. You don't have to be so
surprised at the brevity of the name—only the
Dragons of the Blue Flame were famous for their long
names. It was thought that the longer the name, the
more powerful the Dragon...A bunch of nonsense. The
true name of your Totem, my second son and your
brother is Shiel. By the way—I haven't seen him for a
week—is he all right?"

At this point I had to recount to Renox how my
Shamanic powers had been stripped from me, how I
had summoned my Totem without knowing I wasn't
supposed to and how Draco was currently in the
Anhurs public library terrorizing the librarian. I don't
know what he was looking for, but Draco had flown
there with some purpose in mind. So let him study.

"In that case, I have nothing further to tell you,
son," said Renox, settling down on the earth and
propping up his head with his tail.

"And yet I have a further question," I settled

down beside Renox. "For example, what were the War Lizards so famous for that they earned their place in the Chess Set?" Since you helped Karmadont create this masterpiece, no doubt you know more about them than I—especially since I don't know a thing about the War Lizards."

"Lizards? Hmm...Are you sure you want to find out about them?"

"Judging by your question, there's some kind of restriction here?"

"Yes. Karmadont understood that only he who is worthy could open the door to the Tomb, so he made a deal with me right away—that I would never tell anyone about more than one figurine. It seems to me that as far as the reasons for being part of the Chess Set go, the Emperor of Malabar is the most complicated. After all, it was Karmadont himself who founded the Empire and there weren't any Emperors in Malabar before him. Even the name 'Malabar' only appeared three hundred years after Karmadont's death. In his time the Empire was called Berimor."

"You want I take a guess?" I smirked. "The Emperor of Malabar in Karmadont's Chess Set is the Emperor—or his analog—of Calaan, the human homeworld. Correct?"

"Yes. You're right. It is Lait, the Prime Priest, demigod, Emperor and simply a great sentient, who ruled his people for several millennia. His deeds were so great that even across centuries, people still..."

"Renox, I asked you to tell me about the Lizards. I have nothing but utter respect for Lait and everything related to him, but let me find out his story from someone else, not you. I still have a ways to go before I get to the Emperor. Meanwhile, I can start on the Lizards even now. So, let's talk about them..."

"I'm sorry, my son," the Dragon shook his head sadly. "You were the one who began the conversation about the Emperor...I haven't the right to tell you about the other figurines after naming this great sentient."

I simply can't describe the emotions that flooded me at that point. What had caused me to open my mouth like that? The Emperor must be crafted from Blue Diamond, which requires Level 500 Jewelcrafting to work with. Considering that I hadn't even reached Rank 3 as a Jeweler yet, I still had vast amounts of hard work ahead of me before I it was Lait's turn.

"What does Prime Priest mean?" Doing my best to calm myself, I began to ask Renox about Lait. I don't know how I managed to let this chance to find out about the War Lizards slip away—why that's just...I haven't the words, only feelings!

"It's not difficult to guess—the Prime Priest is the first priest of god. As for Lait—he founded the original temple to one of the Calaan gods and began to develop it. Gradually adding the lesser gods to the pantheon, he engendered a new power in Barliona, which the original gods decided to destroy. A war broke out, which brought to..."

With Renox's every word about Lait, I became more and more interested in this person. Like Karmadont, Lait started out from the very bottom and gradually rose to such heights that his name was remembered even after the resettlement to Barliona. Lait was generous to his friends and inhuman in his cruelty to his foes. When Renox told me of the time that Lait and his partner or companion forever imparted the soul of one of their enemies into a slug, I completely fell for this great man. It was doubtless that a sentient of his caliber had every right to be included in the Chess Set as a King.

Renox told me of Lait's victories and defeats, his pain and happiness, hate and love, fears and noble deeds—and all of a sudden I realized that I was in Design Mode and that there was a person there looking at me who resembled an Elf but was definitely human. Renox never said a word about Lait's class, yet in my sub-consciousness he turned out to be a Death Knight. Clad head to toe in menacing steel, Lait held in his hand an unusual staff that seeped black fog. Succumbing to a sudden premonition, I added an Imperial crown to the King piece and engraved several scars on his face, imparting Lait with the appearance of a seasoned warrior.

The thought that I still had a while to go before working with Diamond receded in some mysterious way as if it were some minor detail. Without even leaving Design Mode, I recreated the Blue Diamond from my bag and merged it with the Lait figurine.

Congratulations! You have continued on the path of recreating the Legendary Chess Set of Emperor Karmadont...

Item created: Diamond Emperor of Malabar (Legendary Chess Set of Emperor Karmadont). Probability of finding items increased while in possession: +50% (Unusual), +40% (Rare), +20% (Epic), +5% Unique and +1% (Legendary).

+1 to Crafting. Total: 14.

+5 to Jewelcrafting (primary profession). Total: 139.

You have created a Legendary item. +500 Reputation with all previously encountered factions.

"That's precisely how I helped Karmadont create the Chess Set," Renox bared his enormous teeth in a smile. "He had no Jewelcrafting at all, so I had to channel all my skills, memories and thoughts into him. I am confident that you will be able to handle the War Lizards on your own, but I couldn't not help my son craft the King. I was very apprehensive of our meeting. I delayed it as much as I could and made Kornik promise that he wouldn't bring you here, but all my fears turned out to be in vain. There are no more Dungeons left in Barliona that would be of interest to you, and the information that is useful to you is confidential, so teaching you how to create a figurine was the only way I could find to thank you. Now you may go—working with the foundation of this world takes a lot of energy. I will have to sleep for the next month, so even if you return to Vilterax, we won't be able to meet. Perhaps this has been our last conversation. I would like you to know that I am proud to have a son like you..."

"*Dan, I don't care if you're free or not! I'm summoning you to my location. I'm putting you up against the wall and forcing you to tell me how you managed to craft the King Piece!*"

Your other half wishes to summon you to her location. Do you accept?

I glanced at Renox and smiled bitterly—the Dragon had fallen asleep. Eyes shut, Renox was breathing heavily, the tip of his tail jerking nervously as if he was having a nightmare. I placed one paw on the sleeping Dragon, saying farewell to this Imitator, and pushed the 'Accept' button. It looked like this was our last time seeing each other. In the future I'd be under the tutelage of the Patriarch of Vampires.

* * *

"Greetings dropout," hissed Nashlazar as soon as I appeared beside Stacey. She turned to the girl: "A power of the flowering Ying-Yang, correct?"

Stacey, who was in her Siren Form, gave a barely perceptible nod. The girl's full attention was directed at keeping her balance—she was standing on a thin cord stretched across a basin full of green, boiling liquid. I even began to wonder how Stacey had managed to summon me.

"All right, my pupil. Your lesson is complete for today. I will be waiting for you tomorrow. We will continue to work on your balance. Since you somehow managed to summon your other half, be prepared for gusts of wind to impair your balance tomorrow."

"Hello, Danny," said Anastaria, descending from the tightrope. The basin vanished, as did Nashlazar, giving the girl the opportunity to jump down and turn into her human form. By the way! I'm still in my Dragon Form! Stacey waited for me to return to my normal form, kissed me warmly and, rubbing her hands, said with a sly smile: "Let's see what you made."

I offered the girl the King figurine and used the opportunity to embrace her in my arms.

"Dan?" Stacey protested coyly, making no attempt to wriggle away. "Whoa! Can you imagine what'll happen if you bring this figurine on a raid with you? Particularly if it's a higher-level Dungeon...Did you consider sharing it with Magdey and Clutzer?"

"When? I only just crafted it and...Hang on—how much time has elapsed since we saw Kreel?"

"A day! A mere day—although it took you like a week to craft the other Chess Pieces. I have this impression that this King..."

"Was prepared for me ahead of time," I completed Stacey's thought. "And that he was developed a long time ago and simply inserted into the game now...I didn't even have to try very hard to make him—Renox did everything for me...You know, it seems like the Corporation really wants someone to open the Tomb."

"You can say that again. As I hear it, the craftsmen working on the key in the Celestial Empire on the neighboring content, also have one item remaining. Only instead of the Chess Set, they're crafting swords—they've already crafted five Legendary Swords and have one left...You're probably right—the Corp is trying to even the playing field between our continents. And yet, we still have an advantage because we know where the entrance is!"

"Speaking of that, you didn't find a way in, did you?"

"No. Neither magic, nor force can open it—the entrance is part of the landscape and has no Durability stat. So we need the other Chess Pieces. Did you check out the King quest? It's supposed to be the most difficult! I'm even curious what all they put in it."

I looked up the properties of the King but encountered an astonishing phrase:

The quest for this Chess Piece cannot be issued until you complete the preceding quests.

"I don't play like that," Anastaria pouted and then grinned. "It's too bad. I wanted to test myself. I looked at the Giants' riddle, but it didn't seem interesting, so we won't even bother checking the coordinates. We have little time as it is."

"How's your training moving along?" I changed topics, putting away the King. I'd make up my mind about sharing with Magdey and Clutzer sometime later—an item like this could be useful for me too.

"As you see—I'm practicing my balance and concentration. In order to level up my Siren, I need to complete a special test, the gist of which is a run-of-the-mill obstacle course. I've already failed it twice, so Nashlazar said that I won't get a third attempt until I learn how to keep myself balanced on a tightrope...And here I am. How's it going on your end?"

"I'm still working on that list we drew up. All that's left of the fourteen items on the list is, uh— hang on, let me see—right, the second Dungeon, the Pirates, the Widow's Eye, the Chess Set (I have one other set of figures to make), reaching Gem Cutter Rank 3, for which I need eleven points in my profession and to pass the training with the Patriarch. Why look at that! Six of the fourteen, including the Pirates and the Eye, don't count. And I'm already making progress on the Chess Set and earning Gem Cutter Rank 3.

"Hmm...Really," Anastaria said pensively upon scanning the list. "I'll admit I thought it would take you longer. But I wouldn't strike out the meeting with Kreel just yet. It's premature to consider this task complete until we've done the quest with him. You jumped the gun with your pupil too—she hasn't completed her trial yet...Plus..."

Stacey began to smash my pie in the sky ideas about having made progress: This isn't done, this isn't ready, this isn't quite complete, that still has a detail or two missing... Really, what a brat she can be!

"But on the whole, you're moving in the right direction," Stacey concluded. "Where to now?"

"Now?" I echoed, finding myself brought back down to earth. "Now I'll turn my attention to my student. Not far from our castle, there are several villages. We'll go there and do some quests. I'll evaluate how she handles them."

"Got it...I have another two weeks to spend here," Anastaria said sadly. "Any news from Plinto?"

"Nope. Dead silence. I imagine he's also working on his coordination—balancing on a rope above a green puddle."

"That was acid."

"What?"

"The basin was filled with acid that would instantly dissolve me and send me to respawn. The first time I fell into it, I turned into a human...I don't know why but Nashlazar started hollering for some reason...Then she lifted me high up into the air and dropped me...By the way, try and become a Harbinger as soon as you can—you'll be much better off facing players of any level. It takes a second—you teleport up to them, grab them around the waist, teleport high up into the air, drop them and teleport back to earth. Meanwhile, your foe plummets swearing like a sailor...I never imagined that a free fall would cause me to curse like that."

* * *

I returned to Altameda only the next morning—and that was merely because Nashlazar kicked me out...

"Mahan, I can't maintain this pace of work!" Barsina collapsed into a chair and rubbed her eyes. "All these letters are beginning to show up in my dreams! 'Let me join your clan,' 'please let me join your clan,' 'how can you have a clan if I'm not in it...' At first I figured that hiring people for the clan would be interesting and fulfilling, but the more I do this job, the clearer it becomes that we need a specially-designated person for it. I mean, it's a miracle if we receive less than a thousand letters a day! My in-game day starts with opening my mailbox, reviewing applications, then reviewing applications some more. It ends with—you won't believe this—reviewing some applications! I'm a mercenary, damn it! I'm supposed to be running around Dungeons with Clutzer, leveling up my character—yet here I am dealing with this nonsense."

It was looking like the girl had had her fill. I had never seen our little Druid so stressed out. Abandoning both Anhurs and her training, my deputy had arrived in Altameda that morning to express her irritation.

"Barsa, I'm not opposed to it—let's hire someone. Aren't there clans that specialize in recruitment? Or if not clans, then players whom you can pay to find people for you. Let's ask them for someone we can use. You don't have to be a hero..."

"That's basically why I came here," the girl said in a calmer tone, realizing that I wasn't opposed to spending resources or delegating responsibility. "I already have a contract with some players who do recruiting, and it doesn't cost too much money actually—twenty thousand gold a month. Given the size of our clan, we need about five people who will do the hiring, build an incentives and categorization system, determine growth priorities for the various ranks...Damn, I sound like a human resources manager, don't I?"

"I'll reiterate—I'm all for it, Barsa! If it helps our affairs, then...Wait, how many people are in our clan? I have to confess, I kind of stopped paying attention..."

"In our clan? Just over two-and-a-half thousand people."

"But you said that the Azures and the Heirs were massacring us so bad that we started losing players?"

"I did and we were...And I mean we were losing masses of people, especially all of the ones who'd joined because of Anastaria's fame and then realized that being in the same clan as her didn't really do anything for them. To the opposite, they found themselves hunted. And yet after you captured Altameda, after Armageddon and especially after you created the Stone of Light, there're new players coming in non-stop. Every day, we're getting hundreds upon hundreds of applicants, and not merely warriors—we're getting craftsmen and gatherers too. Leite's rubbing his hands from these numbers—even though he's over here all the time, he still manages to draw up and sign new contracts for mining work. Basically, our clan is easily in the top 500 of Malabar at this point, even though we're only at Level 6."

"So you're thinking of wandering around some Dungeons?"

"To be honest, not really. If you don't mind, I'd like to work a little closer with Leite…"

"What do you mean?"

"You allowed him to govern the three villages. I want to take part in that. Playing and leveling-up is one thing…But I really liked administration and I'd like to keep working in that field."

"How much?" I understood what the girl was getting at. Barliona was not only a game where you could pass your time or earn a livelihood. One of the popular functions of Barliona was the education it offered—albeit one clad in a fantasy guise. Education, management, marketing, chemistry, physics—hundreds of various courses were taught by Imitators in specially-purposed Dungeons. The only drawback to these classes was their cost—from forty to two hundred thousand gold per course.

"To become eligible for certification, I need to complete three courses, costing all together two hundred thousand. I don't have that kind of money at the moment, but I am willing to pay it back gradually."

"Send me the contract," I instantly made up my mind. I know firsthand how important it is to develop one's skills. If Barsina decided to give up being a mercenary in order to become a manager, why wouldn't I help her? Especially, since she seemed to have such a knack for it.

"Here," the girl, who had come prepared, smiled and sent me the contract. Glancing at the document's terms and conditions—the money would be paid back over the course of a year or in one lump sum if Barsina left the clan—I signed the contract with my digital signature. Immediately, I was confronted with a prompt to approve the fund transfer. The girl had anticipated even this. It was as if she hadn't doubted for a second that I would give her the money. Now how do you play with people like that?

The next two weeks turned into an unending festival of crafts for me—Clutzer and Magdey got on my case and announced that until I craft clan rings for their Raid Parties, they wouldn't let me leave Altameda. Leite and Barsa seconded them. They poured three mounds of jewels onto the table and forced me to get to work. I resisted up until the point that Fleita informed me that she had to study for exams and wouldn't be in game for two weeks. Or rather, that she'd be there only for an hour a day, no more...

So in general, the way things worked out meant that I had no choice and had to occupy myself with my crafting. The upshot of those two weeks was that I finally earned my eleven points for Jewelcrafting and leveled up to Gem Cutter Rank 3—and therefore crossed this item off my list.

A week remained before we would set out with Kreel to kill the sleeping dragon when early one morning Fleita showed up and offered me a sheet of paper.

"What's that?" I asked, taking the document automatically.

"My report card for the semester! I got straight A's! Now Evolett can't bug me about my studies!"

"Well...In that case, get your things together!"

"Where are we going?" the girl asked, surprised.

"Since you've completed one part of your education, it's time to start another one! It's time to find out what you're capable of as a Shaman!"

CHAPTER SEVEN
THE OUTSKIRTS OF CARNUE

"I DON'T GET IT. What are we doing in this village?" Fleita grumbled yet again. "I can't believe you're forcing me to do ordinary quests! I bet all you deal with are epic and legendary ones, but I have to do whatever comes along."

By 'village' Fleita was referring to Carnue—the capital of Lestran Province. Paying a visit of honor to our Governor, I reported on the progress we had made with the villages under our governance. And there really was something to be proud of. Before departing, I'd met with Leite to find out what had been accomplished, since I could hardly believe my own ears: The population of all three villages had grown by 50% since we took over. We were beginning to build new manufactories, since the old ones were at full capacity. The village craftsmen had completed their training, causing their goods to reach new peaks of quality. On the whole, the growth of the villages was pretty evident. Leite welcomed the news that Barsina wanted to join his governance endeavor. Noting that she was one of the most capable women he knew (after his wife and Anastaria naturally), he immediately called her and began to discuss the degree of her involvement.

The Governor listened to my report, reassured me yet again about his friendship and unflinching support, after which we set out to stroll around the city. Carnue was a city for players up to Level 100 inclusive, so I had high hopes of encountering quests here that would test Fleita as a Shaman. It's one thing to know how to summon Spirits—it's another to allow oneself to be guided by one's premonition during the game. And it was this second thing I wanted to test...

"Can't you tell him, Draco?" The girl refused to give up, appealing to the objective (in her view) arbiter who was my Level 78 Totem. The three weeks that my Totem had spent in the Anhurs City Library had earned him 24 Levels. It had also earned me negative twelve thousand gold for the damage he had caused to library property. It turned out that my Totem was a very emotional kind of reader and had for three months now been obsessed with reading Shakespeare's *Romeo and Juliet*. The problem that Draco encountered with the book was that, as an NPC, he could not open the book at the last place he had been reading at. As a result, the Totem knew the first twelve pages of this play by heart but could only cast longing glances at what remained. So when he discovered that he had a full two months in Barliona, the first thing he did was rush off to read the entire text. *Romeo and Juliet, Eugene Onegin, Venus and Adonis, The Importance of Being Earnest, The Adventures of Tom Sawyer* and *Huckleberry Finn*...Draco consumed one book after the next without pausing to take a breath—and whenever he encountered some poignant moment, the Totem did not hesitate to express his own emotions without concern for his surroundings. Joy, tears, sorrow, pleasure, anger...Even though the Library had the cheapest chairs in Barliona, Draco managed to run up a bill of five thousand gold in them alone.

"No need to look at me like that! Draco flicked his tail. "If Mahan thinks you have to do it, then you have to do it!"

"You're always on his side!" Fleita pouted her lips. "Where are we going anyway?"

"We're just strolling around the city..."

"Oh sure—'strolling!' I know all about you and your 'strolls'..."

"The old hag has respawned once again!" Tearing through the city's monotonous hubbub, an unusual phrase reached my ears. I turned in the direction of the voice and saw Wild Catwick—a Level 75 Hunter. He was standing sideways to us, facing the city guard. Following his gaze, I saw an elderly woman, a little granny, who seemed to be looking for someone in the crowd. Judging by her properties, this lady belonged to the hallowed NPC tribe, so it was quite odd that Wild was speaking to her like this.

"Hi Wild!" I addressed the Hunter. "Do you mind

telling me why you're talking to her like that?"

"Mahan?" Judging by his surprised face, the player knew who I was. "You feel like being a White Knight or something?"

"Nah, I'm just curious. It's pretty rare for a player to be angry at an NPC—and you seem like you don't seem merely crazy, so I became curious."

"Oh! I see. Well, see that hag over there?" Wild nodded at the grandma.

"Is she looking for you?"

"What? Oh—no! She's looking for any player who has zero reputation with the Province. If a player like that comes across her sight, it's curtains for him!"

"Does she eat them or something?" I grinned, not understanding what Wild was talking about.

"If only. That old bag of bones issues an impossible quest that you can't refuse. Do it or don't do it, you'll end up losing."

"How interesting." I pricked up my ears. Social quests popped up frequently in Barliona, but I'd never heard of one that was impossible to complete.

"Oh please! This isn't the Dark Forest or Altameda. This is nothing short of a trap that the devs have laid for unwary newbies."

"So tell me more. Maybe I should stay away from her too..."

"There's not much to tell. As soon as the hag spies a player with a Neutral reputation with the Province, she runs over and asks him to rid her vegetable garden of some rats."

"Excuse me?"

"Yeah! An ordinary quest, just like in the Tutorial, and the reward is about right too—several silver coins. Some players agree to do it. Out of naïveté I guess or kindheartedness. Maybe it's the chance to relive those first few moments, pretend you're a rat exterminator...But then comes the catch. If you refuse the quest, you earn -400 Reputation with the Province, as though the granny is the Governor himself! And your Attractiveness with her and her sisters drops to zero, which means that you can't talk to them again. The old lady has two sisters—one's the owner of the local grub joint, the other's the owner of the potions store. Pretty vital NPCs to be able to talk to when it comes to this location...However! Even if you refuse once, the hag'll offer you the chance to go rat hunting in an hour! And the penalty for refusing is the same: -400 Rep with the Province...et cetera et cetera...Do you get the picture?"

"What picture? An ordinary social quest that you have to complete in the right way. What's there to get heated about?"

"It's ordinary and all but then again it isn't. Since most of the players who come here initially have a Rep of zero, basically all of them agree to do the quest. By the way, I forgot to mention, the hag will give you +400 Reputation for killing the rats. And so, the old lady asks you to rid her garden of the pests. You go there and start hacking away at the rodents. Everything's just like in the Tutorial, only the rats are like Level 70–75. After you kill about 15–20 of the critters, a mini-boss shows up: A Ratherd goblin.

Ratherd isn't his name—it's his occupation, like swineherd. He drops a rag that's required for the quest—'a goblin cape.' Well and he also drops a healing or Mana potion, depending on the roll. Sometimes it'll be a ring or an amulet, though I'm not sure because I've never seen it firsthand. But again, that isn't the point..."

"Wait, so you're trying to say that the hard part is killing the boss?"

"No, just hang on! The hag takes the cape and says something like 'so that's where the good tablecloth's been,' and then she ends the quest and you get your reputation reward. Seems like everything's nice and peachy. You get a handful of silver and an Attractiveness bonus with her sisters. But here's the snag—that night, someone offs the hag. As in like the revenge of the Ratheards' Union or something. The two sisters blame you—saying that you didn't finish the quest all the way and the dear old grandma-sister bought it because of it...As a result, your rep with the Province drops by 1500, with all that entails...A week later the hag respawns. Can you believe this crap?"

"Got it...Hang on, didn't you say she only asks you to 'rid the garden of rats,' not exterminate them? What if you try to scare them off or something?"

"Check out the big brain on Mahan! You think you're the only one who's thought of that? Why the players have tried everything they can think of! They tried merely catching the rats, putting them in cages and taking them to the hag. But it wasn't that easy: If you catch too few, the hag won't count the quest complete. And if you catch too many, the Ratherd shows up and it's back to square one. But let's say that you hit the sweet spot and catch just the right amount. First of all, you get half the rep—a penalty for scaring the old lady. She's terrified of rats it turns out. Secondly, there's no Ratherd, so no loot—although that's not a big deal. If you release the rats, even all the way in Kartoss, or if they escape somehow—you're awarded the 'Liar' Achievement and your Reputation with the Province drops by 3000. If you slaughter the rats after the quest's been marked complete—the hag dies that night. That's the deal and that's why she's an old hag. Our only hope right now is that she catches someone unimportant and leaves the square. She'll get offed tonight then and we'll have some peace for the new players for a week."

I looked at the NPC looking for her 'prey' with astonishment—she seemed a fairly respectable old lady...I was filled with such a desire to solve this riddle that I asked Fleita to stay in place and approached the grandma. There aren't any penalizing quests in Barliona! There are only players who fail quests by doing them wrong.

"Greetings, madam!" I said to the old lady, who had an odd sounding name: Agrippina Dormidina. "Do you require some assistance? You wouldn't happen to have some chore you need done?"

"Why, yes I do, young man!" The old lady perked up. "A neighbor of mine, the Happy Milkman (that's what people call him—I don't remember his name) has lost a cow. She tore the rope, the silly heifer, and wandered off into the forest. He's so distraught, you should see him. He's not here looking for help because he's back home waiting for her. Could you, kind stranger, pay a visit to my neighbor and help him with his sorrow?"

Quest available: 'The Sorrows of the Happy Milkman.' Description: The Happy Milkman's cow escaped from her pen and ran off to the forest. Find the lost little cudster and bring her back to her owner. Quest type: Common. Reward: A jug of milk, +40 Reputation with Lestran Province, +200 Experience. Penalty for failing/refusing the quest: None.

Why look at that! So it turns out that my Exalted Reputation keeps the granny for offering me the rat-catching quest, so she's given me some other quest to find a cow! Thanks, but no thanks! I didn't come here for this! Accepting the quest so as not to upset the grandma, I decided to ask her some more questions:

"Thank you, I will make sure to go visit your neighbor and find out what happened to his cow. I heard that you've been having some trouble with rodents—maybe I could help you with that too? I'm a very good rat catcher!"

"Oh but it wouldn't do for me to ask a nobleman like yourself to bother with such a trifle," said the old lady bashfully. "If the Governor catches wind that I've asked an Earl to root around my vegetable garden, why, he'll confiscate my land so that I don't trouble the aristocracy in the future. Please don't be cross with me, your highness—I can't ask you to do such a thing."

"So it's all right to ask me to go find a cow, but rat catching is out?"

"A cow is a cow! A cow is a livelihood. Bringing her back is the noblest thing anyone could do. There are others to take care of the rats."

"What about me? Will you give me the quest?" said Fleita, ignoring my request to hang back.

"Oh god almighty! An undead monster!" The old lady jumped back in fright. "What is the world coming to? A hideous cadaver terrifying honest citizens in the town center!"

Bystanders began to notice us at this point—players, NPCs, and I even noticed the town guard pop up in the near distance—so I began to feel a bit uncomfortable. I will have to have a chat with my student about obeying my orders.

"I'm not hideous!" Fleita pouted, crossing her arms over her chest. "I want to help you kill the rats!"

"Why, you could simply take a walk through the garden and all the rats would drop dead from the sight of ya," someone yelled from the crowd around us. This was followed by further jeers, which at first were relatively harmless but gradually grew meaner as the spectators got a chance to appraise the girl's costume. Fleita craned her neck left and right trying to get a look at the hecklers, but the old lady drew closer to her and asked with an intrigued voice:

"Did I hear you say that you want to kill some rats?"

"Yes." When Fleita understood that looking for the hecklers was hopeless, since the whole crowd was heckling, she turned back to the old lady—who grimaced, but didn't jump this time.

"I won't let you into my house," the old lady decided. "You might ruin it. As for the rats—since you're volunteering your service, you are more than welcome. Come by my vegetable patch today around four. I'll show you where those pests are hiding. Will you come?"

It looked like a quest notification had popped up for Fleita because she spent several minutes staring dully into the distance and then finally nodded with satisfaction.

"I'll be there!" the girl replied decisively.

"Very good!" the granny grinned. "In that case, I'll go take a stroll around my vegetable patch. Just don't come any earlier than four. I won't be home."

The crowd began to gradually dissolve, though several individuals couldn't help but make several more remarks about Fleita's intellectual capacity for volunteering to destroy her own reputation, so I took the girl by the arm and led her in the direction of the city gates.

"But the old lady said it's still too early," the girl tried to resist, but it wasn't so easy to knock me off my path. The time had come to dot all the i's and cross all the t's.

"And why have we stopped?" Fleita asked after

several minutes, once we had left the city and stopped not far from the entrance to the village where the old lady and the Happy Milkman lived. "There's that village!"

I got the protective shroud from my inventory—without which Anastaria wouldn't even sit down to eat—and activated it, hiding us from any prying eyes and ears. Then, I sat down on the ground and gestured to the girl to sit down beside me.

"What is it now?" came the question, but the girl took her seat.

"You know, Fleita, the time has come for us to have a chat."

"About what?"

"About you, about your training and behavior. Of cabbages and kings."

"Cabbage? What's that have to do with it?" the girl asked, surprised.

"Never mind, we'll drop the cabbages and kings, since you don't seem to get the joke anyway. But tell me—why the hell would you get involved with the granny?"

"I wanted the quest..."

"Great! And what had I told you to do?"

"To hang back. But what are you, my dad or husband, to order me around, to tell me what to do and what not to do?"

"Didn't you agree to do as I commanded if I became your teacher?"

"For you to be my teacher, you actually have to teach me. Have you even once tied to instruct me how a Shaman should behave?"

"Do you not have the brains to figure out that your training is already under way at full steam? Do you need a little sign that says 'training ongoing?'"

"What are you getting all aggro with me for all of a sudden? Big deal—so I got a quest..."

"It's not about the quest. It's about your attitude. If you want to keep being my student, you'll have to follow certain rules."

"You said yourself that there aren't any rules for Shamans. That they make the rules as they go! So it looks like you really don't follow rules, but I have to deal with one restriction after another!"

"Fleita..." I sighed deeply, calming my nerves. "Let's try again. I don't like it when you don't do what I asked you to do directly. If you feel like continuing in that vein, then let's part ways. If you were an NPC, I'd understand why you act like you've just graduated kindergarten. But you're a grown up girl, so I'd like to treat you as such."

"Mahan, I really don't understand you. At first you'd say that, as a Shaman, I have to follow my feelings in how I act. I started doing that and then you tell me off and scold me like a dad scolds some naughty girl who's stayed out too late!"

"You're telling me that your premonition told you that you should approach the old woman and take the quest?" I smirked.

"Well, yeah! Stop laughing at me!"

"Tell me, how old are you anyway?"

"Seventeen, but I'll be eighteen soon..."

"I'm thirty-two. I'm practically twice as old as you are. And yet you keep poking and messing with me as if I'm someone your age. Did I miss the part where we decided that we'd be equals?"

"But this is a game." The girl's eyes filled with such a deep puzzlement at my words that I even began to feel a little awkward. "Everyone acts like this with one another here...So you're bothered because I don't talk to you like to my *dad*?" The last word was marked with such evident irony that I all but started.

"You've misunderstood me again..."

"So then explain...please...more accurately what you would like from me...sir!"

I shut my eyes wearily, realizing that our conversation had reached a dead end and that I'd only made things worse. I hadn't managed to get my position across to the girl, nor managed to understand where she was coming from. What I should do right now is stand up, tell her that our meeting had been a mistake and then simply head back to Altameda—forever forgetting about the Zombie. But I recalled what Kornik had asked me. An NPC of his level wouldn't forgive me just like that. It follows that someone's pulling the strings somewhere and the last thing I should do is abandon the girl's training. There was nothing left to do but take ahold of my emotions and make another attempt to explain myself:

"Fleita...I really dislike it when you act inappropriately and when you ignore what I tell you to do..."

"There you go! You sound just like my dad now! This is impossible! This sucks...I came to this game in order to get away from all the rules and it turns out that there are more of them here than back in reality! You're right—if this keeps going on like this, then it is better if we go our separate ways! I thought that you were a true Shaman! But you're just like everyone else! Feelings, emotions, the way of the Shaman...It's all talk—all you care about is proper behavior."

Jumping to her feet, the girl dashed out from under the protective shroud and ran in the direction of the village.

"You know, brother," Draco said pensively, looking after the receding girl, "If you ever catch me behaving like that, promise me that you'll scold me and remind me of this...Why didn't you put the little brat in her place?"

"Fleita is right though—I am a nobody. She and I aren't even officially teacher and student. We're just two Free Citizens, of which one asked another to teach her something. It seems like I'm not meant to be a true teacher, since I utterly have no idea what's going on in the Zombie's head...But okay, what's the point of regretting something that never was. Let's go see the Milkman—we need to find his cow."

"You're not going to help her take care of the rats?"

"No. She made her choice..."

"It's too bad about the granny. They'll kill her..."

"She knows how to return from the Gray Lands...She's a pretty strange NPC, don't you think?

Hardly an ordinary villager, that one...Where'd she come from anyway? Did the Emperor place the Seal of Return on her?"

Only having said this out loud did I suddenly realize that the granny really was not what she appeared to be at first glance. It wasn't even the rats—pretty much all the NPCs would fall ill if you failed a quest. Their Hit Points would drop to single digits and they'd temporarily go somewhere. But no one ever died in Barliona—to return again one week later. Even when there'd be a city raid, the NPCs would survive...Something tells me—hello, premonition, my old friend—that I should take a closer look at this old lady.

"Draco, do you mind if I ask you watch over Fleita?"

"But you said that you don't want to help her."

"I didn't say help, I want you to watch over her. And not even her, so much as the rats. Remember Beatwick?"

"Is that where I played with Clouter?"

"Yup. So, if you remember, there weren't any rats there. At all. And yet here there's not only rats, but even a Ratherd. We need to figure out where they come from."

"All right. I'll do it. Say, you're at Dragon Rank 11 now. Did you see our father?"

"Yes. We had a chat about the history of Dragons in Barliona. It's a good thing you asked. I completely forgot about it during that week I spent crafting the clan rings. Anyway, our father told me that..."

Your Totem has gained a level...
Your Totem has unlocked a new ability: 'Whirlwind of Time.' +300% to airspeed for five minutes. Ability cooldown time: 50 minutes.
Your Totem can now carry a player.
The duration your Totem may spend in Barliona has increased to 7 hours per day.

"So that means that I had another brother? That my name is really Shiel and that dad will die in a month?"

"That is correct."

"So why haven't we gone to Armard yet?"

"Where?"

"The capital of the Shadow Empire? All Barliona is talking about is how the Free Citizens are marching to its walls and vanquishing all the servants of Shadow in their path...We should be there with them!"

"Draco—I mean, Shiel—what do you want me to do? All my Shamanic powers have taken a two-month-long sabbatical."

"But you're still a Dragon! Come on, brother! It's only now that I've reached Level 103 that I'm starting to understand that the most valuable thing in life is family. Friends come and go—students do too...you saw how she ran off...But if our father leaves us, there won't be anyone to take his place! And...you know what...When you told me my name is Nilirgnis, I asked you to keep calling me Draco. I'd prefer if you did the same now too... Maybe in Vilterax I'm Shiel, but here my name is Draco..."

"You're right," I said pensively, shooting Draco a sidelong glance. My Totem had grown—and not merely physically. The Dragon wheeling around me right now was three-four meters from nose tip to tail tip—and was no smaller in spirit. Draco had become...well...perhaps not an adult, but certainly a teenager. It was like he was now 17–18 in human years... "Okay, let's wrap it up here and go do that Dungeon with Kreel. We'll help him kill a Dragon of the Blue Flame and go to Armard afterwards."

"Who is Kreel?"

"A Titan..."

"Another foe?" Draco smirked. "You seem to be collecting enemies—first a Siren, now a Titan. All you're missing is a Minotaur and a Cyclops and you'll have the full set."

"But you know yourself now that the list of our so-called enemies includes several races that we know of only by name. And that Titans as it turns out aren't the great enemies they were made out to be. If we speak honestly, it was we who were the enemies of the entire world..."

"You are right. Now I know...I still can't believe it. Okay, let's head out. I will look after Fleita, while you deal with the Milkman. The sooner we wrap it up here, the sooner we can go save our father..."

The house of the Happy Milkman was really situated beside the granny's house. Fleita was sitting in front of the gate to the latter, acting like she didn't know I was there. She even turned away demonstratively when Draco cracked up at her turned-up nose. She really was a girl with a character—and not the sweetest one...I wonder if she's like this in real life too...

"Greetings, your highness," a man in a white frock said to me. He was fiddling with a torn rope and bell in his hands and kept looking in the direction of the woods.

"I heard you need help..."

"What? Who? Are you here to see me?" the NPC said puzzled. Then, however, he gathered his thoughts and told me about his tragedy—how his only livelihood had run off to the forest which was brimming with wolves. And how he'll never get first prize in dairy expositions now and how, in general, all the cows of this world have it in for him.

"Why'd you decide that all of a sudden? It's not like cows have a professional guild whose leader has decided that you should punished."

"What else am I supposed to think when these ungrateful beasts slip out of their pens every day and run off into the woods? In the five years that I've been in the dairy business, I've gone through five hundred cows. All of them run away to the forest first chance they get. Sometimes they're brought back by kind strangers like you, but the brainless things still only want to get back to the woods, where the wolves eat them sooner or later. These overgrown babies are so fearless and obsessed with dying that the cow vendor is all but camping in front of my house. By the way, you don't feel like hunting some wolves, do you? I have nothing to give you as a bounty, but I heard that Zane the Tanner likes a good wolf fur. He'd be happy to take a dozen off your hands, and I wouldn't mind seeing some payback for my little heifers."

"How can you afford all this?" I asked surprised. "A cow isn't cheap."

"Every time I buy a new one, I insure it with the Mayor. They even came to check on me already—to see if I don't let the cows out on purpose to collect on the insurance. And, can you believe it, the cows just scurried past the investigators into the forest! They caught one and put her back into the pen, and came back the next day to check again. And that mad cow galloped off into the woods again...Oh...How I'm tired of all this! Five years and every day it's the same old thing. They've even started calling me the Happy Milkman as a joke—I've never even tried a drop of my cows' milk. I never manage to milk them in time!"

Quest available: 'Wolf Hunt.' Description: Kill 10 wolves in the forest outside of Carnue and bring 10 wolf furs to Zane the Tanner. Quest type: Common. Reward: +40 Reputation with Lestran Province and +200 Experience. Penalty for failing/refusing the quest: None.

"I'll do both—kill the wolves and find your heifer," I assured the Happy Milkman. "Or what's left of her—so don't worry. Tell me instead the direction she ran in."

"Over there," the man pointed at the tree line. "Escaped this morning...No doubt she's already been eaten, the poor thing..."

Leaving the Happy Milkman, whose name was actually Amir—a very odd name for an NPC by the way and odder still since his neighbors were named Zane and Agrippina—I headed towards the forest. As we had agreed, Draco stayed back to watch what Fleita would do, so I walked alone and...found myself really enjoying myself. How I missed this—walking through the forest all by myself without anyone to distract me with conversations, buzzing in my ear, asking for favors...The weather was excellent, the sun was out, the birds were singing, a cool breeze played around me scattering the sun's heat but not blowing so hard as to give me a chill...How great life was!

I tore the wolves to little pieces—literally. My Dragon Rank allowed me to use Thunderclap, which was an Intellect skill that launched a sonic boom at my enemy. So in short order, all that remained of the Level 65 wolves who'd come out to see their uninvited guest was their furs, which I needed to complete the quest. It turns out that I'm not that weak of a Dragon—as long as I used my powers right.

Roar—fur, another roar—another fur. Despite the fact that I'm only a Rank 11 Dragon, I was a Level 130 player—which in some mysterious way strengthened my Dragon Form. I had no idea how and didn't feel like thinking about it. The day was just too nice for it.

"Moo..."

It took me half an hour to locate the 'cudster.' Having played their role by dying and dropping their furs, the wolves had disappeared as if there hadn't even been any of them in the forest, so I walked along the ordinary grass of a leafy forest enjoying my stroll. In truth, you couldn't even really call this a forest—it was too well taken care of, without a single fallen tree or branch. There weren't even any leaves on the ground—just grass. And very green grass at that. I got the impression that I was strolling through a city park, instead of a forest brimming with predators. It seems that the developers had missed their mark here a bit. During my entire journey through this forest park I only encountered one ditch, in the center of which as if following the rules of the fantasy genre, stood the cow lowing bitterly, bemoaning her horrible fate. She could easily have stepped out of the ditch if she just turned around and gone home, but wishing to escape Amir, she stood there against the far wall of the ditch looking up and bellowing across the whole forest in her wild inhuman voice. Stupid cow...

The animal reacted fairly calmly to my appearance, as if she was used to seeing me every day and in general we were friends that went way back. I tossed a rope over her neck but the cow went on mooing sadly and looking up without making any attempt to turn around.

"What do you have, a nest there or something?" I muttered, turned into my Dragon Form and flew up into the air. It was odd—the cow wasn't even afraid of a toothy monster like me. She reacted so little that you could think that there were flocks of Dragons flying around her head every day.

Rising above the ditch didn't clarify anything for me—it was quite ordinary. Earth, grass, the odd pebble—there was nothing else there—neither a cave nor a hole—nothing that could possibly cause the horned beasts to run away from home and come here every day. What else could it be? I opened my map and saw that, in effect, the cow had traveled in one continuous path: If I connected the three points—Amir's house, the entrance to the ditch and the current location of the cow, then I'd get a straight line. That meant that the cow had some goal in mind and I simply had to find out, life or death, where this line led.

I marked the direction on my map and turned to the cow, transforming back into my human form. Taking the rope, I sighed bitterly—it looked like I'd have to do some heavy tugging. Only instead of a ship, I'd have a cow, and instead of water, I'd have the grass that this dumb beast would dig into with all four of her hooves. I considered turning into a Dragon and carrying her in my paws, but instantly rejected this idea—I had nothing to grab onto and might hurt her with my claws. I doubt that Amir would be very happy with that outcome...

Including my battle with the wolves, I had spent thirty minutes looking for the cow—but it took me two hours to haul her back. The cow resisted with all her strength and kept turning back to the ditch as soon as I let any slack accumulate in the line...Nothing helped: neither my pleading, nor my yelling, nor my attempts to bribe her with sweets that I had picked up in the Golden Horseshoe way back when...If anyone had seen me then, they would've died laughing: Shaman Mahan offering an NPC cow food from the finest dining establishment of Barliona—and she just flicks her tail idly and turns up her snout as if I'm offering her trash. I had nothing else to do but grit my teeth and yank the dummy after me...

"Bessie!" yelled Amir, as soon as we emerged from the woods. My Energy had decreased to thirty points for the third time and a notification appeared to warn me that I was exhausting myself. Stopping to rest, I was surprised to see the mean and very rude cow—who had only several seconds ago tried to entrench herself into the earth with all four hooves—lifted her tail and happily trundled off towards her owner. Wagging her tail left and right, she looked exactly like a dog.

"Oh thank you, Mahan!" Shutting the cow in her pen, Amir approached me. "I thought that the wolves had already eaten her, but you found her, the sweet darling. And the wolves? What about them? Did you see them?"

"I saw them and collected ten furs," I replied, receiving the reward for bringing his cow back from the Milkman. "Who do I give them to? You or do I need to take them to the Tanner?"

"You can give them to me. I'll pass them on," Amir said, marking the second quest complete as well. Since my Attractiveness with this NPC had now surpassed 45 points, I decided to ask Amir some more about his cows and odd name.

"Oh! That's an interesting story," smiled the Milkman, inviting me into his house. "Please, make yourself at home! You brought back my Bessie, so I owe you at least a story about how a resident of the famed city of Cadis ended up so far away from his native land—and in a little village to boot."

Amir's house turned out to be fairly comfy and urbane: It was filled with thoughtfully arranged, plush furniture and a fireplace which would be out of place in a typical village hut where ovens were the norm. Several shelves, a pair of paintings, white curtains— the interior of this place in no way resembled that of a dairy farmer's abode...It was too reminiscent of an urban residence.

"What kind of tea do you prefer? Black or green?" Amir called from the kitchen.

"Black as a rule, but if my honorable host doesn't mind, I'd like to treat him with a tea brewed according to a rare recipe," I offered on a hunch. Something told me that the more Attractiveness I'd earn with Amir, the more interesting our conversation would be. By making tea for this NPC, I should definitely boost this stat by a few more points.

"Oh! With pleasure! I adore tea and try to learn anything I can about it. What do we need to make your recipe?"

Opening my cookbook, I found the recipe for Aromatic black tea and grinned, remembering how I had offered it to the old ladies...Though, truth be told, I had slipped them some liqueur to turn the tea into something more 'dazzling' so...I wonder whether the same trick will work on Amir?

"Nothing special—Leaves of the highland tea tree and a little liqueur."

"Liqueur?" Amir asked surprised. "For what?"

"It's a secret," I smiled. "Let's just wait till I make it and you can try a sip."

"Okay...I am curious! Let's do it—I'll get you the leaves and liqueur. Then we'll see what kind of tea you brew..."

"...And then the city council kicked me out of the city like I was some stray dog," Amir concluded his tale in a mumbling voice and took another sip of tea. "I came here five years ago and have been trying to create the same heavenly flavor, but...It's some kind of curse or something! The cows are conspiring against me!"

"Why here though?"

"Where else was I supposed to go? Kartoss is scary—there aren't even any humans there—just orcs and goblins. Lestran happened to be on my way and it so happened that the village elder instantly gave me a house...So I've grown comfortable here..."

Amir's story really was quite interesting, for me at any rate. About ten years ago, Amir, a resident of Cadis, encountered some imported butter at a market. It was ordinary butter from cow's milk, which nevertheless tasted so good to Amir compared to the other butter he had tried that he bought the entire shipment. Amir was overjoyed when he received the hundred crates of this unearthly delight in his cellar. And it really was heavenly, since it would be pointless to compare ordinary butter with the one the merchant, who always wore a hooded cape, brought to Amir. Amir invited his neighbors to taste the new butter and even dared offer some to the city Mayor, who liked it so much that he asked Amir for some more of this dairy spread. The Mayor was receiving some guests and he decided to treat them with this wondrous dish. That's when the strange things started happening...

Overjoyed, Amir returned from the Mayor's house, ran down to his cellar where he kept the butter, opened the door and froze in his tracks—the cellar was empty. Not only had the butter vanished but also several wines that Amir was keeping for a rainy day, some cured meat that he had saved for his guests and some dried fruit...The cellar was so bare that, at first, Amir assumed that he had opened the wrong door. That was when the guards the Mayor had sent for the butter showed up—as it happened, the Mayor had already bragged about the delicacy to his guests and now wanted to treat them. But there were no treats left...

The next day was a nightmare for Amir—at first the shop was closed, ruining the harmony of the neighborhood, then someone set fire to the house, though thankfully the servants subdued the flames quickly, and after that the city council summoned Amir and declared him persona non grata for tricking the Mayor and embarrassing him in front of his guests. Amir was given a day to gather his belongings, sell his house for next to nothing, since no one wanted to buy it, and then he was literally thrown out beyond the town gates. The tragedy he'd suffered was so great that Amir promised himself that he would learn how to make this heavenly butter himself. Settling near Carnue, Amir began to pursue his life's goal—until he came up against the bovine conspiracy. The cows simply refused to give him their milk and ran off into the woods every chance they got.

"Now, you tell me, Mahan, what is this ill fortune?" Amir asked me with a wavering voice. It turned out it took very little of my tea to give him a buzz. "What have I done to offend Eluna that she sends me such trials and tribulations?"

"Maybe it has nothing to do with Eluna? Maybe it's your own fault?" I replied with a wavering voice as well. "Maybe you're meant to be a Smith, but you stubbornly insist on being a Milkman? How could you know?" I raised my index finger to emphasize my point.

"Why I'd be an awful Smith...I can't even hone a knife properly..."

"Brother!" Draco burst into the house, busting down the front door. "Hurry—Fleita is about to die!"

It occurred to me that respawning never really hurt anyone, but my body was already moving on its own without heeding whatever my mind was occupied with: Downing the rest of the tea, I darted after Draco to the street, turned into my Dragon Form and soared into the air to Amir's shocked gasp.

"Over here, hurry!" It was a short flight of no more than thirty meters, but Draco was rushing me so urgently that you could have thought that Fleita was on her last breath.

"Everyone stop!" I roared and landed heavily on the ground. Since in my Dragon Form I was a four-meter tall beast, everyone should probably be terrified of me. Even dumb, scripted mobs.

Fleita really wasn't doing so hot—her Hit Points were blinking red and she was down on the ground, meaning that her Energy was exhausted. Three giant rats were skittering around her. The Ratherd completed the scene—a goblin in a soiled cape, with a staff that resembled a crutch and that had some kind of beads wrapped around it. The rats didn't react much to my arrival—they squeaked, perhaps telling me what they thought of me, and turned back to gnawing on the girl's toes. The Ratherd, however, was more appreciative—his red eyes turned black for a moment, he froze as if refusing to believe his sight, but regained his composure and re-donned the grimace of an aggressive mob. Too late! I had already understood that I shouldn't kill him.

"Draco—take the rats!" I sent my Totem to Fleita's rescue and turned back into my human form. It would take several hours for the Level 80 Ratherd to kill little old Level 130 me. I stepped between the girl and the goblin and said, "Hang on! Let's talk!"

Right...The goblin instantly heeded my advice and in a clear and articulate manner elaborated the gist of his complaint...Like hell! Though this wrinkled green raisin had been momentarily afraid of the Dragon, when I became human, it seems that his brain short-circuited. I could clearly see the wheels spinning up there—'I'm looking at a person, so I have to kill him. I can't talk to a person...'

To my surprise, the Ratherd was a Kartossian Dark Shaman. He began to summon Spirits against me, babbling in Kartossian. At least it became clear where the goblin had gotten his get-up from. With his cape and staff, all he lacked was a fitting hat to look exactly like a High Shaman.

The hairs stood up on my nape as a shiver coursed down my spine.

High Shaman...A Dark High Shaman...A dark goblin who was also a High Shaman...A dark goblin...the Romeo and Juliet Achievement!

It took me a second to turn back into a Dragon, upon which I let the Ratherd have it with my tail, knocking him several meters back. Then, I cast Thunderclap. All foes within a 40 meter radius froze for a minute. More precisely the Ratherd and his rats froze, while I soared up into the sky and darted for the village center where the vendor's stall was supposed to be. I only had 60 seconds...

"I need green paint, a lady's leather skirt, a lady's leather tunic, a dark wig with long hair and a bone!" I fired in one go, falling right at the feet of the vendor. To give him his due, the guy wasn't taken aback for a second by the sudden appearance of a Dragon. Commerce trumps all. 20 seconds...

"I have what you want, but..."

"One thousand gold for the lot of it!" I interrupted the vendor.

"Two!" the jerk parried. No big deal—I'll remember this. Later.

"Agreed! Hand it over!"—40 seconds.

"Pleasure doing business..." the vendor began, but I could hardly hear him. Tossing the items into my bag I surged back into the air. Damn it—I'm running out of time. The minute's done...

"Draco—Thunderclap!" I yelled, banking and wheeling down toward the old lady's vegetable garden. The Ratherd had come to and was shaking his head, trying to clear his mind. Draco had finished off the three rats and was now glancing askance at the Ratherd without however aggroing him. What else— oh! Fleita's Energy had restored to the point that the girl could sit up and look around at what was going on. Let her spectate then—as long as she doesn't hurt the Ratherd...

"Fleita, help me!" I asked, realizing that I didn't have enough time. Slathering the paint on my face and arms, I threw on the skirt and jacket and stuffed enough grass under my shirt to give myself a female shape, but I didn't have time to shape the bone into a nose.

"What do you want me to do?" Judging by how promptly the girl took her place beside me, her Energy was coming back quickly.

"Take the bone and wire. I need to attach this to my nose. Make the clamps."

"Got it—I need a couple seconds."

A couple seconds...I remained focused on the Ratherd and was realizing to my great chagrin that we didn't even have that much. Just ten seconds...

"Time's up—give me what you have," I ordered. "Now take Draco with you and get out of here!"

"Argh! I'll kill you!" yelled the goblin coming to his senses, but I took several quick steps, stuck the bone onto my nose the best way it would fit, and sang in a mellifluous voice:

"Mmm...Hey handsome! Are you here alone, or what?"

Somewhere behind me I heard Fleita roaring with laughter—meaning she hadn't forgotten her Kartossian.

"What a babe!" The Goblin stopped and 'Charmed' appeared in his status effects. "I must have you!"

"Only if you catch me first!" I replied coquettishly and began to flee ladylike to the stunned amazement of Draco and the roaring laughter of Fleita. "You'll never catch me! You'll never catch me! Ha-ha-ha!"

Oh kill me.

I almost stumbled when I glanced back at the goblin who had now also gained the 'Aroused' effect—the entire fence was smattered with the heads of players watching the farce, while up in the air above us, some more players were spectating from their griffins. To my great disappointment, their cameras were all recording, meaning I was done for.

"Argh! I'll catch you!" screamed the goblin,

undistracted by the players. In fact I don't think anything could distract him right now—the Aroused effect had taken ahold of him too firmly.

I stopped and took out my Mallet and when my 'Romeo' came running up, desiring to envelop me in his embrace, I let him have it with the Mallet flush on his head, adding for good measure: "Yuck—what a monster." Fleita doubled over laughing, while the goblin received the 'Flirting' buff, upon which all three status effects united into one larger one: 'Love.'

I had attained my goal.

"Argh, what a beauty!" the goblin's red eyes turned dark, meaning that this mob had ceased to aggro.

"If anyone kills this mob," I yelled to my audience, warning the players, "he will become my personal nemesis! And if I assemble another group for a foray in the future, I certainly won't invite him! This is my mob that I need for a quest!"

Since the viewing public had already climbed over the fence, wishing to get closer to the spectacle, it stood to reason that there would be several dimwits among their number who would kill the goblin simply because they had the chance—so I figured a warning was in order. It'd be useless to try to scare them with the Sword of Damocles—i.e. Plinto—whereas banning them from future adventures would actually mean something to them. Since the public is recording video, they know who I am, which means they know what I've been up to.

"What's a beauty like you doing in a hole like

Malabar?" the goblin started up again, politely having waited until I'd done yelling at the bystanders.

"I'm looking for a true warrior worthy of my love!" It was hard to speak in a high-pitched voice, but I did my best.

"Me! I'm a true warrior! I defeated the Bloody Greemik, vanquished Lastirans and thrice took first place in my tribe for cleaning duties! My earring is the biggest, my staff is the hardest and longest among all the Shaman goblins. I'm that warrior that will have your love!"

"Why how can I love you if you keep pestering this town with your rats? What warrior would fight an old granny?"

"Oh great beauty! Don't believe your eyes! That monster you call a granny is a terrible witch! My tribe has a leader—the vile witch poisons his life! I am a great warrior. We've killed the old hag many times, but she continues to live! Every week she returns from the Gray Lands and does her black magic. My chieftain is ailing more and more, but we do what we can."

"We?"

"Me and my brothers from the tribe. Every week one of us is killed, but we must do as our chieftain commands—the granny must die! If we attack during the time of the sun, then at night the old woman goes to sleep and we kill her!"

"What do you need rats for though?"

"The witch is very clever and powerful. If she doesn't kill one of us, we can't get to her! The rats force her to bring Free Citizens who kill one of us and allow the rest to creep up to her at night. It was my time to die, but I have met my one true love and now I want to live!"

"Yes, truly you are a great warrior and I can love you," I told the goblin, stroking him between his ears a bit—and with my mallet smacked his hand, which had begun to reach for my uh, let's say, softer areas. "But you must prove that you are as great as you say you are. I want to speak with your chieftain. Who knows, maybe I'll be able to help him...will you let him know?"

"Of course, oh beauty, I will report to him immediately. I have to run, but...What about the witch?"

"I will deal with her, don't worry!"

A look of immense happiness appeared on the goblin's mug. He hopped up to kiss me—I managed to turn away in time and his kiss landed on my cheek—and then he vanished. Why look at that! There goes yet another Harbinger just wandering around and I'm not even aware of it!

"Mahan, my quest has been updated," said Fleita in Kartossian as soon as the goblin vanished. "I need to see the old lady and ask her some questions about witchcraft...Mahan...will you go with me? I'm sorry I behaved like an idiot...I realize that I said a bunch of things I shouldn't have and that I was mean, but...Can I be your student again?"

"What—to finish driving me insane?"

"But I apologized!"

"That's what I'm talking about…"

"Why, you no good…!" A litany of curses streamed from Fleita. I'd never imagine that such a young girl could possess such a lexicon of crude expressions!

"Let's do it this way—we will deal with the granny together and then decide what we'll do about your being my student. Just send me the quest…"

Quest available: 'Rat-catcher, Cont'd.' Description: You have spoken with the Ratherd and discovered that the old lady is a witch who is cursing the Ratherd chief with various ailments. Solve this issue with her. Quest type: Rare. Reward: +200 Reputation with Kartoss, −200 Reputation with Malabar and +600 Experience. Restrictions: Only for subjects of the Kartoss Empire or players from Malabar who have reached Friendly status with the Dark Lord.

Ta-da! A rare Kartossian quest found only in Malabar lands! Just sign on the dotted line!

"Does that mean that the first quest you received is gone?"

"No. It's marked completed. When I said the quest was updated, I didn't look in the right place—here it says 'Continuation,' do you see?"

"Yeah, I see, I see…Do you understand what this means?"

"Uh…no…should I?"

"It means that the Ratherds are the servants of

some guy from Kartoss who is causing trouble in Malabar!"

"And so what? I'm from Kartoss after all."

"But I'm not!"

"Oh—did you kill the rats already?" The granny approached us, interrupting our exchange in Kartossian and waving her arms happily. "And the Ratherd, curse his stars, was he here too?"

"He was, but he's gone now," I assured the old lady. "The Zombie scared him so much that he said he won't set foot here again."

"Oh I understand him very well. I all but went to meet Eluna when I first laid eyes on Fleita. To imagine what terrible black magic was used to raise someone from the dead and instill them with reason! Pure terror, no less! But I won't go back on my word—I gave you the quest, and I'll give you the reward for its completion…"

"Madam," I stopped the old lady as she was about to head off. "Could you be so kind as to treat us weary travelers to some tea? We're so tired after our rat catching that we can hardly move our feet. Some tea would help us immensely…"

Since I had Exalted status with the Province as well as various buffs that increased my Attractiveness, the old crone could hardly refuse me. Or so I thought…

"Oh no! I haven't cleaned the house. There's dust everywhere…and there's no tea! It wouldn't do to invite an Earl into a hovel like mine. So, please forgive me, your highness, but I can't treat you to tea…And anyway, you should wash up. Green make-up is unbecoming for an Earl..."

"Stacey, hi! I really need your help."

"What's up?"

"There's this NPC that I need to convince to invite me in for a chat. I'll share the quest with you when you show up. Are you at Friendly status with the Dark Lord?"

"Like you need to ask! So you're in Kartoss?"

"That's the point—I'm in Lestran..."

"Summon me!"

"Greetings!" sang Anastaria to the old lady in a voice so sweet that thousands of players would have gone mad hearing it. It took the girl several seconds to familiarize herself with the quest, make up her mind and put her plan into action. "Would you be so kind as to show me your teacup collection, Agrippina Dormidina? I've been dreaming of seeing it my entire life!"

"You look great by the way, Dan! Green really suits your complexion well!"

"Oh daughter—you should first recover your lost powers before trying to manipulate people! And even then, know who you're dealing with before trying!" the granny replied and, even as she spoke, she transformed to the point that I hardly recognized her. Despite her age, it seemed like the NPC standing next to us now was incredibly mighty and had some special skill that forced players to cower in fear before her. The Emperor, the Dark Lord, the High Priestess had this ability—as did this seemingly ordinary village granny, who respawned weekly.

You should have seen Anastaria's face. Her impenetrable mask twitched, revealing for a moment bafflement with a touch of shock. Stacey was at a loss...

"Please forgive me oh High Priestess. I was blind." In a flash, the girl bent her knee and bowed her head penitently.

"Oh come now, come now! I left that post a very long time ago, passing it on to a younger and more energetic Priestess. It was oh so very long ago...All right, let it be. I'll invite you in for some tea. But let me be very clear—that Zombie won't set foot in my house! I'll burn her alive...er, undead!"

"Dan...I don't know what to say...but oh do I love you! You've dug up the High Priestess of Eluna who abandoned her post fifty years ago...This is none other than Elizabeth's mentor!"

CHAPTER EIGHT
RETURN TO NARLAK

"WHERE DID YOU find a Zombie anyway?" Agrippina asked as she poured us some tea. The granny met my offer to help her make some tea with a sly smile and an astonishing familiarity with the consequences of adding liquor to tea. Telling me to go wash off the green paint, the old lady hauled the water herself and brewed her own tea.

"She's my student," I replied. I had returned to my typical human guise, picked up my cup and got comfortable in my chair. Agrippina's house turned out to be very comfortable and done up in hues of blue. Even the several houseplants on the windowsills had blue flowers.

"Who has ever heard of a Dragon taking a Zombie as his student?" Our host raised her eyebrows in surprise and turned to the girl: "Anastaria—why didn't you intervene?"

To my surprise, Fleita reacted quite normally to

being barred from the house. If she was offended, she didn't let it show. I sent her to the Milkman to discuss the broken door—since Draco had knocked it down, it was up to me to reimburse him.

"My husband is a mysterious being," Anastaria replied with a smile, avoiding for now the main subject of our conversation. Oh how tired I am of all this etiquette! Until you've spent a few hours discussing the weather, no one will get to the business at hand.

"What's true is true," Agrippina agreed. "Daughter, you are the only Warrior of Light to become a Paladin Captain in the past five years. I've met some Lieutenants, but no Captains yet...I'm curious to see how far you will go in your service."

"In three months I will have my trial to receive the rank of General," Anastaria replied, surprising both the old woman and me. Such seminal progress through her class was quite a thing! Although...No, I won't consider my own progress here—it's just me after all.

"So it's like that, huh? Have you been to Eluna's Chambers?"

"That was where I did my training to become a Captain and prepared for General rank. Eluna gave me time to get used to my new powers, but this Heart of Chaos..."

"Yes, that Geranika has lost his marbles completely..."

"You know Geranika?" Anastaria asked with some surprise.

"Why, who doesn't know that Shaman? Just because I live in a village doesn't mean I don't keep up with world affairs. I know all about Geranika, as well as Mahan's creation of the recipe for the Stones of Light. I haven't turned senile quite yet..."

"The Ratherd called you a witch." I grew tired of going in circles and decided to guide the conversation to the topic at hand. "He even gave us a quest to solve this problem..."

"A quest?!" the granny threw up her hands dramatically. "What else would you expect from a goblin?"

"Dan, don't rush things. Let me work on her a bit..."

"Please forgive my husband's impatience," Stacey took ahold of the conversation. "He's tired from his battle with the rats. The goblins wanted us to resolve the issue with you. I am naturally outraged that my husband negotiated with the Kartossians instead of destroying them outright. However...as I mentioned, he is a special person."

"Sorry, Stacey, what do you mean you're 'outraged?'"

"Just help me out here, Dan. If I call you an earthworm, you'll need to crawl on the floor. You've stumbled on a rare quest and we can't fail it. Try to be more open-minded to what I say!"

"You're a bit mean..."

"Mean but loving..."

"To resolve the issue..." Agrippina echoed. "So his affairs are so bad that he's even willing to use someone else to fix things?"

"Please forgive me, mother, but is there some way we can help you?" To my surprise, Anastaria dropped the topic of the goblin and steered the conversation in the direction of a new quest.

"No," the old lady shook her head, "you two can't. Perhaps you on your own can help, but your husband can't. He has too much...I don't even know how to describe it...wants and desires. Impulsiveness."

"Teacher?" the vision of Fleita that appeared in my mind was so unexpected that I said her name out loud. *"Teacher—I found the one who sends the Ratherds to the old lady. It's the Milkm—Oh!"*

The vision vanished and was followed by such a wave of sharp pain that I fell out of my chair and doubled over on the floor. Though it didn't last very wrong, it took a while for the pain to dissipate and fade. My vision darkened and a metallic taste filled my mouth. When I regained my ability to see and think, a notification had appeared before me:

Your student has summoned the Air Communication Spirit. Under the teacher-student rules, you have received 30% of the discomfort felt by your student. We request that you remind your student to follow the rules...

"Is everything all right with you, Mahan?" Anastaria asked anxiously out loud. It seemed that my convulsions had jammed our telepathic link.

"I need to get to Fleita," I wheezed getting to my feet. "My student..."

"Not out loud Dan. I understand—she's contacted you with a Spirit and channeled a portion of her pain to you. But...okay, go find her. I'll wrap it up here with Agrippina and then go force the Corporation to explain why the hell they're allowing such a link to exist between players. The teacher-student rules only apply to NPCs and players, not between two players."

"You know about that?"

"I've taught three NPCs. Trust me, I'm well acquainted with this issue. That's it—go!"

Even though they were neighbors, there were about forty meters separating Agrippina's and the Milkman's houses, so it took me about a minute to reach my destination. The door that Draco had torn down was already back in its place and bore no indication that something had recently happened to it. I paused before it, considering whether I should enter without knocking or be polite—when it opened and the Happy Milkman cast me a suspicious glance.

"Are you alone?" he asked with surprise. "Where are the guards?"

"There won't be any guards," I replied calmly. "How is Fleita?"

"She's alive and sleeping at the moment. I didn't wish to disturb her."

"She's sleeping?" I asked surprised. Fleita was not a prisoner and would most likely log out if she felt pain, not sleep.

"Come in, since you're here," the Milkman

stepped back allowing me to enter and instantly see the girl: Fleita's transparent projection was lying on the couch in the living room. My student had logged out of the game after all. However, following the quest requirements, she would return to the Milkman's house instead of to my side. By the way, we still hadn't gotten around to binding ourselves to each other...

"I never imagined that an Initiate Shaman could summon a Spirit of Communication," Amir said pensively, looking at the girl. From his perspective, she hadn't gone anywhere but merely fallen asleep— and that sleep could last five minutes until Fleita came to again as well as the rest of his life if she decided to stay out of Barliona for good. It was at this moment that I realized that the Corporation had officially confirmed that she was my student. It remained to be seen what Anastaria would uncover— but until her trial, Fleita was my student. It's odd—I wonder why the Corporation acquiesced to all this in view of my status as convict in Barliona.

"So what happened?" Without waiting for an invitation, I sat down at the same table where we had just recently taken our tea and cast the Milkman a glance. "Fleita shared with me the quest to resolve the issue with Agrippina."

"You're not from Kartoss," muttered Amir, taking a seat beside me.

"True, but I know the Dark Lord quite well." Opening my reputation stats, I sent a link to the Milkman. "I won't start hollering 'Help! Save me!

Guards!' until I've gotten to the bottom of what's going on. Please start with the cows. Why do they keep running away from you?"

"Because the stupid creatures can't stand being near an Incubus." It seems that these words were difficult for Amir to say because his face grew very grim. Maybe he expected me to jump up and start dashing around his house screaming my head off. Weird bunch, these NPCs.

"So your pretty story about the butter was just that, a fairy tale?" I asked calmly, thereby deeply shocking the Milkman.

"I am forbidden from lying. The master who summoned me a hundred years ago, bound me to speak only the truth...But he granted me the freedom to determine which truth I told."

"Who is your master then?"

"I will pretend like I didn't hear your question. Otherwise, I would have to attack and kill you. The master is long since playing with the cherubim in the gardens of Tartarus. Accordingly, a portion of his orders have waned in power. Still, there is no need to test them, Dragon."

"I understand...Amir, I would like to hear the full tale of how you came to Lestran, or that part of it which you are free to tell," I added, noticing that the Incubus had tensed up.

"Very well. I will try to satisfy your curiosity...The gist of my tale remains the same. A merchant brought some butter with a unique flavor to Cadis. I really did buy some, but not for me—rather for my master's descendant. I have been serving his house for hundreds of years. And I really did advertise the butter's heavenly taste until the Mayor himself was my acquaintance. But my master's descendants turned out to be weak, will-less and petty people...They ruined the shipment by putting it out into the sun and relishing the sight of the butter melting away into the earth. Even this was not enough because then they cleared out the rest of what was in the cellar. They drank the wine and tossed the cured meats to the dogs. When the town guard came to me with the Mayor's request for the butter, I had nothing to give him...Everything had been ruined. The city council exiled my master's descendants from Cadis—and me too among their number. My house was sold for next to nothing—and then the most terrifying thing came to pass: I was rejected. I gained my liberty. I spent several years wandering the world, stumbling from town to town, until I encountered the Ratherds in the Free Lands. These goblins were so hounded, so tattered, that I took pity on them and became their leader. The slave had become the master. A year later the Magister contacted me with an offer to settle near Carnue. Kartoss had certain designs on this territory—I'm sorry, but I can't tell you about them. Either way, to put the plans in effect, I had to kill an old lady. And moreover I had to do so with another's hands so that nothing would point to Kartoss's involvement. The deadline I had to do this has long passed. I already received a letter from the Magister stating that he was disappointed in me—and yet I have nothing better to do with my life...So this is what I do. My cows flee constantly. I ask the Free Citizens to find them as a form of entertainment. And later I send my Ratherds to my neighbor's vegetable garden. I don't have anything further to add...I was happy when this Kartossian girl appeared. I told her about my task here, but she summoned a Spirit of Communication and then fainted."

"That's not true. I didn't faint right away," Fleita protested from the couch. "First I said what you were up to and only after..."

"Good morning, student," I grinned.

"So you forgave me after all?"

"We'll see about that. So you summoned the Spirit?"

"Well...when I found out about the Incubus, I knew I had to tell you right away, since you went off to deal with this issue with the granny...I became very worried that you'll kill her and...I don't even really know how I managed to do it. I simply wanted to very badly, so I recited my poem and..."

"Poem?"

"Kornik taught me," Fleita's already pallid face grew even whiter. "*One, two, three, Shaman flee—to your feelings and be free!*"

"E-ehh..."

"Well it helps me, all right? If I recite it like a mantra, I can work with the Spirits...So that's what I...Oh damn! Say, does it always hurt this bad?"

I had already opened my mouth to reply when another thought occurred to me and refused to leave.

"Kornik, my dear teacher, why didn't you, oh most honored one, tell me that thirty percent of the pain I've been feeling was being channeled to you?"

"How many times do I have to tell your dimwit self that you can't get in touch with me! You don't have your Shamanic powers! And anyway, were that not the case, do you think I'd humor and tell you?"

"No, but..."

"So forget about it! And remember—you don't have your powers so stop screwing around!"

"Are you even listening to me, Mahan?" Fleita flared up again. "I'm telling him about how much I'm hurting and he just stands there with his eyes all glassy and stares into nowhere! That's not fair!"

"Just hold on a second please, Fleita," I replied and reached out to Anastaria in my mind:

"Stacey, what's going on with Agrippina?"

"Nothing. She's been living here about fifty years and she's already grown accustomed to the Ratherds that have been hunting her for the past ten years or so. Unlike Slate, whom the Emperor has cursed to respawn once every six months, Agrippina has been cursed by Eluna herself. She was the High Priestess after all. This is why she gets reborn once a week. Initially she tried to deal with the rats on her own— then she gave up and started hiring Free Citizens to do it. The sisters that live here are her acolytes, who followed their High Priestess into exile. What about you? What do you have?"

"I have a hunch that we should invite Agrippina over to the Milkman's house...There's something she'd

want to know over here..."

"...And that's the way things stand," I came to the end of my tale and reclined in my chair. The idea of having Amir meet with Agrippina came to me spontaneously, so I trusted my premonition and arranged for a grand meeting where I told the full story of what was going on. About the Magister and about the High Priestess and about the state of humanity. "I'll point out right off that the Empires are at peace right now, so there's no point in maintaining hostilities or seeking vengeance against each other. Let's just chat..."

"And there I was trying to guess why his cows keep running off to the forest...I thought that something was summoning them. I even tried to go looking for them myself, but this..." the former High Priestess said pensively, avoiding her neighbor's eyes.

"And I kept wondering at your ability to return from the dead," added Amir, studiously examining the tablecloth of his table as if he'd never seen it before.

"Dan, I have a suspicion that you found another launch point for Kartoss. The High Priestess, Kartoss, the attempts on her life...I'm starting to wonder if there are some Transformers nearby? We'll have to take a look..."

"All right guys," I made my decision when it became clear that the NPCs weren't going to keep talking. "Mark our quests completed and let's get on with life. You can figure out the problem between you without our help. Amir, just stop sending your Ratherds. Don't you feel sorry for them? They keep getting killed...Stacey, Fleita, let's go...There's nothing more for us to do here..."

Leaving Amir and Agrippina on their own, we stepped out on the street.

"You know, Mahan, when that video of you painted green shows up, I'll be sure to save it for posterity," smiled Anastaria. "When I saw you, I almost lost my ability to speak—particularly once your right boob slipped down to your belly. Maybe warn me the next time you decide to cross-dress. Where are you off to now?"

"To Altameda. We only have a week before we have to meet Kreel. I want to craft some more rings so that Clutzer and Magdey will leave me alone."

"I heard that you gave Barsina money to take classes?"

"She's done a lot for the clan. I mean, she effectively made the clan what it is, so it was the least I could do to thank her. Fleita," I looked over at my student, "are you with me?"

"Yes," the girl nodded immediately. "I'm definitely not leaving you now. The way you handled those two quests was so cool..."

"In that case, let's make an agreement," I grinned. "Either it's time we introduce some punishment for bad behavior..."

"*Keep in mind,*" Stacey butted in telepathically, "*that tonight I will come visit you and I demand you punish me, 'cause I've been behaving very badly...*"

* * *

"Say, Viltrius," I said to my majordomo the morning after we returned to my castle. "Can Altameda teleport anywhere on the continent?"

"Since the castle originally belonged to the Free Lands, yes. The castle may teleport anywhere in Kartoss, Malabar as well as the Free Lands. However, the appearance of the Shadow Empire changed this. We have nothing to do with it, so we can't open a teleport to a location within its boundaries. And yet we can still summon any sentient from any point on the continent—excluding from jail."

"Why?" I asked surprised.

"Because special spells are employed when jails are built that block teleportation. Are you planning on going somewhere, Master?"

"Not really, but...Tell me—could you send me to the following coordinates?" I dictated the coordinates of the buildings in Narlak that belonged to Astrum. As I was going through my mail today, I stumbled across Kalatea's explanation for how teleportation across the continents worked:

Hey Mahan!

A mere thank you wouldn't really do justice to your discovery. You're right—the building on your continent at the coordinates you sent really is Astrum territory and as a Harbinger I can teleport there without any problem. This really grants me new options for travel. I won't be able to meet you personally to give you my present, and I won't send it by post either. But I'd like to see your face when I hand it to you, so I asked the residents of one of those houses to confirm their receipt of the package and send me a recording of you opening it. Accordingly, you should check out the house at the coordinates you sent. I'm sure you'll like the present I've prepared for you.

Good luck!

Kalatea, Harbinger of Astrum.

"Pardon me, Master, for reasons unknown to me, I cannot open a portal to that location."

"Then cast one to a nearby point and be prepared to haul me out at a moment's notice. Draco—do you feel like dropping in on Narlak and causing a little ruckus there?"

"Like you need to ask!"

"Fleita?" I smiled at the pouting girl. A single signed document and I was now facing the perfect student—no arguments, no cursing, no yelling. Sheer constructive criticism and positivity. It's too bad it was temporary, since soon enough she'd forget all about our contract...that's the kind of person she was.

"If his majesty deigns to bring along unworthy old me, then of course I want to go! Is there a reason for causing a ruckus there?"

"Sure—Mahan is at Hatred status with that city," Draco showed off his erudition. "As soon as he shows up, he and everyone with him will be arrested and taken to jail. And later kicked out of town..."

"Hatred? Is that even...Well, whatever, I want to go! Big deal—jail!"

"Viltrius, cast the portal..."

The door with the four-leaf clover against the background of a yellow sun had not changed one bit since the first time I saw it. I entered the portal last so that I could immediately dash into the Astrum house and ask to be let in—but my precaution was unwarranted: Our appearance in Narlak went entirely unnoticed. There were no guard patrols nearby, so I calmly approached the door and knocked.

"Who's there?" came the question from behind the door.

"Shaman Mahan with two companions. I was told that you have a present for me."

"Please enter," the door opened to reveal a woman who resembled an Indian, ushering us inside. To create the impression of a foreign environment, the woman spoke with a heavy accent, as if she'd never become fluent in Malabarian. "Beg your pardon—not everyone has woken up yet, so I will take you to the living room and call our boss."

"Of course, we'll be happy to wait," I assured her, taking my seat on the indicated couch.

"Mahan—why are we here?" Fleita sat down beside me and began to question everything. "Keep in mind that I don't have a lot of time today. I promised mom to go to the store with her after lunch."

"It won't take long. They'll give me the prize and we'll be on our way."

"Prize? Cool! For who? And from whom?"

"Yes, a prize. For me from a Harbinger. You owe me three hundred gold."

"Huh?" Fleita paled.

"How many times have I told you to stop asking me questions about every little step I take? Remember the demon who tried to get you to pay? Well, I've decided to follow his example and make some profit from your incessant inquiries."

"That's not fair! I'm simply curious. How am I supposed to find out without asking you?"

"You could always eavesdrop," replied a tall, old man who had entered the living room. "Or you could interrogate, steal or blackmail to get the information you want. Really there are many options for obtaining information, my dear guest. Allow me to introduce myself—I am the Astrum envoy to Narlak, General Cortes."

"It's a pleasure to meet you, General," I stood up from my couch and warmly squeezed the man's hand.

"I am a plainspoken man," Cortes went on, once we'd sat back down, "so allow me to get right to the business at hand. I don't like to beat around the bush much."

"I am fully in agreement there," I replied with relief. "We are of one mind when it comes to this..."

"In that case, let me warn you ahead of time that Kalatea asked that our conversation be recorded onto a crystal. The Harbinger wished to see your reaction to her present. If you have objections to this, it would be better if you stated them now."

"Kalatea warned me about this, so everything is

all right."

"Well...Since we have dispensed with the formalities, please accept the present that our Harbinger prepared for you. I really do hope you will find it pleasing."

Cortes produced a small case from among the folds of his uniform and offered it to me. I'll admit that I was counting on some unique Shamanic item, so I opened the case with a little puzzlement and stared dumbly at the document inside.

Hello again, Mahan!
Don't even ask how I managed to come by this—there definitely won't be a second opportunity like this. Enjoy!
Kalatea, Harbinger of Astrum.

Why is it that girls always like to make such a hubbub about presents, drop all kinds of hints and enigmatic allusions—to hand you a gift certificate for a pair of socks? And then they tap their toes in expectation of your oaths of love and devotion...What could be so unique and amazing about a piece of paper?

Mahan!
I invite you and your spouse to take part in the celebrations of the thousand-year anniversary of my reign. The event will be held in two months at the Astrum palace. My Mages will arrange for a portal for you.

Almazitor, Ruler of Astrum.

The system informed me that the two tickets I had received were for admission to the celebration at the Astrum palace, but I was in such a state of shock that I paid this no attention. To visit the palace of the Emperor—or Ruler, to be more precise—which was located on the neighboring continent, is an insanely expensive gift from Kalatea. I can't even imagine what I'd have to do to receive something like this from my own Emperor.

"This was the very reaction that Kalatea warned me about," smiled Cortes, recalling me back to my senses. Draco and Fleita were impatiently waiting to see the gift that had turned their Shaman into a statue, so I made the invitation's properties available to them and placed the document back in its case.

"Whoa! Will you summon me, brother?" Draco instantly asked.

"The letter doesn't say that I can't summon my Totem."

"But it does say that you can only be accompanied by one person," Fleita muttered, crestfallen. "I've never visited the Dark Lord, nor even the Emperor of..."

"Gentlemen, I must request you leave this house now. The Guardian has informed the Council of your arrival in the city and the town guards have already been waiting for a minute for my permission to enter this house and arrest you. Pursuant to the laws in force, I am allowed to bar them for no longer than two minutes—after which the guards are free to enter whatever they wish."

"Viltrius," I called my majordomo, "summon us back! We're done here..."

"Please forgive me, Master, but that is not possible..."

"Viltrius?"

"If understand our demon correctly, you are not technically located on our continent. The demon we are employing is not capable of summoning you from a different continent...I can try and find a more powerful demon, but I will need several minutes to do so and our costs will double. Shall I find a different demon?"

"It's not necessary," I barked and hung up. It took me just a few moments to make my decision: "General, do you have a rear exit?"

"I'm sorry, but there are no exits that you could use to escape. The house is fully surrounded by the guards, who will enter in twenty seconds..."

"Fleita, just don't start hollering—you're about to ride on a Dragon. Draco, get ready—as soon as we step out, we're taking off. Let's go! General, thank you for your hospitality and please forgive the inconvenience."

"I understand. It happens." Cortes shrugged his shoulders, yet I couldn't even see him. I couldn't turn into my Dragon Form inside the house—I might get stuck, so...

"Mahan! You and your companions are under arrest!" As soon as I opened the door, three spear tips pointed at my throat, while the system notified me that all spells—including portals—were blocked in a ten meter radius around me. I hadn't even managed to turn into my Dragon Form! As far as I'm concerned, respawning isn't such a big deal—however, if they kill Draco, he'll lose ten levels, and I really don't want that...

"We give up," I agreed, wishing to keep my Totem safe. Trying not to provoke the guards, I turned my head and saw them cast several metallic nets over Draco, wrapping him from nose to tail while likewise brandishing spears in his face. I wasn't sure what had become of Fleita because she was behind my back.

"You shall be incarcerated in Narlak jail for 24 hours, after which you will be escorted from the city's territory. If you are seen in this city again, you shall be detained for another 48 hours. You must answer for your trespass!"

There was no trial as such—with a reputation like mine, there wouldn't be one anyway, so hardly several minutes passed before the heavy iron doors clanged shut, cutting me from the game for 24 hours. It's a good thing at least that this is merely a gameplay imprisonment because otherwise I'd be back in Pryke Mine right now back at square one.

All three of us had been placed in different cells. Fleita was sent to a special women's cell and only received a sentence of two hours—for being in my company. Draco and I, however, were issued the full sentence.

"Stacey, hi! What are you doing?"

"I'm trying to complete another of Nashlazar's trials. What about you?"

"Sitting behind bars in a dank dungeon...a young Dragon stripped of his freedom."

"What bars? Crap! I failed the trial again...Where are you?"

"In Narlak...Sitting here, bored..."

"But you're at Hatred status with them! For how long?"

"24 hours..."

"Got it...Well it's not a big deal. Sit it out. It'll do you some good."

"Hey! I'm talking to you!" Someone flung me around roughly, tearing me from my pleasant chat. Raising my head, I was so stunned that for a moment I forgot that I was in a game. Before me stood a gigantic, unshaven thug with the fancy name of Calrandos. He wasn't wearing a shirt, evidently wishing to show to the world his triangular torso—the fantasy of women and envy of men. He was also missing two teeth and bore a very unfriendly expression on his face, which promised me nothing good. Calrandos was quite the terrifying sight. "You better sit still and stay quiet! Stool pigeons like you are the last thing we need in our cell! Get in your corner!"

Why look at that! Welcome to Pryke Part 2! The three months I had spent in the mine instantly flashed before my eyes, so instead of submitting to the bully—and in terms of Strength, this monster really did have me beat, a fact made worse by the unavailability of magic in the cell—I straightened my shoulders and gave this gorilla an assured look. I'm going to let some program browbeat me? In its digital dreams! Even Prontho couldn't manage that!

"How dare you speak to me like that, maggot?" I said the first thing that came to mind. "To your knees this instant—you are facing an Earl!"

My 88 points of Charisma with all its attendant bonuses granted me the hope that in several minutes I would become the 'boss' of this cell. The Imitators simply have nothing else to do than to follow my orders, which is why I didn't anticipate the stiff straight that sent me flying across the cell. The last thing I saw before losing consciousness was a message that I had taken damage and received the 'Disoriented' debuff for ten minutes. After that, my eyes shut and I along with my Level 88 Charisma drifted off to non-being.

"...Say, he hasn't moved in a while," said a creaky senile voice through the murk of unconsciousness. "You didn't off him by any chance, did you?"

"Ah he's a Freemie. If you off them they vanish and come back again later. He's fine. No but did you see what an ass he was? 'On your knees...!' Argh. Could the boss really find no better rat?"

"You'll pay for that." Back at Pryke, I had learned once and for all—never let anyone humiliate you, or you'll be far worse off later. Since I have 24 hours ahead of me here, I'd prefer to pass it in peace and harmony—that is, without listening to endless insults from some overgrown Imitator. On the other hand, I knew I'd have to earn the respect too.

"I told you he's fine," said Calrandos, at which point I felt my head shatter into a hundred little shivers that all went flying every which way. Thankfully, the system informed me that I was okay but had to sit out another 10 minutes. He'd used his foot that time...

"...Eh, I wish I'd ran into this Freemie on the seas," Calrandos' wistful voice broke through the film of fog and ushered me back into the game. "I'd have a nice chat with him..."

"So what's the problem?" My words didn't come out very clearly as if my mouth was full of cotton and I had to spit a couple times to keep talking. "Once we're out, we'll head to the sea. We can settle our accounts there and let it go which way it will."

"Hold on, Calran," spoke up the now familiar senile voice. It sounded like the thug was about to knock me unconscious again. "The sea doesn't care for empty words, Freemy! If you have a ship, let's see who has the better crew! Are you ready to wager two months' work on my ship if you lose?"

Oh no way—these guys are pirates! Sitting up on the floor I looked at the gaunt old man. I didn't pay any attention to the musclehead—one way or another my conversation would be with Darius, as this prune was called.

"I don't have a ship at the moment." The fire in Darius' eyes went out, as he'd expected more from me, so I went on: "But I won't refuse your bet. As soon as I get out of here, I'll get a ship. Surely Grygz the Bloodied Hoof will let me borrow one of his ships. I'll think of something for the crew on my own."

"You know Grygz?" The old man's face changed to such sincere astonishment that I couldn't help but laugh. Opening the properties for 'Pirate Brethren, Step 1,' I sent the quest description to Darius. There's no harm in letting the NPC see it, especially considering he's a pirate.

"Well then, Freemie, now we're talking," the old man perked up. I have a task for you. I need you to deliver something to Grygz..."

"Darius!" yelled the thug, but the old man silenced him with a glance.

"We're to be hanged on the morrow—and not even from a yard or a measly mizzen. No, they want to hang us from a landlubber's gallows..."

"Why did you suggest the bet then?" I asked surprised. "If tomorrow you're to be..."

"Tomorrow's a ways away!" the old man cut me off. "When tomorrow comes, we'll talk about it. For the moment life goes on as it always has! Will you do what I ask?"

"What do I need to deliver?"

"A message...word for word. It's too bad I don't have any paper to write it down."

"I have paper, but that can wait." A plan was forming in my mind. If I was about to get another pirate quest, then it wouldn't do to accept it without Evolett. "When's the execution?"

"Your mail won't work here," smirked the ruffian

when I received a notification that my message would be delivered only once I'd been released from jail. "And messages inside the clan as well. They want to do us in early in the morning so they can feel good the rest of the day..."

It was only then that I noticed the utter silence in the clan chat—it was dead empty as though all the players had logged out to reality, leaving me one on one with the game's limitations. Were I an ordinary player, I'd pop out to reality myself, get in touch with Evolett and advise him to storm the town and the jail, but of course I wasn't allowed to do this...

Then again, I always have Anastaria!

"Stacey, hello again!"

"What—are you bored again and want me to keep you entertained?"

"Situation's changed drastically. You'll have to act as my messenger again. I will have to take breaks to let my Energy recharge but I need you to listen to what I want you to do..."

It took me about a half hour to describe the action. Most of this time I spent drinking whatever elixirs of Energy remained in my inventory. Telepathy sure does cost a lot of Energy.

"All right guys—now I have a lot of questions about Narlak's defenses." An hour later I returned to the pirates. Stacey told me that not only was Evolett interested in assaulting the city, but he was already mustering his players and by seven o'clock in the morning Narlak would come under attack—which no doubt would interfere with the execution. However, I needed to come up with whatever intel I could about this city.

"We don't really know that much," Darius replied indecisively, still unable to believe that some 'Freemies' would risk Hatred status with such a politically important port city over a bunch of pirates. "But there a few tidbits I can share. It's like this..."

The patrols along the walls reported back to their commander every minute by amulet. If even one report failed to come in, the city would raise a general alarm. Narlak knew what it meant to be careless with pirates around. It was better to apologize an extra time to some inconvenienced citizen and bawl out a careless guard than risk the city being plundered. Considering that about half of the city's armed forces were stationed at various castles like Glarnis, twenty minutes after the general alarm, the city's assailants would receive a hefty blow to their rear. You could of course assemble such a large army of players that any reinforcements would be crushed to dust, as would the city, but firstly, such an army would earn almost no loot—each player would gain a crumb or two—and second, there was no way to get it together in one night. I needed to mull things over...

The city was even better defended from the sea—catapults, ballistae, searchlights, magical shields—it would be easier to come in from the air...

The air!

"*Stacey, tell Evolett that the plan's changed. There's no need to take the city by storm—he won't manage it without good planning and the pirates we need will be fish food by then. I need a pair of Assassins who can infiltrate the city and break us out of the city jail."*

"I'll let him know—but Evolett really has his mind set on capturing Narlak."

"And he still can—but only after we break out of this place..."

"You want to fly out?"

"You bet!"

"Okay. Hold on. In an hour, one of our kobold acquaintances will pay you a visit. If Reptilis can't get into that cell, no one can..."

Waiting for something you have absolutely no control over is one of the most difficult things to do in this life. Until I made good on my promise to set everyone free, I didn't really exist for the pirates—why comfort yourself with a million to one chance? I was left alone, yet no one was overly friendly either. The developers really had created some colorful characters. I'd need to see if I could hire them somehow. But all that was for later. For now we had to wait for Reptilis.

"Boy, they really did tuck you guys away!" About five hours later we heard a smothered whisper, which caused the pirates to jump to their feet, arrange themselves back to back and clench their fists in anticipation of a brawl. By their faces I could tell that my cell mates were ready to give their lives—even though they still had no idea where the voice was coming from. And neither did I, for the cell door remained shut...

"Would you believe it? You two are truly a scary pair. I can hardly keep from shaking!" giggled Reptilis, as this was the voice of my kobold friend, and one of the cell's shadowy corners materialized into a smallish, green crocodile. "Well, what are you staring at? Are you going to bust out of here or what?"

"Mahan, is this your kobold?" Darius asked carefully.

"Not really his," Reptilis answered for me. "In fact, you could say, I'm not his at all. But I'm with him, yes. As I understand it, you lot need to come with too, right? You there—steroid junkie," the kobold's crooked finger pointed at Calrandos, "you wouldn't happen to know how to be skinnier? Sewage pipes are, uh, not really meant for waste of your girth."

"Can't we just open the door?" I asked Reptilis, shocked at his manner of infiltrating our cell. Unlike players, most NPCs played their roles perfectly—and this included going to the bathroom when necessary, which meant that most buildings had plumbing as well, but escaping through the sewage pipes...I wouldn't dream of it. Compared to our last meeting, Reptilis had grown a lot. I was now looking at a Level 212 Assassin, glimmering with the star of a First Kill. He was also the lone member of the 'Reptilis' Exclusive Clan for Himself' clan. The guy really had a sense of humor about him...

"Sure, if you want the entire city guard to show up here. There're so many spells on these doors that unless you really roll up your sleeves and break them the right way, which would take four hours or so, there's no point in even touching them. So the problem remains—unless this heap of flesh can suck it in and I mean really suck it in—we can't do anything with him."

Seven out of eight, including the leader—Darius—was a pretty good escape rate, but I had a bad feeling about leaving the giant. Even though Calran had really let me have it a couple of times, this enormous NPC had something about him that wasn't evident at first glance, but that was still very much there. I was curious to find out exactly what...

"Will the others get through for sure?" Calran asked.

"Who knows?" Reptilis smirked. "Maybe they will, maybe they won't. But you're a lost cause, that's for sure."

"In that case, I'll remain here," Calran said decisively.

"Okay, but spare us the grandiloquent speech asking us to tell your offspring to not sell the family farm," Reptilis jeered, after which he turned to me and pointed at the toilet. "Since everyone's ready, then, after you, your highness..."

"Get the pirates out," I made my decision, "and then open the door. We'll escape through the roof..."

"Your cell is located at the bottom floor of this building. There are twelve floors above us, including several dungeons. As soon as the cell is opened, as I already explained, the entire city guard will rush here...Naturally, I couldn't care less, but Anastaria requested that I break you out. She didn't say anything about adding an escape attempt to your sentence."

"Reptilis—get the pirates out," I reiterated implacably to the mini-crocodile. "We'll figure out my escape after that's done."

"Goddamn idiot," Reptilis said to himself, shook his head and made one more attempt to appeal to my reason. "Do you even realize that you're currently obsessed with saving a piece of software code?"

"Are you still here?" I arched an eyebrow in surprise. "I thought you had no time to spare..."

The kobold again muttered something to himself about my intelligence and then demonstrated to the pirates the correct way to dive into a toilet. Watching the sinewy pirates struggle to squeeze through in his wake, I knew for certain that I wasn't going to follow them...It wasn't even about the smell—it's simply unbecoming of an Earl to go crawling around some pipes...Okay, okay, that's a lie—it was very much about the smell.

"Can't do much damage with empty hands," Calran mused sadly. "Eh...If I just had a scimitar right now—boy I'd show these scurvy dogs how to sail straight and true..."

"*Stacey, Reptilis came by and picked up the pirates. One of them remained. I'm planning on making my way out through the roof with him. Send Reptilis a Level 200 scimitar, will you? We're going to swashbuckle a bit here.*"

"*What, without me? And you call yourself my*

husband! So be it—you'll have your scimitar."

"Reptilis, are you with us or what?" I asked the kobold when he reappeared and, without saying anything, pulled a scimitar out of his inventory and handed it to me. "As I recall, you really like gassing everyone around you. That could be really handy right now."

"I still can't figure out what Stacey saw in you..." said Reptilis instead of answering my question. He approached the door, leaned back on his tail and froze. His narrowing and widening eyes told me that Reptilis was occupied with lockpicking—without using his hands somehow. I'll have to look up exactly how that's supposed to work.

"Okay, here's the deal—there are five protective spells on this door and one lock. I can break the lock and dispel three of the spells, but the remaining two will take me up to two hours each. That is—it could take ten seconds if I guess the code on my first try, or it could take two hours if I have to go through all the possible permutations. It's five in the morning right now. The hanging, as I understood it, is scheduled for seven, so you two need to make up your minds: Are we going to break out quietly but without any guarantees of success or are we going to cause a ruckus but leave here no matter what?"

"What's all the security for?" I said with surprise, handing the scimitar to Calran and forming a raid group out of the three of us.

"I'd guess you've really hurt the locals' feelings?" Reptilis shrugged. "Anyway, what's our move?"

"Who will be notified by the remaining two spells?" Calran asked.

"How would I know?" Reptilis replied. "Since everyone's ready—I'm opening her up..."

The siren began to blare as soon as the door cracked open. Reptilis hummed to himself thoughtfully, as though something had gone differently than he had expected, and then said:

"Follow me."

Even though the kobold was helping us, I had no illusions about his intentions: The first time we met, this player was ready to sacrifice me to complete one of his quests, so it was a bit difficult to believe in his altruism. No doubt he had in mind to dig around the local castle to see what loot was lying around, which meant that our escape was little more than a diversionary tactic for him.

"Halt!" the door we were rushing toward flew open and three Level 150 guards burst through it.

"Mine!" Calran yelled, rushed ahead and swung his scimitar several times. The system announced that I'd received experience, even though Calran couldn't actually kill the guards—at one Hit Point, they just collapsed to the floor and lay there awaiting healing. "Where to next?"

"Up the stairs until they end!" ordered Reptilis and began to ascend. We could hear the clamor of running feet and the clatter of steel coming from the doors we ran past, but we continued up the stairs without even a thought of stopping.

"Through that door—move it!" Reptilis yelled. He

stopped and cast a cloud of venomous-green gas. "I don't know what you did to piss off the locals, Mahan, but I know they don't send gnashers after any old runaway.

"Gnashers? What is that—some kind of monster?" I asked with surprise, dashing through the door that Reptilis shut right behind me.

"They're really annoying guards," Calran replied. "You only find them in treasure vaults brimming with gold...Reptilis—are you sure that was a gnasher?"

Was I tired—or did I detect a note of curiosity in Calran's voice? There's a pirate for you! Even in the face of death he won't miss a chance to get his paws on some loot.

"I'm sure. I stunned him for a little while. When he comes back to his senses...well, this door sure won't stop him. I got a look at his Level though—he's a 300."

"That means thirty tons of gold at least," Calran concluded in an expert's voice. "Where could the treasure vault be?"

"People! What treasure vault?" I objected. "We need to reach the roof!"

"We are in a castle," Reptilis began, utterly ignoring my objection. "The jail was down below, so it won't be down there, that's for sure. A gnasher never strays far from the treasure vault. The glimmer of gold sustains him. Therefore, the vault's either on this floor or the next one."

"Shall we check it out?" asked Calran, adjusting his grip on the scimitar and turned to me: "Mahan—I understand everything perfectly, but Grygz will have my hide if he hears that I passed up a chance to get into the vault. Reptilis—lead on. You can have half."

"The hell! The most I'll give you is a fourth. And even then exclusively due to my immense respect for you."

"Guys, maybe we'll stop arguing and divvying up what we don't have?" I asked when the door shuddered from a blow. It looked like the mysterious gnasher had come to and was following us again.

"No way Freemie, my share's half. You forget that there's two of us, so each one will receive a fourth. You can set out on your own, but you better consider now how much you'll be able to carry while fleeing from a gnasher..."

"Are you trying to say," Reptilis inquired, "that you know how to get rid of this bastard?" The door shook again and cracks appeared in the wood, indicating that in another couple of blows, the gnasher would stop in for a chat.

"Half?" The pirate answered the question with a question.

"Deal! If you manage to..."

Calran didn't let the kobold answer, throwing the door wide open. Now that I saw the gnasher up close, I realized that I didn't feel much like becoming a treasure hunter. On the other side of the door stood a two-meter-tall dog with two heads that bore a close resemblance to the mythological Cerberus, if you ignored the fact that this beast was made entirely of gold.

Showing utterly no fear of this monster, Calran jumped up to it and with a wild swing slammed the pommel of his scimitar right on the nose of the right head. The pirate didn't seem to care one bit about the difference in levels, nor that he did effectively no damage—it's not easy for a Level 230 Warrior to scratch a Level 300 dog, much less cause it any damage, and yet...

"After him!" yelled Calran when the gnasher yelped like a puppy whose paw had been stepped on and darted up the stairs with his tail between his legs. Both of the gnasher's heads were howling pitifully and casting the 'Slowed' debuff on us, causing the treasure vault's two-headed guard to steadily pull ahead of us. Yet it's also worth mentioning the positive aspect to the dog's rabid state—climbing two floors, the dog ripped a side door from its hinges and disappeared down the corridor destroying everything in its way. And by everything, I mean mostly other guards who'd come running out of the adjoining rooms and hallways.

"How?" asked Reptilis, snipping the purse from another guard that the gnasher had knocked to the ground.

"Another twenty percent for our share," Calran replied over his shoulder with a grin.

"Twenty?" Reptilis even whipped the wall with his tail at such temerity, but quickly made his decision. "Ten and it's a deal. Twenty is too much."

"Thirty, Freemie," Calran was now openly enjoying himself. "You seem like the type who likes to creep around castles, so the secret to dealing with a gnasher will cost you eighty percent of the loot that we're about to get. If you want your half—by all means. I don't insist...Oh! I think we're here!"

The gnasher took another couple turns and stopped before an enormous steel door—at which he began to whine and scrape his paw like a dog begging to be let in.

"Back already?" The door opened with a slight squeak as though it hadn't been oiled in several years, and a fat goblin appeared on its threshold. It took me looking at his properties to see that we were facing the Narlak palace majordomo, the goblin Uveritus. "If you've already killed the escapees, why is the siren still screaming? All right, wait here, I'll go check it out and..."

Here, the goblin noticed us. At first his face expressed puzzlement, then recognition, and finally utter terror. The gnasher paid us no attention and darted through the steel door, preventing the goblin from slamming it shut and giving Reptilis the time to cast another cloud of gas that paralyzed the majordomo.

"We have twenty minutes," said Calran, "before the gnasher calms down and starts chasing us again. And mind you, the second time we won't be able to stop him...So, Reptilis, what do you say to taking twenty percent as your share?"

"Bunch of bastards, you NPCs," cursed the kobold and barked: "The hell with it—tell me how you dealt with the gnasher."

"Here's the description." Calran handed Reptilis a sheet of paper. Recalling our recent conversation about how the poor pirates had no paper on which to send Grygz their message, you could think that even on their deathbed, they sought to eke out a little profit by saving on stationary—and yet knowing the ins and outs of Barliona dispelled such ill thoughts of the pirates. When an NPC gives information to a player, he always does it in a letter in order to create a paper trail. Otherwise, what if a player claimed that he hadn't heard properly in order to get the NPC to speak louder? By passing the info on a piece of paper, Calran ensured that I wouldn't overhear it. It looked like if I wanted to discover the secret of dealing with gnashers, I'd need to spend some money. No thanks— I have Magdey and Clutzer who could whip that dog without any extra discussions—and gain some XP in the process.

"You don't have the right!" the goblin began screaming when he regained some composure. Calran tied his hands and feet, assuring us that even the majordomo wouldn't be able to escape such bonds, and so Uveritus had nothing else to do but curse and watch as Reptilis studied the enormous safe.

"This city must have some crazy security nerds living in it!" he exclaimed a minute later. "Two levels of physical security, four magical, several traps, and a honeypot with an alarm...Only a lunatic could make a safe like this!"

"Can you crack it?" I asked the kobold.

"There's nothing in Barliona that I can't crack,

given time. Calran—how's the corridor looking?" Reptilis asked the pirate who was guarding the entrance.

"Quiet so far. The gnasher scattered everyone on this level so quickly that there wasn't any time to warn anyone, and we tied up the majordomo right away, so...I figure we have about twenty minutes—right as the dog's regains his senses. How much time do you need?"

"Why is everyone so impatient?" muttered Reptilis, whose hands were flashing with his full set of lockpicks. "Unlock this—rescue that—how much time do you need...No, Mahan, I really can't understand what Anastaria sees in you at all. There doesn't seem to be anything special about you, even despite the movies they made, and yet...Got one! At least Mirida explained why she wanted me to find you, but Stacey...It really is utterly mystifying...There! Got another one..."

"What do you mean Mirida explained why she wanted to find me?" I asked, my heart skipping a beat at the name of the girl that I so badly needed to have a chat with.

"This heap of meat here has the right idea: If you want to know something, be ready to pay for it. I'm happy to tell you everything I know but it'll cost you a third of the loot. Agreed?"

"Sorry, but no way. I immediately dug in my heels. "Crack the safe!"

"Already done," smirked Reptilis, stepping aside. "Behold in amazement and wonder—the Narlak palace treasure vault!"

"You don't have the right!" the goblin squealed again, but no one heard him, for just beyond the enormous safe's door was an ordinary, static portal— the same exact kind used in Altameda to access its storage vaults.

CHAPTER NINE
THE PIRATES

"WELL THIS IS A BIT OF LUCK," whistled Reptilis when we crossed the portal's threshold. Calran insisted we lock the safe from inside—after which the kobold wrecked the two physical locks as much as he could. We wouldn't have any visitors for some time.

Narlak's treasure vault was an enormous cave filled with heaps of gold coins—which from a player's perspective were nothing more than scenery as you couldn't actually pick them up. One of these mountains was crowned with the gnasher's bed, which suggested that as soon as that beast came to and understood that he had no way of going back home, he'd smash the palace to pebbles in a fit of rage. As Reptilis pointed out, this creature lost its mind when kept from gold for too long, and this meant that we'd have several extra hours to peruse the treasure vault.

"It's not super nice of you to leave me in jail, brother!" Draco complained as soon as he appeared beside me. Remembering that I'd left him in Narlak city jail and the guards there could kill my Totem by way of revenge, I did that which Kornik had told me I couldn't do—I released the Totem back to the Dragon world and instantly re-summoned him—after all, the Totem was bound to me and not to his last location in Barliona. I'll confess that I was a little worried whether it'd work or not, but since Draco appeared beside me without losing any levels in the process—it worked! It was too bad that Fleita had already been released, since her sentence was only for two hours. "Oh! Where are we? Wow! No way! I'll be a flying gecko! Brother, do you mind if I look around a bit?"

"Just don't even think of taking something without asking first," Reptilis reminded him, casting a measured eye across the sea of loot before us. "Hmm...I get the feeling that the three of us are too few for all this stuff."

Ignoring the mountains of gold, we turned our attentions to what we could carry: ingots of various metals, elixirs, and the most desirable thing for all players—items. Heaps and heaps of items...

"The Narlak armed forces captured several merchantmen brimming with this stuff," Calrandos answered our unasked question. "What you're looking at is in effect Narlak's loot."

"I only have fifty free slots in my bag," said Reptilis. "I can't drop anything either...Damn it! I wish I'd known."

"Maybe we can summon someone to this place?" I asked.

"Summon?" Reptilis smirked. "Are you a Mage and are there three of you? You can't teleport into a treasure vault—there aren't any coordinates here. All you can do is teleport out. Okay, let's see—this thing I can get elsewhere," the kobold turned back to cleaning his inventory. "This I can buy from Arkandios...And this..."

"Stacey, hi!"

"There you are! I left you alone on purpose. I was waiting for when you'd call me. A brief update—the Nameless Council is complaining to the Emperor about your escape from jail and I've already had a Herald come visit me to tell me to tell you that the Emperor intends on giving you a stern talking-to. He just can't wait to speak to you, but he can't get in touch with you directly for whatever reason. You're probably in the Free Lands or in Kartoss. Anyway, just keep in mind that as soon as you are done there, you'll be taken to see the Emperor. What did you want?"

"Reptilis, one of the pirate NPCs and I are currently in the Narlak treasure vault with the entrance barricaded. Consequently, we're having issues with our location and our location coordinates. According to the rules, no one can teleport in here, which is why I need your help."

"I need ten minutes to buy three bags of 200 slots each. A player can't have more than two...Dan...How did you end up there? I sent Reptilis to break you and the pirates out...How did you find your way into a

treasure vault?"

"Well...are you going to argue or go get those bags? We're here now—what do you care?"

"Brother! Look what I found!" When I was done speaking with Anastaria, a very excited Draco swooped over to me, holding in his paws a metallic sphere with a golden sheen. My unconsciousness began to scream that I'd seen something like this before and that I even remembers its name—the Crastil of Shalaar, so I wasn't super surprised when I read the properties of the item Draco'd found.

'The Crastil of Gwar.' Description: Rastukal, who snarfed the prarqat in rurna, managed to glass the pralix of kurlex. Only the rhims qrijoplix gurt-gurt can take the Crastil of Gwar. Item class: Unique.

The difference between the descriptions was a single word. And yet there wasn't a single hint that the items were part of a set. It was a simple sphere of gold—just like the silver one in my bag.

"If you like, that piece of junk will be part of your share," Reptilis smirked, reading the item's properties and immediately losing any interest in it.

"Why piece of junk?"

"Because I have one just like it and haven't found any use for its whatsoever. There isn't a single antiquarian who knows what that thing is, so you can rest assured that it's some joke on the part of the Corporation. They just made some spheres, added a nonsense text that sounds like it's saying something but is really just a random collection of letters—and then they goad the players into racking their brains what the purpose of these things is. I was actually just about to toss a similar item. You want I give it to you? I won't even charge you!"

"All right," I instantly agreed to such a unique and generous offer. Even if these spheres don't do anything—I can arrange them in my castle like decorative stones for guests to look at and wonder at the sick imaginations of the developers. Oh! By the way...

"Stacey?"

"A couple more minutes..."

"No, I'm wondering about something else. Did you ever figure out the riddle of the deck of cards?"

"Cards?"

"The Deck of 52 Cards. You were going to figure out what its purpose was..."

"Oh! I did figure that out—the deck of cards is for playing card games. No less, no more...It's an ordinary McGuffin that the devs put in the game to mislead the players. Look, I've got to go—I'm busy here."

An ordinary deck of cards and ordinary spheres...There sure are a lot of ordinary things lying around Barliona. Reptilis finished digging around his bag and offered me another sphere, of a copper color—the Crastil of Levaar. The description also differed by one word, so I took out all three spheres and placed them beside each other.

"You're missing at least three Crastils there,"

Calran said in passing as he stuffed his pockets with gold coins. Unlike for players, the heaps of gold were real for the NPCs, so the pirate was currently having a field day of it. What were items to him when he could fill up on sweet, sweet gold?

"Three?" I echoed surprised.

"The wood one and the clay one that Grygz has and the glass one that, they say, is in the possession of the High Mage of Anhurs. I didn't know about the gold, silver and copper Crastils, so you can assume there are others too."

"What are they for?"

"Crastils? Why, nothing, obviously! They're ordinary spheres. There's nothing magical about them. Grygz holds onto his solely because it says 'Unique' in the description. Otherwise, he'd've tossed them ages ago. Their only decent use is for throwing at enemies—even the clay one won't break if you bounce it off someone's brainpan."

"I'm ready Dan—summon me."

"Reptilis, do you mind if Anastaria joins us?"

"Here? Mahan—I already told you: You can't cast a portal to a treasure vault!"

"No one's going to cast any portals," I shrugged my shoulders. "I'll assume that you don't mind..."

"Hello everyone! Reptilis, Mahan," Anastaria greeted everyone as soon as I summoned her over. "Oh! Will you please introduce me to this handsome young man, Mahan?"

You should have seen the pirate's face. In general, the Imitators that represent the various in-game fraternities have extremely emotional algorithms governing their demeanor. Accordingly, Calran now froze rooted in place with his mouth agape and his eyes fixed on Anastaria like Eluna herself had appeared to him. Truth be told, to some degree I understood how the program felt, since Stacey really looked stunning—having put away her golden armor, she was now wearing a green skirt with some kind of red fringe which, along with her green boots, did good justice to my wife's perfect legs. And after all, her avatar was an exact replica of the girl in real life...Stacey had braided her glorious chestnut hair in a wondrous braid, and the overall effect of a green fairy was completed by a roomy, emerald blouse. Stacey was so impressively fresh and shining that even I—as used to her appearance as I was—caught myself standing in place smiling at her dumbly.

"*Stacey, you look maddeningly gorgeous!*" I told the girl telepathically, trying to come to my senses.

"*Thank you! I tried extra hard for you. Introduce me to the pirate—I want to have this quest too!*"

"Anastaria," I croaked, my throat having gone dry from the girl's appearance, "allow me to introduce to you Calrandos—a member of the pirate brethren. Calrandos—allow me to present to you Anastaria, my wife. Now since we have observed all the necessary formalities..."

"M'lady." Utterly ignoring me, the enormous pirate bent down to one knee and bowed his head. "Allow me to introduce myself. I am Calrandos Furioso—but you may call me Calran. Captain of the

Fearless, the right hand of Grygz the Bloodied Hoof—head of the pirate brethren—I am now and eternally your true, obedient servant..."

Try and doubt your premonition after that...

"Please rise, brave Calran," Anastaria spoke in a voice filled with such grace that I even felt a knot forming below my heart, full of burning envy towards the NPC. With several steps, the girl floated over to the pirate and placed her hand on his shoulder. "I accept your offer, Calran. However, I request that you keep in mind that I have a spouse."

"If the hour comes when your paths shall fork," the pirate said, getting to his feet, "I will be happy to see you as my wife!"

Welp. Now I've heard it all. Even the Imitators want to put horns on my head and take my lawful (in-game) wife. Like hell!

"Guys, can we cut it out with the soap operas?" Reptilis quipped. "I love her, I want him, but she's his wife...Ugh...We're here to stuff our pockets with as much loot as we can before they fix the entrance—not to figure out who Anastaria belongs to. Stacey, did you get the bags?"

What followed was a full-fledged plunder of the Narlak City treasure vault. We didn't manage to clean out the entire cave—even the three extra bags didn't suffice for this, but we did teleport to Altameda over-encumbered with loot. Stacey and Reptilis preferred items—Reptilis even found some new gear to equip there and then. I, on the other hand, focused on resources. Imperial Steel, Oak, Flowers—anything that would bring in money at auction, found its place in my bags. Items come and go, but resources and profession levels—which they help develop—remain.

"And so, according to your contract," said Stacey when we had filled the last bag to its rim, "Reptilis, you owe three million, three hundred and twenty thousand gold—for this list of items. I assume that you have your own distributor equipped, so you can double-check on your own."

"Yeaaah," droned the kobold thoughtfully. "I kind of overdid it with my plunder...But all right. I need everything I picked up, so charge that amount to my account. You lot can figure the rest out among yourselves, so please excuse me—I'm out. By the way, Mahan—do you want me to send the funds to the clan account or your personal one?"

"Send them to the clan," I said, deciding to make Leite a present. I need to pull my weight on the monetary side of things when I can too.

I received a message that a payment had been made to the clan account, after which Reptilis cast a portal and vanished.

"Well, I guess the time has come for us to go too," I said. "Calran, I invite you to check out my castle. We can take a portal to your people from there. By the way, Stacey, where did Reptilis take the pirates?"

"If they're not in jail, we can summon them," said Calran, his eyes still glued to Anastaria. "Will your castle allow us to do that?" He made a great effort and turned to look at me. Only here did I notice that my Attractiveness with him, which had earlier been at 45, had fallen to 35. Why, this NPC has decided I'm his rival in love! What is the world coming to?!

"Yeah, it will," I assured him and called Viltrius to ask him to cast us a portal to the castle.

"Greetings, Earl!" As soon as I set foot in Altameda, a Herald appeared beside me. "Please follow me—the Emperor wishes to see you."

I transferred the loot from the Narlak treasure vault to Viltrius—just in case—and asked Anastaria to entertain our guest. Then I hopped into the Herald's portal. Who knows what the Emperor wants with me...

"Mahan, please follow me," said the palace steward whom the Herald delivered me to. Good news already—since they didn't send me directly to the Emperor, then nothing too bad has happened.

Naahti received me in his office, most of which was taken up by a massive round table. Unlike my previous audiences with the Emperor, Tisha was not with her father. It was as if our conversation was to be man to man.

"Have a seat," the Emperor said, looking up for a moment from the documents before him. Finishing up with some paper, he offered it to me from across the table, and the sheet floated across and over the air to my hand as if carried by some invisible assistant. "Read it. I'd like to hear your thoughts..."

To the Emperor of Malabar from the acting

Guardian of Narlak, Geranika, the Lord of Shadow.

RE: Complaint.

Honored colleague! I hereby bring to your attention that one, Shaman Mahan, a Dragon and Earl of your realm and holder of Altameda Castle, and, further, a player of your acquaintance, is doing his utmost to violate our agreement regarding Narlak's autonomy. I request that your Highness impress upon this subject the main points of our agreement. Otherwise, I will be forced to complete the transformation of a certain lady near and dear to you— to one of my subjects forever. All the best...

Geranika has Tisha?

"No, Tisha is safe," the Emperor replied, as though I had asked the question aloud. "He's referring to a different lady...Tisha's mother."

An oppressive silence descended on the office. I was feverishly trying to remember what I knew about Tisha's mother, but all I could come up with was that she was dead.

"Many years ago," Naahti began, reclining in his chair and slouching his shoulders as if from an unbearable weight, "back even before I went to Beatwick, my wife left this world. As a Priestess of Tartarus, it was her duty to perform certain rituals beyond the Nameless City. One time her group did not return. Search parties were sent out, but it was no good. Half a year later, the High Priestess, whom the Dark Lord had put the Death Seal on, returned and announced that mysterious creatures had attacked and killed all of them. My wife did not bear the seal, so she was reckoned as dead...Right until that moment when you took over Altameda and removed her from Glarnis. Geranika understood that neither I nor Regul would allow him to remain the temporary Guardian of Narlak, so he gave us ironclad proof that my wife was in his hands. And fighting against one's wife, even if she's been turned to a subject of Shadow...Geranika promised to return her if we left him alone in Narlak for another two months—until his post as temporary Guardian expired, so we acquiesced...My Heralds kept a close eye on the movements of my subjects near Narlak, strongly warning Free Citizens to stay away from its environs, and yet you teleported there directly, bypassing their jurisdiction."

"Evolett, the head of the Dark Legion has decided to attack Narlak," I said immediately. "At my prompting, to be honest, but he is already gathering people for the attack."

"A couple hours ago, the Dark Lord met with him and told him what I'm telling you now. There will be no attack on Narlak..."

"Why isn't Geranika reacting to our attempts to capture the Heart of Chaos? He could blackmail you there too."

"Because he's bound by his oath of Emperor. When he proclaimed himself the Lord of Shadow, Geranika swore an oath to Barliona and now he must perform it."

"An oath?"

"To be an Emperor is not merely to exercise enormous might and power—there are also responsibilities and duties you cannot violate. The Creator keeps a very close watch over these matters...As soon as Geranika tries to use Adelaide to protect himself, he'll cease to be the Lord of Shadow. He knows this and does so only in his capacity as Guardian. When it comes to our host, he will have to do battle with it on his own."

"Does that mean that the Creator hasn't left Barliona?"

"He never left it. He ceased to rule it, leaving our world to his sons—and when they left, to the gods they had created. But he has always watched over this world. It is his child, after all..."

"As I understand it, I'm not allowed to show up in Narlak for the next two months, correct?"

"Yes. You may keep the loot you obtained in the treasure vault, but I request that you stay away from that city. This is a request, not an order. At least for two months. The Dark Lord and I already made a decision that as soon as a permanent Guardian appears in Narlak, the city will return to my jurisdiction. I've had enough of indulging the local authorities with extra freedom—but that will take place only in two months..."

"I understand and I promise you that I won't set foot in Narlak for the next two months. If I may, I have one question—how is it going with the Heart of Chaos? How is the war coming along?"

"There is progress. It is incredibly slow, but it is

there. The allied forces of Malabar and Kartoss are sorely lacking the assistance of Hellfire, Anastaria, Plinto and other high-level Free Citizens. As a result, the advance on Armard is going very slowly. We have lost nine out of the eleven battles we fought. In most cases, our forces are simply too outnumbered. Geranika doesn't seem to have a single warrior weaker than Level 250. Most of his forces seem to be at Level 330, so we are having a very hard time of it."

"I must ask: Why make a head-on assault if we could just fly there on griffins?"

"There is much you don't know about the Empire of Shadow," smiled Naahti. "Flying over this Empire is prohibited."

"What about using Assassins or Rogues?" I recalled Reptilis, who had snuck into the Narlak palace.

"The only sentient I am aware of who could sneak past Level 330 guards is Plinto the Bloodied. But he has another month before he regains his powers. There aren't any others capable of this in Malabar. Even the kobold that helped you plunder Narlak failed all six of his attempts. He was captured and sent to respawn. Therefore, our only option is brute force, and there we are desperately missing the players I just named…"

"So the Empire of Shadow has the same flight restrictions as the cities?" I clarified.

"I understand your desire to save Renox's life. Don't be surprised. I am aware that you have this information. However, I must disappoint you—even if you force your way into Armard, there is nothing there for you except for another respawn. On your own, without your Spirits...Even if you take a companion with you, the idea is pointless. Don't think that I'm trying to dissuade you—I merely wish to give you some perspective if you decide to try to get to Armard in your Dragon Form. You have my condolences, but Renox will depart this world..."

"He already has..."

"I have told you everything I wanted to," the Emperor concluded, standing up. "It's up to you to decide how you will act now. The Herald will take you back..."

* * *

"So then the wife of the Emperor is also the mother of the Dark Lord and she's alive and in Geranika's hands," Anastaria said more to herself than anyone else when I related the gist of my conversation with Naahti. "And Geranika is blackmailing both Emperors with this fact, keeping them from approaching Narlak. Why?"

"'Why' what?"

"Why does Geranika want to be a Guardian? That's a very large responsibility that surely distracts him from the war being waged in his lands. Why does Geranika need this city?"

"It's a port," said Calran, who had begun following Anastaria around like a dog. A real mighty pirate this one...

"A port?" Even Stacey looked at the pirate with puzzlement, unable to understand why Geranika would need a port.

"If I understood you correctly, the main thrust of the allied armies—you could say, the only thrust—is taking place overland. Meanwhile, no one is even trying to reach Armard by water. Considering that there is a major river running within a hundred kilometers of this city, it's mystifying that no one has thought of using this fact."

"You have a map of the Shadow Empire?" Anastaria perked up.

"Only of its waterways. We never passed very deeply into the Shadow Realm. There's nothing for us to do there. But we did chart the major rivers. Plus, we have an active trade with the people of Armard. We supply them with slaves. Malabar and Kartoss have a single access point to the sea—Narlak, which is currently controlled by Geranika. Naturally he isn't interested in handing over power to someone else, since this is almost a direct path to his capital."

"Dan, are you thinking what I'm thinking?"

"Most likely. I think it might be a good idea for our raiders to make an outing on a ship. We'll bring Plinto along too—he needs to take a break from all the bloodsucking he's been doing."

"Tell me, Calran, what are relations like between the pirates and the Empire of Shadow?" Stacey asked the pirate. "Are you its subjects, allies, partners, or were you merely passing by and decided to stop in?"

"I'd say the last. Our main base is in Cadis.

That's where Grygz's fleet is moored, but Shadow allows us to use Verdax as a base too—an enormous city on the coast."

"In other words, if we approach Grygz with an offer to wage a little war with Shadow, he might agree?" Stacey went on interrogating the pirate in a musical voice that carried notes of the Siren song.

"Everything depends on the price you name," Calran replied truthfully. "If it suits Grygz and his officers, myself included, then yes we will be ready to wage a little war against Shadow, as you put it. We will be acting as ordinary mercenaries, so it won't be a complicated issue."

"You said 'officers.' How many of them are there altogether?"

"Five, if you count myself. Normally, we get together once a month and boast of the loot we've plundered, but this time I was unlucky—the storm cast us against the defensive dome and the Narlak Mages bound the ship..."

"When is the next officers' meeting?"

"Tomorrow." It looked like Anastaria had turned her Charm up to 11 because Calran had begun to tell us things that players weren't supposed to know. "The next meeting will take place at the Three Squids tavern in Cadis, at two o'clock. All the approaches to the tavern have already been closed off, so the meeting should take place as per usual—without any incidents."

"Can you get us into the meeting?"

"Yes, I am allowed to bring three companions.

But normally, that's Darius—my first mate—and two captains from my ships whom I select based on their performance in the past month. It would be very difficult for me to explain why I brought three Freemies instead of the pirates everyone's used to.

"Ahem." A Herald's polite cough sounded beside us. "Anastaria, please forgive me, but I am forced to issue you another warning for your abuse of the Siren's power. You have only three warnings remaining—please be careful. With great power comes great responsibility, please remember this."

"Three?" I asked surprised once the Herald had dived back into his portal and Calran froze with the 'Petrified' status effect for 20 minutes. "I thought you had three before...?"

"So you were listening! I knew it!" the girl exclaimed in a satisfied voice. "Father told me that the creator of a cursed item may be present at its first use, but I didn't believe him—there was no precedent of it. And you kept mum about it all this time? And you call yourself a husband! It's rude to spy on your wife, by the way!"

"At the time, you weren't my wife. And in general, I considered you an enemy of the people who wanted to seize the Chess Set from me," I parried. "But you still haven't answered my question."

"So I take it, I'm no longer an enemy of the people?" the girl smiled. "You're a mischievous one. As for the warnings—every six months, one of them is struck off, allowing me to charm someone else. Obviously you didn't know this, since Hellfire never told you, right? What a sleuth you are, darling..."

"We'll still see about which one of us is mischievous," I muttered. "What are we going to do then?"

"First of all we need to meet Grygz and figure out why we were allowed to encounter the pirates to begin with. Note that in the fifteen-and-a-half years of Barliona's existence, no one has managed to make contact with them. At any rate, I've never heard of it. And after all, this is almost like an in-game El Dorado—everything from the First Kills of various monsters of the deep to trade and safe passage to other continents. The important thing is to use this opportunity properly, so make sure to bring me with you to the meeting. I am confident that Evolett will take Zlatan with him."

"Who?"

"He's got this brainy guy. Hang on, I'll call my uncle real fast..."

During the twenty minutes that Calran was in a frozen state, the population of Altameda increased by two. As Anastaria guessed, Evolett arrived with Zlatan—a hulking Level 288 orc Mage. The 'brains' of the Dark Legion had chosen such a plain face for his avatar that one look at this creature was all it took to make one's conclusions about his intellectual prowess. Or, rather, its utter absence.

"M'lady, forgive me. I somehow fell asleep," Calran boomed when he came to. "It seems that my incarceration took its toll on me...Who are these two Kartossians? I don't remember being introduced to them..."

As we had agreed, Evolett showed his quest to meet with Grygz to the pirate and in so doing aroused a certain curiosity—it turns out that Calran had never seen a living orc before. Or rather, he had, but only as a slave or an enemy with whom he couldn't talk. So he attached himself to Zlatan, asking him about all kinds of trivialities—where and what and where and why. The pirate was interested in all things orcish, but after ten minutes I noticed that Zlatan and Anastaria had somehow turned the conversation upside down and began to ask Calran the questions— which he was happy to answer. It was true that the questions didn't directly concern the number of officers or sailors under Calran's command or in the brethren as a whole, yet his answers to questions like 'how many bags of food do you have to take with you on a voyage?' or 'and is it difficult to find a place to stay after a voyage?' revealed a lot more than the pirate suspected. I watched the players' cross-examination of the pirate with immense astonishment, understanding that I really was out of my depth around those two...They were out of this world...

As soon as Anastaria and Zlatan had pried everything they could from Calran, we made the decision to travel to Cadis and begin our pirate quest. Neither Evolett nor Anastaria saw any more reasons to put off the quest, so I had nothing to do but agree with them. Having brought the pirates that Reptilis broke out of jail to Altameda, we opened a portal right to the center of Cadis. Thankfully none of us had negative reputation with this Free City. We still had almost a week left until our next meeting with Kreel, so we had the time to deal with the pirates and with Renox...

Outwardly, Cadis was no different than the other cities in Malabar I'd seen along my journey—ordinary architecture, vendors, guard patrols and, what was most surprising, crowds of players. Starting from Level 250 Kartossians and ending with Level 38 minnows from Malabar. Cadis united the players of both empires who never even imagined attacking each other. I was extremely surprised to see messages like 'gathering a raid, need players of Level 150+ from any Empire. Translation provided' or 'guys, help me with this quest—I can't kill these mobs' popping up in the city chat in both languages at once. Who could have thought that the players could live harmoniously in a single city?

"Grygz is at the Three Squids tavern," said Calran, deeply inhaling his native air. "I won't go with you—I can't show up before him without reporting first. Good luck! Follow me, you vagabonds," Calran said to his pirates. "Let's go see what we can replace my little swallow with..."

"Okay, the Three Squids tavern is located in..." Zlatan began, but I cut him off.

"Wait!" I produced one of my amulets and spent several minutes hypnotizing it, trying to get a response. The word 'swallow' had jogged something in my memory and I couldn't rid myself of the thought that Calran had mentioned it especially for me. Or, more accurately, in order that I took another player with us—the owner of a unique means of transportation that he too called his 'swallow.'

"If this isn't about an inheritance of twenty million, then you are definitely disturbing me," sounded the impatient grumbling on the other end of the 'line.'

"Happy to hear your voice too, Plinto. I need you. Teleport to Altameda, and from there to Cadis. Viltrius has the coordinates. You have one minute."

"Hey, Mahan!" came the Patriarch's voice. "Plinto cannot abandon his training. He only has..."

"I need him to save Renox," I blurted out. "We are about to go meet the pirates in Cadis and then we'll sail in a ship to Armard. Please don't ask what Renox has to do with the pirates, but if Plinto doesn't come with us right now, we won't be able to rely on his help."

"One week..." replied the Patriarch after a little thought which made me think our connection had been interrupted. "You have one week. After that Plinto must return..."

"We won't need any more," I assured the head Vampire of Barliona, after which two sentients appeared beside me—a slightly surprised Plinto, who hadn't anticipated such a sudden jump, and the Patriarch, who looked at me with his black eyes, nodded a greeting at Anastaria and dissolved, returning to his forest.

"Hey! Well met, people!" smirked the Rogue,

recognizing who stood before him. "Two former bosses, a current one and an orc, by whose face I can tell that even in Kartoss, Zlatan continues to play the fool. What'd you call me for?"

Relating to Plinto the gist of what was going on and remarking to myself that I really could use his fine sarcasm, we headed out to meet Grygz. The time had come to meet the pirates at long last.

* * *

We had been trying to get into the Three Squids tavern for two hours already...

"I've told you a hundred times, the tavern is closed!" droned the Level 300 bouncer, barring our entrance to the Three Squids. "Come back in two days..."

"*Stacey, maybe you can make him fall in love with you?*" I asked the girl in desperation. "*I can't bear another hour of this...*"

Nothing we said budged the guard blocking our path:

"Need to get into the tavern? No problem. Come back in two days..."

"Grygz is expecting you? No problem. Come back in two days..."

"You want to give me money to let you pass? Hand it over. I like money. Come back in two days..."

"You want to force your way in? Good luck. There's a guard patrol passing right there..."

All of the various formulations and appeals that

Anastaria and Zlatan came up with, shattered against the cliff of the bouncer's granite implacability. After our second time bailing out Plinto—who tried to sneak in through the window but only encountered the same bouncer, who then handed him over to the guards—it became evident that if we were ever to meet Grygz it would have to be in two days.

"I already tried my Charm on him," Stacey now grumbled aloud. "It doesn't work. He's wearing an amulet of self-absorption."

"In that case, maybe we should come back in two days?" Evolett said what everyone had been thinking for at least forty minutes. As pathetic as it is to admit it, the NPCs simply don't want to see us.

"Ahoy, vagabond!" smirked the bouncer, stepping aside. "Drop anchor in my gullet if isn't the scourge of the seas!"

The NPC that walked past us was decked out head to toe with swords, miniature crossbows, throwing knives and various other dreck for cutting and piercing things. Showing something to the bouncer, the pirate passed inside with a happy smile, as if he'd been awaiting this day for several years. For a moment, we heard joyous cries sound from the tavern and then everything went quiet as the door shut.

"Stacey, how can we become pirates?"

"We can't. Players can't be pirates..."

"Just like they can't be Sirens, Dragons, Vampires or Titans. Stacey, I'll ask again: How can we become pirates?"

Evolett was right of course—we probably simply needed to reconvene in two days and decide this thing then—and yet I simply hated this awful feeling of being limited by some kind of dumb scenario.

"Where did Calran go anyway?"

"Who knows..." Zlatan replied. "He went to go look for his 'swallow...' I figure he's at the wharf somewhere."

"There are three wharfs in this city, Mahan," Anastaria added, realizing what I wanted to do. "It'd take us three days to find him!"

"Us—yes," I smiled. "But not them!"

"Who?" Evolett managed to ask before I typed into the city-wide chat:

"I'm looking for an NPC named Calran. I'll pay twenty thousand gold to the first player who submits accurate coordinates of his whereabouts!"

The chat came alive with the babble of players. And of course while some of the coordinates were located in the city, other were pointing to somewhere deep in Malabar. The trolls were alive and well in Cadis too...

Five minutes later, the Imitator I had set on this task informed me that I had received three similar sets of coordinates which differed only in the final digits. Telling everyone to follow me, I ran in the indicated direction, afraid of missing the pirate. Judging by the map, Calran really was at one of the wharfs. The important thing was to not let him get away.

"Mahan!" Grygz's officer exclaimed joyously upon

seeing me. "I thought you had gone to the Three Squids?"

"I did and now I've come back," I replied, sending the player who had submitted the first set of accurate coordinates the money I owed him. "I have some business to discuss with you. How can we become pirates?"

"Pirates?" Calran asked surprised. "Why do you want to be a pirate?"

"Well, you see, I realized that the sea is my true home. I know how to rob and kill, but I have never yet set sail on the seas. One should try everything in this life; otherwise, what will I tell my grandchildren in my dotage?"

"The high honorable Earl, the owner of that huge castle, wishes to become a pirate?" Calran still refused to believe his ears.

"He's not the only one," said Evolett, surprising me along with Calran. "I too do not wish to appear before Grygz as a common landlubber. If he is ready to meet us, I wouldn't like to insult such a great pirate."

"So that's it! In that case, I see..." Calran shook his head agreeably contemplating something. "It's no good, it's no good...You're right about that...He doesn't much take to landlubbers...It's no good, yes..."

"Perhaps I'll become a pirate too?" meowed Anastaria when the silence grew too long. Calran remained standing in a stupor, muttering something to himself and utterly refusing to make any kind of decision. It looked like his strong Attraction to Anastaria was having its effect.

"M'lady?" the poor pirate's eyebrows hiked way up on his forehead. "Why would you want something like that?"

"A handsome fellow offered to become my husband. If for some reason it doesn't work out with my present husband, I wouldn't like to be without a means of income. But as a partner. A partner on the seas!"

"What the hell? I'll kill you!"

"Like hell you will..."

"Free Citizens have never become pirates before. In any case, the fraternity never had any among its number." The pirate stood no chance against Anastaria. "But you saved my people and me from jail and I am ready to take a risk...Darius!" Calran shouted.

"D'you call me, Cap?"

"To the registration office double quick and have them draft a patent of piracy. For Captain Anastaria and two junior Captains under her command—Mahan and Evolett. Do you need two ships or three?" Calran asked us.

"Two," Stacey replied. "Mahan and I will take one ship. Then I'll make him walk the plank if he..."

"Put in a request for two ships." The giant scratched his chin in thought and added: "You can't be a pirate without a ship...We need to think which type of vessels you'll need..."

"Types of vessels?" Evolett asked carefully.

"Novice pirates typically get little frigates, with a crew of ten. Those don't cost too much and teach the pirates a sense for the sea...Darius, are you still here?!"

"I'd prefer to start out in a normal ship," Evolett said. "If I'm to be a pirate, then I'd like to do it right and for the long haul, and not just to sail around in some tub. How much does a normal ship cost—one that can fit a boarding party?"

"I can tell right away that we'll get along well!" A smile bloomed on Calran's face. "A medium-class vessel costs three million, while the perfect vessel, one that you could compare to my former 'swallow' costs ten. That one will fit two hundred sentients comfortably with room to spare for loot..."

"I guess I'll take a swallow then," said Evolett. "And if she'll be as good as you say, I'll even give you a zero-interest loan towards a swallow of your own..."

"Zero-interest?" Darius immediately latched on. "For how long?"

"Let's say, eight months..."

"A year," Darius began to haggle. "A window of a year and...Cap, what do you say?"

"M'lady, what ship would you like?" Calran asked, ignoring his assistant.

"I think I'm with Evolett in this. If we're going out to sea, then let's do it right...I'll also have a ship worth ten million..."

"*Stacey! We don't have that kind of money!*" I almost yelled out loud but controlled myself at the last moment and sent the girl the thought telepathically.

"We do not. But I do. She will be my ship, not the clan's, so relax. The money isn't a problem. I'll be a pirate."

"Did you hear that, Darius?" The enormous captain asked his first mate. "A captaincy patent, two for junior captains and three licenses for five-masted galleons! We'll have our beloved *Fearless* again!"

It was like the wind carried away the old man—despite his respectable age, he literally sprinted into the city, waving his arms fantastically to maintain his balance—and it occurred to me here that back in the Narlak jail, the pirates had pretended that Darius was the one in charge in order to conceal their chain of command.

"I confirm it," said Evolett, staring with glassy eyes at the nearest wall. "The conditions suit me just fine. I look forward to working with you in the future."

"Excellent, excellent," Calran rubbed his hands in satisfaction. As I understood it, the two had just concluded an agreement and the money the captain needed had been sent over from the Dark Legion's account. "In that case, I propose we consider the issue right away—where are we going to get a crew?"

"What do you mean, 'where'?"

"Wrong question. Do any of your Freemies have the Seafarer skill? You've got no business going out to sea without an experienced skipper. And you'll need a boatswain to ensure that the loafers don't loaf, and a first mate who can take care of the necessities, a cook so that the crew doesn't starve, a pilot if you want to traverse the shallows..."

"And naturally a talented captain like you," Anastaria meowed, forcing another puppy-eyed smile from Calran, "knows just where we can find such a worthy crew with which we won't be afraid to set out against the terrible sea monsters..."

"I will select both the ships and the crew for you—one that will go anywhere with you—even into the maw of the dreaded Squidolphin!" the mighty captain said triumphantly and a notification appeared before me:

Patent of junior captain received. New ability unlocked: Seafarer.

"What the hell is a Squidolphin?" Zlatan asked. "I've never heard of it."

"Agreed, it's quite an odd creature," Calran grew grim. "It destroyed three of my ships—and we didn't even know what hit us. Just, poof, and the ship's gone—and naught but some lumber floating on the surface...It's a quick creature, like a dolphin, and yet it has tentacles, like a kraken. No one really knows what this monster looks like. The ships that it attacks tend to vanish along with the crew—and none escape to tell their tale."

"Then why do you think the thing has tentacles? Maybe it's a giant spider or, for example, simply a whale..."

"Because one time we got tired of sharing the seas with that beast and we—and by 'we' I mean the entire world—set out against it. Never had the sea monster faced such an Armada—and yet the Squidolphin didn't care one bit. It surfaced from the deeps, wrapped its tentacles around our ships and pulled them down to the abyss. Krakens aren't capable of this—we already caught one once...One of the ships had a barrel with magic paint in it, which doesn't sink in water. With my own two eyes, I watched the trail of paint sweep out to sea at an incredible speed. Not only does this beast possess terrifying tentacles, but it swims faster than anything we've got, so we named it a Squidolphin...But enough of these horrors! You have your patents, so let's go buy our ships! In all of Cadis, there is only one place where we can purchase a worthy vessel—from Master Ravzan. That's where we'll go now..."

"Dan, I'll pay for the crew as well," said Anastaria, as soon as we signed the contract to hire the crew. Thirty-two mangy-looking NPCs greeted Anastaria as their leader, and we set out to board our new ship, built by Master Ravzan in a matter of seconds. That's what it means to be a Master Shipbuilder in a computer game. In the real world, a vessel like that would take at least several months to build.

"*And why are we being so generous all of a sudden?*" I asked.

"*What's so generous about it? The sea is large and the quests and First Kills available in it are as many as grains of sand on the beach. For the past sixteen years, no one's explored the piracy content in this game. I want to be the first. By the way—it's only on our continent that players haven't been able to do this. Other continents have had their Free Pirates for ages. At least seven years."*

"Captain," Lom, the first mate, turned to me. "You still haven't named the ship. We can't set out to sea in a nameless vessel. If our bodies are destined to remain out there in its abyss, it'd be better if we were remembered somehow."

"I'll make sure to name the ship," I reassured Lom, familiarizing myself with the controls. Like Altameda, the ship had an immense number of settings, most of which were entirely mystifying to me. The length of the first mainmast, the girth of the second mainmast, the lumber that the mizzenmast was made from...Gaffs, booms, sprits...Despite the fact that I understood the letters, the words that they formed were utterly unfamiliar to me—and that went double for the settings that dealt with the names of items. Afraid of messing something up, I left it all on default, hoping that the crew would let us know at the right time what we needed to adjust. No, Stacey really is just too kind, too kind! She buys a ship and then just gives it to me to manage as her junior captain— since, naturally, it wouldn't do for a senior captain to go digging around the subtler settings of a ship! Her business is the finer stuff, like strategy. And of course I owe her a big thanks for the book on seafaring which explained all the terms, but it's all a bit too much, isn't it?

"Have you thought of a name?" smiled Anastaria

when Lom went off to attend his business. "Evolett named his the *Butterfly*. He says that his ship will float over the waves like a moth that is oblivious to the weather. I haven't seen my uncle this happy in ages. I'll let you in on a secret: The sea is his passion. He can talk about sailing ships for hours. He even bought himself a retro sailboat in real life—one that looks quite a bit like that galleon. You are his favorite now. It's rare that my uncle speaks of anyone with such respect."

"Sorry, but no way. It's your ship, so you name it. I've always had problems with coming up with stuff to say. There's no point in forcing a weak brain to do what a good brain can! You can name the ship yourself and until you do, we'll just sit here in port like dead weight."

"I knew it!" Stacey said with a grin. "All right, I've had a name in mind for a castle for a long time, but it'll do for a ship too. Name the ship *Vraanakush*."

"*Vraana*-what?" I echoed puzzled, trying to repeat the strange combination of sounds.

"*Vraanakush*," Stacey repeated and sent me the correct spelling. "I want that to be my ship's name."

"What does that even mean?" I couldn't help but ask, entering and confirming the ship's new name.

"That was the name of one of the greatest Sirens of Barliona—the teacher of Nashlazar, who taught her everything she knows. Plus, this name has one particular feature to it, if I apply it to something I own."

"What's that?"

"Captain, the crew is ready," came Lom's voice from behind me.

"Why, this one," Anastaria smiled. "Turn and see…"

No, I really have been building up my immunity to miracles. Only two months or so ago, I would've jumped back several meters—now, however, I merely cursed, looking at the first mate, Lom, impatiently beating his tail against the deck, eager to set out to sea as soon as possible. I looked behind Lom's back and understood that he wasn't the only one who'd changed. The entire crew we had hired thirty minutes ago had transformed from people into…

"M'lady, didn't I tell you that I'd find you the best seadogs?" Calran approached us with a satisfied smile, completely ignoring the crew's metamorphosis. "Lom is a trueborn seafarer. He can't be anything else—it's in his Myrmidon blood."

"Stacey, what is this? Where did this come from?" I asked the girl mesmerized when I understood what just happened—by giving the ship a special name, Stacey had completely altered the history of the crew we'd hired. If, earlier, Lom had been an ordinary, if rather hale, human, now he was a Myrmidon—a modified Naga. And no one was one bit surprised by this besides me and Plinto—who hummed several times upon seeing the updated crew and shook his head. Barliona's Imitators adjusted to the new histories of these thirty-five people very quickly, smoothly integrating them into this world.

"Nashlazar told it to me when she turned me

into a Siren. It was long ago, but there wasn't an occasion to use this little move. When I was in Phoenix, everything belonged to my dad. I couldn't afford a castle, but this ship...Now I have some Myrmidons of my own!" Stacey said satisfied, looking almost lovingly at how the serpentine creatures slithered along the vessel.

"Yeah, Stace..." said Plinto, "it's been a while since I've been this...let's say...surprised, although a better word would do here. Sailing with beauties like this is a sheer pleasure...Shall we set out to sea?"

"Let's do it," Stacey nodded and yelled in my direction: "Captain! Weigh anchor and cast off! *Vraanakush* is setting out on her maiden voyage!"

"State the purpose of your visit to Cadis," ordered the customs inspector, jotting down our answers into a thin ledger. Calran had warned us that all new ships had to undergo a customs inspection—even if their owner was Grygz himself. Why this was done and who had thought of this, no one remembered, but the city Mayor dutifully sent his people to check, knowing full well that they wouldn't find anything. Or rather, if they did find something, they'd be bribed—Calran even gave us the prices: 10 gold for a slave, 5 for tobacco, 100 for improperly filed papers. And of course the papers were always filed improperly, even if the inspectors themselves had filed them—such was tradition, and on the seas, tradition was serious business.

"To make an appearance, show off our fine new rigging and check out what's going on," I replied, placing my wallet on the table with a hundred gold in it.

"Showing off is a noble purpose," the inspector said officiously, as the wallet vanished from the table. "In that case, we will write as follows: 'tourism.' You can dock the ship at that berth over there," the customs inspector pointed to the side, but I didn't even bother looking. I had Lom for that.

"Ahoy, vagabond!" the Three Squids bouncer greeted us when we entered his sight. He'd spent two hours driving us insane, barring us from entering as ordinary players, but as soon as we got our hands on a ship: 'Ahoy!' "Drop anchor in my gullet if it isn't the scourge of the seas!"

"When I get my powers back," Plinto muttered under his nose, "I'll show you an 'ahoy!' And then I'll drop an anchor down your gullet for good measure."

"Before I let you inside," said the guard, as if he didn't remember us at all, "there is one formality we must take care of. Please show your ship license and piracy patent, if you could be so kind!"

Plinto and Zlatan stayed outside—only captains were allowed to enter—and I could tell by looking at the Rogue's face that he was going to come up with some way to erase this bouncer from Barliona's history—Plinto never forgave easily. Could the reference to the swallow have been about the ship and not him after all? Had I confused something?

The Three Squids was crammed full—about forty people, goblins, elves and various other races of Barliona were all crowded in an area of ten square meters. It was astonishing how they had all fit into this hall, as well as that they were all happily chatting, drinking beer, arguing and yelling.

"Look, newbies!" yelled the pirate closest to us, regarding us with a drunken eye. "They're Freemies to boot! Who let Freemies into our tavern?!"

As if at the wave of a magic wand, the clamor died and forty pair of eyes and eye-patches fixed on us. The silence was so oppressive that I found nothing better to say than:

"Ahoy, vagabonds! Did you not expect a Free Captain? We're a new breed! Remember my name—I am Mahan, captain of *Vraanakush*! Drinks are on me—we need to celebrate our arrival to this port!"

"Drinks are on Mahan!" echoed approving cries, cautiously here and there. "I'll have one too! Spare no expense—don't you see the Earl is moneyed! A toast to the captain of *Vraanakush*!"

It took the tavern a few moments to decide that if we're willing to pay for the drinks, then we can stay. And since we can stay, then there's no point in paying attention to us. Who cares why an Earl decided to become a pirate? It's his personal business ultimately...

"Grgyz wishes to speak with you," a voice sounded in my ear. I started but beside Evolett and Anastaria there was no one beside me.

"Catch, captain," the voice sounded again and I

realized that it was coming from overhead. Looking up, I couldn't help but exclaim in surprise—four Level 400 Assassins were hanging over our heads, wrapped from head to toe in a dark material. Their eyes, which even the ninjas leave unobstructed, were covered with blindfolds. Four dark figures were hanging upside down, like bats, and one of them was indicating three thick tow lines hanging from the ceiling. Grabbing one of these cables I felt the floor drop out beneath me as in one sharp jerk, I was hoisted into the air without anyone bothering to make sure whether I had gotten a good grip or not.

The Three Squids turned out to be a tavern with a surprise. The main floor, accessible to any captain, was filled with a celebrating crowd of pirates who'd come to the tavern. But on the second floor, situated almost right under the roof and hidden from the revelers below by a magic screen and a fake ceiling, the elites of the pirate world had gathered for a meeting. I say 'elites' because Grygz (who turned out to be a normal NPC despite his strange name) was Level 500. Yet another Emperor, albeit of a unique Empire—that of the pirates.

"I heard you really stuck it to Narlak," Grygz said in a low voice. In his appearance he didn't look much different from Calran—he was large, muscle-bound, covered in scars and bare-chested as if the chief designer of these characters was a young lady with certain ideas of the male physique.

"Yes, I can't say I've managed to become friends with the Nameless Council," Evolett replied, since it was clear whom the pirate leader was addressing.

"Very good," Grygz said slowly. "I also heard that you saved Calran from the noose."

"No—from jail. We never even saw the noose," I replied, since this time the pirate was speaking to me.

"And you plundered the Narlak treasure vault along your way," Grygz said emphatically, as if this information wasn't news to him.

"Narlak owed us for the time we'd spent in jail, and we couldn't well ignore such a howling injustice..."

"Dan, try to be more serious. This doesn't feel like a friendly meeting. They're about to spring something on us."

"Owed indeed," smirked Grygz. The pirate propped his cheek up on his chair's armrest and began to think aloud:

"Several months ago we received a report that someone had incurred Hatred status with Narlak. I became curious and decided I'd like to meet such a desperate band of people. Afterwards, I was told that there were now two groups from two different Empires, which interested me even more. A very strange coincidence. I have had quarrels with Narlak for a long time, and fresh blood could come in handy..."

Grygz fell silent as if collecting his thoughts and at this point, I realized what he was getting at. Understanding that I was taking a huge risk and that if I was wrong Anastaria and Evolett would have my hide, I said:

"And that is precisely why we're here. I understand that you wish to maintain Neutral status with Geranika and that you periodically run small errands for him. I'm sure you knew full well that Calran would not be harmed—Geranika would not hurt your right-hand man. Perhaps, he merely wished to scare him a bit to keep him away from Narlak. But if we don't stop that mad Lord of Shadow, in a month, Barliona will be plunged in utter darkness. And not the same kind that you find in Kartoss—no—an entirely other kind of darkness which is the enemy of all that lives. To use Shadows and to be a Shadow are two absolutely different things, and this is precisely why we are here. We're not here to satisfy your curiosity. I have a ship and a crew, but it's not enough. We need another dozen ships. No one sails into Shadow unassisted, right? I'm not asking you to act officially—I want to hire you as ordinary mercenaries and take all the responsibility myself."

A silence followed as Grygz considered my words. At last came the reply:

"Geranika promised to make me and my people immortal for handing over you and your companions to him. Can you offer me anything better than that?"

CHAPTER TEN
THE SECOND-RATE POWER

"I HAVE SOMETHING I CAN OFFER," Anastaria spoke up, drawing Grygz's glare onto herself. "They say you like unique items. Here is a list. All this could be yours."

The pirate leader glanced at the list that Stacey held out to him and smirked:

"You wish to offer me some trifles in exchange for immortality? You, madam, must be as stupid as you are pretty."

"Just take a look before you make your decision," Stacey parried. "I'm not asking you to agree right away."

"Agree to what?" Grygz asked surprised. "At the moment, I am looking at three captains of two vessels who thanks to Calran have acquired piracy patents and wish to hire me and my people as mercenaries. Meanwhile, Geranika's offer is that I hand two of you over to him. What is there to agree to? And another thing...You know, Siren, your fame has reached as far as Cadis, and I'm sure I can name three of the items on your list without looking at it. Those would be the Horn of Priol, the Scroll of Razmuradji and the Lirenean Shade—all of these items were once located in Dungeons which I can tell by simply looking at your face you have completed. No doubt the list you are offering me contains another three items that would suffice for me and my officers, but you have made a mistake. It would be stupid to trade immortality for unique, but ultimately simple items. But, okay, I will take a look." Grygz took the document, glanced at it and burst out laughing. "I see I should consider a career as an antiquarian!"

"*Checkmate*," Anastaria's thought occurred in my mind. "*It seems that the info I have on this guy isn't very good...Oops. Dan, you gotta save us.*"

"*Save you? What's with the list? What did you offer him?*"

"*The stuff that my dad gave me after our raids. I'll show you the items later. They're in the bank. I offered him three Legendaries and three Uniques...*"

"I believe that Anastaria began the conversation on the wrong foot." Deciding that I'd talk to Stacey later, I redirected the pirates' attention back on myself. "Geranika is offering immortality and it's almost impossible to offer anything much more valuable. But only almost. Grygz, surely you can understand what it means for the Lord of Shadow to grant you immortality? He'll turn you into Shades and you will spend all eternity casting about the world doing his bidding. You'll have neither freedom, nor free will. There will be nothing but Geranika's bidding. If that suits you, then I don't understand why he's not here already, nor why we're still talking. But since we are, I'd like to offer you something else, something similar to immortality. I offer you remembrance...The remembrance of heroes that will live for many centuries."

"Remembrance?" Grygz echoed with amusement. "I will already be remembered as the leader of the mightiest pirate fleet in all of history!"

"And then one day, one of your successors will assemble a larger fleet...No! I am offering you the chance to enter the pages of history as the vanquisher of the Squidolphin!"

"What?" Grygz froze.

"*What?*" Anastaria asked simultaneously in my head.

"I'm offering to help you kill the Squidolphin. Even if Geranika makes you immortal while allowing you to hang onto your body, a sea monster like the Squidolphin won't leave you in peace. More so if you're immortal—it'll consume your ship and then you'll spend the rest of eternity on the seabed or in its gullet recalling the good all days without even having the option of being properly digested. Some immortality that will be. Does languishing in stomach acids for thousands of years strike you as fun?"

Quest completed: 'Pirate Brethren. Step 1: Pleased to make your acquaintance.' Rewards:

+1000 Reputation with the Pirates of the South Seas and Grygz's ship for hunting the Squidolphin.
Quest available: 'Pirate Brethren. Step 2: Thar she blows!'

"Hmm..." I heard Evolett say, as the quest update notification flashed before his eyes. Once again, the reward and penalty varied and the quest came with the same clan restrictions—but at least we had made progress. All that was left was to catch the Squidolphin and the pirates would be on our side.

"*Your turn, Stacey. I need to know everything there is to know about this monster. It's not possible that there's no information about it.*"

"One doesn't utter words like these in vain, Free Citizen," Grygz said pensively, playing his role to a T. "You have three days to kill the beast. I will give you ten ships from my personal fleet and will come with you myself. Anyone willing can join our hunt and if we succeed, we will discuss a campaign against Armard. But no sooner...The countdown begins the day after tomorrow. Tomorrow, I invite you and your spouse to our meeting. I will announce what you said there and then...Now go—I must think!"

"Grab the line," said the voice from above me, but I was already ready for this means of conveyance. It beat being sent to Geranika in a cage. By the way, I wonder if he would have arrived to pick us up on his own or whether that would have constituted a violation of our (the players') rights to free movement. Or perhaps in this scenario these rights would no longer apply? Damn it! What am I thinking about? I have a hunting expedition ahead of me!

"In that case, I'm headed back to training," Plinto announced as soon as I told him what we had agreed to. "You can catch the fishy without me just fine. What about you, Stacey?"

"Thanks but no thanks—Nashlazar can wait! The name itself—Squidolphin—makes me want to see it with my own eyes, and knowing Mahan, he'll stumble on it for sure."

"Shall we make bets?" quipped Plinto. "Let's see who knows our boss better?"

"What?!" Anastaria exclaimed. "A bet?"

"Should I maybe step out or something?" I grinned, but no one paid attention to me.

"Let's put it in writing!" said Plinto. "And we'll let a third party hold onto the betting document—may as well be Mahan actually. We won't even look to see what the other wrote. The result will speak for us."

"What do you wager?" Anastaria asked. I never imagined that she had such a taste for gambling. She seemed unshakeable to me, but in the company of Plinto, the Iron Lady turned into some monster that didn't resemble my Stacey.

"Me?" Plinto took his time thinking and then continued: "My swallow."

"WHAT?!"

Besides Stacey and me, Evolett and Zlatan also exclaimed in astonishment.

"My swallow," Plinto shrugged. "I've had plenty of time to study our fearless clan leader, so I'm pretty confident about what he'll do. In two days, you'll see that I'm right..."

"If I lose the wager, you can have the Kalrinian Tear," Anastaria said enigmatically. Judging by Evolett's and Zlatan's stunned expressions, they understood exactly what she was talking about.

"Activated?" Plinto inquired.

"Of course not. How will we check to see who was more accurate?"

"We'll sign a betting contract and load an Imitator. It'll determine who was closer to the truth."

"Guys have you lost your marbles?" I yelled when all of this had finally ceased to amuse me. It's cool and all when people make bets about you—as long as it's in jest. But Anastaria and Plinto were going too far now and this was no longer sounding like a joke to me at all.

"Do you agree with my conditions?" asked Plinto, ignoring my objection. It looked like the Rogue had already sent Stacey the contract.

"In full!"

"*Stacey, stop!*" Realizing that no one was listening to me, I resorted to my other 'channel.'

"*Dan, it's okay...This little know-it-all needs to be punished...I'll send you all there is to know about that dolphin in two days! Don't spoil my chance at pulling one over Plinto!*"

"*Stacey!*"

"*The issue's closed! Sorry Dan, but this argument goes back a long time for me. The chance to win Plinto's phoenix comes around once in a lifetime. Don't meddle and focus on the game."*

Utterly stunned, I watched Anastaria scribble on a piece of paper how she envisioned I would deal with the Squidolphin. For the first time since our virtual wedding, Stacey was acting against me, placing her personal desires ahead of what was best for us. Perhaps she'd done it earlier too, but never so obviously...I don't even know...This was an unpleasant feeling...

"Here, boss," said Plinto, pulling me back to the game and handing me two folded papers. "Keep these safe like they were your birth certificates. And don't look at them. We could have used another player, the mail, the Bank or a simple contract, but it's cooler if you're involved."

"Uh-huh, we'll see how you handle yourself," Stacey smiled, as if she hadn't put me in my place a moment ago.

"First of all, you can both go to hell," I said through my teeth, taking the two notes and putting them in my bag. So they place bets on me and assume I'll play along like a good boy? Thanks but no thanks. "Neither of you will get bonuses for the next three months. I realize it's dumb to punish a player who bought a ship with her own money, but...Imitator, please record my words. Second of all, neither one of you will be a part of this quest. Stacey, your ship is moored at the wharf. Figure out how to sail it yourself. Remove me from its settings. Tomorrow at my meeting with Grygz, I'll request that he exclude you from the hunting party. Plinto—I'm sorry that I distracted you from your training with the Patriarch, but you are free to return to him. I hope that Evolett will take me aboard his ship," I glanced over at the man who'd grown serious in the meanwhile and received a supportive nod in response. Well that's good at least! "Third of all—guys, I have a lot of respect for you as players, but as friends, what you just did was very…Well, you're simply insane!"

"*Dan, I…*" Anastaria began, but I managed to cut her off mentally:

"*Stacey, this isn't funny! The hell with what Evolett thinks. The hell with Zlatan and what he'll think, but Stacey! How am I going to look in front of you? Little Stacey decided to gamble on me, and I'm supposed to grin and bear it? After all, what can I say when the interests of her highness are at stake?*"

"*Dan, we're talking about the phoenix here…*"

"*The issue's closed. I've said my part. Good luck to you and your ship. Try not to drown…My Energy's running out…*"

It occurred to me that I was acting like a child, but it had been a very long time since I'd felt anything like this. It's incredibly unpleasant when a person who does such a thing to you is the person whom…whom yes…whom you love! I loved Anastaria, god damn it!

"Thank you everyone for coming here," I went on calmly, more for Evolett's benefit than anyone else's. "We'll meet up here tomorrow…"

Your patent for junior captain is no longer

valid because you have lost your vessel. You are now a pirate novice.

As soon as Anastaria removed me from her ship, the system glibly demoted me to the very bottom of the pirate hierarchy. I had no reputation and no ship...To hell with it all!

Plinto didn't even bother to say anything to me. He only smirked, cast a portal and returned to his training. For their part, Evolett and Zlatan announced diplomatically that they wished to go see the city and left me alone with Stacey—as alone as we could among the bustling streets.

"Dan, what's with the tantrum?" Stacey asked. "I swear you're acting like a child. If there's anyone who should understand that Plinto's phoenix is worth grinning and bearing it—it's you!"

"Stacey, I'm sick and tired of constantly grinning and bearing it. With the pirates I have to grin and bear it. With Plinto I have to grin and bear it. But when it comes to real life, I don't even have a say in the matter. I'm a prisoner here! Maybe enough?"

"Are you confusing something?" The girl's eyes narrowed. "There's the game, in which the rules are clear, and there's reality in which those same rules are very different. If in the game you have to grin and bear something to get a unique thing, then you should grin and bear it. In reality, it's your duty to voice your disagreement, but not here Dan! In Barliona both you and I and whoever else will grin and bear whatever they need to at that moment. Look at Plinto—he's even received the nickname 'the Bloodied' for all the craziness he pulls. And you can see for yourself just how crazy he is. Please, don't confuse Barliona and reality—I'm begging you..."

"Don't confuse the two? For the next seven years, Barliona is my reality!" Unfortunately, I couldn't control my emotions. I wonder whether Stacey had brought up the example of Plinto on purpose. There's a lot in a name. What if I too become known as Mahan the Grinning Bear...well, it's got a ring to it!

"Dan, I love you very much, but please consider again what will happen in seven years. Barliona will cease to be your reality and become a game again...I'm already twenty-eight. In seven years, I'll be thirty-five...Our healthcare is excellent, and I'm very fit, but thirty-five...it's...I want to have a child as it is, and I don't want my future husband to run away from me to be in his 'reality'—in Barliona. Even though you still have a lot of time ahead of you in Barliona, you need to remember that it's just a game..."

A state of permanent shock is my customary state when I talk to Anastaria. First they made bets about me, then they told me to keep out of it, and everything ended with the girl admitting that she wanted to have a child. What is even going on here?

"Truce?" meowed Anastaria, pressing up to me with her body and wrapping her arms around neck.

"Truce," I sighed at an utter loss about what to do. I couldn't remain angry at the entire world, but I couldn't forgive Stacey that easily either.

"Then let's do it this way—I will log out to reality right now and come back tomorrow around lunchtime, and then we'll spend the rest of the day together and do nothing but meet the pirates. What do you think of my offer?"

"Let's try it," I agreed again, understanding that I shouldn't argue with Stacey at the moment. I didn't have any arguments to make...

"In that case, until tomorrow." Having kissed and evaporated in my embrace, Anastaria logged out to reality. Now at last I could take my anger out on someone. The important thing was not to get sent back to the mine in the process...

"Dearie, could you help a helpless old woman?" The NPC's boilerplate request for aid caught me as I was wandering around the city contemplating my revenge against Stacey and Plinto. More so against Stacey, since Plinto simply started the argument. Once I had calmed down, I considered that Stacey was a mature person with her own issues and insecurities, so it would be utterly inappropriate for me to try to break her and change the way she was so as to suit me better. Given the way I felt about her, I wanted to be constructive, but I also couldn't ignore the way she acted either. I needed vengeance, preferably of the pettier variety.

"Dearie, could you help a helpless old woman?" the granny repeated, addressing some other player. I glanced at the time—it was 3 p.m. and I had most of the day ahead of me, so I could easily put some work in. I couldn't come up with a preferred plan of vengeance—all of my ruminations ended either in the bed of a tavern or the Dating House, so I decided to distract myself. Sending everything to the devil, I made a beeline for the old lady—social quests can be interesting too. I knew this from experience.

"How can I be of help, madam?" I asked the old lady who was sheltering in the shade of one Cadis' many stone buildings.

"A pirate?" smirked the old lady, giving me a sidelong glance. "Move along, dearie."

"So you do not need help?" I asked with surprise.

"From a pirate, certainly not!" The hag cut me off, turning sideways and calling out to another player.

"Why I'm hardly a pirate!" I exclaimed, my premonition warning me that I shouldn't let this quest slip away. "I don't even have a ship of my own. I don't belong to the pirate brethren. So you're being unfair..."

"You're not part of the fraternity?" The old lady, whose name was Tanuvern, asked. "How is that possible?"

"I've been a pirate for all of two hours—here: The ink on my patent isn't even dry yet," I took out the document and showed it to the old lady. She examined it very carefully as if she were a customs officer or something, scratched her head and then asked me a question that killed me:

"So what do you need, little pirate?"

I just about bit my tongue off, shutting my

mouth which was about to ask the old lady if she hadn't confused something. Luckily, I noticed that I'd just gained ten points worth of Attractiveness with this NPC.

"I wish to accomplish a great deed so that Grygz will take me on his crew. But I don't know what that deed could be. Maybe you can help me?" I began carefully, feeling out the situation. Unlike other players, I had received a unique chance to get the old lady to talk, and as a result, even my quarrel with Stacey was relegated to the back burner. If there are any player-pirates at all, surely not many of them do social quests...

"So you wish to be a pirate?" the granny asked me, indicating that I was digging in the right direction.

"You didn't understand me," I changed tack. "Simply...I love the sea very much. You could say I'm crazy for it. To see the waves, the pretty sunsets, to visit new lands and climes...Pirates are the only faction that traverses the sea freely. That is—the only free maritime faction. I don't want to be a merchant or mercenary on a trade ship. As a result, yes—to make my dream a reality, I can only join the pirates. I can't live without the sea."

"Why exclusively the pirates?" the old lady asked in a friendlier tone. "There's another faction that sails the seas freely..."

"What's that?" I couldn't help but ask, already understanding that she was talking about the Narlak fleet.

"You should first go into the service dearie," the old lady reprimanded me. "You can ask your questions after you've done that. Everyone's always looking for a free ride around here. It used to be different in the good old days..."

The various slogans that you hear in the cities of Barliona are basically all the same—love your loved ones, take care of the elderly, make this world a better place, the grass used to be greener and the sky used to be bluer. Which all begs the question of how this world tolerates people like me...

"So what needs to be done?" I asked, when Tanuvern paused to take a breath.

"For me—nothing," the old lady surprised me again. "Not far from here there's a village called Gumtrees, it's right on the coast. You should go there. Ask for Rastman. He'll tell you what you need to do for him and the village. If you do what he wants, he'll give you a confirmation document. Then we'll talk about the free maritime faction. You should go now—you're blocking my sun..."

Considering the old lady was in the shade of the building, she'd just sent me to hell. There really is a lot of that going on today...It doesn't bode well. Accepting the 'Help Gumtrees' quest, which appeared as a waypoint on my map, I just about cursed out the old hag—'not far from here' meant 200 kilometers to the east of the city. If I rode a mount or flew in my Dragon Form, it'd take me a day to get there. I'd have to use a portal. Eh...more expenditures...However, before calling Viltrius, I decided to make another call:

"Hi, Fleita! What are you up to? ...You're still angry about the jail? Oh come off it. Anyway—I need you here. I'm sending you an invite."

I tussled Draco's scruff and called my majordomo to ask him to summon me to the castle. If I had to go to Gumtrees, why not take my student with me? Our previous adventure had ended fairly well, so I could give it another shot...

"Master, the esteemed treasurer has asked me to prepare a financial report for you for the last two weeks," Viltrius said by way of greeting as soon as I appeared in Altameda.

"Show it to me. By the way, why didn't he prepare it himself? Do you have access rights?"

"Now I do. Master Leite granted them to me. Since Barsina and he began to govern the villages, he hasn't had the time to pay attention to anything else."

"Is he here?"

"No. You and Barsina are the only members of the Legends of Barliona present on the premises."

"Tell me where she is and then send over my student to us," I asked Viltrius. It had been a while since I'd seen the little Druid—almost a week—so I should stop by and say hi.

"Mahan!" the girl greeted me warmly, looking up from some paperwork. "What's up? Listen, this is some kind of treasure trove!"

"Where?"

"Why the villages we're governing! Have you read the financial report for our clan?"

"No, I just arrived and stopped by to see you."

"Read over it. You'll find it very interesting. Leite and his wife are working miracles!"

"I'll make sure to read it," I assured the girl. "What about you? How are you?"

"Oh, don't even ask. I can't believe that I wasted so much time trying to be a mercenary...I thought that the money was in the quests and Dungeons...What a fool I was! This is where the real money is," Barsa gestured around her. "Storage vault rental, transportation services, and much more—check out the reports. Listen, thank you for giving me the chance to prove myself. Where's Stacey?"

"She's out in reality. When's the last time you were out there?"

"Hmm...It's been several weeks now...Maybe you're right. I should take a little break. Otherwise, I'll turn into a zombie....Speaking of zombies, how's your student progressing?"

"Fine, I think. Listen, Barsa, would you consider yourself a cruel woman?"

"E-ehh..."

"You see, I need to come up with a revenge against Anastaria."

"What do you mean, 'revenge?' Why would you want vengeance against your wife?"

"To show her that I have feelings as well..."

"Hmm...You know, without knowing the full story, I can't really tell you anything. Will you tell me, or is it something between you two?"

"Not anymore...I want revenge because of something that happened not between the two of us but with other people. But okay, it's nothing worth hiding from you...Basically, this is what happened..."

"Mahan, are you sure that Stacey really needs that phoenix?" Barsina asked after I'd finished relating to her what had just happened.

"What do you mean?"

"You see...I don't even know how to explain it to you...Would you ever act the way she did?"

"Of course not. That was..."

"And we both know who Anastaria is and what she used to do earlier..."

"You mean her working for Phoenix as an analyst?"

"Therefore," Barsina went on, without answering my rhetorical question, "we can conclude that Stacey surely must have foreseen the consequences of her behavior, right?"

"Well...Yes, but I don't understand what you're getting at..."

"Let me go on. Plinto, whom you haven't seen or heard from for almost a month, suddenly offers a wager about how you'll act and then he bets something that Anastaria effectively doesn't really need—she already has a pretty decent griffin. And yet she accepts the wager. I might say some bad things about our Stacey right now, so don't take my words too seriously, but Mahan, are you sure that Anastaria is really on our side?"

"Okay, now I've really lost your thread..."

"She doesn't need the phoenix—that's a fact. But you couldn't find a single player in Malabar who doesn't know about how badly Hellfire and Ehkiller want to get their hands on that bird. They're ready to give a lot for it too! Anastaria was in Phoenix and supposedly left it, yet she agrees to make the bet over an item that she doesn't need. I told you I might say something bad, but...With all due respect to that girl, Mahan, what if she's still working for Phoenix under a different banner, so to speak? Do you have a contract with her?"

"Obviously." Barsina's suggestion stunned me. My little Druid really was getting at something beyond the pale.

"In that case, I don't know," Barsa shrugged. "Forgive me—lately, I've been imagining enemies all around us who want to infiltrate our clan and co-opt what we're doing, so I'm a little paranoid...and tired. You're right, I need to take several days' break and spend some time at home, away from Barliona. It's not so simple to change professions. It's just that I used to wonder how is it that Anastaria manages to get Phoenix's help, considering she's no longer part of that clan. Were I the leader of Phoenix, I'm not sure I'd be ready to help her. After all, you have to consider...Well, sorry, I can't really help you. You can see yourself that I'm so tired I've begun talking nonsense. I'm going to go, okay?"

Barsina jotted down several notes, cast me an apologetic look and dissolved. The entire time that the Druid was making her preparations to leave, I remained standing staring at my feet, trying to gather my thoughts.

Barsina's words had struck me in the gut...

No, there had to be a reasonable explanation for everything—Ehkiller was Stacey's father and would always try to help her. And, perhaps, Stacey leaving Phoenix was just show for Hellfire and Rick...both of whom nevertheless remained in the clan without changing even a bit...Damn! What if Stacey really only joined my clan to be deputy for six months and then, when she learned that I had Karmadont's scroll, had come up with a plan B? No—nonsense! After all, she'd summoned the Emperor to witness her oath while swearing that she'd never seen the scroll before...Damn it all! Why did I tell Barsa about my quarrel with Stacey?

"Master, I have brought your pupil," Viltrius said, bringing me back to reality. I glanced at the goblin's bowed head and a new thought struck me like a lightning bolt. I reached for an amulet and made a call:

"Hey Clutzer! Listen, I need you to do a small thing for me. Can I summon you to me? Viltrius—summon him please."

The Rogue had gained his freedom by paying the not insignificant (by current measures) debt to the government. And he had asked me not to tell anyone that I knew this...especially...especially Anastaria.

"So what do you need?" The Rogue appeared before me a moment later. Sending Fleita off to level up her Intellect at one of the castle's training areas, I waited until she left and then cast my protective shroud over us—even though it was impossible to eavesdrop on me inside my castle.

"I am going to do the talking. I want you simply to listen. You're free now which means one thing—your twenty-something million debt to the government has been paid. You couldn't have paid this amount on your own, so it follows that someone paid it for you, forcing you to sign some contract first. I suspect that the contract includes a nondisclosure clause, which stipulates that you can't let anyone know of your freedom, whether by a word, a gesture or some other means. But you found a way to let me know the happy news without violating your contract...This means that it's not immaterial to you...But okay, I'm interested in something else. Who paid for your freedom? I have several suspects in mind, and I don't like any of them. The first is the Corporation, who might wish to have someone near me to adjust my actions if the need arises. I can't imagine why they would need to do this and any reasons I can think of seem ridiculous under closer scrutiny, but the thought still remains. The second candidate is some enemy clan that's ready to pay money to find out the secrets of our clan. I realize that this sounds even nuttier than the first option, so I will be more concrete...Phoenix bought your freedom—though I have no idea why they would need to do so. Moreover, Anastaria knows that you are free...And you know, I suspect that you're bound not only by an in-game contract, but another one in reality...But again, for the life of me, I can't figure out why anyone would do this."

"So what do you need?" Clutzer asked again without so much as twitching a muscle during my speech. "While you're thinking, I wanted to ask you—I recently saw that global message that the Emperor Chess Piece had been crafted. Can I look at it? It's quite amazing that you managed to craft it out of sequence ..."

"I need to come up with a way to pay back Anastaria," I said pensively, removing the protective shroud. I got the impression that by asking about the figurine, Clutzer was only cobbling together an excuse for our conversation and I wanted to help him out. But had I really been mistaken in my assumptions? Thinking a little longer, I showed the Lait Chess Piece to Clutzer. "Will you help me?"

"Sorry, I have a raid coming up and don't have the time. But if I had the chance, I'd be more than happy to help you. If there's anything I learned back in reality, it's coming up with dirty tricks. Damn! And you kept mum about it all this time?" the Rogue exclaimed. "Have you seen the king's properties?"

"Like you need to ask...I'll tell you right now: Don't even think of asking for the figurine. I need it..."

"Greed is a bad habit," Clutzer remarked philosophically. "That's it. I have to run! Good luck with the other Chess Pieces and tell Viltrius to send me back—I'm not some millionaire's son to go jumping around Malabar on my own dime."

My majordomo returned Clutzer to the castle portal, leaving me to my sad solitude. I figured that I'd get at least some hint about what was going on, but it all ended in...

The Chess Set of Karmadont!

Clutzer had quite openly told me that Anastaria had paid his fine, since he'd "be more than happy to help" me, but didn't have the chance because of some chess pieces! Like hell!

Realizing that I was running in mental circles, built mostly from my own stupidity, paranoia and god-knew-what-else, I opened the clan settings, looked up the player contracts and selected the one for Stacey. We really had signed a contract with her which—and here a cold sweat struck me through and through—which ceased to be effective as soon as she quit being deputy! The boilerplate contract between the clan head and his deputy had been terminated due to her quitting that post! Memories of our meeting at which I had proposed she sign a contract began to flash through my mind, since who could I trust if not Stacey, but...

"Mahan, I'm sick of crushing the training dummies," came Fleita's voice. "Did you invite me here to do just this?"

"What?" I asked, still turning my new outlook on Barliona over in my mind.

"I said, I wish you'd stop sitting there with glassy eyes. Let's go take on some real enemies," the girl said. "And I don't want to end up in jail again. It's wet and cold there!"

"Gumtrees."

"What gum trees?"

"We need to go to Gumtrees," I explained, still

not entirely myself.

"Well that tells me a lot," Fleita quipped. "Are you at Hatred status with Gumtrees as well?"

"No...yes...Listen Fleita, give me a couple hours to think...I don't feel like doing quests right now..."

"Like hell!"

"That's a trademarked phrase you're using there..."

"We can share it. Come on—we'll go to your Gumtrees. You should look at yourself in the mirror. Even when I'd only just shown up in Barliona, I looked better than you do at the moment. And keep in mind that being a Zombie is pretty disorienting the first few minutes. We rise howling from a mass of dead bodies, like this..." Fleita imitated herself rising like a zombie with her arms outstretched and her head crooked. "So all in all, I can assure you that you don't look so hot right now."

"Maybe you're right," I said, trying to come to my senses and rid myself of these oppressive thoughts. Even if Stacey was an agent of Phoenix, she wouldn't receive the quest. I needed to craft one more figurine in order to open the Tomb, so I should occupy myself with that first, and deal with the other stuff later. "Let's go..."

* * *

"So this is Gumtrees?" Fleita asked skeptically when we popped out of the portal into the central square. It was another standard layout reminiscent of Beatwick:

an immense wooden house, village elders, a stockade, dogs barking, NPCs scurrying about their business...Just like an ordinary old village. "Where do you even find these locations? This is the middle of nowhere..."

"Who are you?" came a gruff male voice. I turned in its direction and saw a sinewy, thickset man regarding Fleita with an unkind eye. It was only my presence with my Attractiveness bonuses that kept this grim Level 250 NPC from attacking the Zombie. "What'd you want?"

"To speak with you," I replied, checking his properties: Alderman Rastman. "Tanuvern sent me to you, telling me that you have a job for me and my companion."

"The old lady has never sent two before," Rastman narrowed his eyes suspiciously. "Not to mention a Zombie and a pirate."

"So there have been others before us?" I asked, ignoring Fleita's surprised exclamation. I'd fill her in about the pirate business later.

"Of course there have! I reckon we've had twenty guests in the past ten years. But not any that were like you...I think, it'd best if you went on your way..."

"Give us the document that says we completed everything and we'll be gone without a trace," I jumped at the opportunity to complete the quest in record time.

"Document, you say?" Rastman's face went smooth for a moment. "That's a thought. Come on, I'll write one right now. Do you have some paper?"

Even in such trifles as stationary, the Corporation did its best to extract money from the players. Any little occasion to profit would do for them!

"Mahan, we can't just leave this place," Fleita said, watching our conversation. "There's something here that's...I can't say what it is, but...I have this strange premonition that it's not a good idea to leave..."

"So, will you give me some paper?" the alderman raised his eyebrows inquisitively, but I decided to trust my student. I hadn't felt anything myself, as if I'd grown old and insensitive, but since Fleita was feeling something, it'd probably be best to heed her.

"Never mind about the paper," I sighed. "We'll deal with it later. What's the job? What do you want us to do?"

"So you don't want to take the easy way," grumbled Rastman. "Have it your way...I do have something for you and your Zombie pet to do..."

Quest completed: 'Help Gumtrees.'
Quest available: 'Clean the pigsty.'

"Will you take it?" grinned Rastman. "It's been a month since it's been cleaned. Even the flies refuse to go in there."

"We'll do it," Fleita announced calmly. "We've seen worse..."

"A pigsty?"

"Well...We'll be like Hercules," my student

shrugged as soon as Rastman indicated where we needed to go. He didn't want to accompany us, owing to the smell. Maybe this NPC was sure that he was seeing us for the last time in his life and didn't want to gum up his memory with useless data.

"Listen brother, I just remembered that I forgot to do my homework," said Draco when about three hundred meters remained between us and the large stone building. Situated on a hillock—which made it impossible to use Hercules' trick of cleaning the stables by diverting a river into it—the pigsty was a sad sight indeed. It was dirty, foul-smelling, weathered by time and full of broken windows and the mad squealing of swine.

"Mahan, I'm not sure I want to go in there either," Fleita joined Draco. "Maybe you'll deal with it on your own?"

"What? You're the one who took the quest! Don't even think of shifting it on me. Grab the shovel and let's go do some cleaning..."

Next to the door holding on by one hinge lay two shovels—as if the devs knew ahead of time that there'd be two of us doing this quest.

"How do these animals survive in here?" croaked Fleita, frowning from the mortifying smell. I have to admit that the developers had really pulled out all the stops. My student informed me that she'd received a warning that the olfactory component of her sensory filters had been turned off, which meant that she was smelling the same odor I was. The pigs—that is the enormous, lazy monsters called Swinesnouts—were lying on their sides in large puddles of mud, making bubbles and oinking in contentment. They seemed completely unfazed by their surroundings, as if living their lives in the manner was completely acceptable to them.

"Let's get out of here," I barked, almost running out of the sty. It was impossible to remain inside of it and terrifying to think that we'd have to clear those enormous mounds of excrement on our own. By the time we'd clear one side, a similar pile would have been made on the other. It looked like we'd been forced into a Sisyphean task. I needed to mull things over...

"I'm not going back there again!" Fleita announced flatly, as soon as we'd gotten a breath of fresh air. Even though the air beside the pigsty wasn't much, it was fresher than what we'd just breathed.

"I agree. We need to find some other way. Did you notice that that place hardly has a roof?"

"You mean all the holes in it? I noticed..."

"Well, I did too. If we can shovel the excrement, then we can move it some other way too."

"And so what?" the girl asked puzzled, failing to understand what I was getting at.

"And so nothing!" I raised one finger meaningfully, got out my amulet and called Clutzer: "What's up! Listen, I urgently need four Water Mages who can cast a rain shower that doesn't do damage...Yup, just a huge torrent of water falling from the sky...No, it's not for a date...You know what? Throw in one more—scratch that—two more Druids.

We'll need to bind a hundred or so mobs in place temporarily. I'm sending the coordinates. I'll be waiting."

* * *

"How do you like the piglets?" Rastman asked, barely containing his laughter. "You gave up a little quickly. Ordinary Free Citizens take a little longer to come and complain."

"We've completed the task you gave us, esteemed alderman," I replied, paying no attention to his conceited tone. "How else can we help you?"

"Completed?" the alderman's brows hiked up to his forehead as his jaw dropped to his chest. "But how?"

"You haven't replied to my question. How else can we be of assistance to your village?"

It'd be a mistake, I think, to inform the locals that we'd just almost drowned their bacon in a lake of filth. Clutzer's Mages called down such a torrent that the pigs that we'd bound to the earth, could do nothing but scream and complain about the unfairness of life. We'd even had to resuscitate one of them after the water had receded—the dumb beast had managed to drown. But the result was satisfactory—the pigsty was sparkling clean and the animals had re-assumed their original color—pink. Pink Swinesnouts...What could be more terrifying...

"I will...send someone to make sure..." the alderman muttered, still not believing us.

"However...Maybe...That's right! I have one more job for you, Free Citizen! We have this one problem—every month a monster comes from the sea seeking to destroy our village. Luckily we are protected by the magical beacons situated along the coast. All we have to do is charge them and the village will be left untouched. Just such a beacon is located right here in the village. But there are another 22 beacons along the coast and we've never managed to light all of them at once—three of them are very difficult to get to, and a beacon stays lit only for 24 hours. Plus we only have two crystals to activate them with, so you and your companion need to hurry. Will you accept this quest? The monster will show up tomorrow morning. I can show you right now how to activate the beacons with the one in the village and then I'll give you a charging crystal apiece. If you manage to activate all 22 beacons in time—eleven on each side of the village (I'll mark them on your map)—I'll give you the note you need for Tanuvern. But if you don't make it in time, come back in a month and you can try again. I really want to see what all these beacons are here for."

Quest available: 'Activate coastal defenses.'

"We'll do it!" I replied in Fleita's place. There'd be no problem reaching the beacon—I'd send Draco and Fleita in one direction and head in the other in my Dragon Form. Unless there'd be some problem with the actual activation—this quest was a shoo-in.

"I'll warn you right off though—you won't be able

to fly there!" Rastman said. "Griffins get scared for some reason and refuse to fly over the coast. You can only complete this quest over land."

"We'll see about that," I replied ambiguously, knowing full well that Draco had no problems flying in this area. And if he can, why couldn't I? I'm a winged lizard too, aren't I?

"Beacon four activated—we're headed for the next one!" Fleita reported over the amulet. "How are you coming along?"

"I'm a hundred meters from the sixth. You must be dragging your wings!" I smirked. The activation procedure presented no difficulties—as soon as I held the charging crystal up to the special device, a spark flashed and a message appeared that the beacon had been activated. The beacons themselves were three-meter-tall posts of some strange metal with unreadable properties. And yet the devs had situated them in such strange locations that unless you knew how to fly, you'd be utterly out of luck: in a deep canyon with sheer cliffs for walls, at the top of a hill, on an island several hundred meters out to sea...Not a single of the beacons was easy to get to, as if doing this quest required twenty-two players assigned to one beacon each—as well as three Mages with an endless supply of Mana in order to teleport each player and crystal to the required locations.

You have activated the coastal defense against the monster of the deep. The coast will be safe from the monster for the next six months.

And that's it? Nothing about what the monster would drop if we slayed it? A simple announcement that it'd be barred from this area for half a year? By the way, what harm could the monster cause anyway?

"See that hill there?" Rastman pointed in the distance when I asked him this question. Upon our return to Gumtrees, Fleita and I were met by a village in celebration. I'd never imagined that I'd find so many people so far away from the large cities—the entire town square was brimming with revelers, celebrating their safety for the next half year. As soon as we landed, the alderman marked both of our quests completed, while our Attractiveness with him soared through the roof to 38 points. "Once upon a time, that was our farm, but the sea monster appeared and destroyed it, consuming all our swine. Since then, we don't build our farms near the sea."

"What did it look like?" Fleita inquired. "I'd never heard of sea monsters that could crawl out to land."

"I don't even know...We were hiding in our basements at the time. The village is protected, but I ventured a peek...It had a long body like that of an enormous whale—with long tentacles like an octopus. I can't say anything else about it....Tomorrow morning, if you like, you can see it for yourself—it tries to break through to the village directly at first, but as soon as it encounters the magical barrier it shifts its attention to the neighboring areas. Here— this is your paper for Tanuvern—you've done a great deed for our village..."

"What kind of monster is that? An octopus and whale in one creature?" Fleita asked, surprised. "Does that exist?"

"I guess it does...Let's go back to Cadis and complete this quest. We'll come back here afterwards. I kind of want to take a look at this monster of the deep..."

When I handed her Rastman's note with his words of gratitude and a description of what we had accomplished for Gumtrees, the old lady spent about five minutes studying it, turning it from side to side and even testing it on her tooth like it was printed on gold leaf or something. Considering that during this entire process, the NPC's eyes turned into two glassy orbs, I could safely assume that she was downloading new data, as if this Imitator hadn't expected us to succeed.

"I don't even know what to say," Tanuvern's eyes finally regained their sight and she addressed us. "I remember issuing the quest, but the Zombie had nothing to do with it."

"This is my student, madam," I immediately covered for Fleita. "I have been charged with the vital task of setting her on the Way of the Shaman and it is not in my power to object to the will of the Supreme Spirits. From now on, she follows me wherever I go and does the same quests I do. Such is the fate of all students..."

"I can see that she's your student," the old lady muttered, "I wouldn't even have mentioned her otherwise...Okay, let it be so, I accept your note. Remind me—what did you want to know?"

"You were going to tell me about the faction that sails the seas as freely as the pirates. I can't live without the sea, you see..."

"That's right—the faction...Well, north of our continent lies the city of Radring. The ruler of this city and its surrounding lands is King...hmm...I forgot the new fellow's name, but that's not the point. The important thing is that he rules this kingdom with the help of the Sea Wolves—the people who hunt the pirates. If you're so crazy about the sea but don't want to be a pirate—ask any guard in Radring, complete the quest he gives you, then the training and you'll become a Sea Wolf!"

"Radring?" I asked, staring at Fleita's puzzled face. I had figured that I was about to find out about the Squidolphin and how I could defeat it, but the old granny launched into a spiel about some new city instead. "I've never heard of that place..."

"Don't yell!" the old lady whispered and looked around like some spy on a mission. "Radring and Cadis have a very poor relationship. In fact, put simply, they're at war. I spent thirty years before the mast in the service of that mighty kingdom, but now I spend my time finding people like you—who can't imagine themselves away from the sea and don't want to be—or cannot be—pirates. I've sent about three thousand Free Citizens from here to my native land. Now your turn has come. So—will you go?"

**Quest available: 'A Sailor's Apprenticeship.' ...
Quest type: Rare.**

"Mahan, let's take it! What do you say?" said Fleita, who'd received the same message.

"Why did you send us to Gumtrees then?" I asked the old lady, feeling no urgency to accept her quest. No doubt the three thousand Free Sailors she'd helped recruit had already unearthed all the secret quests available in Radring. Meanwhile, there hadn't been any pirate players before me as I understood it.

"Where else could I send you?" the granny replied with surprise. "All of the surrounding villages are allied with the pirates. They outfit them with supplies and the quests there are all the same—catch the fish, plant a tree for a ship, steal a sheep for supper. Gumtrees is one of the few locales that the pirates haven't captured yet. Something to do with monsters of the deep or something. So it was either Gumtrees or Gorlov, Shady Trees or Wellbeckstein. I'll confess that I don't send players to Gumtrees often— it's a bit far, but...Why would I send a pirate to his favorite village anyway? Especially considering he managed to pick up a Zombie along the way. I assumed that you were a pirate agent come to catch me—meanwhile Rastman has a cleaning quest that no one's been able to complete yet. I wanted to get rid of you—it was a mistake I...You're a dependable guy, one of our own...So, will you go to Radring?"

"Sure, I'll go check it out," I accepted the quest, thinking to myself that no one could force me to do it, and this way, if things didn't work out with the pirates, I'd have a backup...It was too bad that I didn't have much time available to me.

"So when do we go to Radring, Mahan?" Fleita asked impatiently as soon as we stepped away from the old lady. Tanuvern had played her role as contact person and now turned back into an ordinary NPC with a quest to offer. By her own words, three thousand players had already spoken to her and set out on the path of subjugating the seas among the Sea Wolves' ranks...Was I going to follow in their wake? I didn't much feel like it...

"You don't want to take a look at the sea monster anymore?" I asked surprised.

"I do and all, but..."

"But?" I hitched an eyebrow.

"But this is an adventure! Sea battles, endless expanses, the sway of the deck, the courageous seadogs and daring pirates," Fleita's eyes lit up as if the girl was already imagining herself on the deck of a ship, sailing straight at the enemy fleet.

"Adventures are nice. Are you sure, however—as a Shaman—that you have taken care of all your business in this area?"

"As a Shaman? What do you mean?"

"I suggest you listen to your feelings and say to yourself, 'I'm going to Radring; there's nothing else for me to do here in Cadis.' If nothing holds you back..."

"That's not fair!" the girl exclaimed. "You can't just shift responsibility to someone else like that."

"I don't follow you..."

"I want to go to Radring. I want it very much...But I want it with my brains. In my heart, I know that I need to return to Gumtrees...You see, when I said that we needed to stay there, I felt something...I felt something that forced me to stand up to you even though we have our agreement. It was the same feeling that led me to you originally...And it's the same now: My head is telling me that I need to travel to the Sea Wolves as soon as possible, while my internal voice is forcing me to go to Gumtrees...Only I can't understand how it is that I feel this...I feel like I'm going crazy, so I'm still for us going to Radring."

"You're not going crazy," I grinned. "That's called the Way of the Shaman, and you have only just set foot on it. Your job as a player is to follow it as much as you can. Only then will you be able to complete your class initiation and receive your unique Totem. I'm telling you this as a player who has traveled along the same Way...And another thing...Let's decide now—if you feel something that contradicts what we're doing—you tell me right that instant. Please, I beg you, don't mess with your feelings by throwing tantrums. Nothing good will come of it."

"In that case, let's head back to Gumtrees," Fleita offered a little uncertainly (though I was happy with even that). "Thank you! I just understood why you brought me along on these quests..."

"Back already?" Rastman asked with astonishment when we reappeared in Gumtrees. "Did the old lady not accept my letter?"

"The letter went over fine, don't worry," I assured

the alderman. What a difference +13 to Attractiveness makes! The new opportunities are invaluable. "We wanted to see the monster that haunts these lands. Your description of it really piqued my interest. When did you say, it'll show up?"

"Typically early in the morning, around four or five. It tries to break through the barrier for about an hour and then gives up and heads off to destroy everything else it can get its tentacles on ..."

"Wonderful! Could you tell us where we can rest until early morning?"

"The tavern might have some free rooms available. We don't get much tourists around here typically."

"Typically? So some do come by every once in a while?"

"Of course! Not very long ago, about two months or so, we were visited by a Free Citizen, a kobold named Reptilis Y'allgotohellis, I believe. He declined the quests I offered him, but sojourned in our village for a few days, constantly creeping around the hills. I have no idea what he found here, but he was positively glowing on the last day...Before him, we had some other guests stop by..."

Rastman went on listing the players who had visited the village, but I was already barely listening to him. The news about Reptilis was much more interesting to me—what did that snooper want here? In view of the immense speed at which this player was leveling up, I couldn't help but be curious about him...

"Mahan, I've spent too much time in-game as it is today and I need to get up early tomorrow. May I leave?" Fleita asked awkwardly, sitting down on the edge of the only bed in the room. As Rastman had assumed, there was indeed space for us in the tavern—only this tavern came with a surprise: It only had a single room. One room with one bed. A player could of course sleep in any position and any place, but purely from a psychological point of view, ordinary beds retained their appeal. Therefore, when Fleita saw the room we were offered, she went chalk-white. It's no simple matter to sleep in a single room with a strange man: To do so in one bed is overboard for a 17-year-old girl.

"Go on," I smiled, understanding perfectly well the way she felt. Despite the fact that were I even free, I couldn't do anything to her (in Barliona, all erotic contact was banned until the age of 21), I'd never insist on Fleita spending the night beside me. It was looking like our relationship was growing closer in its teacher-student aspect, and the last thing I wanted was to spoil the beginnings of our mutual understanding.

Glancing at the watch, which read nine in the evening, I set my alarm for three in the morning and went to bed. I had a hard day ahead of me tomorrow...

CHAPTER ELEVEN
THE SQUIDOLPHIN

"WAKE UP!" I heard Fleita yell as my bed began to rock left and right. "Get up! You'll sleep through the hunt!"

I opened my eyes and saw the Shaman above me, her white eyes shining in the room's darkness.

"It's not even 3 o'clock yet!" I muttered, turning off the alarm. A mere ten minutes remained before it was supposed to ring—but they were MY ten minutes!

"Don't grumble," Fleita parried. "I brought you some breakfast."

And indeed—next to my bed stood a small tray with a piece of toast, a bowl of oatmeal and a pitcher with some liquid I didn't feel like investigating. After eating at the Golden Horseshoe, other food elicited nothing but condescension.

"Thanks," I told the girl regardless, consuming the food mechanically while trying to ignore its flavor. With all due respect to the local cook, even I, with my

32 points in Cooking could had prepared something that tasted better.

Nighttime in Gumtrees met us with silence and pleasant coolness. There were neither bustling passersby, nor children playing, nor a smith forging, nor a tanner blackening the sky with his fumes. Silence, coolness and the alderman standing near the tavern, waiting for us. I wonder why he isn't sleeping...

"I'm tired of hiding," he explained when Fleita and I approached him. "I've never seen all the beacons activated before, so the monster can't do anything to us. I'll at least have a look at it, since the opportunity presented itself...Where are you going to look at him from? WHAT THE HELL! A DRAGON!"

No sooner had I turned into a Dragon than the alderman changed completely too. He collapsed to the ground and began to crawl back like a crab until he encountered the nearest wall and began to crawl in place. And the most curious thing was that Draco, who had been with me the entire time, hadn't elicited this reaction—yet when I turned into my Dragon Form and flew up into the air to look for a convenient vantage point...

"What are you hollering for?" I asked the alderman, turning back into my human form. "So it's a dragon! Have you never seen a Dragon before or something?"

"No, your highness," the alderman whispered, his face as pale as Fleita's. If earlier he had paid no attention to my title—an Earl in Malabar isn't an Earl in the Free Lands—then now it was as if Rastman's eyes had opened for the first time. Here is the power of true terror—the fear of Dragons at a genetic level. I'm starting to understand how Casper felt!

"In that case, here's your chance to look at one. Just don't yell. I don't like yelling! Draco," I turned to my Totem. "You're carrying Fleita again. Will you give her a ride?"

"Sure," my brother nodded. "Where are we going to observe from?"

"I think that we can..."

BOOM! A sound reminiscent of the ringing of an enormous bell resounded throughout our surroundings. It was deep, saturated, clear and it forced all your organs—or whatever it is in-game avatars have—to vibrate.

"It has begun!" the alderman paled even further—his fear of the monster seemed to be greater than his fear of the Dragon—and yet, to his credit, he didn't crawl away or try to fade into the wall. "It's come earlier today for some reason..."

Paying no attention to Rastman's ravings, I turned into my Dragon Form and rose into the night sky of Barliona. Draco with Fleita stayed beside me, but I didn't pay any attention to them either—utter chaos reigned only a hundred meters from the coast. In a cloud of sea spray, foam and muck, an amorphous shape was trying to break through to the shore—encountering with its tentacles the barrier that stood between it and the earth. As soon as the thing touched the wall, a shower of sparks flew up and the tentacles retracted back into the cloud of spray and foam. It didn't seem at all that the monster was somehow restrained or paralyzed, so I flew up closer and...

"Mahan!" Fleita yelled. "That's no monster..."

"I can see that..."

When a mere twenty meters remained to the barrier, the monster's outlines grew sharper and I gained access to its properties. The properties of the object—not the monster—that we were dealing with...

Minor Squidolphin (Level 1). Object type: Sub/surface vessel. Crew size: 7. Owner: None. Status: Feral.

Velocity...Armament... Armor... Maximum operating depth... Other bathyscaphic characteristics...

Well, damn!

The Squidolphin really was a sight to behold—a long sleek body with a flat deck on which I could clearly see three rows of seats. Or perhaps a nave in the creature's body that resembled seats. Long appendages were situated along her sides, where ships had oars. The appendages looked almost exactly like a squid's tentacles, but several times longer and thicker...The Squidolphin's nose had a toothy mouth and two red eyes that were staring at us with open hostility. A Minor Squidolphin...Considering that this monster was about twenty meters long, it was hard to imagine what a Normal Squidolphin, or for that matter, a Large or Giant Squidolphin looked like...

The amulet around my neck began to vibrate, so I turned to activate it.

"M-Mahan," came Fleita's voice. "We need to train it..."

"Her—she's a ship. But yeah, that's a reasonable idea—do you have any suggestions about how we might do that?"

"No...Yes...Maybe..."

"Fleita!"

"She needs to be tamed like a stallion!"

"What?"

"We need to saddle her and try to hang onto her until she stops kicking...That's what I think at any rate...While you try to break her in, I'll go to the village and bring back some fish. A lot of fish. Like five barrels' worth, I guess. She's just a child after all. We need to feed her."

"Fleita, what the hell are you talking about?" I asked surprised. "What do you mean we need to break her in? Don't you see she's got the red eyes of an aggressive mob?"

"I see it, but Shaman Mahan!" steely notes sounded in the girl's voice. "On your mark, get set, and grab that ship! Your orders are to hold onto her until I bring the food!"

A pause followed, and then Fleita added in an apologetic voice:

"Sorry, but you said yourself..."

"Oh go and get the fish!" I barked and soared up higher. I rose over the barrier and then dove while trying to avoid the tentacles. It seemed that it was easier for an Initiate Shaman to sense this world than for me now that I had passed Level 100. After all, even Antsinthepantsa had told me that I'd start having inaccurate and misleading sensations...In my case—I didn't have any at all. Since Fleita was sure, I'd have to trust her...By the way, something tells me that she might be ready to do her initiation trial. As a Shaman, Fleita was already well on her way—everything else was a matter of technique.

The deck, if I could call the Squidolphin's back a deck, was slippery and wet—and not at all designed for a Dragon, so I had to turn into my human form in order to take one of the seats. As I did so I kept dodging the tentacles.

You have stepped aboard a feral Minor Squidolphin. The taming process has begun...

A status bar with the label 'Taming' appeared and was followed by a series of instructions, demanding I do various things.

When the Squidolphin turns right sharply, you must shift your center of mass to the right, forcing the ship to straighten out. Try to do this now...

My foal (that's what I'll call the Squidolphin) suddenly banked right sharply, leaving the shore. The acceleration was so abrupt that the inertia pressed me into the left side of the ship, immobilizing me.

"Where are you going, Mahan?" Fleita shouted into the amulet, while another message appeared:

Steering maneuver failed. Number of attempts: 1 of 3. Please try again. When the Squidolphin turns right sharply...

It took me all three attempts to summon enough balance to successfully counterweigh the ship. Shifting my body to the right, I beheld a welcome message:

Right turn successful.
When the Squidolphin turns left sharply...

The training went on for several hours I believe. I was taught how to straighten the vessel out as she turned. What to do when she submerged (a dome appeared over the seats, allowing me to breathe underwater), when she jumped out of the water, how to dodge her tentacles' attacks, how to stay calm when the monster bellowed, and how to hold on when she stopped abruptly. The system dutifully repeated the ship's various actions, preparing me for the scariest maneuver of all—the underwater roll.

Training exercise complete. Taming will commence in 60 seconds...

"Catch the fish!" yelled Fleita, hanging over my

head. The Squidolphin was gathering strength and her tentacles were submerged in the water, so Draco flew up to me and Fleita dropped down a giant barrel of fish.

"Thank you!" I yelled in reply, not quite sure why the ship needed food. But since Fleita thought that it could come in handy, I'd leave it...The important thing was that she didn't get in the way as the ship rolled.

Prepare yourself! Taming commencing in 3...2...1...

The bank to the left again pressed me into the ship's right side, while an error appeared before me:

Number of errors: 1 of 10.

The Squidolphin straightened out, allowing me to regain my original position, and instantly dove under water, throwing me onto my back.

Number of errors: 2 of 10.

A sharp turn to the right...Abrupt braking...Left...Right...

Getting to my feet one more time and noticing that I only had two attempts remaining to tame this ship, I found a moment to smirk at myself—I really wasn't acting like a Shaman here. I get the impression that along with my powers, I had also been stripped of the most valuable thing that Shamans have—my premonition. I was trying to react to events as they happened instead of seeing ahead...It wasn't right...

Number of errors: 9 of 10.

As soon as I saw this message, something clicked in my head. I lost all interest in whether I'd succeed or not, whether I'd manage my nerves or not—I simply stood up on my feet and leaned right. For, at the moment, everything was right...

How can a Shaman be a Shaman if he's ruled by his mind and not his feelings? Lean left. After all—they had locked my summoning powers—not my ability to sense this world. Lean forward. No one could ever divert me from the Way of the Shaman, except myself. Lean back and jump, forcing the foal to calm down. Kornik tried to get this through to me, as did Prontho, but due to all the problems that had fallen to me lately, I had forgotten who I was in this world. Lean right, dodge a tentacle and lean left immediately, dodging a second tentacle. I am a Shaman! Lean right. And no one could convince me otherwise, whatever powers I lost. Lean forward.

Not a single thought remained in my head. The feeling of complete relaxation was so surprising and alluring that I was making various turns and banks without paying any attention to the 'Taming' bar which was slowly but steadily filling with green progress. But even that didn't matter right now. I didn't even feel—I saw what the foal was about to do and had the time not only to prepare myself, but to steady myself as well.

The Squidolphin has been tamed. Rest time: 30 seconds.

The 'Taming' status bar stopped at 50%. The system began the countdown, allowing me time to rest, or perhaps loading new, still unused, combinations of moves—when my attention was drawn to the barrel of fish, which hadn't budged an inch this entire time. Placing both hands on the ship's body, I shut my eyes and following Anastaria's example mentally offered the ship a snack. She had to regain her strength after all...

Like a giant hammer, a tentacle slammed next to the barrel and carefully, like a child's hand, embraced it and lifted it from the deck. I heard a munching sound, mixed with the sound of splintering lumber, and the 'Taming' bar filled up by another 10%. The ship had liked my snack...

"Fleita, bring me another barrel!" I managed to yell into the amulet as the time for rest ended and the next dance began. The dance of feeling and premonition...

"How hungry she is!" said Fleita with surprise when the third barrel of fish vanished down the Squidolphin's gullet. The second wave of taming was no less intense than the last and if I hadn't continued to work at the level of premonition, it would not have ended well. The speed with which the ship went from one maneuver to the next had increased several-fold, forcing me to dash back and forth along the foal's body. When the 'Taming' bar was at eighty percent the ship got tired again and I managed to feed her another barrel of fish. There was no third wave, as if the Squidolphin had eaten her fill and was waiting for another portion, her tentacles rummaging around the place where the other barrels had been placed.

"That's true," I agreed, and a whole litany of messages began to scroll past my eyes:

Achievement unlocked: 'Sea Devil.' You have become the owner of a unique vessel. +20% to surface speed.

Vessel acquired: Minor Squidolphin.

You have acquired a personal vessel. Please speak to the registrar to receive your captaincy license.

You have acquired a nameless vessel. Please name her.

+4 to Spirituality. Total: 89.

+5000 Reputation with all encountered maritime factions.

New title available: 'Tamer of the Seas.' +10% to Squidolphin speed.

"Mindblowing," Fleita muttered, stepping onto the ship's deck. "Never in my life would I imagine that someone could sail in such a monster!"

I didn't reply and looked at the girl carefully. She was wandering around the deck, wondering at the chairs and the tentacles that moved like oars, carrying us along the shore, and doing so quite rapidly. I was looking at an ordinary girl of whom there were very many in Barliona, and yet I suddenly realized that our brief acquaintance had come to its end. I had nothing more to teach this Shaman. She had proven today to everyone, including myself, that she was ready to complete her trial to become an Elemental Shaman. And the hell with the fact that we had scheduled it for several months from now...

"Kornik..." I whispered into the air. For some reason, I had no doubts that the goblin would hear me. "She is ready..."

"Are you sure?" my teacher's voice sounded to the right of me. To my surprise, there was no trace of mockery in his voice.

"Yes, absolutely. I don't doubt it for a second. She is ready."

"In that case...Fleita!" yelled Kornik. "Come over here!"

"Kornik?" Fleita asked, surprised. "What are you doing here? Have you come to check out Mahan's ship as well?"

"You think I've never seen a Squidolphin before? Back in the day, it was the only way to travel. We have other business at the moment. Get your things— your next trial awaits you."

"But it's still five months away!" the girl exclaimed with astonishment.

"Your teacher says that you are ready—so you're ready. It's not up to you. Let's go. The Supreme Fire Spirit is expecting you."

"But...am I really ready, Mahan?"

I nodded to her silently and smiled. My teaching had ended—it was time for Fleita to become an Elemental Shaman. It was looking like a new Shaman had appeared in Barliona—one who would give me as well as Antsinthepantsa and Kalatea a run for our money. Fleita was singular and she had to continue to grow. It was too bad that it wasn't going to be with me—the girl had to follow a Way of her own.

"It's too bad," muttered Kornik before vanishing, "that you couldn't wait another couple weeks. I would have won my bet with Prontho...I guess I'll have to buy him a case of the best vintage at the Golden Horseshoe...That damn orc. I bet you two are in cahoots! Coincidences like this don't just happen on their own!"

Fleita cast me a farewell glance and vanished, leaving me alone with my new ship. A notification popped up telling me that my student would do her trial in a week after some extra training with Kornik, and I sighed bitterly—I would miss the annoying little brat.

Not wishing to overthink things, I named my living ship *Nautilus* (I hope Jules Verne doesn't sue me) at which point an ordinary ship interface appeared before my eye—though, after studying it for several minutes, I understood that perhaps it wasn't so ordinary after all—there was no mention of masts, but there was an extra tab dedicated to the ordinance. Ordinary pirate ships were armed with several nose harpoons and some boarding hooks. There weren't any cannons in Barliona, which was a good thing. Why would a ship need extra weapons anyway when you could just fill it with a squad of Mages who would do much better than a dozen cannons. And yet my *Nautilus* did have plenty of non-standard equipment.

First of all, the tentacles acted not only as oars but also as both cables for boarding and ordinary melee weapons that could break the hull of an enemy vessel under water. Having the option of submerging to a depth of ten meters, *Nautilus* was a very dangerous threat. Sonar was unheard of in Barliona after all. All I'd have to do was approach an enemy ship from beneath, hit her hull with all twenty tentacles and, poof, the enemy ship was sunk. Time to deal with the next one. Now I understand how the Squidolphin destroyed the ships of pirates and merchants—she approached them from below, grabbed onto them and then dove deeper, pulling her prey down with her. In this manner, I could safely reckon that my Squidolphin and the one that we had to hunt were different creatures. I wonder—is it possible to tame the large one as well?

Second of all, my ship had another weapon at her disposal—a mouth filled with teeth, which would enable me to ram enemy ships with ease—with all the attendant consequences. The Squidolphin really wouldn't be bothered by ramming her nose into a hull, so if I really wanted to have fun with my foe, I could play chicken with them to see who'd squawk first.

Third, the Squidolphin could emit a black liquid

called 'toxic ink.' This did damage to all organic matter but had a downside as well—it did damage to the Squidolphin as well. With that said, the effective radius of the 'toxic ink' was quite small—only a couple meters. All I had to do was exit the cloud of ink and its negative effect would cease, while another five minutes later, the 'toxic ink' would dissolve in the water. A pretty double-edged weapon this, but since I have it, I'll have to try it sometime.

Getting familiar with the controls took up so much time that I didn't even notice the sun rise in the sky. However, I did manage to learn two more aspects of *Nautilus*. The first was that the beacons that Fleita and I had lit, had absolutely no effect on her. The ship could crawl out onto land and then crawl back into the seas. Another surprising capability with uncertain applications.

Before returning to Narlak, I decided to stop by Gumtrees and tell Rastman that I had caught the monster. I'm sure that a new Squidolphin will show up in some amount of time and will begin to terrorize the village all over again. But for now that wouldn't happen. And yet I did not for a second anticipate the astonished reaction of the Gumtrees resident...

"A MONSTER!!! RUN FOR YOUR LIVES!!!" Rastman's wild yell shattered the morning calm of the village, forcing me to smile. And why not? Bypassing all of the defensive barriers, the monster sailed right up to the pier. Pure terror, nothing less!

"Rastman, calm down! It's me, Mahan! The Squidolphin is mine from now on!"

"Mahan?" The alderman, perhaps by habit, was once again on his back trying to retreat in a crawl against a building's wall. "The Dragon?"

"The same one," I replied with a grin, docking to the pier and hopping down from my vessel. "From now on, this monster is my ship!"

"Nice ship, what can you say," a deep voice sounded behind my back. I whirled around and like the village locals, stared agape at the two-meter-tall Water Spirit that had taken a seat on the edge of the Squidolphin and dangled his tail into the water—the Level 500 tail of the local Guardian... "But you'll have to pay the toll. It's not proper without paying the toll, you know."

"Toll?" I echoed surprised. "For what? As soon as I get back to Malabar, I'll pay it..."

"Not the one for your ship," the Water Spirit waved his arm. "I'm talking about a different toll—the road toll. Or the water one, if you prefer. You owe me five thousand gold for using the ocean, considering the power of your ship and her number of tails. You got lucky too that your registration isn't in the capital—otherwise your toll would be a lot more. Anyway—I can't spend a lot of time out in the air, so why don't you go ahead and pay. It'll be easier for everyone that way..."

Road tolls! What a bunch of jerks, those devs. They try to make money from everything, even such trifles! And this is money players have to pay!

"Sorry to pile on, Mahan," Rastman said, coming to his senses. "But you owe me six hundred gold for three barrels of fish. If you had sailed off right away, I wouldn't've said a word, but since you came back...By the way, do you need any more fish? We could get you some in a jiffy!"

All I could do was grin, hand the alderman a wallet with the money and order another four barrels of fish. I had discovered a surprising detail about my ship—I had to feed her. Otherwise, she would fall asleep. The ship needed a standard barrel of fish once a week—and there was even space to store five such barrels in a special hold. So once a month I would buy five barrels and then I could avoid worrying about such trifles for the rest of the month. With all that said, it's important to note that the Squidolphin's main hold was in her belly. I could store food, loot and items in there—that part of the stomach was like an ordinary cargo hold. A pretty convenient fish, this Squidolphin. I wonder why they aren't more common?

"Dan, where are you?" Anastaria's telepathic question popped up around two in the afternoon. Judging by the map, there was no way I'd make it back to Cadis by three. In five hours, I had covered 150 km—the Squidolphin did about 30 km/h with her bonus to speed. She was only a Level 1 vessel after all, so I couldn't complain.

"I'm out at sea, breaking in my ship," I replied flatly, not wishing to explain everything that had happened now. I'd rather it be a surprise...

"You bought a ship? Why? I thought we'd already decided everything?" Anastaria's irritation was so evident that I could even feel it in reality.

"It just happened this way, Stacey..."

"Daniel, oh Daniel...What an overgrown bungler you are! All right—come back. When should I expect you?"

"In about two hours. I won't make it back earlier than that..."

"Hold up! What do you mean two hours? Where are you right now?"

"Out at sea. My Energy's running out. Call me on my amulet..."

"All right, out with it—what'd you do?" Stacey asked a moment later. "I know you didn't spend ten million on a ship. You don't even have that much!"

"I don't," I agreed. "I didn't buy a ship. I acquired one."

"Want to tell me about it?" came the question. "He acquired a ship...It was delivered to him."

Even though my gloomy thoughts about Anastaria were still fresh in my mind, I didn't want to pick a fight with her right then. I just didn't have enough information and all my assumptions could be shattered in a matter of minutes. I also didn't want to bring up my feelings about our relationship, so I summoned her to my location. I guess I'd deal with the problem as things developed.

"Well I'll be god-damn-ed," slowly, stretching each syllable and savoring it as if it was a sip of the most expensive wine from the Golden Horseshoe, said Anastaria after she appeared on *Nautilus* and got a chance to look around. "I mean, *goddamn*...Okay, Dan, tell me what happened..."

"...Only 30 km/h despite the bonuses," I came to the end of my tale, explaining the reason I was going to be late. We only had sixty clicks to Cadis, so *Nautilus* still had two hours' worth of hard work with her tentacles ahead of her.

"So does this mean that we'll be hunting the same type of ship?" Stacey asked the question that, as usual, held the most promise to herself.

"Yes, only she won't be a little one like this one. Something tells me that we're going to go up against this one's mother, maybe even grandmother. And she'll be capable of pulling a ship down to the bottom and breaking it to pieces."

"A Squidolphin...I read so much about her today and it turns out that it was all wrong. Nowhere did it say that she was a ship and that you could capture her. Did you look through our papers?"

"The ones you drew up when you made the bet? No," I said gloomily, since Stacey had broached a very unpleasant topic for me. I really didn't feel like talking about that.

"You know, we'll have to warn my uncle that we'll be several hours late!" Anastaria changed the subject abruptly. "Let him meet the pirates on his own and...Dan, did you get a chance to test *Nautilus*?"

"Sorry...What do you mean by test? We're already sailing at full tentacles, if you could call it that—she can't go faster."

"I don't mean that. Look," Stacey pointed at the horizon. Looking in the indicated direction, I noticed the outline of a vessel headed in our direction. "Are we pirates or what? Shall we try it?"

"You want to attack a ship without even knowing its Level? Stacey, at our Level they'll destroy us and not even break a sweat!"

"Dan...If something goes wrong we'll just dive as deep as we can and lose them. Don't you want to see what *Nautilus* can do?"

"If that ship is carrying players, I'll be sent back to the mine in an instant," I made a last attempt to avoid the adventure Stacey was proposing, even though she had struck the most painful chord for me—I desperately wanted to find out what the Squidolphin could do before facing her ancestor.

"It's not a problem—you can just make me captain for the time being. If that's a pirate ship, then there can't be any complaints. If it's a merchantman, then we get loot and as a Siren I can raise it from the bottom of the sea, assuming the depth here is less than one kilometer. If it's someone else, like a cargo ship from a different continent...Too bad for them. It's what they get for sailing in our waters. Shall we attack, captain?"

"Full tentacle ahead, junior captain," I agreed, granting Anastaria access to the ship controls. "Look—this is how we dive and this is how you attack with the tentacles and this is the ramming procedure..."

"Got it," Stacey nodded, all but rubbing her hands at the prospect of battle. The girl was so enthused that I couldn't help but get into it too. Really—what could one ship do to us if we attack it from under water?

"They're headed in our direction," Stacey concluded when the distance between us and our prey began to decrease. Not wishing to cause panic in the enemy, the girl submerged our ship into the water, leaving only the top of the deck on the surface and allowing the waves to wash over us. If it weren't for the protective dome, I'd be neck deep in water right now. Additionally, in order to maintain stealth, Stacey did something with the tentacles and forced them to work not like enormous propellers, but as the legs of a dog treading water. I couldn't believe it...I'd never imagine that you could make adjustments like that.

"We're diving," said Stacey and *Nautilus* submerged beneath the waves for the first time since I'd acquired her. While I had been testing the ship, I hadn't gotten around to trying this—and to be honest, I'd been a little scared to go under. What if something went wrong? "Do you see them?"

If from the surface the sea seemed dark and terrifying, then from underneath it was transparent and captivating. All kinds of fish were swimming around our ship—from tiny herring to giant rays. The beauty of it all was so enticing that for a second I forgot why we were even down there. Who can think of war amid such beauty?

"Target straight ahead!" said Anastaria, seemingly unconcerned with our surroundings. The girl's eyes were focused on the ship sailing ahead of us. Judging by its properties, we were dealing with a

Level 12 cargo ship from the city Verdax in the Shadow Empire. Consequently, there definitely wouldn't be any players aboard, "Depth three meters. They can't see us. We'll get closer...Three seconds until contact. Two. One! Contact!"

The Squidolphin gently attached herself to the bottom of the ship, revealing yet another interesting capability—suction cups. All of the tentacles attached themselves to the hull, securely fastening the Squidolphin to it—at which point we were turned around sharply as our target began to drag us, slowing in the process.

"Gran'rag rarra?" Even through the hull, we could hear the cargo ship's captain call out. I'd need to find some way to learn the language of Shadow. If we were going to fight a war against this empire, we'd need to understand what our prisoners said. After all, there would be many prisoners.

"Shall we?" Stacey asked and, without waiting for my reply, engaged the tentacles. "We shall..."

"Narda'elok! Narda'elok!" The screams of terror drowned out the splintering of timber. To my immense surprise, *Nautilus* didn't hurry to deal with the hull of the ship. A 'Durability' bar appeared and began to crawl very slowly, as if unwillingly, towards zero. The Squidolphin's tentacles hammered at the hull without pause, but the actual result was not the way it seemed. I had thought that it would be enough to approach the enemy ship and deal one blow to it to sink the target, but the in-game reality turned out to be quite a bit stricter. If you wanted to sink a ship, you had to destroy her hull's Durability first, which could regenerate too it seemed!

"They're repairing their ship from inside," Stacey exclaimed, playing the role of Captain Obvious. "At least they can't do anything to us, since we're..."

Your ship has been damaged...Two tentacles have been frozen...Damage percentage is...

"Let's go!" I ordered, taking the controls away from Anastaria. The Mages in charge of security on the target ship weren't sleeping on their jobs—nor were they afraid of our monster, nor did they use their Mana for nothing. All in all, all these 'nors' came out to 10% damage to our ship.

"Depth seven meters...eight...ten...that's it, we're at our limit!" Stacey helped me keep track of the readings while I steered the ship. The mages were sending giant blocks of ice onto us from above, which I was maneuvering to avoid. In addition to the damage that each block of ice did to the Squidolphin, it froze our ship and, weighing her down, forced her deeper. For a Level 1 ship like *Nautilus*, diving too deep could cause her to rupture and be completely destroyed.

"I could be wrong, but I think they're chasing us," Anastaria pointed out, observing the cargo ship's actions. She had abandoned her prior course and was following us as if the ten meters of water between us did nothing to hide us. In order to make sure, I changed our course several times and watched as the cargo ship turned to follow each time.

"Oh! We've been repaired as well," Stacey said with surprise and immediately explained what had happened: "It cost us two barrels of fish. All that's left is...Be careful!"

The girl's scream coincided with a sharp maneuver to the right, which I made in order to avoid an enormous iceberg. Not only could they see us— they were targeting and trying to destroy us!

"When will their Mana run out?" I managed to mutter as the water overhead suddenly grew dark and a gigantic chunk of ice descended right onto the center of the Squidolphin. My head exploded in a hundred rainbow shivers, my vision grew dark, yet before losing consciousness, I managed to see two notifications:

Nautilus has been destroyed. Owing to the absence of an insurance policy, your vessel cannot be restored.

You have lost your vessel (Nautilus).

Darkness...

"...pull him...."

"...you go...I'll deal with him..."

"...pull us out! Hurry..."

Snippets of a shouted conversation pierced the darkness around me, but I couldn't summon the strength to concentrate on them. I had just lost Nautilus. A minor trifle like respawning didn't upset me one bit. Although, I did feel bad that Draco had lost ten levels...

"Where did this happen to you?" Ehkiller's voice sounded beside me, yanking me from the comfortable darkness of non-existence back into the game. Through my closed eyes, I could see the various auras from the debuffs that were currently on my character. The lengthy list included 'Stunned' which lasted thirty minutes and caused the world to spin like a helicopter around me.

"At sea. Mahan found a Level 1 ship. We tried to attack a Level 12 ship and this is what came of it. They dropped an iceberg on us. Mahan's Totem and I dodged it, but he...It's a good thing it didn't flatten us."

"Are you going dispel his debuffs or is he just going to lie there like a ragdoll for the next half hour?"

"I don't have a way to dispel them. I don't have my Paladin powers, remember? But I'm glad you're here. Tell me, how's that thing I asked you to do coming along?"

"Now I've seen it all! My own daughter—instead of visiting me in real life, prefers to meet me in-game. What is the world coming to?"

"Dad!"

"All right, all right. The business is moving along fine. They promised to have a decision for us this week. You know yourself how the bureaucracy likes to drag its feet. When are you going to tell Mahan? If I were him, I'd have asked you a long time ago..."

At this point, the light waved a farewell and darkness descended upon me to melancholy music. I wonder what I was supposed to have asked Anastaria a long time ago...

"Wake up, Mahan," I came out of non-being within a second. The debuffs did not leave a 'hangover'—the bubble removed anything that the system considered a negative aura. "Have you recovered?"

"Where...? What's with the ship?" I didn't want to let on that I had accidentally overheard Stacey's conversation with her father. What if it was merely the fruits of my feverish imagination?

"We're in Altameda. Your ship has been destroyed. Evolett called five minutes ago. Grygz is super pissed with us for not showing up to the captains' meeting. Especially since he'd invited us personally. Dan, please forgive me—I never imagined that it would work out this way...Do you want me to help you catch another Squidolphin? I'm sure that there are plenty others swimming around the seas of Barliona...Dan, are you listening to me?"

"Give me a minute..."

"Like hell...By the way, that's a pretty useful phrase you came up with. Anyway, don't dwell on it, please. The loss of *Nautilus* is my fault and I'll make it up to you. From now on, my *Vraanakush* is yours. I'll file the necessary documents when we return to Cadis."

"What does your ship have to do with this? That was a Squidolphin!"

"I understand. Again, forgive me. I miscalculated its strength. And please note—I'm not saying that you agreed to the attack yourself. It was my idea and I'll hold myself responsible for it. Get up—we need to go to Cadis."

"I'm not going anywhere today," I cut her off. "Since we already missed our meeting with the pirates, I don't feel like doing anything until tomorrow. You have no idea what it cost me to get that ship. I had almost reached Cadis! And if the pirates had seen the Squidolphin, I could have received new quests!"

"You think I don't understand that, Dan?" Stacey parried. "I blame myself fully, but what's done is done. Let's look at the bright side—now we know how to kill the Squidolphin."

"Do we now?" I couldn't help but remark sarcastically. "*Nautilus* was a minor Squidolphin. We're planning on hunting a real, mature, enormous monster. It'll drag our ship underwater without even noticing what level it is."

"That's precisely why I want to go to Cadis right now. I have an idea and I couldn't care less that it contradicts what I wrote in the wager note. Plinto will get his Tear after all."

"What is your idea then?" I couldn't help but grow curious. No one had canceled our quest to catch the monster, and Renox still had to be saved, so I could whine and mourn my ship's passing some other time.

"We know how the Squidolphin attacks. It swims up underneath and tries to pull the vessel to the seafloor. But what if we do the following..."

Listening to Stacey, I couldn't help but be

astonished at her daring. She had learned every little lesson she could from our battle with the Shadow cargo ship—she even pulled up the video she had recorded and pointed out the illuminated porthole which the enemy had used to track us. If we had closed that window somehow, the Squidolphin would still be alive...But all right. Anastaria was right—why cry over something that was gone? However, if I manage to catch another Squidolphin, Stacey won't be allowed to set foot on her.

"You're mad!" Grygz retorted when Anastaria related her idea to him. "The sea won't stand for this. We shall be smashed against the first cliffs in our path."

"Does the wisdom of the mighty pirate really submit to tradition?" Stacey asked with surprise. "You do understand that this is our only chance to catch the monster?"

"There has to be another way!"

"There isn't. The Squidolphin can drag a ship down to the bottom like a turtle snapping up a pond lily. If we don't bind the ships together into one whole, the pirates will forever remain a second-rate power in this part of the ocean. If that suits you, then..."

"We were never a second-rate power!" Grygz exclaimed enraged. "If we have to break with tradition to catch the monster—I will do it! All of the smiths and shipwrights of Cadis are at your command! Do what you must—tomorrow we set sail and I will personally lead the monstrosity that you will cobble together! The ships allocated to the hunting fleet are moored at the second wharf."

Anastaria's idea was as simple as 2+2. The Squidolphin dragged ships down to the seabed as if they were pond lilies. That was a given. Consequently, it could take two ships at the same time too—but with a little effort. But even for a monster of the deep it would be incredibly difficult to pull down three ships at once. Therefore, if we bound together four ships—to be safe—there wasn't a Squidolphin out there that could take them to the sea floor. The monster would have to attach itself to the hull of each ship separately and hammer at it with its tentacles. And that's when we'd give it an icy welcome...

The most difficult step in Stacey's plan was binding the ships together. They would have to be attached so tightly to each other that even if one ship was dragged underwater—the others would go with it. For that we needed smiths and many kilometers of thick chains with hoisting winches. None of this was impossible, however, so an hour later the Cadis wharf was bustling with work as the shipwrights created a four-decked ship, with all the decks at one level.

The captains whom Grygz had put under our command wept as holes for chains were drilled into their beloved vessels. And every gang of four captains cast lots to see which ship would be the most unlucky—Stacey had been taken with the idea of making a porthole for observation by hacking one into the hull of a ship and glazing it with a magical shield. Doing this caused the ship's Durability to drop by 20%, but everyone understood the need to observe what the Squidolphin was up to, so they stayed silent and accepted their fate.

The work went on into the night, and in the morning the townspeople of Cadis awoke to find six enormous conglomerate vessels of four ships each. *Butterfly* and *Vraanakush* did not go untouched, being bound to the ships of Grygz and Calran. From the perspective of power, this was our flagship and the vessel we placed most faith in.

"The ordinance has arrived," announced Evolett when a portal appeared and began disgorging players. Mages, Druids, Hunters—Evolett had brought everyone who could do damage from a distance. Once more, we'd had to pony up for a portal, since the Kartossian scrolls were only effective in the territory of that Empire and couldn't transport anyone to the Free Lands.

"And here comes our ordinance," I said, when the stream of Kartossians ended and our boys from Malabar began to arrive. I didn't want to invite strangers, so our side consisted only of fifty warriors. However, almost all of them were at Level 200. Basically, I doubt that the sea creature would be very happy to see them.

Despite the realities of life, in my heart of hearts I hoped that the Squidolphin we were about to set out after was the same kind of ship like *Nautilus* and I could get a chance at 'saddling' her. With this goal in mind, we stored ten barrels of fish in the hold of Stacey's ship. Who knows—maybe they'd come in handy. All in all, we were well prepared.

"Captain, we are ready to set sail!" Lom reported when we had taken our stations. With Grygz' and Calran's agreement, Anastaria—as the plan's author—took over the command of our squadron. To do this, all of the ships' steering wheels had been moved to our vessel and connected to the rudders with magic. I do love magical games—there's never any problem with technical details.

"Full steam ahead!" Stacey ordered, turning into the same girl who had wrecked my Nautilus. I guess Evolett's thirst for the sea runs in the family.

Over the next two days that we spent wandering around the ocean looking for the Squidolphin, I managed to learn to hate the sea. The sea, the sea, the sea again and some more sea. And endless waves, tossing the ship up and down. Then a calm and then more waves. Repeat x times, until you're utterly nuts. We passed through all the points where ships had vanished previously, but encountered nothing. One time a sail appeared on the horizon, but the captain of that vessel wisely decided to avoid our armada and fled before we could take a closer look at him. I hoped that that wasn't the same cargo ship that had sunk my *Nautilus*—I'm never opposed to an act of revenge.

"We have a day left," Grygz said in a torpid voice, heading into his cabin. "If we do not encounter the Squidolphin in the next day, I will hand both of you over to Geranika...It'll be some small compensation for all the holes you've put in my ships."

The pirate leader had almost reached his cabin when the creaking of the rigging was drowned out by a thunderous ringing:

DONG! DONG! DONG!

"All hands on deck!" Not a trace of lethargy remained in Grygz's voice. "Man your stations!"

Three tolls of the magic bell meant only one thing—we had found the target of our expedition...

CHAPTER TWELVE
THE BATTLE AND ITS AFTERMATH

"TARGET STRAIGHT AHEAD!" reported the player we'd assigned to the viewing porthole. His task was simple—report everything that the underwater creature does, where it goes and what it's about to do. All six of our 'squadrons' had players like this, who reported through their amulets to the captains. Even though this caused a lot of noise over the 'airwaves,' the information was invaluable. "Distance—who the hell knows! Depth is 50 meters and it's moving incredibly fast. It's headed in our direction but not surfacing. This beast is enormous! It's a real doozy!"

"Doozy?" Calran asked Anastaria in puzzlement.

"A hundred meters," the girl explained. "Maybe longer—but a more precise estimate is unnecessary."

"What a pithy word," Grygz nodded his approval. "I'll need to remember it."

"Twenty tentacles on one side, fifteen on the other—something's chewed at it a bit!" the lookout went on with his report. "The monster's stopped right before us. I get the impression that it's looking for a target. Sending a projection now..."

The amulets were working perfectly and in several moments, several steps next to Grygz, there appeared a 3D spatial grid in the middle of which floated the Squidolphin.

"A real doozy," Grygz concluded meaningfully and I could not help but agree with him. *Nautilus* didn't even come close to this beast—I'd never seen a creature of this size in Barliona. "So this is what the monster looks like..."

Unlike the Squidolphin I was already familiar with, the current member of this species had a number of further characteristics—there were fins along her spine and stomach which it seemed would allow her to break ships; her tentacles terminated in what looked like claws or fingers, and bristled with hooks in addition to their suction cups. And that was only what I could see of her additional weaponry. I was afraid to imagine what remained hidden inside this miracle of the seas...

"The monster's too far. I can't get a read on its properties," the lookout continued. "Attention! It's headed for squadron number three! Tell them to prepare for collision!"

The third squadron, which consisted of four pirate ships, was one of our weakest links. Only one of the ships was at Level 10, the others were barely Level 7. After the sinking of *Nautilus*, I took a look at the distribution of ships in Barliona and almost growled with rage—it began at Level 1 and ended at Level 20. This meant that by attacking that Level 12 cargo ship while at Level 1, we were quite consciously committing suicide. We had had no chances of surviving. When I showed her this part of the manual, Anastaria grimaced guiltily and confessed that she was actually quite familiar with this aspect of the game, but had reckoned on us calmly escaping underwater. This had turned out to be a failure and she again offered I take her ship as partial compensation. I had to refuse once again—I didn't feel like having to deal with an enormous chunk of wood. I'd rather wait half a year, solve all the current problems and find myself a new Squidolphin. But I did make the necessary notes in the margins...

"Thirty meters until collision! Ten! Contact!"

The squadron of ships beside us shook noticeably and rose out of the water, after which the ship nearest to us began to go under. In the projection it was clearly visible how the Squidolphin had attached itself to two ships at once with her tentacles and began to gnaw at the hull, trying to tear it to pieces.

"I've got a readout of the properties!" the lookout went on as if nothing had happened. "Sending it now..."

Giant Squidolphin (Level 20). Object type: Sub/surface vessel. Crew size: 50. Owner: None. Status: Feral. This creature has reached her maximal level and can no longer be tamed.

"We'll attack at the count of three," Anastaria announced. The girl had waited for the creature's properties until the last moment, hoping that the Squidolphin could be captured and tamed, but now it was clear that this was pointless. Since we couldn't train it, we'd have to destroy it—which is what we were about to do. The third squadron of ships was creaking at its seams and groaning, yet holding on despite the Squidolphin's best attempts. "Aim straight for the center. One...Two...Three!"

For a moment Barliona's bright sun went dark—more than a hundred Mages, Druids, Shamans, Hunters and Eluna-knew-what other classes, struck one joint blow at the Squidolphin. Lightning, ice, branches, arrows, Spirits...It was quite the spectacle!

"Target hit! 10% damage to Durability! One of the tentacles has fallen off! Attention—the monster's released some black liquid! It's released our ships and is retreating!"

"Third squadron—retreat from the black liquid immediately!" Stacey yelled into her amulet over the joyous yells of the players. The four ships that the Squidolphin had attached itself to, jumped out of the water like a cork from a bottle—and slammed back down raising great clouds of spray. "Faster! It's eating everything!"

"The monster is targeting squadron four! Distance one hundred! Forty! Contact!"

"We're going down!" the third squadron began to scream suddenly. "Two of our ships have lost their bottoms! Save yourselves whoever can!"

"Fire at will!" Anastaria commanded and turned to Grygz: "Cast hooks at the third squadron and begin hauling! We need to pull it out of the toxic ink!"

"Get it done!" the pirate leader called to his men as Anastaria returned to the projection.

"To all ships—hoist sails and move ahead!" the girl issued another order. "We need to avoid the clouds of toxic ink! What's the status of the monster?"

"Durability is at 78%. It's finishing off the second ship of the fourth squadron. If we don't stop it, in twenty seconds it'll sink them..."

"Squadron three is gone," Evolett remarked calmly, looking on as four ships crumbled to pieces. Both players and NPCs were in the water now, but not everyone managed to remain on the surface. Only about a third of the crew managed to escape the Squidolphin's tentacles and its toxic ink—almost all of them higher-level players and NPCs. With only 10–20% Hit Points remaining, the sailors were swimming in our direction.

"The third ship in the fourth squadron has been breeched," the lookout reported. "Only one remains. It's currently..."

The Squidolphin didn't bother battering the last ship, grabbing her instead with her tentacles and pulling her into the depths. Since three of the other ships already had broken hulls, this wasn't too difficult. Emitting one more cloud of toxic ink, in order to kill whatever survivors remained, the Squidolphin dove sharply, taking her prey with her. No one survived from the fourth squadron...

"Target lost! Continue the search!"

"Shannaya will kill me," Grygz said philosophically, removing his hat in memory of the drowned men. "Lartan was an honorable pirate!"

"The monster is returning! It's aiming for squadron number five! Fifty meters till contact...Ten...Contact! No! Belay that! It's heading for squadron number six! Contact! Again belay that! The monster's coming around for another pass!"

"It's using its fins to attack!" announced a player either from the fifth or sixth squadron. "It's coming past us at full speed under our hulls and cutting our Durability by 20% with each pass. The NPCs are already making repairs...But we just lost another 20%! We can take only four more attacks—you have to do something!"

The Squidolphin had radically changed tactics. Choosing two squadrons that were near each other, she began to dart between them using her upper fins like a plow. Everything the players and NPCs aboard those ships tried to stop the monster had no effect— her Durability had dwindled to 70% but it was already clear that the fifth and sixth squadron were doomed...

"To all Mages—get the crews off the ships immediately!" ordered Anastaria. The downside of the squadrons was that they were not mobile and so we hadn't the time to come to the aid of the sinking ships. We had only one thing left to us—save as many of the players and pirates and concentrate everyone on our four Level 18 ships—our main strike force against the Squidolphin.

"Say, Evolett, you don't by any chance have a Scroll of Armageddon?" I asked. "We've already lost twelve ships and only done 30% damage to that thing. It's not a very fair trade..."

"It won't help," Anastaria muscled into our conversation. "The Squidolphin has very strong armor. Even if the detonation takes place right next to her, the monster will barely notice it. You can see yourself—we're exhausting all our Mana, but all we're causing are scratches. In terms of power, we've already poured an Armageddon-worth of spells into her, but only done 30% damage."

"That's only if we detonate the scroll from the outside. What do you think will happen if we set off Armageddon inside of her?"

"But how...? Uh-huh...Evolett? We'll take care of the money later."

"I don't have any. I gave you the last one for the castle."

"Hi Killer," Anastaria instantly called her dad. "I need a Scroll of Armageddon urgently. I'll fill you in later. Do you have it?"

"...?"

"Yes or no?"

"I think I do...but why don't you summon me over there? I'd like to take a look at what you're up to."

"Mages—summon Ehkiller this instant! We'll summon you in a second, just make sure to bring the scroll with you."

"Five and six have gone down," reported the

lookout. While we were deciding what to do next, the Squidolphin had continued to destroy our ships' hulls. "We've transferred a fifth of the players and main NPCs. We're hauling out the ones in the water right now. The monster's cast toxic ink next to each ship, the bitch!"

"Squadron two—head towards us," Anastaria ordered and turned to Ehkiller who had just appeared on deck. "Hey! Have you brought the scroll?"

"Never leave home without it," the Mage shrugged. "What are we hunting here?"

"Killer—how many Level 300+ Mages do you have at your disposal right now?" I asked the head of Phoenix. "Can we borrow them for an hour?"

"Just a second," Ehkiller's fingers began to wriggle, indicating that he was typing something into the chat, after which he replied: "At the moment, we have seventeen people online. Do you need help?"

"Stacey, summon them over here. Summon anyone who can help stop this beast. If what I have in mind doesn't work—we'll have only one option..."

"Want me to do it, brother?" Draco appeared beside me and looked decisively at the Scroll of Armageddon that Killer was holding in his hands.

"No, Draco. This one's mine..."

"The monster's turning to attack the second squadron! They don't have time to reach us!"

"Mages—iceberg!" yelled Anastaria. "We'll combine forces. Whoever is low on Mana, drink an elixir. I need a second iceberg next to the first thirty seconds from now! On the double!"

Since it was impossible to stop the Squidolphin—at the speed she was going at, the second squadron would be destroyed like the other two, after which the monster would turn her attention to us—Anastaria made the only correct decision under these condition—she put an iceberg under our squadron. It would keep our ships safe from the Squidolphin's fin attacks, and yet make them vulnerable to the toxic ink.

The Mages managed to do as the girl commanded only by the time the second squadron had 32% Durability remaining. And they did such a good job that the enraged Squidolphin didn't have the time to evade and smashed into the mountain of ice with the full immensity of her torso.

"22% damage to Durability," the lookout reported. "It's got 47% left!"

"Remember, Mahan, the scroll can only be activated while in battle—and 60 seconds after it begins. But until the monster's attacked these ships, we're technically only bystanders to the battle," Ehkiller began to explain, handing me the Scroll of Armageddon.

"We were in battle with her, but the monster dove deep and broke contact with us, removing the 'Battle' buff," Stacey explained the reason for why four ships brimming with players and NPCs had done nothing to save the sixteen sunk vessels.

"I see. As soon as the scroll is activated, the activation point appears in its properties and then it will detonate three seconds after any text appears there. That text field, as I'm sure you understand, is editable. You'll have three seconds to remove your equipment, otherwise...Well you know yourself what'll happen."

"How are you planning on approaching the monster?" Anastaria managed to inquire, as the Squidolphin pulled another trick, crawling up and out onto the iceberg.

"Squadron two, get out of there immediately!" I yelled, but it was already too late. The squadron was too close to the iceberg and couldn't do anything when the hundred-meter-long torso of the enraged Squidolphin collapsed onto it, snapping its masts.

"Farewell all! Don't forget to write," I muttered turning into a Dragon. The three hundred meters between the two squadrons were a matter of several flaps of my wings, so I could already receive the 'Battle' buff.

My Thunderclap only stunned the Squidolphin for 10 seconds, instead of the minute I had counted on. By that time, her immense body had broken through the upper deck and descended to the hold, flailing and whipping her tentacles around herself as she went. Still, the ten seconds gave the pirates time to jump overboard and the players to inflict two or three more attacks.

Throwing all caution to the wind, I landed onto the Squidolphin's back, turned back into my human form and took cover under the protective dome that blocked out the water. If this monster dives again, we'll go under together...I didn't want to lose my

'Battle' buff and I still had to wait 60 seconds...

You have stepped aboard a feral Giant Squidolphin. Taming is not available ...

Swiping away the notification, I dodged to the side—right where I had been sitting, a tentacle descended with immense force, leaving a clearly visible dent where it had struck. Now that's what I call strength! I surrendered myself to my premonition and began to waltz along the Squidolphin, dodging attacks. The Squidolphin continued to wreck the ship but also assigned two tentacles to deal with me. As a result, I didn't have much time to enjoy the spectacle of the ship's destruction. Dance, dance and some more dance...One-two-three...One-two-three...One-two...

"*Dan, you're under water and the minute's elapsed—you can activate the scroll!*" Anastaria said telepathically, almost knocking me off rhythm. The Squidolphin continued to beat herself with her tentacles, trying to swat the fly on my face and—what was quite surprising—ended up taking her Durability down to 30%.

"*Dan, we've lost you. All that's left is our squadron. We've rescued half of the pirates and players and we're currently next to the iceberg, but the monster shouldn't be able to reach us. What's going on with you?*"

"*Sorry—can't talk—dancing...*"

After another ten seconds or so, the Squidolphin

stopped trying to knock me off. Instead, she began to row frenetically with her tentacles and dived almost vertically towards the bottom. If it weren't for the protective dome which kept me safe from the water, the mounting pressure and the abrupt acceleration—the Squidolphin remained beneath my feet, while the world spun around us—I can't imagine how I would've survived at this depth. At first the light grew dim and teeming darkness filled my field of vision—then, what I had assumed to be darkness vanished too and was replaced by absolute gloom. Still, the Squidolphin continued her descent. In any case, her body never once straightened out to cease her dive into the ocean's depths...Damn! I'm getting a little scared here, even though all this is a game...

Then there was a light...A small point of light straight ahead, which gradually grew, filling everything before me. We were still heading down vertically, so it took me a couple moments to realize that I was seeing the ocean floor. The soft phosphorescent light was coming from everywhere, as if each grain of sand tried to cast a tiny bit of light onto this world. Considering that we were in a game, the light meant only one thing—I had reached a location that had been designed with the players in mind. Otherwise, who was the light for? Very interesting...

Though the Squidolphin straightened out and slowed down before reaching the bottom, she still slammed fairly heavily onto the ocean floor, stirring up a cloud of sparking silt. Thank god for the protective dome—it again saved me from unnecessary difficulties which included a mud bath in this case.

"*We've arrived,*" I messaged Anastaria telepathically, yet the system returned an error message as if mocking me:

You cannot send out personal messages when you are in the Oceanic Abyss...

No way! Does that mean that if I die here I won't respawn on the surface either? What's this?

Slowly, at a rate of half a percentage point a minute, the Squidolphin's Durability began to regenerate. Here's a dilemma then: Either I set off Armageddon here and hope for a miracle, or I can wait until we return to the surface and then look for a way to get inside the monster...The second option sounds a bit crazy, if I'm honest with myself...As for my worries about not respawning up on the surface, if worse comes to worst, I can push the 'Character Stuck' button and then figure out how to escape this Oceanic Abyss. Or I could call Viltrius—though it seems that my signal's pretty poor down here.

It's decided then! I'll blow up the Squidolphin before she has a chance to fully restore herself...

As Anastaria already pointed out, it'd be pointless to activate the scroll up on the surface...You can't sink a beast like this with Armageddon, especially when it has 32% Durability. Not seeing any other options, I got out my beloved pickaxe and walked over to the deepest dent the tentacle had made. Since I can't step outside and make my way inside the creature through some natural opening along her body—and I shuddered at the thought of what such openings could be—I had to fashion one of my own. After all, by and large, the Squidolphin was no different than a ship in which you could drill a hole. The preparations we had made yesterday for the hunt were a perfect example of this.

After the first dozen strikes, I thought that I wouldn't achieve anything—the pickaxe didn't even leave a mark on the Squidolphin's body. But after a minute, when a small piece of the outer shell broke off, I understood that my plan was indeed possible. The important thing was to persist and hammer away at one spot and particularly one spot between the humps. Rine had taught me this well...

Thirty minutes of hammering a hole in the Squidolphin ended in an entire avalanche of consequences. First of all, the monster's Durability regenerated by 15%, though this in no way affected the ruckus I was causing. The Durability regenerated in some other part of the creature. Second of all, twelve giant pieces of Squidolphin meat found their way to my bag. As soon as a blow from the pickaxe dislodged a hunk of meat, I immediately picked it up, since it seemed to me like an interesting item that demanded further examination. What if I could use it to make a stew? Third of all, my pickaxe floated away to some unknown destination. The last blow I landed caused the dent that the tentacle had made to pop like a champagne bottle being uncorked. The explosion was so intense that the pickaxe, which had become stuck in the surface, was ripped from my hands and carried away. And fourth of all, water gushed into my protective dome from the hole I had created.

The space under the dome was filling second by second, and yet I didn't feel any pressure, as if the dome continued to protect me from this aspect of the environment. A system notification appeared, informing me that my Diver skill was at Level 1 and I could remain underwater for three minutes and change. Meanwhile, the Squidolphin's body began to heal right before my eyes, as if the creature was now concentrating on this area. It took me a single glance at the 1.5 meter thick armor to understand that if it weren't for the dent and the internal pressure, I would've been digging here until the end of time. This one thought blocked my other one: "Save yourself now." While my mind was considering how many years I'd be hammering away at the armor, my body already did as it felt like—I dove headlong into the Squidolphin.

I don't know where I ended up, but what I saw was something large, about two meters in diameter, green and pulsating. Without thinking, I turned into a Dragon and latched onto this something with my claws. I began to tear at it left and right. I had all of three minutes to enjoy my destruction of this monster, after which I was going to activate the scroll and enjoy my hard-earned rest. But first I wanted to cause some damage to this pulsating something...

I don't even know where all this anger had come from...After five seconds I was using my teeth, then my tail which whipped at everything it touched, while my claws went on tearing to pieces this pulsating sphere. I even cast Thunderclap several times to add insult to injury. I wanted to take out all the frustration I had accumulated on this poor creature— for Stacey, for the bungling players, for the bad weather and for my imprisonment in Barliona. I simply wanted to destroy and crush everything in reach...

When the sphere exploded, pushing me away with a wave of warm, green blood, I felt completely satisfied. I only had a minute of air remaining, so now I could detonate the scroll and stop worrying about...

The speed with which the Squidolphin changed her position was so great that I was thrown onto my back and pressed into the wall. The dome was no longer protecting me from the changes of direction, so I began to crawl along the wall in the direction of the tail. Even despite the fact that I used all the claws I had, my wings and even my tail, the speed with which the Squidolphin was rising was so great that all my progress was for naught. The only good news was that the water began to empty from the monster's insides allowing me to take a breath. I wish I hadn't...

I had never experienced such a revolting, mortifying smell in my life. Thanks to the fact that I was in my Dragon Form, the poisons didn't affect me, but it wasn't any easier to breathe for knowing this. Losing my balance due to the foul odor, I rolled along some strange corridor located along the Squidolphin in the direction of the tail. It was looking like this was her gullet and I was on my way to her stomach where I would be digested...Ugh...

After about thirty meters, I managed to grab onto another pulsating thingy. It wasn't as large as the one from before—only about a meter—and yet there was something inside this sphere. Knowing that I could always activate the Armageddon scroll, I began to hack at this sphere as well—again gnashing with my fangs and tearing with my teeth at this soft pulsating part of the Squidolphin—and knowing that if it popped I would continue my fall.

When the sphere burst, I managed to do two things at once—avoid from falling further and catch the item that the sphere had released. This turned out to be a silvery cocoon about fifty centimeters in length, soft and springy like a ball.

Acquired item: Giant Squidolphin Embryo (Level 0). Item class...

To activate, place the Embryo in warm water...

I stared at the cocoon for about a minute, afraid to even breathe on it lest it vanished. So this means that my Minor Squidolphin would forever have remained a Minor Squidolphin, even if she had reached Level 20? The item I was holding in my hands made me, and I mean me, and not someone else, the foremost power of our continent's southern seas. Well

I'll be...

In the position I was in, it was extremely difficult to activate my inventory bag, so I retrieved my Mailbox with my free paw, wrote myself a letter and attached the Embryo. When I return, I'll show it to Stacey—and trigger another spasm of wanting to somehow get her hands on this thing. By the way, speaking of Stacey!

"*Earth calling Mars, come in Mars, what's the word?*"

"*You're alive, Dan! What's the Oceanic Abyss? What did you see there?*"

"*Stacey, we are surfacing, get ready to summon me over on my command. Okay?*"

"*I'm ready. I'm sending the summons. When you're ready, just hit accept.*"

The scroll was also in my personal bag, but I had sagely assigned it to a quick item slot, so after waiting long enough for the notification that my other half wished to summon me to appear, I opened the scroll's properties and entered a single word into the special text field: 'Die.' A countdown immediately appeared, so I didn't stick around to see the result. Releasing the scroll, I accepted the summons. I'm coming, Stacey...

Achievement unlocked: 'Corsair of the Century.' +30% to vessel damage.

+5000 to Reputation with all encountered maritime factions.

Level gained!

The Legends of Barliona Clan has slain a Giant Squidolphin. Reward: 250,000 gold.

As soon as I appeared beside Anastaria, seven Levels fell to me in a row. Judging by the happy faces around me, everyone received something from Barliona—some a Level, others an Achievement or Title.

"A DRAGON! WHAT A DOOZY! TO ARMS!" Grygz's shout thundered across all four of the ships that had survived the battle, so I was forced to soar up into the air. Evasive maneuvers, so to speak...

"Stacey, tell them to chill out, please."

"Come on down, my speckled dove," the girl replied after a few seconds. *"They've promised not to kill you right away."*

"Look!" came another yell, from a player pointing at the water. "The monster's remains!"

Truly—from the depths of the ocean a huge, one-hundred-meter-long body floated up to the surface. According to the mechanics of Armageddon, it should have been torn to pieces, and yet the Squidolphin's remnants refused to bow to the laws of logic or physics. Until the players got a chance to collect their loot, it's difficult for a mob to depart this world.

"Mahan, fly over there please and take a look at what we earned," Anastaria said in such a soothing and pleasant voice that I couldn't help but grin—were it up to her, she'd kill all the players right now, kick them from her group, drown the pirates and, for safety's sake, wipe out the maritime fauna in the vicinity just to take a look at the loot she'd gotten from this unique ship. Effectively, what had just happened was a First Kill—it was quite ominous that we hadn't officially received an Achievement. Could the players of some other continent have defeated a similar creature? Although, I think we have different Achievements...But all right, let Stacey worry her head about that—it's not like she has it just to look pretty. And I have to admit that sometimes she does have some good ideas...

"*Loot will be distributed by an Imitator,*" Anastaria instantly announced in the raid party chat. I hovered over to the Squidolphin's floating cadaver and carefully landed on it, hoping that I wouldn't weigh it down too much. Then in my properties, I opened the loot bookmark and without looking at what was in it and what wasn't, dumped it all for common access. Imitators are a cruel race—if they notice you staring at something too long, they'll never let you have it. What pleased me most was that the Embryo that I had found inside the monster was formally mine—I had acquired it in battle, not in its aftermath. So anyone who wanted to lay a claim to it could take a walk. It was mine according to all the rules and regulations of Barliona...

Money earned: 334,558 gold, 34 silver, 18 coppers.

Item acquired: Piece of Squidolphin Heart. Attributes: Hidden.

Acquired   item: Squidolphin   Scales

(Ingredient: Smithing). Attributes: Hidden.

"Hmm...You can come back. I've explained to them that the Dragon is you..."

Stacey's face suggested that this was not the result she had expected from the loot. I landed on the deck, returned to my human form and was immediately embraced by Grygz—who began to clamor about how now he would be remembered for centuries! The pirate leader was swearing he'd put a fleet at my disposal as early as tomorrow and that we'd sail to Armard, yet I didn't pay him much attention—instead, I kept my eyes focused on Anastaria. The girl's glassy eyes and twitching head told me that she was carefully studying the list of loot that I had published for all the players to see. The list included the Imitator's distribution of items—who'd get what and how much of it—as well as various information about each item and why it was allocated to the player in question. I never imagined that Anastaria would be that interested in such information. It was evident that there weren't any global item drops...neither Legendaries, nor Uniques...It's odd, by the way. Why is this?

"Daaaan?" a minute later, the girl's unsettled, drawn out voice appeared in my head. *"Were the pieces of the heart really the only thing that you got down there? How's that possible?"*

The emergency siren instantly went off in my head, indicating that she had just riffled through my bag to see what I had acquired, realized that there wasn't anything valuable there and began to complain.

"*Stacey, it wasn't really a situation that gave me time to think about loot,*" I shrugged, dodging the question.

"*But you did take the pieces of the heart.*"

"*It was a trade, and not even a fair one,*" I objected. "*That monster took my pickaxe!*"

"Grygz, we've done as we promised," said Evolett when he had finished going through his loot. "What do you say now? Are we setting out against Geranika?"

Quest completed: 'Pirate Brethren. Step 2: Thar She Blows!' +4000 to Reputation with the Pirates of the Southern Seas.

Quest available: 'Pirate Brethren. Step 3: Armward Ho!'

"In that case, we will set out in a week. Any objections?" Evolett said, looking around at everyone present, and then turned to me: "Armard will take up a lot of time. I'll need to sign out to reality. We still have about a month to recapture the Heart of Chaos, so we should have enough time."

"Agreed, let's meet in Cadis in a week," I nodded to the Priest and addressed the pirate leader: "Grygz, do you know a suitable place to celebrate our triumph? It wouldn't do to not have a drink!"

"Ahoy, friend Mahan!" Grygz clapped me on the shoulder so hard that my jaw almost dropped to the deck. Taking into account the recent hike in reputation, I'm one of the boys now for the pirates, and my 74 points of Attractiveness with the leader makes me something like his brother. "Only a true pirate thinks of loot after a battle and only then about drinks and only after all that about women! A toast to our new brother! From now on he is a captain without a ship! Such is my word!"

New title available: 'Pirate Captain.' This status does not depend on having a ship.

A 'hip-hip-hooray' sounded three times from the ships around us and the pirates began to celebrate, while the players began to cast portals and head back to their customary haunts. I walked over to Stacey who was staring out at the sea sadly and embraced her shoulders.

"What's wrong, baby?"

"I lost my bet...Let's summon Plinto, what do you say? I'd rather deal with this right away."

"What did you bet anyway?" I asked, still embracing the girl. "What's the Tear?"

"An access key to a unique location that was designed for Rogues. It's the only item after the Phoenix Bridle for which Plinto is ready to do anything—even sing a song and dance a jig. And in reality too. Can you imagine? An enormous, clumsy, bald guy dancing a jig in front of you so that he can get a series of bytes in Barliona...You should have seen the look on his wife's face—I shudder to recall it."

"Forget it. Maybe the Imitator will decide the bet in your favor. You don't know what Plinto wrote after all."

"That's why I want to summon him now. If I lost, I want to pay immediately..."

"Hello everyone! Oh look at that—you've killed the fishy! Excellent. Without even knowing what happened, I'll venture a guess—Mahan rescued everyone while busting his butt once again!" Plinto's mocking tone and sarcastic demeanor was a good match for Anastaria's downcast look. "Well, shall we open it?"

"Okay," said the girl, sighing like someone consigned to defeat, and glanced over at me: "Get the betting contract and summon the Imitator. Let him make the comparison..."

Plinto's note: *"What I think: Mahan will encounter the Squidolphin, most likely on a pirate vessel, something will go wrong, most likely everyone will die or almost die. Anyway, Mahan will turn into a Dragon, since he's not much of a Shaman at the moment, and he'll fly over to the fishy and kill it. Specifically, from within. I have no idea how he'll get inside it, but that is the most unrealistic option."* Accuracy percentage—98%.

Anastaria's note: *"A pirate fleet will set out to seek the Squidolphin, led by me and not Mahan. There will be no fewer than 20–25 ships. The Squidolphin will destroy most of the fleet, at which point the scenario will permit Mahan to use his Dragon's breath. Mahan will kill the Squidolphin in his Dragon Form and receive a unique or legendary item that has something to do with the sea."* Accuracy percentage—91%.

Anastaria's eyes became two narrow slits and fixed on me like two laser beams. Without saying a word, she retrieved the Mailbox and put it on the floor, looked at it, at me, again at the box, and now understanding where the unique item was, got out the silver tear and handed it to Plinto. And she did all this in silence, moving abruptly and basically without looking away from me. Damn it all!

"How did you say you killed the monster?" the girl asked once she was sick of playing the guessing game.

"Forgive me for interrupting your conversation," Ehkiller wedged himself between us. "I have to run. But I cannot leave without discussing the cost of the scroll. In view of our partnership, I'm ready to give it to you almost for free—a mere ten million gold."

This bit of news almost knocked the breath out of me. What ten million? From where? What was *this*?

"Evolett asked for seven," coming to my senses, I tried to bargain, while Stacey stepped right up to me, utterly ignoring her father and distracting me from my negotiations.

"Let's not bring that up. Evolett had his own interest at stake, wishing to gain access to the pirate quest. I on the other hand, don't really profit from this. I'm basically selling you this scroll at cost as it is."

"Nine," I made a last ditch attempt to save a little money. The clan currently had sixteen million in its treasury and losing ten of them would severely curtail our budget. It's very difficult to haggle when your wife is staring right at you waiting for an explanation.

"My condolences, but I want either ten million or some equivalent. For instance, the Eye of the Dark Widow is an option, or give me another scroll of Armageddon if you can find it for cheaper. That's my final word. I request that the Imitator record it and I request that you pay me the indicated amount. Mahan, there's no point in ruining our relationship over some business—if the scroll belonged to me, Ehkiller the player, personally, I'd give it to you without even thinking about it. But as the head of Phoenix, I don't have the right to spend clan resources as I wish. You have two days to give me the money, the scroll or the Eye. All the best!"

Ehkiller teleported out, leaving me effectively one on one with Anastaria—who went on staring at me.

"I propose we go somewhere else," Anastaria said, casting a portal and gesturing at it. "After you..."

Shaking my head in puzzlement and still not fully understanding what the girl had in mind, I nodded at Grygz, assured him that I would make sure to stop by for the feast later, asked Draco to be careful and not get into any fights, and finally dived into the portal.

A frigid, Alpine wind enveloped me from every

direction, forcing me to shiver. It took one glance at the stone wall several steps away to realize that Anastaria had brought me to the entrance to the Tomb of the Creator that she had found. I wonder why?

"Anything you want to tell me?" the girl started up again, appearing beside me.

"Nope. I do have a question though—where are we going to get ten million?"

"Forget it. I request the Imitator to formally record my words—the question of the Armageddon scroll does not concern the Legends of Barliona. I will take care of it myself," a glowing aura of confirmation appeared around Stacey.

"Hang on, what do you mean you'll take care of it yourself? I needed the scroll!"

"I told you—forget it! So you don't want to tell me anything?"

"Okay, I will. Stacey, I found something down there," I had to surrender since I didn't feel like arguing. But Stacey was also the one who taught me the value of revealing information slowly and bit by bit, so I went on: "It's dumb to hide it now. But, before I showed it to you, I wanted to arrange everything so that it would be a surprise. Damn! I still want to make it a surprise, so I will dig in until the end. Stacey, I promise you'll like what I got down there. But give me time to arrange everything the way I want to..."

"I'll kill you! Do you hear me? If I learn you lied to me one more time, you can forget I exist! I can live with everything except lies! When?"

"When what?" I was taken aback at seeing Stacey like this. The woman standing before me right now wasn't the Anastaria that all of Barliona loved, but nothing short of an exact copy of Nashlazar in her worst mood. You could love and cuddle the Stacey I loved, but the woman before me now was better feared and avoided.

"When am I going to see my present?"

"It's a surprise," I corrected the girl.

"When am I going to see the surprise you've prepared for me?"

"If you go on in that tone of voice, then never," I struck a pose. "What's with the aggression, Stacey? If I acquired something illegally, the Imitator would send me straight to the mine, since other players would have been involved. Therefore, this conversation ends here. Whatever I found is mine legally. I decided to make it a surprise for you, and here you are pressuring me—what, where, when...Doesn't it seem a little strange to you?"

"So it's like that? Pressuring..."

"That's right! You're the best damn analyst in this game—try and look at your actions objectively! I get the impression that all you care about is items, while people and feelings are merely the tools by which you can obtain them..."

"So that's how it is! I guess then you think I'm using you? That I'm only interested in Shaman Mahan because he has a heap of unique toys? Is that right? Here," Anastaria offered me several documents. "I also had a surprise for you..."

Emphasizing the word 'surprise' like it had once been truly epic but had now become distasteful to her, the girl fell silent, giving me the chance to study the contents.

"What is this?" I asked stunned, glancing through the document but not reading closely. It looked like Anastaria had brought me some kind of contract and called it a surprise. How odd...

"It's a contract for a loan. It states that a certain Anastaria, aged 28, shall borrow a sum of 94 million and change from the central bank of our sector and uses it to extinguish the debt of one Daniel Mahan, aged 33. Taking into account my social status, my recommendations and the cosigners—my father and uncle—I will be issued this amount for five years with an APR of 2%. As my family lawyer informed me, you would never get a loan of this size, even if you put up your castle as collateral. So this is my surprise...I also prepared it in secret, hoping to make my beloved husband happy, and then it turned out that I was lied to. I hate people who lie to me. And you know what, knowing full well ahead of time that you'd never just let me gift you the money, I prepared a second contract which stipulates how you're going to pay me back. Later...Sometime...There's no deadline, but just in case, it begins with the same five years. This is what I've been busy with for the past couple months—and that's why I was signing out to reality so frequently."

My head had grown so heavy all of a sudden that it felt like it was made of stone and if I moved it even a bit it would fall off and roll away. For some reason, someone had made Barliona start skipping and dancing and I had to take a seat to avoid collapsing.

A way to freedom!

"Does your dad know?" I asked an absolutely idiotic question, trying to gain my bearings. On the one hand, Anastaria was offering me a fairy tale. On the other hand, to owe over a hundred million credits to someone...It's too much...I wasn't ready for this...

"Yes. He helped me. As soon as they give final approval to my loan and you're released, we'll hire you the best lawyers we can and try to have the case retried. My family lawyer said that you made an enormous mistake by turning yourself in, so there's remedies available to us. The important thing is to get you out of Barliona. It'll be easier after that."

"In other words this contract isn't effective yet?" I asked.

"It's a draft. We're hammering out the final details with the payment. As soon as everything's confirmed, it'll be given to you for your signature, so I had to warn you ahead of time. Initially, I ALSO wanted to surprise you. I imagine that the details will be taken care of in the next two to three weeks and you'll be released. But goddamn it, Dan! How could you lie to me?!"

"Stacey, I...Baby, please forgive me..." I embraced the girl who was on the verge of tears and pressed her to myself. "I'm sorry, honey, I simply lost my mind..."

"How could you, Dan?" Anastaria couldn't

control herself and tears began to stream down her cheeks. "I'm sure that if I had been in your place that you would do the same thing. We've been together only for half a year, but I feel like I've spent an eternity with you and I really can't imagine myself or my future without you...But I never expected you to do this..."

It was impossible to describe my feelings at that moment. They were completely contradictory—joy and anger, happiness to utter desolation...it's difficult to find the epithets for the sensations that had flooded my mind.

"I'm sorry, Dan, I need to sign out to reality. I'll be back soon." With a tear-stained face, Anastaria moved away from me and shrugged her shoulders guiltily. "Wait for me here, all right?"

Anastaria kissed me and dissolved as usual. Wait for her? Am I supposed to pitch a tent here until she returns? How could I suspect this girl? What an idiot I am!

My feelings were so vivid and contradictory that I wanted to sing, dance, cry, scream, celebrate and do something unreal and impossible that could extinguish the guilt I felt before Anastaria. Submitting to the urge, I opened Design Mode and began to craft. I'm sure that when Stacey returns, she'll wake me up.

The Tourmaline War Lizards...the final pieces of the Chess Set.

I had never seen any war lizards and therefore had no idea what they should look like. But this didn't stop me at the moment—the greenish

Tourmaline took its place before my eyes, all but yelling: 'Here I am—use me, hurry!'

What had the lizards done to be remembered? No doubt they had...

Oh to hell with this! I'm not doing the right thing! I'm filled with so many emotions that I can't possibly concentrate! I need to find some other way!

Giving in to my emotions, I lost all touch with reality. Only the sad Tourmaline remained before my eyes. If you were to ask me how I had decided that it was sad, I'd twirl my finger at my temple, questioning my own mental state. But at the moment the stone was sad because I had given it all the joy that had filled my being. The expectation of liberty—Anastaria's present—the chance to see Stacey in real life. There was so much joy that the Tourmaline became too joyful...Too much of something is harmful, so I imbued it with all the sadness and sorrow that filled me at that moment. My mistrust of the girl, my folly, my desire to hide the truth...The Tourmaline filled with strength and began to glimmer like a light that had been turned on, yet I didn't like how one-sided its emotion was. In the life of any creature, be it man or jewel, there are many more emotions and more suffering than mere happiness and sadness. And I was about to share all of this with the Tourmaline...

I gave it the triumph I felt at defeating the Squidolphin...

I gave it the fear I'd felt when I descended to the Oceanic Abyss...

I gave it the love I felt for Anastaria...

I gave it the pride I felt for my student who had surpassed her teacher...

I gave it the pain I felt at summoning the Rank 100 Spirit...

I gave it all of myself, without holding back, since this was the only way to create a masterpiece. This is not a piece of this world—this is a piece of the player's Soul, separate from whatever the developers invest in their creation. Without the player, the algorithm remains dead. With the player, with his emotions, desires and feelings the world blooms with colors that make it better, more perfect...

I don't need to see the War Lizards. I don't need to understand their history—that's unnecessary. I used to think that it takes love to create the figurines—love that the originals had felt for this world...How wrong I was! The figurines are created not through love exclusively—they are created through emotions! Through feelings! Through sensations! The important thing was to share instead of keeping them to myself...everything else would happen on its own...It couldn't not happen...

Congratulations! You have continued along the path of recreating the Legendary Chess Set of Emperor Karmadont, the founder of the Malabar Empire. Wise and just...

You have created the Tourmaline War Lizards from the Legendary Chess Set of Emperor Karmadont. +10% to Movement while the pieces are in your possession.

+1 to Crafting. Total: 15.

+5 to Jewelcrafting (primary profession). Total: 160.

You have created a Legendary item. +500 to Reputation with all previously encountered factions.

"Danny, you did it!" I heard Anastaria's joyful squeal and felt the girl embrace my neck. "You made it! You're the first in all of Barliona! You even beat the Celestial Empire!"

Opening my eyes, I gazed at the small figurines in my hands. The Tourmaline lizards...Once, long ago, I watched a movie about dinosaurs—specifically about a T-Rex that ate anything that moved—while anything that didn't move was moved and then eaten as well. In my hands now I held two miniatures of this very T-Rex, saddled and bridled like horses.

Quest available: 'Tomb Raider.' Description: Find the Tomb of the Creator of Barliona, use the Chess Set to unlock the Tomb and complete the Dungeon inside.

Attention to the Creator of the Chess Set! You have discovered the location of the Tomb of the Creator. Do you wish to unlock the Tomb? Warning! This process lasts 30 minutes and cannot be interrupted.

I peered deep into the magically-beautiful eyes of Anastaria and pushed the 'Activate' button. Stacey had dreamed of this moment her entire gaming life, so why not make this dream come true for her right this instant?

The Tomb of the Creator is being opened. Time remaining: 30 minutes.

"You unlocked it?" Stacey asked with excitement, giving me another kiss, after which a new message appeared in the clan chat: "*The Tomb's unlocked and opening as we speak. We're on location!*"

"At last!" After several moments, Barsina appeared right beside us and began examining the gates like they were to her own house. "You were right yet again, my dear..."

"Naturally," Anastaria laughed. She looked me up and down and added: "Can you imagine it, mom, he has no idea what's going on! It's so easy to manipulate him..."

Mom?! Manipulate?! What the hell is going on?

"All right, the activation will take another thirty minutes," Barsina went on, taking a seat on the boulders. She got out her amulet and made a call: "Magdey, jump on over here with your raiders, we'll need to protect the entrance." Thinking a little longer, Barsina made another call. "Hi honey. We've done it. Send Hellfire over to us, please. It's time we return to the clan..."

Eyes as big as saucers I looked from Barsina to Anastaria, utterly dumbfounded at what was going on. Barsa is Anastaria's mother? Our little, one-meter-tall-with-her-cap Druid is my mother-in-law?

"Stacey, while we wait, do you want to play the villain from a sappy movie?" the Druid asked, turning to Stacey. A portal opened, unleashing my raiders led by Magdey. Mounting griffins (I didn't even know they had griffins!) the raiders soared up into the sky and vanished among the mountain peaks, leaving two warriors with us.

"You want to finish him off completely? You really are quite cruel, mom! Sometimes what one doesn't know is much more pleasant."

"Hence my offer!" Barsina giggled maliciously. "You have no idea how sick I am of playing my part..."

"Ladies, maybe you'll clue me in about what's going on here?" I asked, finding the strength to smirk. This was all starting to resemble a really cheap prank, so it seemed dumb to take it seriously.

"All right, since he's asking for it himself," Anastaria said. Sitting down beside me she looked at me and began: "My dear, I must disappoint you—you're a dummy. The most natural, ordinary dummy! You...Hmm...I don't even know where to begin." Stacey seemed to be relishing the situation so much that she could hardly keep from laughing. "Okay, I'll start at the beginning...In Anhurs, not far from the clan registration office, stands a small house that's called the Hall of Fame. It contains a gallery with the images of all players who have received First Kills. And it is this place that, one day, received information that four players had appeared in Barliona who had earned these First Kills. The first to approach Phoenix with an offer to join it was Clutzer..."

"Clutzer came to Phoenix?" I narrowed my eyes. This was no longer resembling a prank.

"Clutzer, teleport to the Tomb entrance, will you?" A message from Stacey appeared in the clan chat, after which she continued: "Surprised? Too bad. Not only did he come to us, but he brought with him the entire trio. Ah! There he is. Clutzer," the girl said to the Rogue, "I hereby remove all disclosure restrictions from you. We have what we wanted...Now please explain how it all happened."

"Mahan, Mahan...I let you know that I was free and asked you to think!"

"Excuse me?" Anastaria interrupted. "Mind clarifying that?"

"Forget it," Clutzer smirked in reply. "Check the Imitator—I haven't violated anything. As you taught me yourself—you always have to predict all the possibilities, even the least likely ones. So you can chill out—I'm clean as far as the law goes. I'll pay my debt soon enough. I've done everything by the rules of our contract, oh Great Anastaria!"

Clutzer all but spit out this last word, demonstrating what he thought of the girl.

"Since this pig," he went on with a nod in Stacey's direction, "wants me to tell the whole story, well, why not? As soon as we left the mine, I headed to Phoenix. Starting a clan with four prisoners is utter nonsense. I was welcomed with open arms, taken care of, tested. Basically, they did all the due diligence. Once I passed the tests, I was granted an interview, since the Imitator supposedly determined my skills. Obviously trying to ingratiate myself, I told her everything about the four of us and our desire to start a clan. I didn't fail to mention the strange behavior of our Shaman who, at Level 12, could draw rings that were quite a deal better than the standard ones. That was when they became curious about you. It was a cinch to entice Eric, Leite and Karachun into Phoenix—the cons of them being in other clans were obvious, but you ended up in Beatwick, so we forgot about you for a while. Or, more accurately, until the pair of oafs from Phoenix encountered you in the forest. At the time, Hellfire mentioned that everyone was already in the clan and you were the only one out, but due to the specifics of the scenario you couldn't be invited into Phoenix then. After that, you began to interact with Anastaria a lot, who realized that you were the creator of the Chess Set. It was then, at a strategy briefing that I floated a plan that took into account your psychological profile, which I had managed to study while were in Dolma Mine. We were planning on starting a clan by then and I had learned what Karmadont's Scroll said, so I suggested that Phoenix allow us to make our clan and proposed that we slip in a person from Phoenix. At first that was supposed to be me, but Ehkiller decided that Anastaria would be better—they still didn't fully trust me..."

"You joined Phoenix?" I asked him angrily.

"Of course! I knew you all of several weeks. Why would I trust you? You're a prisoner—who knows what skeletons are in your closet? My own hide is worth more to me, believe me. But I suggest you don't get hung up on details and focus on the main points. We decided to create a sister clan to Phoenix and transfer Anastaria to it—for no longer than two months, so that she could receive the Tomb quest. Meanwhile, we were all forced to sign nondisclosure agreements. If we violated them, we'd be sent back to the mines, so we kept mum. Karachun was the exception—he felt so indebted to you for the First Kill that he wanted to meet with you. So we had to come up with a fairy tale that he defected to Phoenix, while we three had remained stalwart soldiers immune to fairy tales..."

"Unfortunately, I hadn't planned on you becoming acquainted with Reptilis," Anastaria cut in. "Everything went according to plan at first—the clan, the game with your feelings, which I didn't even have to predict—I could see your mouth water when you looked at me from a kilometer away. But then, as they say, a force majeure situation arose, which we had to deal with as quickly as possible. So we sent Barsina to you."

"Barsa joined the clan before I got the scroll."

"Reptilis refused to give us the scroll and threatened to hand it over to the Emperor or to the creator of the figurines, so we decided not to risk it. Mom deleted her former Mage and in several days we leveled her up to Level 147. Clan leveling programs can work miracles. When Clutzer told us that you were looking for an extra player, it became clear that this was our chance. Initially, Barsa was going to be leveled up to Level 250 and then introduced to you—but we had to work with what we had. That's how Barsina ended up with you."

"I guess the first question I'd ask if I were you," Barsina approached us, "was how a mercenary—for whom this game represents her livelihood—was supposedly only at Level 147? Either she's a crappy mercenary, or she's no mercenary at all. And yet to my utter surprise, this never even occurred to you! All I had to do was write you a message and that was it—I was one of the gang. Joining the clan was only a matter of time after that. And, what amused me most of all—Mahan never wondered how a simple mercenary would have experience managing personnel. What kind of person does business like that?"

"When you kept missing out on scenarios in the Dark Forest, I was grinding my teeth, but I kept quiet," Anastaria began once again. "By that point it became clear that you had acquired the scroll, so we decided that I would join your clan in order to keep Barsina safe. So that you'd never suspect her."

"The nonsense with Rick and Hellfire was my fault," Clutzer shrugged sadly. "By that point, I hadn't yet figured you out entirely, so...As you see, no one even bothered to come up with some logical explanation for Anastaria's appearance. As for putting Rick and Hellfire in their place, well, you couldn't think of a dumber idea, but you ate it up without a second thought...And so my plan came to fruition:

Anastaria and Barsina were in the clan and all three of us were ready to pick up the fallen banner of the deputy at any moment—to hand it to Phoenix later."

"As I predicted, you read the scroll and began to accuse me of supposedly being with you only for the sake of the Chess Set. In some sense you were right!" Stacey started laughing but then controlled herself and went on: "I summoned the Emperor and looking right in your eyes sincerely swore that I'd never 'laid eyes on this document or its contents' in my life. Notice that I didn't say I didn't know what it said—only that I'd never seen it. Then, I asked you to remove me from my position as deputy. You were so predictable that you did exactly what I wanted—and made mom your deputy. She immediately began play her part as deputy as actively as she could, recruiting players who wanted to join Phoenix and testing to see how good they were. We killed two birds with one stone—we managed to test the new players in the context of a real clan, while meanwhile you were kept from any doubts about Barsa's abilities. All that we had to do after that was wait two months until she received her buff, force you to craft the unfinished figurines, convince you to activate them and that's it—your part in this game has now ended. Shaman Mahan is no longer of any use to anyone..."

"After the Dark Forest, Anastaria signed an agreement with us and Phoenix paid our debts, putting us on an installment plan," said Clutzer. "Around this time I realized that I didn't want to be in Phoenix at all and that the Legends had become family for me. I began to look for a way to let you know and even found it in the end—but you didn't understand...It's too bad...It's just too bad..."

"They paid your debt after the Dark Forest?" I noticed an inconsistency in the testimony of the trio before me. "Leite took out a loan to pay his debt..."

"Which yet again reinforces the fact that you absolutely do not read the documentation," Anastaria cut me off. "I almost killed him when in your mournful tone you told me that Leite wasn't in the game—but then I came up with the story of the loan. And yet if the highly-esteemed (in some circles) Shaman had actually bothered to do his homework, he would have been surprised to learn that the law prohibits prisoners from being issued loans. But you're too predictable...Take for example the loan contract I told you about—I simply got sick of waiting for you to get to the next figurines, so I found a way to prod you along. Mom sowed doubts about me in your mind, using the pretext of my bet with Plinto. And then I sold you on it by briefly removing the 'Stunned' debuff after we'd been sunk by the cargo ship and allowing you to overhear my conversation with dad about the bureaucracy. *Et voila!* Like a calf to a teat, Shaman Mahan dashes off exactly where I need him to. I had filled you with such emotions that you had no choice but to pour them out into your crafting. And to ensure that you wouldn't make something abstract, I brought you to the clearing before the Tomb first. You had no choice but to create the last two chess pieces."

"Emotions? What are you talking about?"

"Ah but of course! You think you're a heavenly craftsman...Do you mind if I bring you back down to earth? Remember when we met and I told you that Rick was only at Level 14 or 17 in his Crafting? I didn't want to brag about him being at Level 39 to you, so that you wouldn't feel inferior. At the moment, Rick's already at Level 112 and I doubt he'd give you a second thought. You're a shit Craftsman...You know what is the only thing that I'll miss? The projections! They're the only thing that you managed to get your hands on that I don't have. Everything else you've acquired—either I already have it or I destroyed it. Like your Squidolphin. I couldn't let you keep such a powerful ship—it would be too great of a weapon for a lone player."

"Lone?" I was feeling worse and worse with every word that Anastaria, Barsina and Clutzer said to me. It was incredibly difficult to learn that over the past six months I'd been fed and fattened like a pig to the slaughter...

"Maybe not entirely alone," came Leite's voice, "but you certainly won't have three thousand players with you as before. Everything's ready on my side, Stacey."

"Wonderful! You know, Mahan, you are so utterly predictable that even now when we're dragging you through the muck, you still behave exactly as your psychological profile says you will. If you don't mind, I will take these things—they're much safer with me, isn't that right, dear?"

The Eye of the Dark Widow, the Crastils, the Squidolphin Scales I had found in the Oceanic Abyss—everything that I had worked so hard to acquire in this game appeared in Anastaria's hands. She had unfettered access to my inventory! Why hadn't I shut her out the moment when all of this had begun?

"I suppose I'll take the Chess Set as well." Before I could cut her access, I was robbed bare. "After all, we're husband and wife and should share our assets in the game!"

"What about the Ying-Yang? How did you get it to bloom?"

"Elementary—in that moment, I simply forced myself to believe that I loved you. You see, love is like a buff—it's there and then it's not. In fact, the part with the stone was quite simple."

"Ready?" Hellfire asked Stacey.

"Let's do it. It's time to go home..."

My clan's insignia faded over the girl's head and in its place a bright phoenix flared to life—the girl had returned to her father. The same transformations began to occur gradually to the other players around me, while a series of notifications raced past my eyes:

Your deputy (Barsa) has left your clan. Pursuant to your contract, you hereby receive monetary compensation in the amount of 12,000,000 gold...

Your treasurer (Leite) has left your clan. Pursuant to your contract, you hereby receive

monetary compensation in the amount of 10,000,000 gold...

Your raid leader (Magdey) has left your clan. Pursuant to your contract...

"I do want to thank you for Leite—being able to test the quality of a treasurer in a real clan setting is invaluable. Especially since this treasurer had full access to your clan vaults..."

WHAT?! N-N-O-O-O!

Opening my clan properties, I blocked all access to money and resources. I was the only one who could approve any transaction from now on, and yet...

"Yes, we've received everything. Thanks, Leite. We'll transfer the required funds now...

Clan achievement unlocked: 'Deal of the Century.' You have sold 50 million gold worth of goods. +1000 to Clan Reputation with all mercantile clans.

"You won't need all that Imperial Steel, will you, honey? And you can't accuse us of being unfair—your treasurer had the authority to sell it at 40% of its market value. You signed the agreement with him yourself...And so, what do you have left?"

"But why now?" I blurted out. Even if they had crushed my spirit, if they were waiting for me to attack them with my fists and get sent to the mines, they were deeply mistaken. I can contain my rage. I can contain it and channel it in the necessary direction.

"Because you're now useless! Your job was simple—open the Tomb. Everything that will happen after this doesn't concern you. If you think that you're a successful player who sees everything that others don't—I'm sorry to disappoint you. During our acquaintance, you managed to miss out on at least three continental events. Three! For example, the last one with the High Priestess and the Milkman. What kind of moron do you have to be to assume that that was just another launch point for the Kartoss scenario? It's a good thing I managed to deal with it in time and assign some people to that quest chain. So that's it—you, Mahan, are now wasted material. The Tomb is an ordinary Dungeon. Until I complete it, no one will even come close to it and, what makes me happiest, is that Nashlazar will be so proud of me."

"Nashlazar?"

"Of course! This is the prettiest way to defeat the Foe! You think she forgot the past? Hah! I have finally been promoted to Rank 50!"

"I'd like to be there when you look Eluna in the face after this," I said. "A Paladin of Light indeed..."

"Oh! I will look her in the face quite calmly! After all, from the game's perspective nothing terrible has happened! I simply switched clans, neither betraying the Empire nor my ideals. This isn't reality, Mahan. There are different values here...Oh! Here's that call I've been waiting for! Speaking!" the girl said into the amulet.

"We're in position and ready to attack," said the

voice in the amulet.

"Do it..."

Your castle (Altameda) is under attack! Hurry to its aid! Attackers...

"It's not in my interests to allow you to keep a Level 24 castle," Stacey finished me off completely. "It shall be reduced to Level 1, and then I will have achieved my goal—the Dragon will be crushed."

My amulet began to vibrate. I picked it up without thinking.

"Master! We're under attack!" yelled Viltrius. "We need assistance urgently!"

"Viltrius, teleport the castle!" I yelled, noting Stacey's narrowed eyes. I guess she didn't know I'd given an amulet to my majordomo...

"I cannot!" the goblin sounded disconsolate. "We still have a month before we're allowed to teleport and the cost of a forced teleport is fifteen million. I don't have access to that kind of money..."

"I grant you permission to withdraw money from the clan account! Choose a location in the Free Lands and teleport there! Block access to the castle to everyone but me! And do not reply to any calls!"

"Yes, Master," the goblin replied joyfully.

A notification appeared before me requesting me to confirm the withdrawal.

Yes, I confirm it!

A sharp pain pierced my body and the world grew black.

Player Barsina wishes to revive you. Do you accept?

"He managed to do it, after all," smirked Stacey. "It's okay. We'll find the castle sooner or later anyway. But we won't kill you. I want to see your face when the entrance to the Tomb opens and you understand once and for all that everything you've worked toward for the past half a year is beyond your reach. One shouldn't let moments like that slip away..."

The countdown timer for the gates was on its last minute. I looked at Anastaria and Barsina who were smirking, at Clutzer with his head bowed in guilty, at Hellfire and Magdey, opened my clan properties and almost cursed—there were just over four hundred players left in my clan. I had just lost almost two-and-a-half thousand players...

A new notification appeared, announcing that I had received a lot of gold, so I made sure that the available balance was sufficiently large and whispered:

"I call upon a Herald. I request your assistance...I wish to extinguish my debt to the government from the clan account." I was leaving Barliona...

Are you sure that you wish to pay 94,883,998 gold as monetary compensation?

Yes, I'm sure. There's no longer anything for me in this game. I have lost everything—my friends, my love, my clan...Everything that I had, had just vanished...I opened my character's properties and sighed bitterly—over the past year, I had leveled up quite a lot...

Stat window for player Mahan, companion of Anastaria					
Experience	314429	of	750760	**Additional stats**	
Race	Dragon			Dragon Rank	11
Class	High Shaman			Minutes in Dragon F	110
Main Profession	Jeweler			Physical damage	2284
Character level	137			Magical damage	46965.5
Hit points	61930			Physical defense	5206
Mana	114550			Magic resistance	5206
Energy	170			Fire resistance	5206
Stats	Scale	Base	+ Items	Cold resistance	5206
Stamina	64%	79	6193	Poison resistance	100%
Agility	11%	64	2334		
Strength	84%	78	784	Dodge chance	41.20%
Intellect	35%	204	11455	Critical hit chance	25.60%
Charisma	41%	80	88	Shamanic Blessing	10%
Crafting	0%	15	18	Eluna's Blessing	15%
Endurance	43%	154	178	Water Spirit rank:	12
Spirituality	0%	89	98	Totem level	103
Free stat points:			595		
Professions				**Specialization**	
Jewelcrafting	23%	160	160	Gem Cutter	3
Mining	77%	86	86	Hardiness 2	10%
Trade	25%	19	19	-	
Cooking	20%	32	32	-	
Cartography	50%	99	99	Scroll Scribe	10%
Smithing	20%	129	129	Smelter 2	10%
Repair	0%	6	6	Leather Repair	

Goodbye, Shaman Mahan. You were a good friend.

Payment accepted. You will leave the prisoner capsule in 10 seconds...
9...
8...

The last thing I saw before leaving Barliona were the gates of the Tomb of the Creator, slowly swinging open to reveal a dark passage.

END OF BOOK FIVE

Want to be the first to know about our latest LitRPG, sci fi and fantasy titles from your favorite authors?

Subscribe to our NEW RELEASES newsletter:
http://eepurl.com/b7niIL

Thank you for reading *The Karmadont Chess Set!*
If you like what you've read, check out other LitRPG
books and series published by Magic Dome Books:

Dark Paladin LitRPG series by Vasily Mahanenko:
The Beginning
The Quest

The Dark Herbalist LitRPG series by Michael Atamanov:
Video Game Plotline Tester
Stay on the Wing

The Neuro LitRPG series by Andrei Livadny:
The Crystal Sphere
The Curse of Rion Castle

The Way of the Shaman LitRPG series by Vasily Mahanenko:
Survival Quest
The Kartoss Gambit
The Secret of the Dark Forest
The Phantom Castle
The Karmadont Chess Set
The Hour of Pain (a bonus short story)

Galactogon LitRPG series by Vasily Mahanenko:
Start the Game!

Phantom Server LitRPG series by Andrei Livadny:
Edge of Reality
The Outlaw
Black Sun

Perimeter Defense LitRPG series by Michael Atamanov:
Sector Eight
Beyond Death
New Contract

In order to have new books of the series translated faster, we need your help and support! Please consider leaving a review or spread the word by recommending *The Karmadont Chess Set* to your friends and posting the link on social media. The more people buy the book, the sooner we'll be able to make new translations available. Thank you!

Till next time!

97504190R00279

Made in the USA
San Bernardino, CA
23 November 2018